EVERYMAN, I will go with thee,
and be thy guide,

In thy most need to go by thy side

GUSTAVE FLAUBERT

Born at Rouen on 12th December 1821. He had a nervous breakdown in 1843, and lived for the rest of his life at Croisset, near Rouen. His health rapidly declined after 1870 and he died on 8th May 1880.

GUSTAVE FLAUBERT

Sentimental Education

TRANSLATED
WITH INTRODUCTION AND NOTES BY
ANTHONY GOLDSMITH

DENT: LONDON
EVERYMAN'S LIBRARY
DUTTON: NEW YORK

NO. *969*

To
K. O. N.

INTRODUCTION

In the France of the eighteen-forties there existed, not for the last time in history, a generation of young intellectuals in revolt against their environment. Their first quarrel was with the regime under which they lived. Louis-Philippe had been swept to power in 1830 on a wave of popular enthusiasm. Constitutional government, freedom of the press—all the rights which his predecessor, Charles X, had denied—were to be granted to an expectant people. But he had showed no alacrity in carrying out his promises of reform, and by 1840 France was in the grip of a bourgeois reaction. Surrounded by an atmosphere of philistinism, under a Government of elderly mediocrities, the young men felt snubbed, ignored, and frustrated. It was natural that they should seek consolation in literature—in the romantic works of Byron, Goethe, and Chateaubriand, where the youthful hero, if not always successful, never failed to appear dramatic and picturesque. And if life did not come up to literature, so much the worse for life! Escape was always possible; the young romantic could take refuge in an introspective aestheticism, in the cultivation of his own emotions, in the search for an ideal love. He could construct, in fantasy, a private paradise in distant times or places—the Orient, America, or the Middle Ages. He could pose as an artist misunderstood by society, or, in endless discussions and arguments, could build Socialist Commonwealths and Liberal Utopias. 'We were not only troubadours, rebels, and Orientals,' wrote Flaubert of his own youth, 'we were, above all, artists. Like Antony, we carried a dagger in our pockets. . . .'

In 1848 Louis-Philippe fell. Progress had triumphed and the Second Republic was born. No wonder the young men were exultant. 'We shall be happy now,' exclaims Dussardier, one of Flaubert's most sympathetic characters, 'I've just been listening to some journalists talking. They said we're going to liberate Poland and Italy. No more kings, do you understand? The whole world free! The whole world free!'

But the triumph was short-lived. The theorists were in power and they proved unequal to the practical tasks of administration. The Republic disintegrated; and the reaction of 1851 swept it away almost without a struggle. It was the final disillusion of a generation which, as Thibaudet observes, 'wasted its strength and went bankrupt, with the Second Empire as official receiver.'

As a young man Flaubert had shared to the full the frenzied idealism of his contemporaries. At the age of twenty-five he had produced a first and highly romanticized version of *L'Éducation sentimentale*. But in the twenty years that separate this early unpublished effort from the present volume his intellect had rebelled against the romantic school; he had grown to hate their self-dramatization, their contempt for the humble truth, and the distorted view of life which they imposed on their devotees. In *Salammbô* (1862) he had for the time being satisfied his taste for the gorgeous setting, the exotic background. Now he was determined to write a realistic novel about his own generation, to place the passions of his youth in final perspective, and to purge himself, through observation and irony, of the pernicious influences that had once obsessed him. Such was his aim in *L'Éducation sentimentale*; but the design was not completely carried out. Flaubert's emotions were too strong for his intellect; the strain of romanticism in his temperament was ineradicable; and, although the greater part of the book is written in a spirit of detached and sardonic realism, the central subject, the love-story of Frederic Moreau and Mme Arnoux, is pure romance. It is treated throughout, not with the cold objectivity which Flaubert intended, but with a strangely lyrical tenderness.

The explanation of this inconsistency is to be found in Flaubert's private life. Marie Arnoux is clearly identifiable as Elisa Schlésinger, for whom Flaubert had conceived an adolescent passion, when he first met her, in 1837, on the beach at Trouville. It was then that he saved her shawl from being carried away by the tide—an episode which is exactly reproduced in the first chapter of *L'Éducation sentimentale*. The image of Elisa, *la toujours aimée*, perpetually haunted his thoughts, and he once described her as the woman who had 'ravaged his life.' She was never Flaubert's mistress, but she figures as the heroine of all his juvenile novels, including the first *Éducation sentimentale*. This curious unfulfilled passion was in fact Flaubert's own romantic illusion. Elisa Schlésinger was not really an exceptional woman; it was Flaubert himself who, forced by his inner nature, invested her with ideal qualities, and made her typify the perfections of his youthful fantasies. To Flaubert the realities of passion were always distasteful; love was a subjective emotion, best enjoyed in solitary reverie. Even in his affair with Louise Colet, the poetess, he was happiest at a distance from her, and the charm of Elisa was largely dependent on her inaccessibility. She represented for him the joys which he felt had always eluded him, and his attitude is well expressed in his last letter to her, written in 1872, three years after the publication of *L'Éducation sentimentale*. 'The future,' he wrote, 'has no more dreams for me. But the old days come before me, as if bathed in a golden mist, and from that luminous background, whence beloved phantoms stretch out their arms to me, the face that shines out most brightly is yours. Oh, unhappy Trouville!'

This idealization persists in *L'Éducation sentimentale*. Mme Arnoux occupies a position of unique privilege among Flaubert's characters. She alone is spared that deep and devastating analysis to which he was accustomed to subject his creations. Among so many profoundly observed types, she remains a shadowy figure—aloof, mysterious, impenetrable. It is as if Flaubert, obscurely aware of the real deficiencies of his ideal, and fearing to destroy his fragile day-dream, shrank from applying the dissector's knife to his heroine. Sometimes the veil is nearly lifted. '*Quelle bourgeoise!*' exclaims Frederic, in an interlude of clear-headedness; but a moment later he is back in the clouds again. Thus the main theme of the book, so far from being the detached, impersonal narrative planned by the author, becomes a monument, constructed with tenderness and pity, to Flaubert's own frustrated adolescence.

Artistically, this contradiction is of immense advantage. A purely ironic approach to the subject might have justified the charge of coldness and lack of heart so often brought against *L'Éducation sentimentale*. As it is, Frederic's unswerving devotion achieves a certain nobility, and Flaubert's exquisitely poetic treatment of the whole theme perfectly balances the surrounding realism.

When *L'Éducation sentimentale* was first published, in November 1869, it was received with the utmost disfavour. Many critics preferred to pass it over in silence, rather than offend the author of *Madame Bovary* and *Salammbô*. Those who expressed their views were nearly all censorious to the point of malevolence, and the public was not inclined to disagree with them. This almost universal hostility, although it amazed Flaubert, was not really surprising. For the whole tone and atmosphere of the novel is opposed to the spirit of the nineteenth century. Flaubert did not share the inflated optimism or the faith in material values that were characteristic of his era, nor did he conceal his distaste for the bourgeoisie, great and small, who then dominated France. Flaubert's social scepticism was perhaps pardonable in *Madame Bovary*, for the exposure of corruption and hypocrisy in a provincial village might be interpreted as an implied compliment to the capital; but in *L'Éducation sentimentale* the society of Paris itself is made a target for satire—a satire which is all the more penetrating because it is based on meticulous observation and expressed with all the tremendous force of the author's mature style. Flaubert's description of M. Dambreuse, the banker, as a person who 'would have paid for the privilege of selling himself,' with his associates 'who would have sold France, or the whole human race, to safeguard their fortune, to spare themselves a moment's uneasiness or embarrassment, or else out of sheer servility, through their instinctive reverence for brute strength,' was scarcely calculated to secure him the patronage of the wealthy. Moreover, the generation that grew up in the stable, confident decades following the Franco-Prussian War, was satisfied with its surroundings, and had little sympathy with the rebellious Radicalism and the thwarted ideals of Flaubert's young romantics. 'The reaction after '48,' wrote Flaubert, 'dug a gulf between one France and the other'; to the young people of the seventies Flaubert and his contemporaries seemed *de vrais fossiles*.

And it was not only the content, but the form of the book that puzzled and irritated the contemporary reader. Accustomed to the melodrama of Hugo and Dumas, he found Flaubert's unemphatic narrative dull, discursive, and episodic—a chronicle, not a novel. George Sand was almost the only critic who perceived the subtle dramatic structure which knits together the apparently inconsequent incidents of the book. 'The story of the novel,' she wrote, 'as complex as life itself, is bound together and interwoven with remarkable artistic skill. Each character emerges on the surface, but each does so in his turn. . . . They cross the stage swiftly, yet always marking a further step along the path they follow, as they let fall a vigorous summary, a brief dialogue, sometimes a single phrase, a word, which crystallizes, with a simplicity terrible in its strength, the particular obsession of their brain.' George Sand, in using the language of the theatre, seems to have realized how close *L'Éducation sentimentale* is to drama—not, indeed, to the stylized rhetorical tradition of the French stage, but to the modern realistic drama of character, already evolved by Turgenev and soon to be further developed by Tchekov. The writers of this school do not go beyond everyday life for their subject-matter; they avoid stilted plots; they do not moralize. Their main preoccupation is with human psychology; and their seemingly casual and naturalistic dialogue is really selected with extreme care in order to illuminate the characters and their relationship with one another. Once the absolute reality of the characters has been established, the small incidents of their lives become as absorbing as the most sensational melodrama. The broad effects of classical tragedy cannot be achieved by these means; but to a great artist they offer wide scope for delicate pathos and subtle emotional nuance. This was the method used by Turgenev in his exquisite play *A Month in the Country* (1850); and it is exactly the method employed by Flaubert in *L'Éducation sentimentale*. A technical device accentuates the dramatic aspect of the book. In order to bring out the intense and typically romantic egotism of his hero, Flaubert presents nearly the whole story through the eyes of Frederic. The other characters are not depicted, as in most novels, through their thoughts; they are exhibited objectively, from the outside. Arnoux, Rosanette, Louise, and the rest are brilliant feats of characterization, yet scarcely ever do we know what they are thinking; the whole impression is achieved, as in a first-class play, by the subtle selection of dialogue and action. It is worth noticing, too, that Flaubert divides his work into three parts, like the acts of a play, and closes each with a magnificent 'curtain,' reserving, like a skilful playwright, his most telling effect for the end of the second part.

L'Éducation sentimentale is a book about failures. All the characters are frustrated; Frederic is as far from achieving his ideal as Arnoux is from discovering the copper-red of the Chinese potters. Worldly success provides no exemption from the general doom, and M. Dambreuse, the millionaire, is perhaps the saddest failure of all. Nor are these people allowed the consolation of a grand tragic finale, a theatrical funeral pyre. Their exit in the last chapter is abrupt, almost undignified. And, to darken the picture still further, Flaubert attributes their failure neither to the age they lived in, nor to their own weaknesses, but to the futility of life itself, thwarting all endeavour, and, in the last resort, making true happiness unattainable.

Yet, in spite of its pessimism, *L'Éducation sentimentale* is not a gloomy book. Flaubert is a great enough artist to make a success of his chronicle of failure. Life may be futile, but *L'Éducation sentimentale* is not. It brings the reader into contact with all that was best in Flaubert's artistic personality —his wit, his profound wisdom, his immense vitality. And the reader leaves the encounter, not depressed, but inspired.

ANTHONY GOLDSMITH

SELECT BIBLIOGRAPHY

NOVELS. *Madame Bovary*, 1857; *Salammbô*, 1862; *L'Éducation sentimentale*, 1869; *La Tentation de Saint Antoine*, 1874; *Trois Contes*, 1877; *Bouvard et Pécuchet*, 1881.

PLAYS. *Le Candidat*, 1874; *Le Château des cœurs*, 1874.

MISCELLANEOUS. *Par les champs et par les Grèves*, 1886; *Correspondance*, 4 vols., 1887–93; *Lettres à George Sand*, 1889.

COLLECTED WORKS. *Œuvres complètes de Gustave Flaubert*, ed R. Dumesnil, 10 vols., 1945–8.

BIOGRAPHY AND CRITICISM. A. Thibaudet: *Gustave Flaubert*, 1922; R. Dumesnil: *Gustave Flaubert, l'homme et l'œuvre*, 1932; *L'Éducation sentimentale*, 1936; P. Spencer: *Flaubert, a biography*, 1952.

PART I

CHAPTER I

On the 15th of September, 1840, about six o'clock in the morning, the *Ville-de-Montereau* was ready to sail from the quai Saint-Bernard, and clouds of smoke were pouring from its funnel.

Late comers hurried up, panting; barrels, ropes, and washing baskets cumbered the traffic; the sailors ignored all inquiries; people ran into one another; the heap of baggage between the two paddles grew higher and higher; and the general din was merged in the hissing of steam, which, escaping through the iron plates, threw a whitish haze over the whole scene, while the bell in the bows clanged incessantly.

The boat sailed at last; and the banks of the river, crowded with warehouses, yards, and factories, slipped by like two wide ribbons being unrolled.

A long-haired youth of eighteen, with a sketch-book under his arm, stood motionless in the stern. He peered through the mist at bell towers and buildings, whose names he did not know; he took a last look at the Île Saint-Louis, the Cité, and Notre-Dame; but soon Paris was lost to view, and he heaved a deep sigh.

M. Frederic Moreau, who had just matriculated, was now on his way back to Nogent-sur-Seine, where he was to spend two tedious months before going to read for the Bar. His mother had sent him to see an uncle at Le Havre, from whom she had expectations for him, and had provided him with just enough money for the journey; he had returned thence only the previous evening, and he was making up for the shortness of his stay in the capital by taking the longest route back to his country home.

The uproar began to subside; the passengers had all settled down; some stood round the engine, warming themselves, while the funnel spouted its plume of black smoke with a slow and measured snorting. Tiny drops of moisture trickled over the brasswork; the deck shook with a muffled vibration, and the two paddle wheels, turning swiftly, beat the water.

The river was fringed with spits of sand. They steamed past

3

wooden rafts, which rocked under their wash; here and there a man sat fishing in a wherry. Then the drifting mists melted away and the sun came out. The hilly ridge which followed the course of the Seine on the right grew gradually lower, and gave place to a second hill, nearer the water, on the opposite shore.

On its wooded crest stood a row of low-built villas with flat-tiled roofs. Their sloping gardens were separated by new walls and iron railings; there were lawns, greenhouses, and pots of geraniums, neatly spaced along terraces with balustrades to lean on. Many of those on board, attracted by the sight of these peaceful dwellings, felt a longing to possess one, and spend the rest of their lives here, with a good billiard table, a rowing boat, a wife, or some other dream of bliss. The novel pleasure of a trip by water made it easy to unbend. The facetiously inclined began to crack their jokes. Many sang. Spirits rose, and glasses were produced and filled.

Frederic was thinking of his room in the country, of the plot of a play, of subjects for pictures, of future loves. He found that the happiness which his spiritual qualities deserved was slow in coming. He recited gloomy poems to himself; he walked rapidly about the deck, and went forward as far as the bell in the bows—where, in a group of passengers and sailors, he observed a gentleman flirting with a peasant girl, and fingering the gold cross which she wore on her bosom. He was a strapping fellow of about forty, with crinkly hair. His sturdy figure was clothed in a black velvet jacket; two emeralds glittered in his cambric shirt, and his wide trousers fell over curious red boots of Russia leather, which were worked with a pattern in blue.

Frederic's presence did not disconcert him. He turned towards him several times, winking confidentially; then he offered cigars to his entire audience. But it seemed that the company bored him, for he moved away. Frederic followed him.

At first the conversation touched on the different kinds of tobacco, then, by a natural transition, on women. The gentleman in red boots gave the young man advice; explained his theories, told anecdotes, and quoted himself as an illustration. There was something amusing about the paternal solemnity with which he delivered his counsels of corruption.

He was a Republican by conviction; he had travelled; he knew the inner life of theatres, restaurants, and newspapers, and all the celebrities of the stage, whom he referred to familiarly by

4

their Christian names. Soon Frederic confided his plans to him; he viewed them favourably.

Then breaking off, he examined the stack of the funnel; he swiftly muttered a lengthy calculation, in order to discover the exact force of each piston stroke, at so many a minute. Having found the answer, he expressed great admiration for the landscape. He said he was glad to have escaped from business.

Frederic felt a certain respect for him, and, on an impulse, asked his name. The stranger replied, all in one breath:

'Jacques Arnoux, proprietor of "Industrial Art," boulevard Montmartre.'

A servant with gold braid on his cap came up and said to him:

'Would monsieur please go below? Mademoiselle is crying.'

He disappeared.

'Industrial Art' was a hybrid establishment, combining a picture shop with an art magazine. Frederic had often seen the title in the window of his local bookshop, inscribed on enormous prospectuses, which bore the name of Jacques Arnoux in imposing characters.

The sun blazed fiercely down, glittering on the iron hoops round the masts and on the metal plating of the rails, while the prow cleft the sparkling water into two furrows that rippled away to the grassy bank. At each bend of the river the same curtain of pale poplars met the eye. The countryside was utterly deserted. A few small white clouds hung motionless in the sky; boredom, vague yet pervasive, was abroad; the movement of the boat seemed slower and the passengers looked even more insignificant than before.

These, apart from some richer folk in the first class, consisted of workmen and shopkeepers with their wives and children. It was the custom at that time to put on one's oldest clothes for travelling; and nearly all of them wore old smoking caps, or rusty hats, thin black jackets, threadbare and desk-worn, or frock coats with buttons that had burst their covers after years of service in the shop. Here and there a knitted waistcoat failed to hide a coffee-stained shirt of calico, brass tie pins pierced tattered neck-cloths and home-made foot-straps fastened slippers of shoddy felt. Two or three ruffians, carrying bamboo canes with leather thongs, threw shifty glances from side to side, in contrast to the wide-eyed curiosity of the family men. Some stood about, talking, some squatted on their luggage; others slept in corners; many ate. Nutshells, cigar ends, pear skins, and the remains of sausage meat wrapped in newspaper befouled the deck. Three cabinet makers in blouses lounged in front of the bar; a harpist, in rags, was resting, with his elbow on his instrument; from time to time one caught the sound of the coal in the furnace, a burst of voices, or a roar of laughter. The captain paced the bridge unwearyingly, striding from one paddle to the other. On his way back to his seat, Frederic pushed open the grating that led to the first-class deck, upsetting two sportsmen with their dogs.

It was like a vision.

She was seated all alone in the middle of the bench; or at least he could distinguish no one else in the dazzling light which her eyes shed upon him. Just as he passed she raised her head; involuntarily he bowed; he continued his walk a little further, then stopped to look at her.

She was wearing a wide straw hat, with pink ribbons that fluttered in the wind behind her. Her black hair was parted into two broad tresses that brushed the corners of her heavy eyebrows, and, hanging low on her cheeks, seemed to caress the oval of her face. Her dress of pale sprigged muslin billowed out in a multitude of folds. She was working at a piece of embroidery; and her straight nose, her chin, her whole form, stood out in relief against the background of blue sky.

She did not change her position, and he took several turns to right and left, concealing the real object of his movements; then he placed himself close to her sunshade, which was leaning against the seat. He pretended to be watching a rowing boat on the river.

He had never seen anything like her splendid dark skin, her enchanting figure, or her slender, translucent fingers. The sight of her work basket filled him with amazement, as though it were an object from another world. What was her name, her home, her life, her past? He longed to know the furniture of her room, the dresses she had worn, the friends she went about with; and even the desire for physical possession gave place to a deeper yearning, a poignant, limitless curiosity.

A negress, with a silk scarf on her head, appeared, holding a little girl by the hand. She was tall for her age, and had evidently just woken up; there were tears in her eyes. The lady took her on her knee.

'Mademoiselle was a very bad girl, though she was nearly seven; her mother wouldn't love her any more; they were too good to her when she was naughty.'

Frederic listened in ecstasy, as if he had made a great discovery or an acquisition.

6

He supposed her to be of Andalusian origin, perhaps a creole. Had she brought the negress back with her from the West Indies?

A long shawl with mauve stripes hung over the brass rail behind her back. How many times in mid ocean, on misty evenings, must she have wrapped it round her body, covered her feet with it, slept in it! The weight of the fringe was gradually dragging it down towards the water—it was about to fall in. Frederic leaped forward and caught it. She said to him:

'Thank you, sir.'

Their eyes met.

'Are you ready, my dear?' cried Arnoux, appearing in the hood of the companion way.

The little girl, Marthe, ran to him, clung round his neck, and pulled his moustaches. The sound of a harp rang out; the child wanted to 'see the music'; and soon the player, led by the negress, came on to the first-class deck. Arnoux recognized him as a former artists' model; he addressed him as an old friend, to the astonishment of the company. At length the harpist flung his long hair back behind his shoulders, stretched out his arms, and began to play.

It was an eastern serenade—all about daggers, flowers, and stars. The man in rags sang this in a harsh voice; the beat of the engine formed a discordant background to the melody; he plucked harder, the strings vibrated, and it was as if the metallic notes were sobbing out the plaint of a proud and vanquished love. On either side of the river woods leaned down to the very edge of the water; a fresh breeze blew; Mme Arnoux looked vaguely into the distance. When the music ceased she moved her eyelids several times, as though she were waking from a dream.

The harpist approached them humbly. While Arnoux was searching for change, Frederic stretched out his closed hand towards the cap, and, opening it shyly, dropped in a gold louis. It was not vanity that impelled him to make this offering in her presence, but a sense of general goodwill, in which he included her—an almost religious stirring of the heart.

Arnoux, leading the way, warmly invited him to come below. Frederic declared that he had just had luncheon; as a matter of fact he was famished, and he had not a penny left in his purse.

Then he reflected that he had a perfect right to sit in the saloon.

Prosperous citizens were dining at round tables attended by

7

a waiter; M. and Mme Arnoux were at the far end, on the right; he picked up a newspaper, and sat down on the long plush-covered bench.

At Montereau they were to take the Châlons coach. Their trip to Switzerland would last a month. Mme Arnoux accused her husband of spoiling the child. He whispered in her ear—it must have been a compliment, for she smiled. Then he got up and drew the curtain of the window behind her neck.

The light reflected by the low white ceiling was hard and bright. Frederic, opposite, could even make out the shadow of her eyelashes. She dipped her lips into her glass, and broke a little bread between her fingers; her lapis lazuli locket, fastened to her wrist by a thin gold chain, clinked against her plate from time to time. Yet the others in the room did not seem to notice her.

From time to time, through the port-holes, the hull of a small boat could be seen gliding up alongside the steamer, to embark passengers or take them ashore. The people at the tables kept leaning out of the windows and naming each place as they passed it.

Arnoux complained of the food; he made a terrible fuss about his bill, and had it cut down. Then he led the young man to the forward part of the ship for a glass of punch. But Frederic soon made his way back under the awning, whither Mme Arnoux had returned.

She was reading a thin volume with a grey cover. Now and then the corners of her mouth twitched, and a flash of pleasure lit up her face. He was jealous of the man whose words she seemed to find so absorbing. The longer he gazed at her, the more conscious he became of gulfs opening between himself and her. He realized that presently he would have to part from her, without having exchanged a single word with her, without leaving her the smallest memory of himself!

To the right stretched level country; on the left a meadow led gently up to a hill, on whose slopes vineyards appeared and walnut-trees, and a mill among the foliage. Higher up, narrow paths zigzagged along the white rock, which seemed to touch the sky. What bliss to go climbing together side by side, his arm about her waist, while her gown swept up the yellow leaves and he listened to her voice, under the radiance of her eyes! He could stop the boat; they had only to disembark; the thing was simple, and yet it would have been easier to shift the sun itself.

8

A little further on a mansion came into view, with a pointed roof and square turrets. There was a garden in front of the house, and avenues stretched back, like dark tunnels, under the tall lime-trees. He pictured her strolling past the shrubberies. At that moment a young lady and a young man appeared on the steps, between the orange-trees in their tubs. Then the whole scene vanished.

The little girl was playing near him. Frederic tried to kiss her. She hid behind her nurse; her mother scolded her for not making friends with the gentleman who had saved her shawl. Was it an indirect overture?

'Is she going to speak to me at last?' he wondered.

Time pressed. How could he get an invitation to Arnoux's house? And he could think of no better plan than to draw Arnoux's attention to the autumn tints, adding:

'It will soon be winter, the season of balls and dinner parties.'

But Arnoux was preoccupied with his luggage. The Surville shore came in sight; the two bridges drew closer; they passed a rope walk, then a row of low-built houses; on the foreshore there were barrels of tar and piles of shavings; and small boys were running about the sand, turning cart-wheels. Frederic recognized a man in a sleeved waistcoat. He shouted to him:

'Hurry up!'

They had arrived.

With difficulty he sought out Arnoux in the crowd of passengers, and the other replied, as he pressed his hand:

'Till we meet again, my dear sir!'

Once on the quay, Frederic turned round. She was standing in the stern. He threw her a look, into which he tried to put his whole soul. She remained motionless, as though he had done nothing.

Then, ignoring his servant's greeting, he said:

'Why didn't you bring the carriage down here?'

The good fellow made excuses.

'Clumsy fool! Give me some money.'

And he went and had a meal at an inn.

A quarter of an hour later he had a longing to go into the coach yard, as if by chance. Perhaps he might see her again.

'What's the use?' he said to himself.

And the phaeton carried him away.

The horses did not both belong to his mother. She had borrowed one from M. Chambrion, the tax collector, to harness beside her own. Isidore had started the previous night; he had

9

rested at Bray until the evening, and slept at Montereau, with the result that the beasts were fresh and trotted briskly.

Fields of stubble stretched away endlessly into the distance. Trees lined the road on either side; heaps of stones followed one after the other; gradually Villeneuve - Saint - Georges, Ablon, Châtillon, Corbeil, and all the other places he had passed on his journey, came back into his mind, with such vividness that he could now remember fresh particulars, more minute details: her foot, in a thin red silk boot, emerging from under the lowest flounce of her dress; the drill awning that formed a wide canopy over her head, and the little red tassels on the fringe which fluttered perpetually in the breeze.

She was like the women in romantic novels. He wanted nothing added to her, and nothing taken away. The universe had suddenly expanded. She was the focal point of light at which the totality of things converged; and, lulled by the movement of the carriage, his eyelids half closed, his eyes in the clouds, he gave himself up to an infinite, dreamy felicity.

At Bray he did not wait for the horses to finish their hay, but went on ahead down the road, by himself. Arnoux had called her Marie. He shouted 'Marie!' at the top of his voice. His cry was lost in the distance.

A glowing band of purple cloud covered the western sky. Huge haystacks, rising amid the stubble, cast gigantic shadows. A dog barked on a distant farm. He shivered, seized with a nameless apprehension.

When Isidore caught up with him he climbed on to the box and took the reins. His moment of weakness had passed. He had fully resolved to make his way, by hook or by crook, into the Arnoux home, and to become their friend. It should be an amusing household. Besides, he liked Arnoux; and after that, who knew? Then the blood mounted to his face in waves, his temples throbbed, he cracked his whip, shook the reins, and drove the horses at such a pace that the old coachman kept repeating:

'Easy now! Easy! You'll ruin their wind.'

Gradually Frederic grew calm. He listened to his servant's talk. His arrival was impatiently awaited. Mlle Louise had been in tears, wanting to go in the carriage to meet him.

'Who on earth is Mademoiselle Louise?'

'Don't you know? She's Monsieur Roque's little daughter.'

'Oh, I'd forgotten,' said Frederic casually.

And now the horses were tired out. They were both limping; and nine o'clock was striking from Saint-Laurent when he arrived at the place d'Armes, in front of his mother's house. This was a large mansion, with a garden adjoining open country, and it helped to establish Mme Moreau's position as the most highly esteemed person in the neighbourhood.

She came of an ancient and noble family, now extinct. Her parents had arranged her marriage; her husband, who was of humble origin, had died from a sword wound before Frederic was born, leaving her an encumbered fortune. She received visitors three times a week, and from time to time gave a splendid dinner party. But everything, down to the number of candles, was budgeted for in advance, and she waited impatiently for her farm rents to come in. Her money troubles, which she concealed like a vice, gave her a certain sternness. Yet in her charitable works she displayed neither prudery nor harshness. Even her smallest gifts assumed the importance of great benefactions. People consulted her over the choice of servants, the education of young girls, and the art of jam making; and the bishop himself stopped at her house on his episcopal circuit.

Mme Moreau harboured lofty ambitions for her son. She disapproved of criticism of the Government, from a kind of anticipatory discretion. Frederic would need patronage at first; then, rising through his own talents, he would become a counsellor of state, an ambassador, a cabinet minister. His successes at the college of Sens justified her high confidence. He had passed out first.

When he came into the drawing-room the whole party rose noisily to their feet; they kissed him, and moved the chairs, large and small, into a wide semicircle round the hearth.

M. Gamblin at once asked him his views on Mme Lafarge.[1] This case—the rage of the period—inevitably provoked a violent argument; Mme Moreau put a stop to it, to the regret, be it said, of M. Gamblin, who considered the discussion useful for the young man as a future lawyer. He left the room in a huff.

Such behaviour was only to be expected from a friend of old Roque's. Talking of old Roque, they mentioned M. Dambreuse, who had just acquired the estate of La Fortelle. Meanwhile the tax collector drew Frederic aside, to inquire his opinion of M. Guizot's[2] latest work. Every one wanted to pry into his affairs; and Mme Benoît made a skilful beginning by asking after his uncle. How was this worthy relative? Frederic no longer gave them any news of him. Was there not a distant cousin of his in America?

The cook announced that monsieur's soup was ready. The company tactfully withdrew. Then, as soon as they were alone in the room, his mother said to him in a low voice:

'Well?'

The old man had received him cordially, but without indicating his intentions.

Mme Moreau sighed.

'Where is she now?' he thought to himself.

There was the coach rumbling along; she was asleep, wrapped —he was certain of it—in the shawl, and her lovely head was resting against the cushioned seat.

They were just going up to bed when a waiter from the 'Cygne de la Croix' brought in a note.

'What is it now?'

'Deslauriers. He wants to see me,' he said.

'Oh! Your friend!' said Mme Moreau, with a sneer of distaste. 'At this time of night!'

Frederic hesitated. But friendship won the day. He picked up his hat.

'Well, don't stay out long, anyway.' said his mother.

CHAPTER II

CHARLES DESLAURIERS's father, a former infantry captain, had left the service in 1818, and had returned to Nogent to marry. With his wife's dowry he had purchased a position as magistrate's clerk, which barely sufficed to maintain him. His grievances, his old wounds, and his still vivid regrets for the glories of Napoleon, resulted in choking rages, which he vented on his family. Few children were more frequently beaten than his son. The thrashings never broke the lad's spirit. His mother's attempts at intervention met with the same brutal treatment. Eventually the captain put the boy in his office; and all day long he kept him bent over his desk, copying legal documents, which made his right shoulder perceptibly larger than his left.

In 1833, at the suggestion of the president of the court, the captain sold his position. His wife died of a tumour. He went to live at Dijon; after that he made a living by supplying substitutes for military service at Troyes. He secured a small scholarship for Charles, and sent him to the college at Sens, where Frederic recognized him as a fellow townsman; but he was twelve and Charles fifteen—besides, countless differences of disposition and breeding kept them apart.

In his chest of drawers Frederic kept provisions of all kinds, and also such objects of luxury as a dressing case. His pleasures consisted in sleeping late, watching the swallows, and reading plays; he missed the comforts of his home and found college life rough. It seemed good enough to the clerk's son, who worked so hard that by the end of his second year he had actually reached the third form. Nevertheless, either on account of his poverty, or of his hot temper, a veiled hostility surrounded him. On one occasion, however, a servant called him 'son of a pauper,' openly, in the juniors' yard; the boy leaped at his throat, and would have killed him, but for the intervention of three masters. Frederic, in a transport of admiration, clasped him in his arms. From that day forward their intimacy was complete. The affection of a senior doubtless flattered the younger boy's vanity, and the other joyfully accepted the devotion that was offered to him.

His father left Charles at college during the holidays. A translation of Plato, opened by chance, roused him to enthusiasm. He eagerly took up the study of metaphysics; and his progress was rapid, for he approached the subject with the energy of youth and in the pride of a newly emancipated intelligence. He absorbed Jouffroy, Cousin, Laromiguière, Malebranche, the Scotch school—all the contents of the library. He even stole the key in order to get books.

Frederic's pastimes were less serious. He made a drawing of the family tree of our Lord, which was carved on a door post in the rue des Trois-Rois, and another of the cathedral porch. He read medieval drama, and then embarked on books of memoirs — Froissart, Comines, Pierre de l'Estoile, Brantôme. The pictures which these books evoked in his mind affected him so deeply that he felt a longing to create them for himself. It was his ambition to become the Walter Scott of France. Deslauriers meditated a vast system of philosophy which would have the most far-reaching applications.

They discussed these matters during breaks, in the quadrangle, opposite the motto painted under the clock; they whispered about them in chapel. under Saint Louis's beard; they dreamed of them in the dormitory, which overlooks a cemetery. On school walks they took their places behind the others, and they talked incessantly.

They talked about what they would do in later life, when they had left college. To begin with, they would travel, on the money which Frederic could borrow on his expectations when he came of age. Returning to Paris, they would work together, in indissoluble partnership; and as a relaxation from their labours they would have love affairs with princesses in satin boudoirs, or wild orgies with famous courtesans. Their rapturous day dreams were followed by doubts. After a climax of verbal inebriation they would relapse into heavy silence.

On summer evenings they walked for miles over stony paths beside the vineyards, or along the high road in the open country. Fields of corn waved in the sunlight, and the heavy scent of meadow-sweet filled the air. A strange kind of oppression seized them, and lying on their backs they felt deliciously troubled and elated. The others, in shirt sleeves, played touch-last and flew kites. The usher called them. The way home took them past gardens traversed by little streams, and then along the avenues, in the shade of the ancient walls. The empty streets rang under their feet; the iron gate opened; once more they climbed the staircase; and they felt the kind of sadness that follows wild debauchery.

The head master maintained that they over-stimulated one another. Nevertheless, Frederic's present position in the top form was due to his friend's encouragement; and in the holidays of 1837 he brought him home to his mother.

Mme Moreau disliked the young man. His table manners were odd; he refused to go to church on Sunday; he aired republican views. Finally she became convinced that he had taken her son to disreputable resorts. Their relationship was closely watched. This only strengthened their affection, and there were heart-rending farewells when, the following year, Deslauriers left the college to study law in Paris.

Frederic expected to join him soon. They had not seen each other for two years, and, when their embraces were over, they went on to the bridge, where they could talk more freely.

The captain, who now kept a billiard saloon at Villeneuve, had gone purple with fury when his son had demanded from him, as trustee, a full account of his mother's fortune. He had even stopped his allowance on the spot. Deslauriers intended to try for a professorship at the law school later on; having no means of his own, he had taken a post as chief clerk to an attorney at Troyes. By strict economy he hoped to save up four thousand francs; so that, even if he got none of his mother's money, he would still have enough to enable him to work on his own for three years, while waiting for a position. Therefore they would have to give up, at least for the time being, their old plan of living together in the capital.

Frederic hung his head. The first of his dreams had crumbled.

'Cheer up!' said the captain's son. 'Life is long; we are young. I shall rejoin you. Forget about it.'

He shook him by the hands, and, trying to cheer him up, asked him about his journey.

Frederic had nothing much to tell. But, at the recollection of Mme Arnoux, his grief vanished. He did not speak of her; his sense of delicacy held him back. Instead, he talked at great length about Arnoux, describing his conversation, his manners, his connections; and Deslauriers strongly urged him to cultivate this acquaintance.

Frederic had written nothing recently; his literary taste had changed; he now prized passion above all things; Werther,

René, Franck, Lara, Lélia, and others of less distinction, roused him to almost equal enthusiasm. Sometimes it seemed to him that only music could give expression to his inner conflicts; and then he dreamed of symphonies. Then again the surface of things attracted him, and he longed to paint. He had, however, written some poetry: Deslauriers admired it very much, but did not ask for more.

Deslauriers himself had given up metaphysics; political economy and the French Revolution now occupied his mind. He was now a tall fellow of two-and-twenty — thin, with a wide mouth, and a look of determination. This evening he wore a shabby alpaca jacket, and his shoes were white with dust, for he had walked all the way from Villeneuve, especially to see Frederic.

Isidore approached them. Madame begged monsieur to come in, and sent him her cloak in case he felt cold.

'Do stay!' said Deslauriers.

And they went on strolling from end to end of the two bridges, which rest on the narrow island formed by the canal and the river.

When they walked in the direction of Nogent, they faced a group of houses built on a gentle slope; to the right rose the church behind the water mills with their closed sluice gates, and to their left, all along the bank, thick hedges could be seen, marking the boundaries of gardens that were barely visible in the dim light. When they turned round towards Paris, the high road stretched in a straight line downhill, and there were meadows that vanished in the distance, among the evening mists. The night was still and luminously clear. The smell of damp leaves drifted up to them; and, a hundred paces further on, the water of the weir murmured as it fell, with the heavy, soft sound that waves make in the darkness.

Deslauriers stopped and said:

'I can't help laughing when I think of these good folk sleeping peacefully in their beds. Be patient; there 's a new revolution brewing. People are sick and tired of constitutions and charters, hair-splitting and lies. Ah! if I had a newspaper or a platform, I 'd make them tremble—you 'd see! But you can't begin anything unless you 've got money. What wretched luck to be born the son of a publican and have to spend one's youth trying to earn a living!'

He bowed his head, bit his lips, and shivered in his thin clothes.

Frederic threw half his cloak over his shoulders. They both wrapped themselves in it, and walked underneath it, side by side, with their arms round each other's waists.

'How do you expect me to get on without you in Paris?' said Frederic, whose gloom had returned under the influence of his friend's bitterness. 'If only I'd had a woman to love me, I might have achieved something. Why do you laugh? Love is the sustenance of genius—it is the very air it breathes. It is from passion that great works of art are born. But I've no intention of searching for my ideal mate. Besides, even if I find her, she will only turn me away. I belong to the tribe of the disinherited, and I shall go to my grave with a treasure hidden within me, and I shall never know if it is diamonds or paste!'

The shadow of a figure fell on the cobble stones, and at the same time they heard these words:

'Your servant, gentlemen!'

The speaker was a little man in a voluminous brown frock coat, with a pointed nose protruding from under the peak of his cap.

'Monsieur Roque?' said Frederic.

'The same,' the voice replied.

To explain his presence, M. Roque remarked that he had just been examining the spring traps in his garden by the river.

'And so you're back in our parts?' he added. 'Excellent! I heard it from my little daughter. You're keeping well, I trust? You're not leaving us again?'

Then he went away, put off, doubtless, by Frederic's cool greeting.

To tell the truth, Mme Moreau did not call on him, for he lived in illicit union with his housekeeper, and was held in very little esteem, although he was the registrar of elections, and M. Dambreuse's agent.

'The banker who lives in the rue d'Anjou?' Deslauriers went on. 'Do you know what you ought to do, my friend?'

Isidore interrupted them yet again. He had orders to bring Frederic back without fail. His continued absence was making madame anxious.

'All right, all right! He's coming,' said Deslauriers. 'He'll sleep in his own bed to-night.'

And on the departure of the servant:

'You must ask that old boy to introduce you to Dambreuse; there's nothing like having a footing in a rich man's house.

You happen to own a tail coat and white gloves, so you must make the most of them. You must get in with that set. You'll introduce me there later on. A millionaire—think of it! Make sure he likes you—and his wife, too. Become her lover!'

Frederic protested.

'But it's all in the classical tradition! Remember Rastignac in the *Human Comedy*! You'll succeed, I'm certain of it.'

Frederic had so much confidence in Deslauriers that he felt shaken. Forgetting Mme Arnoux, or else including her in Deslauriers's prediction, he could not prevent himself from smiling.

The clerk added:

'One last hint; pass your examinations. A label is always useful; and for heaven's sake give up your Catholic-diabolist poets! Their philosophy is about as advanced as the twelfth century. Your despair is ridiculous. Many a great man has had a harder beginning than you—Mirabeau, for one. Besides, we shall soon be together again. I shall make my old robber of a father cough up. I must be going back now—good-bye! Have you got a hundred sous for my dinner?'

Frederic gave him ten francs—all that was left of the money he had taken from Isidore that morning.

Fifty yards from the bridges, a light was burning in the upper window of a low-built house.

Deslauriers noticed it. Then, taking off his hat, he declaimed with emphasis:

'Venus, queen of the skies, your servant! However, poverty is the mother of continence. Heaven knows we've been slandered enough for that!'

This reference to an adventure they had shared delighted them. They laughed loudly in the streets.

Then, having paid his bill at the inn, Deslauriers accompanied Frederic back to the square of the Hôtel-Dieu—and, after a long embrace, the two friends parted.

CHAPTER III

ONE morning, two months later, Frederic alighted from the coach at the rue Coq-Héron in Paris, and immediately thought of paying his momentous visit.

Luck was with him. Old Roque had brought round a packet of papers which he asked Frederic to deliver personally to M. Dambreuse; and he accompanied the parcel with an unsealed note, in which he introduced his youthful neighbour.

Mme Moreau appeared surprised at these advances. Frederic concealed the pleasure they afforded him.

M. Dambreuse was really the Comte d'Ambreuse; but after 1825 he had gradually discarded both his title and his party, and had directed his attention towards commerce. With an ear in every office, and a finger in each new venture, he was always on the look-out for a good bargain. Combining the cunning of a Greek with the industry of an Auvergne peasant, he had amassed what was believed to be a considerable fortune. In addition, he was an officer of the Legion of Honour, a member of the General Council of the Department of the Aube, a deputy, and likely, sooner or later, to become a peer of France. Accommodating in most respects, he pestered the ministry with continual demands for subsidies, for decorations, for tobacco monopolies; and in his fits of irritation with authority, he inclined towards the Left Centre. His wife, the lovely Mme Dambreuse, was quoted by the fashion papers; she also presided at charity committees. She flattered the duchesses, and soothed the rancour of the aristocratic faubourg, allowing it to be believed that M. Dambreuse might yet repent of his unorthodoxy and render useful service.

On his way to their house, Frederic felt nervous.

'I ought to have put on my tail coat. I shall probably be invited to the ball next week. What will they say to me?'

His self-confidence returned when he reflected that M. Dambreuse was only a business man, and he leaped jauntily from his cab on to the pavement of the rue d'Anjou.

He pushed open one of the outer gates, crossed the courtyard, climbed the steps, and entered a hall paved with coloured marble.

A double staircase, with a red carpet and brass stair rods, ran up the high walls of gleaming stucco. At the bottom of the stairs stood a banana-tree, whose broad leaves drooped over the plush-covered banisters. Two bronze candelabra held porcelain globes, suspended by small chains; a gust of fetid air came from the open vents of the heating apparatus, and nothing could be heard but the ticking of a tall clock which stood at the other end of the hall, under a sheaf of armour.

A bell rang; a footman appeared, and led Frederic into a small apartment. He caught sight of two strong boxes, containing pigeon holes filled with files. In the middle of the room M. Dambreuse was writing at a roll-top desk.

He skimmed through old Roque's letters, cut open the wrapper containing the documents, and examined the contents.

From a distance he could still pass for a young man, by reason of his slender build. But his sparse grey hair, his shrunken limbs, and, above all, the extraordinary pallor of his face, betrayed a ruined constitution. A ruthless energy lay in his greyish green eyes, which were colder than eyes of glass. He had prominent cheekbones, and the joints of his hands were knotted.

Rising at length, he asked the young man a few questions about mutual acquaintances, about Nogent, and about his studies; then he dismissed him with a bow. Frederic went out by another corridor, and found himself in the lower part of the courtyard, near the coach house.

A blue brougham, with a black horse in the shafts, was standing in front of the steps. The door of the brougham opened, a lady climbed in, and, with a muffled rumbling, the carriage began to move across the sanded yard.

Frederic, from the other side, reached the outer gate at the same moment as the brougham. There was not room for him to pass and he was forced to wait. The young woman, leaning out of the window, was talking to the concierge in a low voice. All he could see was the back of her purple cloak. However, he peered into the inside of the carriage, which was upholstered in blue rep, with braid trimmings, and fringes of silk. The lady's clothes seemed to fill the whole interior; and out of this little padded box was wafted a perfume of orris, an indefinable exhalation of feminine elegance. The coachman loosened the reins, the horse grazed the corner stone sharply, and the whole picture vanished.

Frederic walked home up the boulevards. He was sorry that he had not been able to recognize Mme Dambreuse.

A little above the rue Montmartre, a traffic block made him turn his head; and, on the other side of the street, he read on a marble tablet:

JACQUES ARNOUX

Why had he not thought of her sooner? That was Deslauriers's fault. He crossed over to the shop. But he did not go in; he was waiting for Her to appear.

The tall, transparent plate-glass windows revealed to the eye an ingenious display of statuettes, drawings, engravings, and numbers of *Industrial Art*; the subscription prices were repeated on the door, the centre of which was embellished with the publisher's initials. Hanging on the walls could be seen some large pictures, glistening with varnish; at the back stood two cabinets loaded with pieces of china, bronzes, and other fascinating curios; between them was a little staircase, screened at the top by a velvet curtain. A chandelier of old Dresden china, a green carpet, and an inlaid table made this interior look more like a drawing-room than a shop window.

Frederic pretended to be examining the drawings. After innumerable hesitations, he went in.

An assistant lifted the curtain, and in answer to his question said that monsieur would not be 'at the store' before five o'clock. But if the order could be passed on——

'No. I'll come back,' answered Frederic in a low voice.

The following days were employed in a search for lodgings. Frederic decided in favour of a room on the second floor of a private hotel in the rue Saint-Hyacinthe.

He bought a brand-new blotter and, with this under his arm, went to the opening of the law course. Three hundred bareheaded youths were assembled in an amphitheatre to listen to an aged lecturer in a red gown whose voice droned on above the scratching of pens on paper. This hall reminded Frederic of the school classroom; here was the same dusty smell, the same type of chair, the same boredom. He attended regularly for a fortnight. But he gave up the Civil Code before they had reached Article 3, and he abandoned the *Institutes* of Justinian at the 'Summa Divisio Personarum.'

The joys he had looked forward to failed to materialize; he exhausted the resources of the public reading room, he looked over the collections at the Louvre, he visited the theatre several nights in succession. Then he relapsed into the lowest depths of aimlessness.

Many novel experiences increased his gloom. He had to count his linen himself, and endure the concierge, a lout of a man with the appearance of a male nurse, who came in every morning to make his bed, smelling of drink and muttering. He disliked his room, which was embellished with an alabaster clock. The partitions were thin; he could hear the students making punch, laughing, and singing.

Tired of this lonely existence, he sought out one of his old school friends, called Baptiste Martinon. He found him in a boarding house in the rue Saint-Jacques, working away at his procedure, in front of a coal fire.

Opposite him, a woman in a printed calico dress was darning socks.

Martinon was what is called a fine figure of a man; he was tall and plump, with regular features, and prominent, bluish eyes. His father, a well-to-do farmer, intended him for the magistracy—and, in his anxiety to look serious, he wore his beard trimmed in a fringe round his face.

Since Frederic's distresses had no rational origin, and since he could not point to any actual misfortune, Martinon completely failed to understand his lamentations on life. For his own part, he attended the school every morning, took a walk in the Luxembourg gardens, drank his small cup of coffee at the café in the evening—and, with fifteen hundred francs a year and the love of this working woman, he was perfectly contented.

'What happiness!' Frederic exclaimed inwardly.

At the school he had made another acquaintance. This was M. de Cisy, the offspring of a noble family. He was like a young girl, so gentle were his manners.

M. de Cisy studied drawing, and was fond of the Gothic. They went several times together to admire the Sainte-Chapelle and Notre-Dame. But the young nobleman's air of distinction concealed an exceptionally meagre intelligence. Everything astonished him; he laughed immoderately at the smallest joke, and showed an innocence so complete that Frederic at first took this for a humorous pose, and ended by regarding him as a fool.

So there was nobody to whom he could open his heart; and he continued to await the Dambreuses' invitation.

On New Year's Day he sent them visiting cards, but received none in return.

He went back to 'Industrial Art.'

On his third visit he at last caught sight of Arnoux. He was arguing in a group of five or six people, and barely answered his greeting. Frederic was offended. But he did not give up searching for means to access to Her.

His first idea was to call frequently at the shop, in the guise of a picture dealer. Then he thought of slipping one or two 'very powerful' articles into the contribution box of the paper, which might bring about closer relations. But perhaps it might be better to go straight to the point, and to declare his love. So he composed a twelve-page letter, full of lyrical outbursts and invocations; but he tore it up and did nothing, attempted nothing—paralysed by the dread of failure.

Above Arnoux's shop, on the first floor, there were three windows, which were lighted up every evening. Shadows moved behind them—one, in particular—it was hers—and he would come from great distances, just to gaze at those windows and contemplate that shadow.

A negress whom he encountered one day in the Tuileries gardens, holding a little girl by the hand, reminded him of Mme Arnoux's negress. If other women came there, so might she; and every time he crossed the Tuileries gardens the hope of meeting her made his heart beat fast. On sunny days he continued his walk as far as the end of the Champs-Élysées.

Women, seated at ease in barouches, their veils floating in the breeze, passed close to him, while the horses paced steadily along with a scarcely perceptible swaying, that made the polished harness creak. More and more carriages appeared. Beyond the Rond-Point, where they slowed down, they filled the entire roadway. Mane brushed mane, lamp grazed lamp; steel stirrups, silver curb chains, and brass buckles flashed scattered points of light among knee breeches, white gloves. and furs drooping over the crests on the carriage doors. He felt as though he were lost in a remote world. He let his eyes wander over the faces of these women; and vague resemblances recalled Mme Arnoux to his mind. He pictured her among them in a little brougham, like Mme Dambreuse's brougham. But now the sun was setting, and a cold wind stirred up eddies of dust. The coachmen thrust their chins down into their neckcloths, the wheels turned faster, the asphalt grated; and all the carriages swept down the long avenue at a brisk trot, jostling, swerving, overtaking; then at the Place de la Concorde they scattered. The sky behind the Tuileries took on the hue of its slate roof. The trees in the gardens became two solid masses, tinged with purple at the top. The lamps were lit; and the pale green expanse of the Seine broke into shot silver against the piles of the bridges.

He went and dined for forty-three sous at a restaurant in the rue de la Harpe.

He eyed with distaste the old mahogany counter, the stained napkins, the greasy cutlery, and the hats hung on the wall. The company consisted of students like himself. They were talking about their professors and their mistresses. As if he cared about professors! As though he had a mistress! To avoid their happy chatter he arrived as late as he could. The tables were covered with the remains of food. The two tired waiters were asleep in corners, and a smell of cooking, lamp oil, and tobacco filled the deserted room.

Afterwards he went slowly home through the streets. The swaying lanterns threw long yellowish flickering reflections on to the muddy road. Shadows with umbrellas glided along the kerb. The pavement was thick with slime, a fog was creeping on, and he felt as if the moist darkness that enfolded him was sinking endlessly into his heart.

In a fit of remorse he returned to his classes. But as he knew nothing about the matters expounded, he was puzzled by the simplest points.

He began to write a novel entitled *Sylvio, the Fisherman's Son*. The scene was laid in Venice. The hero was himself; the heroine, Mme Arnoux. She was called Antonia; and to win her he murdered several gentlemen, burned a part of the town, and sang under her balcony, where the red damask curtains of the boulevard Montmartre quivered in the breeze. The lack of originality which he observed in his work discouraged him; he gave it up, and his sense of aimlessness grew worse.

Then he begged Deslauriers to come and share his room. They would manage somehow on his allowance of two thousand francs; anything was better than this intolerable existence. Deslauriers was not yet able to leave Troyes. He urged Frederic to enjoy himself, and to cultivate Sénécal.

Sénécal was a teacher of mathematics, a man of powerful intellect and republican convictions—a future Saint-Just, according to the clerk. Frederic climbed his five flights of stairs three times, without receiving any visit in return. He did not go back.

In search of distraction, he went to the balls at the Opéra. These uproarious entertainments chilled him as he passed the door. He was afraid of suffering some financial humiliation, for he supposed that a supper with a domino was a formidable adventure, involving considerable expense.

And yet he felt that he deserved love! Sometimes he awoke with his heart full of hope, and dressed himself meticulously, as if for an assignation; and he wandered interminably through Paris. Every woman walking in front of him, or advancing to meet him, made him say to himself:

'This is She!'

Each time it was a fresh disappointment. His longings drew substance from the image of Mme Arnoux. Perhaps he would find her in his path; and to bring her to him, he invented strange coincidences, and extraordinary dangers from which he would rescue her.

So the days slipped by, in unrelieved boredom, repeating the habits of life into which he had fallen. He glanced through pamphlets under the arcade of the Odéon, he read the *Revue des Deux Mondes* at the café, he dropped in to lectures at the Collège de France, and listened for an hour to a discourse on Chinese or political economy. Every week he wrote at length to Deslauriers, dined with Martinon from time to time, and occasionally saw M. de Cisy.

He hired a piano and composed German waltzes.

One evening, at the Palais-Royal Theatre, he saw Arnoux in a stage box with a woman. Was it She? Her face was hidden by a green taffeta screen which was drawn across the side of the box. At last the curtain rose; the screen was lowered. He saw a rather faded creature of about thirty, with thick lips that disclosed superb teeth when she laughed. She was deep in conversation with Arnoux, and she was tapping him on the fingers with her fan. Then a young girl with fair hair sat down between them. Her eyes were somewhat red, as though she had just been crying. From then on Arnoux addressed himself to her, half leaning on her shoulder. She listened to him without answering. Frederic racked his brains trying to guess what these women could be. They were modestly dressed in dark gowns, with flat, turn-down collars.

At the end of the performance he hurried into the passage, which was crowded with people. In front of him, Arnoux was going down the staircase step by step, arm in arm with the two women.

Suddenly the light of a gas jet fell on him. He wore a band of crape round his hat. Perhaps she was dead?

This idea tormented Frederic so violently that the next day he hurried to 'Industrial Art,' and quickly paying for one of the prints displayed in the window, he asked the shopman how M. Arnoux was.

'He's very well,' the man replied.

Frederic added, turning pale:

'And his wife?'

'His wife is also well.'

Frederic forgot to take away his print.

The winter came to an end. He was less depressed in the spring, and began preparing for his examination. He passed without distinction, and then left for Nogent. To avoid comment from his mother, he did not visit Troyes to see his friend. At the beginning of the next term he left his lodgings and took two rooms on the quai Napoléon, which he furnished.

He had given up hope of an invitation from M. Dambreuse. His great passion for Mme Arnoux was beginning to pass away.

CHAPTER IV

ONE morning in December, as he was on his way to his lecture on procedure, he thought he noticed more animation than usual in the rue Saint-Jacques. The students were hurrying out of the cafés, or calling to one another from house to house through the open windows. The shopkeepers stood in the middle of the pavement, watching uneasily; shutters were being closed; and, when he reached the rue Soufflot, he saw a large crowd assembled round the Panthéon.

Young men, in bands of five to twelve, walked along arm in arm, then joined larger groups that were standing about the square. At the furthest end, by the iron railings, men in blouses were making impassioned speeches, while policemen strolled along the walls, their three-cornered hats cocked on one side and their hands behind their backs, making the pavement ring under their heavy boots. Every one wore a mysterious, bewildered expression; clearly, something was afoot; and on each man's lips was an unspoken question.

Frederic was standing beside a young man with fair hair and a pleasing face. He wore a moustache and a short beard, like a dandy of the period of Louis XIII. Frederic asked him the cause of the disturbance.

'I've no idea,' replied the other, 'and neither have they. It's a habit of theirs these days. What an excellent joke!'

And he burst out laughing.

The petitions for reform,[1] which had been circulated among the National Guard, together with the Humann[2] assessment, and various other events, had led during the last six months to demonstrations of mysterious origin. These took place so often that the newspapers no longer even mentioned them.

'There's a lack of form and colour in all this,' continued Frederic's neighbour. 'I trow, good master,' he added, with conscious archaism, 'that we are a decadent generation. In the good old days of Loys Onze—see Benjamin Constant—there was a bolder spirit among the townsmen. I deem them unwarlike as sheep, stupid as pumpkins, and by my halidom, well besorted to be grocers. And this is what they call the Youth of the Schools!'

He opened his arms wide, like the actor Lemaître in *Robert Macaire*.

'Youth of the Schools, I give you my blessing!'

Then, addressing a rag picker, who was sweeping oyster shells into a pile against the corner of a wine merchant's shop:

'You—are you a member of the Youth of the Schools?'

The old man lifted a hideous face, in which a red nose and two stupid, bleary eyes emerged from a tangle of grey beard.

'No! You seem to me to be more like "one of those men with a hang-dog look who can be seen, in various quarters, scattering money in handfuls." Oh, scatter, my patriarch, scatter! Corrupt me with the treasure of Albion! "Are you English?" I do not reject the gifts of Artaxerxes! Let us talk a little about the Customs Union.'

Frederic felt someone touch him on the shoulder; he turned round. It was Martinon, astonishingly pale.

'Well,' he said with a deep sigh. 'Another outbreak!'

He was afraid of being involved, was extremely sorry for himself. Men in blouses disturbed him particularly, because they were bound to belong to secret societies.

'As though there were any secret societies!' said the young man with the moustache. 'That's just an old hoax of the Government's, to scare the middle classes.'

Martinon begged him to speak lower, for fear of the police.

'Do you really still believe in the police? If it comes to that, sir, how do you know that I'm not a police spy myself?'

And he looked at him in such a way that Martinon, very upset, at first completely failed to understand the joke. The crowd was pushing them back, and all three of them were forced to stand on the little staircase that led, through a passage, into the new amphitheatre.

Soon the throng divided of its own accord; several heads were bared; they were greeting the famous professor, Samuel Rondelot, who, wrapped in his voluminous frock coat, holding his silver spectacles in his raised hand, and puffing from his asthma, was placidly approaching to give his lecture. He was one of the most illustrious jurists of the nineteenth century, rivalling even Zachariae and Ruhdorff. His recent elevation to the peerage of France had not altered his behaviour in the least. His poverty was well known and he was greatly respected.

Meanwhile voices were raised at the back of the square.

'Down with Guizot!'

'Down with Pritchard!'[1]

'Down with the traitors!'

'Down with Louis-Philippe!'

The swaying crowd, pressing against the closed door of the courtyard, brought the professor to a standstill. He paused in front of the staircase. Soon he could be seen on the lowest of the three steps. He spoke; a clamour drowned his voice. A moment ago he had been the idol of the crowd, now he was hated, for he represented authority. Each time he tried to make himself heard the shouting began again. He made a sweeping gesture, to encourage the students to follow him. He was answered by a general uproar. He shrugged his shoulders contemptuously, and disappeared in the passage. Martinon had profited by his position to vanish at the same time.

'What a coward!' said Frederic.

'He's sensible,' replied the other.

The crowd broke into applause. They regarded the professor's retreat as a victory. At every window there were curious spectators. Some struck up the *Marseillaise*; others proposed a march to Béranger's [1] house.

'To Laffitte's!' [1]

'To Chateaubriand's!' [1]

'To Voltaire's!' yelled the young man with the fair moustache.

The policemen tried to pass through the crowd, saying as gently as they could:

'Make way, gentlemen, make way. Move along, please.'

Someone shouted:

'Down with the butchers!'

This insult had become customary since the troubles of September. Every one repeated it. They hissed, they booed the upholders of law and order, who began to turn pale. One of them could no longer restrain himself. Spying a small youth who had come too close to him and was laughing in his face, he pushed him so roughly that he fell on his back five yards away, in front of the wine merchant's shop. Every one drew back; but almost at once the policeman was himself on the ground. He had been knocked over by a kind of Hercules, with hair that overflowed like a bundle of tow from under an oil-cloth cap.

This man had been standing for some minutes at the corner of the rue Saint-Jacques. Quickly dropping a large cardboard box that he was carrying, he had leaped at the policeman. Now he was holding him prostrate beneath him and punching his face with all his might. Other police hurried to the rescue. This tremendous fellow was so strong that it took at least four to overpower him. Two shook him by the collar, two others pulled him by the arms, a fifth pounded him in the small of the back with his knees, and all of them called him a brigand, a murderer, and a revolutionary. With his chest bare and his clothes in rags he protested his innocence; he could not stand by and see a child struck down in cold blood.

'My name is Dussardier! From Messrs Valincart Frères, laces and fancy goods, rue de Cléry. Where is my cardboard box? I want my box!' He kept on repeating: 'Dussardier! Rue de Cléry! My box!'

However, he quieted down, and, with a stoical air, allowed himself to be taken to the police station in the rue Descartes.

A stream of people followed him. Frederic and the young man with the moustache walked immediately behind him, full of admiration for the shopman and disgusted at the brutality of authority.

The further they went, the smaller became the crowd.

The policemen looked round ferociously from time to time; and as the rowdy element found nothing more to do, and the inquisitive nothing more to see, the procession began to melt away. The passers-by whom they met looked at Dussardier, and indulged in loud and insulting comments. An old woman on her doorstep even shouted that he had stolen a loaf; this injustice increased the anger of the two friends. At last they arrived at the guard house. There were only about twenty people left. The sight of the soldiers was enough to disperse them.

Frederic and his comrade boldly asked for the man who had just been incarcerated. The sentry threatened to lock them up themselves if they persisted. They demanded to see the superintendent; they refused to give their names, in their capacity as law students, and solemnly declared that the prisoner was their fellow pupil.

They were shown into a completely bare room, furnished with four benches, ranged against walls of smoke-stained plaster. A hatchway opened at the far end. Then Dussardier's robust countenance appeared; with his dishevelled hair, his small, honest eyes, and his nose with its square tip, he reminded one vaguely of a good-natured dog.

'Don't you recognize us?' said Hussonnet.

This was the name of the young man with the moustache.

'But——' stammered Dussardier.

'Don't go on playing the fool,' went on the other. 'We all know that you're a law student, like ourselves.'

They winked and winked, but Dussardier was still nonplussed. He seemed to pull himself together, then suddenly he said:

'Has my box been found?'

Frederic, discouraged, lifted his eyes to the ceiling. Hussonnet replied:

'Ah! The box you put your lecture notes in! Yes, yes! Don't worry!'

They redoubled their pantomime. Dussardier at last realized that they had come to help him; and he said nothing, fearing to compromise them. Besides, he felt a kind of shame at seeing himself raised to the social rank of a student, the equal of these young men who had such white hands.

'Do you want a message sent to any one?' asked Frederic.

'No, thank you, nobody!'

'But your family?'

He hung his head without answering; the poor fellow was a bastard. The two friends were astonished by his silence.

'Have you got anything to smoke?' continued Frederic.

Dussardier felt his clothes, then drew from the depths of his pocket the remains of a pipe—a beautiful meerschaum pipe, with a stem of black wood, a silver lid, and a mouthpiece of amber.

For three years he had worked to make this pipe a masterpiece. He had taken care to wrap the bowl regularly in a sheath of chamois leather, to smoke it as slowly as possible, never to lay it on marble, and to hang it up every night at the head of his bed. Now he shook the fragments of it in his hand, the nails of which were bleeding, and, his chin sunk on his breast, his eyes staring, his mouth open, he gazed at the ruins of his happiness with a look of unspeakable melancholy.

'Let's give him some cigars,' whispered Hussonnet, making the gesture of producing some.

Frederic had already laid a full cigar case on the edge of the hatch.

'These are for you! Keep smiling! Good-bye!'

Dussardier threw himself on their outstretched hands. He clasped them frantically, his voice broken with sobs.

'What? For me? For me? . . .'

Evading his thanks, the two friends left the police station, and went to lunch together at the Café Tabourey, in front of the Luxembourg.

As he divided the beefsteak, Hussonnet informed his companion that he worked for the fashion papers, and designed advertisements for *Industrial Art*.

'Jacques Arnoux,' said Frederic.

'You know him?'

'Yes! No! I mean, I've seen him. I've met him.'

He asked Hussonnet casually if he ever saw his wife.

'From time to time,' replied the artist.

Frederic did not dare pursue his inquiries; this man had just assumed a position of immense importance in his life. He paid the bill for lunch without the other making the slightest protest.

Sympathy was mutual; they exchanged addresses, and Hussonnet warmly invited him to walk with him as far as the rue de Fleurus.

They were in the middle of the garden when Hussonnet, holding his breath, contorted his countenance into a horrible grimace and began to crow like a cock, which caused all the cocks in the neighbourhood to reply with prolonged cock-a-doodle-doos.

'It's a signal,' said Hussonnet.

They stopped by the Bobino Theatre, in front of a house which was approached through an alley. In an attic window, behind pots of nasturtiums and sweet peas, a young woman appeared, bare-headed, in her stays, leaning her elbows on the gutter of the roof.

'Good morning, my angel! Good morning, my pet!' said Hussonnet, blowing kisses to her.

He kicked open the gate and disappeared.

Frederic waited a whole week for him. He did not dare go to Hussonnet's lodgings, for fear of seeming impatient for a return of his hospitality; but he searched for him all over the Latin quarter. One evening he met him, and took him to his rooms on the quai Napoléon.

They talked for hours; they opened their hearts. Hussonnet longed for fame and commercial success in the theatre. He collaborated in musical comedies that were never produced, 'had masses of plans,' and could write the words of songs. He sang one or two of them. Then, catching sight of a volume of Hugo and another of Lamartine in the book-case, he attacked the Romantics with bitter sarcasm. Those poets lacked both sense and grammar, and above all they were not French! He prided himself on knowing his own language, and he tore the finest phrases to pieces with that malicious ruthlessness, that pedantic taste which characterizes frivolous-minded people when they are faced with serious art.

Frederic was offended at this attack on his favourites; he wanted to break off relations. Why should he not risk, here and now, the question on which his happiness depended? He asked the young writer if he could take him to Arnoux's house.

This was an easy matter, and they agreed to meet next day.

Hussonnet missed the appointment; he missed three others. One Saturday, at about four, he appeared. Taking advantage of Frederic's carriage, he stopped first at the Théâtre français, to get a ticket for a box; he had himself set down at a tailor's, then at a dressmaker's; he wrote notes in the lodges of hall porters. At last they arrived at the boulevard Montmartre. Frederic crossed the shop and climbed the staircase. Arnoux recognized him in the mirror which faced his desk, and, even as he wrote, laid his hand on Frederic's shoulder.

Five or six people, standing up, filled the narrow room, which was lit by a single window opening on to the courtyard. A couch with a brown tapestry cover occupied a recess at the back, between two curtains of the same material. On the mantelpiece, which was littered with papers, stood a bronze Venus, flanked by a pair of candelabra, fitted with pink candles. On the right, near a filing cabinet, a man in an arm-chair was reading a newspaper with his hat on his head; the walls were covered with prints, pictures, rare engravings, and sketches by modern masters. These last bore elegant dedications indicating the sincerest affection for Jacques Arnoux.

'How are things with you?' he said, turning to Frederic.

And without waiting for his reply, he whispered to Hussonnet: 'What's your friend's name?'

Then aloud:

'Have a cigar. They're in the box, on the filing cabinet.'

'Industrial Art,' situated at the very centre of Paris, was a convenient meeting-place, a neutral territory, where rival schools rubbed friendly shoulders. Among those present that day were Anténor Braive, the painter of kings; Jules Burrieu, whose drawings were beginning to popularize the Algerian wars; the caricaturist Sombaz; the sculptor Vourdat; and others, none of whom were at all as Frederic had imagined them. Their manners were simple, their conversation free. Lovarias, the mystic, told a bawdy story, and the famous Dittmer, the inventor of the oriental landscape, wore a woollen cardigan under his waistcoat and went home by omnibus.

They were talking about a certain Apollonie, a former model, whom Burrieu claimed to have seen riding down the boulevard in a carriage and four.

Hussonnet attributed this metamorphosis to her succession of protectors.

'There's not much that old dog doesn't know about the girls of Paris,' said Arnoux.

'After you, sire, if there's anything left,' replied Hussonnet with a military salute, parodying the grenadier who offered his water bottle to Napoleon.

Then they discussed some pictures in which Apollonie's head had figured. Absent colleagues were criticized. They expressed amazement at the prices fetched by their works; and they were all beginning to complain of not earning enough, when there entered a man of medium height, with lively eyes and a rather wild look, wearing a coat that was fastened by a single button.

'What a pack of Philistines you are!' he said. 'Good God, what difference does money make? Those old fellows just threw off their masterpieces and never bothered about the public. Correggio, Murillo——'

'Not to mention Pellerin,' said Sombaz.

But without replying to this sally, he continued to hold forth with so much vehemence that Arnoux was forced to repeat to him several times:

'My wife wants you for Thursday. Don't forget.'

These words recalled Frederic's thoughts to Mme Arnoux. No doubt the little room by the divan led to her apartments. Arnoux had just opened the door to it, to fetch a handkerchief; and Frederic had caught sight of a wash-stand at the far end. Meanwhile a sort of muttering was coming from the chimney corner. It was the man reading the paper in the arm-chair. He was five feet nine inches in height, with eyelids that drooped slightly, grey hair, and a majestic bearing. His name was Regimbart.

'What's the matter, citizen?' said Arnoux.

'Another filthy trick of the Government's!'

He was referring to the dismissal of a schoolmaster. Pellerin resumed his comparison of Michelangelo and Shakespeare. Dittmer was just going. Arnoux intercepted him, and put two bank notes in his hand. Then Hussonnet, seizing his opportunity, said:

'My dear patron, I suppose you couldn't advance me . . . ?'

But Arnoux had resumed his seat, and was shouting at a shabby-looking old man with blue spectacles:

'You're a fat lot of use, Father Isaac! That's three pieces

of work shown up and wasted. Every one's laughing at me. They've got on to it now. What can I do with the things? Send them to Jericho, or to the devil? Hold your tongue!'

This worthy specialized in putting the signatures of old masters at the bottom of pictures. Arnoux refused to pay him, and dismissed him roughly. Then, changing his manner, he greeted a carefully dressed gentleman with side whiskers and a white neck-cloth, who wore an order in his coat.

With his elbow on the window fastener, Arnoux talked to him for a long time, in honeyed tones. At last he burst out:

'Well, count, it doesn't embarrass me in the least to pay commission.'

The nobleman having submitted, Arnoux paid him twenty-five louis, and, as soon as he was outside, he said:

'What a bore these lords are!'

'All scoundrels!' murmured Regimbart.

As the hour grew later, Arnoux grew busier and busier; he sorted articles, opened letters, balanced accounts; at the sound of hammering he hurried to the shop to supervise the packing; then took up his work again, and kept up his repartee even as his pen sped over the paper. He was to dine with his lawyer that evening, and next morning was leaving for Belgium.

The others discussed such topics of the day as Cherubini's portrait, the hemicycle at the Beaux-Arts, and the forthcoming exhibition. Pellerin inveighed against the Institut de France. Gossip and argument met and intersected across the room. The low-ceilinged apartment was so full that movement was impossible; and the light from the pink candles was dimmed by cigar smoke, like sunshine in a mist.

The door near the couch opened, and a tall, thin woman came in. Her jerky movements made all the watch charms rattle on the front of her black taffeta dress.

It was the woman of whom he had caught a glimpse at the Palais-Royal the previous summer. Several of those present greeted her by name and shook hands with her. Hussonnet had at last succeeded in extracting fifty francs. The clock struck seven; every one withdrew.

Arnoux told Pellerin to stay behind, and led Mlle Vatnaz into the little room.

Frederic could not hear what they were saying; they were whispering.

Then the woman raised her voice:

35

'The business was finished six months ago, and I'm still waiting!'

There was a long silence. Mlle Vatnaz reappeared. Arnoux had again promised her something.

'Give me time and then I'll see.'

'Farewell, happy man!' she said, as she left.

Arnoux went back quickly into the little room, put some pomade on his moustache, hoisted his braces to tighten his foot-straps; then, as he washed his hands:

'I want two panels to go above a door. Two hundred and fifty francs apiece. Style of Boucher. All right?'

'Very well,' said the artist, blushing.

'Good! And don't forget my wife!'

Frederic walked with Pellerin to the top of the Faubourg Poissonnière, and asked his permission to call on him occasionally —a favour which was graciously granted.

Pellerin used to read every book on aesthetics, in the hope of discovering the true theory of the beautiful; for he was certain that he had only to find it to be able to paint masterpieces. He surrounded himself with every imaginable accessory—drawings, casts, models, engravings; he searched and fretted; blamed the weather, his nerves, his studio, went out into the street to seek inspiration, thrilled with excitement—he had it! Then he abandoned his work, to dream of another, which would be finer still. Tortured by a thirst for fame, wasting his days in argument, believing in countless absurd notions, in systems, in theories of criticism, in the importance of the codification or the reform of the arts, he had so far, at fifty, produced nothing but unfinished sketches. His strong pride prevented him from feeling at all discouraged; but he was always bad-tempered, and in that state of exaltation, at once real and artificial, which is characteristic of actors.

Entering his studio, one caught sight of two large pictures, the first tones of which stood out against the white canvas in scattered patches of brown, red, and blue. Above stretched a tracery of chalk lines, like the closely entwined meshes of a net. The whole thing was perfectly incomprehensible. Pellerin explained the subject of these two compositions by indicating the missing parts with his thumb. One was to represent 'The Madness of Nebuchadnezzar,' the other 'The Burning of Rome by Nero.' Frederic admired them.

He admired nudes with dishevelled hair, landscapes abounding in storm-shattered tree trunks, and, most of all, free sketches in pen and ink—echoes of Callot, Rembrandt, or Goya, the originals of which he did not know. Pellerin thought little of these earlier works; now he was for the grand style; he held forth eloquently on Phidias and Winckelmann. His brilliant talk drew strength from his picturesque surroundings; there was a skull on a *prie-dieu*; there were scimitars, and a monk's gown, which Frederic put on.

Arriving early, Frederic used to surprise him in his wretched truckle-bed, which was screened by a shred of tapestry; for Pellerin, an assiduous theatre-goer, went to bed late. A ragged old woman looked after him, he dined at cheap taverns, and he had no mistress. His wide, if miscellaneous, learning added point to his paradoxes. He would express his hatred of the vulgar and the commonplace in superb, almost lyrical outbursts of sarcasm, and his veneration for the old masters was such that it almost lifted him to their level.

But why did he never mention Mme Arnoux? Her husband he described sometimes as a good fellow, sometimes as a charlatan. Frederic awaited his confidences.

One day, turning the leaves of one of Pellerin's sketch-books, he came upon a portrait of a gipsy in which he saw a resemblance to Mlle Vatnaz, and, as the lady interested him, he wanted to know all about her.

She had started as a country school teacher, thought Pellerin; now she gave lessons and tried to write for the cheaper magazines.

Her behaviour with Arnoux, in Frederic's opinion, gave the impression that she was his mistress.

'Oh, nonsense! He's got others.'

Then the young man turned away his face—for the vileness of the thought that had come to him made him blush with shame—and remarked, with an attempt at jauntiness:

'I suppose his wife pays him back with interest?'

'Not at all! She's virtuous.'

Frederic was contrite. He visited Arnoux's office more frequently.

The large letters that spelled the name of Arnoux on the marble slab above the shop appeared to him to be of personal application, and to be charged with meaning, like a sacred writing. The wide, sloping pavement seemed to speed his steps; the door opened almost of its own accord, and the handle, smooth to his touch, was as docile and responsive as a hand in his own. By degrees he became as regular as Regimbart.

Every day Regimbart would sit down by the fireside,

seize the *National*,[1] and refuse to give it up, expressing his ideas by exclamations, or simply by shrugging his shoulders. From time to time he would wipe his forehead with his rolled-up handkerchief, which he usually carried tucked between two buttons of his green frock coat. He wore trousers with creases, half-boots, and a long cravat. He was recognizable in crowds, even from a distance, by his hat with its turned-up brim.

At eight o'clock in the morning he came down from the heights of Montmartre to drink white wine in the rue Notre-Dame-des-Victoires. His lunch, which was followed by several games of billiards, took him until three o'clock. He then made his way to the passage des Panoramas, to drink absinthe. After his visit to Arnoux, he went to the Bordelais tavern, to drink vermouth; then, instead of going home to his wife, he often preferred to dine alone, in a little café on the place Gaillon, where he insisted on 'simple home cooking—nothing fancy.' Eventually he moved on to another billiard saloon, and stayed there until midnight, until one in the morning, until the moment when the gas was turned out and the shutters closed, and the exhausted proprietor implored him to go away.

Citizen Regimbart was attracted to these haunts, not by love of the bottle, but by his old habit of talking politics there. With age his enthusiasm had waned; he had become morose and uncommunicative. From his serious expression you might have thought that his head was full of the most profound ideas. But he never expressed them, and no one—not even his friends —knew how he made his living, although he claimed to have an office and a business.

Arnoux seemed to have a boundless admiration for him. One day he said to Frederic:

'He takes a long view, that fellow. He 's an able man.'

On another occasion, Regimbart spread out on his desk some documents relating to deposits of china clay in Brittany. Arnoux put great faith in his knowledge of affairs.

Frederic was very polite to Regimbart—and even offered him a glass of absinthe from time to time; and, although he considered him stupid, he often spent a full hour in his company —for the sole reason that he was the friend of Jacques Arnoux.

Having helped to establish certain contemporary masters, the picture dealer, always progressive, had tried to increase his sources of revenue, while preserving his artistic associations. His aim was the popularization of the arts—the sublime for sixpence. Every branch of the Paris luxury trade felt his influence, which was good in small matters, but disastrous in the larger issues. With his passion for gratifying the public, he enticed able artists from their proper path; he corrupted the strong, exhausted the weak, and turned the second-rate into celebrities; for his connections and his magazine gave him widespread power. Bad painters longed to see their works in his window; and he provided decorators with patterns for upholstery. To Frederic he seemed to unite the attributes of a millionaire, a dilettante, and a man of action. But Arnoux often astonished him, for he was a sly business man.

A picture which he had bought in Paris for fifteen hundred francs would be sent to him from some remote part of Germany or Italy, with an invoice pricing it at four thousand. He would resell it, as a favour, for three thousand five hundred. A common trick of his with painters was to demand, as an extra, a small-scale copy of their picture, on the ground that he was going to publish a print of it. He invariably sold the copy, and the print never appeared. To those who complained of being exploited, he replied with a friendly dig in the ribs.

In some respects he was admirable. Lavish with cigars, familiar with strangers, impulsively enthusiastic over a picture or a man, he sometimes turned stubborn, refused all advice, and scurried about Paris in a whirl of letters and advertisements. He regarded himself as the soul of honesty, and in his moments of expansiveness would give a naïve account of his own misdeeds.

Once he wanted to annoy a colleague who was giving a large banquet to inaugurate a rival art magazine, so just before the party he asked Frederic to write, there and then, some notes putting off the guests.

'There's nothing dishonourable in it, you understand!'

And the young man dared not refuse him this service.

The next day, coming into his office with Hussonnet, Frederic saw the flounce of a dress disappearing through the door which opened on to the staircase.

'A thousand apologies!' said Hussonnet. 'If I'd known there were ladies . . .'

'Oh, that's only my wife,' said Arnoux. 'She's just been up to pay me a visit, on her way.'

'What!' said Frederic.

'Yes, she's going home now, to our house.'

The objects about him suddenly lost their charm. The vague effluence which he had felt in this place had vanished, or rather

39

had never existed. He experienced an immense surprise, and some of the anguish of a betrayal.

Arnoux, rummaging in his drawer, was smiling. Was he laughing at him? The assistant laid a bundle of damp papers on his desk.

'Ah! The posters!' cried the dealer. 'It 'll be hours before I dine to-night!'

Regimbart picked up his hat.

'What? Are you going?'

'Seven o'clock!' said Regimbart.

Frederic followed him.

At the corner of the rue Montmartre he turned round; he looked at the first-floor windows; and he laughed inwardly, pitying himself, when he remembered how lovingly he had often gazed at them. Where did she live, then? How could he meet her now? Vistas of loneliness opened about his desire, which was vaster than ever.

'Are you going to have one?' said Regimbart.

'Have what?'

'An absinthe.'

And yielding to his addiction, Frederic allowed himself to be led to the Bordelais tavern.

While his companion, leaning on his elbow, contemplated the decanter, he glanced from side to side. He caught sight of Pellerin's profile among the crowd on the pavement; he stamped sharply on the ground, and the painter had scarcely sat down before Regimbart asked him why he no longer appeared at 'Industrial Art.'

'I 'm damned if I ever go back. He 's a bounder, a Philistine, a scoundrel, a rogue!'

These insults soothed Frederic's anger. Yet they wounded him too, for they seemed to reflect indirectly on Mme Arnoux.

'Well, what 's he done to you?' said Regimbart.

Pellerin stamped his foot, and blew hard, instead of answering.

He was secretly working at portraits in chalk and charcoal, and pastiches of old masters for ignorant collectors. These daubs filled him with shame, and he generally preferred to say nothing about them. But 'that swine Arnoux' annoyed him too much. He relieved his feelings.

Arnoux had commissioned two pictures from him—as Frederic could witness—and he had delivered them. The dealer had dared to criticize them! He had found fault with the composition, the colour, and the drawing, particularly the drawing,

40

and, in short, would not take them at any price. Pellerin, in difficulties over a bill that had fallen due, had handed them over to the Jew Isaac; and, a fortnight later, Arnoux himself sold them to a Spaniard for two thousand francs.

'Not a penny less! What a swindle! And he's done plenty more like it too. One of these fine days we'll see him in the dock.'

'You're exaggerating,' said Frederic in a timid voice.

'All right! Good! I'm exaggerating!' cried the artist, crashing his fist down on the table.

This violent gesture restored all the young man's self-confidence. Possibly, he suggested, Arnoux might have behaved better; however, if he really thought these two canvases were——

'Bad! Don't say the word! Have you seen them? Is it your profession? You must understand this, my child: I don't accept criticism from amateurs.'

'Well, it's none of my business,' said Frederic.

'Then what interest had you in defending him?' asked Pellerin, coldly.

The young man stammered:

'But . . . Because I'm his friend.'

'Give him a kiss from me! Good night.'

And the painter went off in a rage, without, of course, mentioning the drink he had just consumed.

Frederic, in defending Arnoux, had convinced himself. Warmed by his own eloquence, he felt a sudden affection for this intelligent, good-hearted man, who was slandered by his friends, and was now working alone, deserted. He yielded to a strange desire to see him again, immediately. Ten minutes later he pushed open the door of the shop. Arnoux, with his assistant, was working at some huge posters for an exhibition of pictures.

'Well? What brings you back?'

This simple question embarrassed Frederic; and, not knowing what to answer, he asked if, by any chance, his pocket-book had been found—a little blue leather pocket-book.

'Where you keep your love letters?' said Arnoux. Frederic, blushing like a virgin, repudiated this suggestion.

'Your poems, then?' said the merchant.

He was turning over the placards in front of him, discussing their shape, their colour, their margins, and Frederic found himself becoming more and more irritated by his deliberate air, and especially by his hands, as he fingered the posters. They were large, rather soft hands, with flat nails. At last Arnoux got up, and, remarking 'That's that,' chucked him familiarly under the chin. This liberty annoyed Frederic; he drew back, and then passed through the office door, as he thought, for the last time in his life. Mme Arnoux herself seemed somehow diminished by her husband's vulgarity.

The same week he received a letter from Deslauriers. He would be in Paris on the following Thursday.

In a violent reaction he fell back on this stronger and loftier affection. A man like that was worth all the women in the world. No longer would he need Regimbart, Pellerin, Hussonnet, or any one else. For his friend's comfort, he bought an iron bedstead and a second arm-chair; he divided his bedding; and on the Thursday morning he was dressing to meet Deslauriers when the door bell rang. Arnoux came in.

'Just one word! I was sent a fine trout from Geneva yesterday. We're expecting you in the evening, at seven sharp. 24 *bis*, rue de Choiseul. Don't forget!'

Frederic was obliged to sit down. His knees were shaking. He repeated to himself:

'At last—at last!'

Then he wrote to his tailor, his hatter, his bootmaker; and he had the three notes delivered by three different messengers. The key turned in the lock, and the concierge appeared, with a trunk on his shoulder.

When Frederic saw Deslauriers, he began to tremble like a guilty wife at her husband's look.

'What's the matter with you?' said Deslauriers. 'You must have got my letter, surely?'

Frederic had not the strength to lie.

'Yes, I got it.'

And, opening his arms, he threw himself on his breast.

Then the clerk told his story. His father had refused to give an account of his trusteeship, believing that such accounts were legally limited to ten years. But Deslauriers, with his knowledge of procedure, had eventually extorted the whole of his mother's legacy—seven thousand francs clear, which he had with him now, in an old portfolio.

'That's my reserve, in case anything happens. To-morrow I shall have to find somewhere to put it, to say nothing of a roof for myself. To-day I'm on holiday and entirely at your disposal, my old friend!'

'Oh, don't put yourself out!' said Frederic. 'If you've something important on to-night . . .'

42

'Come now! I should be a selfish brute . . .'

This chance epithet pierced Frederic to the heart, like an insult.

On the table, by the fire, the concierge had spread out cutlets, galantine, a *langouste,* some dessert, and two bottles of claret. Deslauriers was touched by this hospitable reception.

'Upon my word, you 're treating me like a king!'

They talked of their past and their future; and from time to time they exchanged brief, affectionate glances, clasping hands across the table.

A messenger brought in a new hat. Deslauriers commented loudly on the brilliance of the lining.

Then the tailor came in person, to deliver the suit, which he had just pressed.

'You might be getting married,' said Deslauriers.

An hour later a third person arrived and drew a pair of glittering dress boots from a large black bag. While Frederic tried them on, he gave a supercilious glance at the country clerk's footwear.

'Does monsieur require anything?'

'No, thanks,' replied the clerk, withdrawing his old rope-soled shoes under the table.

This humiliation annoyed Frederic. He hesitated to make his confession. At last he exclaimed, as if he had suddenly remembered something:

'Good heavens—I was forgetting!'

'What?'

'I 'm dining out to-night.'

'With Dambreuse? Why do you never mention him in your letters?'

It was not with Dambreuse, but with Arnoux.

'You should have let me know,' said Deslauriers. 'I would have come a day later.'

'Impossible!' replied Frederic abruptly. 'I was only invited this morning.'

And to redeem his fault, and to distract his friend's thoughts from it, he undid the tangled cords of his trunk, and arranged all his things in the wardrobe; he wanted to give him his own bed and sleep in the wood cupboard. Then, just after four o'clock, he began to get ready to change.

'You 've plenty of time,' said the other.

At length he got dressed and went off.

'That 's the rich all over,' thought Deslauriers. And he went off to dine in the rue Saint-Jacques, at a little restaurant that belonged to a friend of his.

Frederic's heart was beating so hard that he paused several times on the staircase. His gloves were too tight; one of them burst, and as he was hiding the tear under his cuff, Arnoux, climbing the stairs behind him, seized him by the arm and led him inside.

The hall was decorated in the Chinese style. A painted lantern hung from the ceiling, and there were bamboos in the corners. Crossing the drawing-room, Frederic tripped over a tiger skin. The candelabra had not yet been lit, but two lamps were burning in the boudoir beyond.

Little Marthe came in to say that her mamma was dressing. Arnoux lifted her up and kissed her; then, as he wished to select certain bottles of wine from the cellar in person, he left Frederic with the child.

She had grown considerably since the journey to Montereau. Her brown hair hung down over her bare arms in long wavy curls. Her dress, which billowed out like a ballet dancer's skirt, revealed her pink calves, and her whole charming person smelt as fresh as a bunch of flowers. She received Frederic's compliments archly; then, slipping among the furniture, vanished like a cat.

He felt completely at ease. The lamps, with their shades of lace-like paper, shed a milky light, softening the colour of the walls, which were hung with mauve satin. Through the spokes of the fire guard, which looked like a big fan, coals could be seen in the fire-place; a box with silver clasps stood against the clock. Here and there homely objects were lying about: a doll in the middle of the settee, a scarf against the back of a chair, and, on the work table, some knitting from which two needles hung point downwards. The whole place had an atmosphere of peaceful, unaffected domesticity.

Arnoux came in again, and, through the other doorway, Mme Arnoux appeared.

She was in the shadow, and at first he could only see the outline of her head. She wore a black velvet dress, and, in her hair, a long Algerian head-dress of red silk ribbon, which was twisted through her comb and fell over her left shoulder.

Arnoux introduced Frederic.

'Oh, I remember this gentleman perfectly,' she answered.

Then all the guests arrived, almost simultaneously: Dittmer,

44

Lovarias, Burrieu, the composer Rosenwald, the poet Théophile Lorris, two art critics, colleagues of Hussonnet, a paper manufacturer, and, last of all, the celebrated Pierre-Paul Meinsius, the last representative of the grand style of painting, who carried in sprightly fashion his fame, his eighty years, and his great belly.

Mme Arnoux took his arm when they moved into the diningroom. A chair had been left empty for Pellerin. Arnoux was fond of him, although he exploited him. Besides, he dreaded his terrible tongue; so much so, that, to appease him, he had published his portrait in *Industrial Art*, accompanied by a lavish encomium; and Pellerin, more sensitive to fame than to money, appeared at about eight o'clock, quite out of breath. Frederic assumed that they had long been reconciled.

The company, the food—everything delighted him. The dining-room had hangings of embossed leather, like a medieval council chamber; a Dutch *étagère* stood by a rack of Turkish pipes; and, round the table, Bohemian glasses of all colours glowed among the flowers and fruit like illuminations in a garden.

There were ten sorts of mustard to choose from. He ate *daspachio*, curry, ginger, Corsican blackbirds, Roman *lasagna*; he drank extraordinary wines—*lip-fraoli* and Tokay. Arnoux took a justifiable pride in his hospitality. With an eye to his larder, he made friends with the conductors of mail-coaches; and he was in touch with the cooks at great houses, who gave him receipts for sauces.

But it was the conversation that particularly amused Frederic. His taste for travel was indulged by Dittmer, who spoke of the East; he gratified his curiosity about the theatre by listening to Rosenwald talking about the opera; and even the horrors of Bohemian life seemed amusing when seen through the gaiety of Hussonnet, who gave a picturesque description of how he had spent a whole winter with nothing to eat but Dutch cheese. Then an argument between Lovarias and Burrieu, over the Florentine school, revealed masterpieces and opened horizons to him, and he could hardly contain his enthusiasm when Pellerin exclaimed:

'I 've had enough of this hideous realism! What does realism mean? Some see black; some see blue; most see wrong. There 's no one less lifelike than Michelangelo, and no one more powerful. This cult of external truthfulness betrays the vulgarity of our age; at this rate, art will become a sort of joke in bad taste, subordinate to religion, like poetry, and to politics, like expediency. You 'll never attain the aim of art—I repeat, the aim of art—which is to give us an impersonal delight—with petty works, in spite of all your finicky execution! Take Bassolier's pictures, for instance; they 're pretty, charming, nice, and not heavy. You can put them in your pocket, or take them travelling with you. The lawyers pay twenty thousand francs for them; there 's not twopence-worth of ideas in them; but, without ideas, there can be no grandeur, and without grandeur, no beauty. Olympus is a mountain! The proudest monument will always be the pyramids. I prefer exuberance to taste, the desert to a pavement, and a savage to a hairdresser!'

Frederic watched Mme Arnoux while he listened to these things. They sank into his mind like metal into a furnace; they joined themselves to his passion, and filled him with love.

He was sitting three places below her, on the same side of the table. From time to time she leaned forward slightly, to say a few words to her little daughter; she smiled, and a dimple puckered her cheek, giving her face a look of rarer goodness.

When the liqueurs were served she vanished. The conversation became very free; M. Arnoux excelled in it, and Frederic was astonished at the cynicism of these men. But their preoccupation with women established a sort of equality between him and them, which raised him in his own estimation.

They returned to the drawing-room. Frederic picked up an album which was lying on the table. The great artists of the period had illustrated it with drawings; some had written pieces of prose, or verse, or just their signatures; among the famous names were many nonentities, and interesting thoughts appeared only among a mass of platitudes. All contained a tribute, direct or indirect, to Mme Arnoux. Frederic would not have dared to write a line beside the others.

She went into her boudoir to fetch the box with the silver clasps which he had noticed on the mantelpiece. It was a present from her husband, a work of the Renaissance. Arnoux's friends complimented him, his wife thanked him; he felt suddenly affectionate, and kissed her in front of every one.

After that they all talked in scattered groups, round the room. Meinsius was with Mme Arnoux, on an arm-chair by the fire; she leaned over to whisper in his ear, their heads were touching; and Frederic would have gladly been deaf, infirm, and ugly, for the sake of a famous name and white hair, for the sake, in fact, of anything that could establish him in an intimacy such as this. He fretted, furious at his youth.

Then she moved over to his corner of the room, and asked

him if he knew any of the guests, if he was fond of painting, how long he had been studying in Paris. Each word that fell from her mouth seemed to Frederic to be a new object, a creation exclusively hers. He gazed at the fringes of her hair, the ends of which brushed her bare shoulder; he stared and stared; he plunged his soul into this white female flesh; yet he did not dare raise his eyes and look her straight in the face.

Rosenwald interrupted them by asking Mme Arnoux to sing. She waited while he ran over the keys; her lips parted, and a sound, pure and long-drawn-out, floated on the air.

Frederic did not understand the Italian words.

It began with a solemn measure, like church chanting, then, growing faster and louder, it burst into repeated explosions of sound, then suddenly died away; and the melody returned lovingly, with a lazy, sweeping lilt.

She stood by the piano, her arms at her sides, her eyes unseeing. Sometimes she thrust her head forward to read the music, screwing up her eyes for a moment. Her contralto voice took on a mournful, icy tone in the lower register, and then she leaned her lovely head, with the heavy eyebrows, towards her shoulder; suddenly she looked up, her eyes flaming; her bosom swelled, she stretched out her arms, and, as she trilled and warbled, her throat quivered gently as if under an ethereal kiss; she sang three high notes, came down the scale, threw out one higher still, and, after a moment's silence, finished with a long-sustained cadence.

Rosenwald remained at the piano. He went on playing for his own amusement. One by one the guests disappeared. At eleven, as the last were leaving, Arnoux went out with Pellerin, under the pretext of taking him home. He was one of those people who say they are ill if they have not 'taken the air' after dinner.

Mme Arnoux had come as far as the hall; Dittmer and Hussonnet were saying good-bye to her; she held out her hand to them; she held it out to Frederic too; and he felt a kind of permeation through every particle of his skin.

He left his friends; he wanted to be alone. His heart was overflowing.

Why had she offered him her hand? Was it a thoughtless gesture, or a deliberate encouragement?

'Come, I must be mad!'

Besides, what did it matter, since he could now visit her at his ease, and breathe the same air as she?

The streets were deserted. Sometimes a heavy cart went by, shaking the roadway. He passed endless rows of grey-fronted, shuttered houses; and he thought with contempt of all the human beings asleep behind these walls, living without seeing her, not even aware that she existed! He was no longer conscious of his surroundings, of distance, of anything; and, treading firmly, striking the shutters of the shops with his stick, he went on walking straight in front of him, at random, spellbound, enchanted. There was damp air about him; he realized that he was on the quays.

The street lamps blazed in two straight lines, away into the distance, and long red flames flickered in the depths of the river. The water was the colour of slate; while the sky, less dark, seemed to be supported by the great masses of shadow that rose on either side of the river. Unseen buildings intensified the darkness. Beyond, over the roof tops, a luminous haze floated; all noises melted into a single hum; a light wind blew.

He had stopped in the middle of the Pont-Neuf, and, bareheaded, his coat open, he breathed in the air. All at once he felt something imperishable welling up from the depths of his being, a surge of tenderness which made him dizzy, as if waves were moving under his eyes. One o'clock struck from a church tower, slowly, like a voice calling him.

Then he was seized with one of those tremblings of the spirit which seem to transport one into a higher world. There had come to him an extraordinary talent, the object of which he did not know. He wondered, seriously, if he was to be a great painter, or a great poet; and he decided in favour of painting, for the demands of this profession would bring him closer to Mme Arnoux. So he had found his vocation! The aim of his existence was now clear, and the future infallible.

When he had closed his door, he heard someone snoring in the dark cupboard, by his room. It was his friend. He dismissed him from his mind.

His own face confronted him in the mirror. He liked what he saw, and stayed a moment to look.

CHAPTER V

BY noon the next day he had bought himself a paint box, brushes, and an easel. Pellerin agreed to give him lessons, and Frederic brought him to his rooms, to make sure that his painting equipment was complete.

Deslauriers was there, and there was a young man sitting in the second arm-chair. The clerk pointed to him and said:

'It's he! Here he is! Sénécal!'

Frederic did not like the youth. His short-cropped hair made his forehead look too high. There was something hard and cold and piercing in his grey eyes; and his long black frock coat, his whole costume, smacked of the pedagogue and the priest.

At first they talked about the topics of the day, including Rossini's *Stabat*; Sénécal, questioned, declared that he never went to the theatre. Pellerin opened the paint box.

'Is all this for you?' said Deslauriers.

'Of course.'

'Well, well! How very odd!'

And he leaned over the table, where Sénécal was turning over a volume of Louis Blanc, which he had brought with him. He read passages aloud in a low voice, while Pellerin and Frederic examined the palette, the knife, and the bladders; then they began to talk about Arnoux's dinner party.

'The picture-dealer?' asked Sénécal. 'There's a fine fellow for you!'

'What do you mean?' asked Pellerin.

Sénécal replied:

'He's made a fortune by means of a vile political trick.'

And he began to talk about a famous lithograph, which represented the entire royal family engaged in edifying pursuits. Louis-Philippe held a legal code, the queen a prayer book, the princesses were doing embroidery, the Duc de Nemours was buckling on a sabre; M. de Joinville was showing a map to his younger brother; at the back could be seen a bed with two compartments. This picture, entitled 'A Good Family,' had been the delight of the middle classes, but the despair of the patriots. Pellerin, in an offended tone, as though he had drawn it himself,

49

replied that opinions differed; Sénécal objected. The sole aim of art should be the moral guidance of the masses. Only those subjects should be represented that encouraged virtuous action; the rest were harmful.

'But that depends on the execution,' cried Pellerin. 'I can paint masterpieces!'

'So much the worse for you, then. You haven't the right . . .'

'What?'

'No, sir, you haven't the right to interest me in matters of which I disapprove. What need have we of such elaborate and useless toys as these Venuses and landscapes of yours? I see no instruction for the people in them. Rather, show us the miseries of the masses! Rouse our zeal for their sacrifices! Good God, there's no lack of subjects: the farm, the workshop.'

Pellerin stuttered in his indignation, and, thinking he had found an argument, said:

'Do you accept Molière?'

'Certainly,' said Sénécal. 'I admire him as a precursor of the French Revolution.'

'Oh, the revolution! What art! There's never been a more woeful period.'

'Nor a greater, sir.'

Pellerin folded his arms, and, gazing straight in his face, said:

'You look to me like a member of our famous National Guard!'[1]

His opponent, accustomed to arguments, replied:

'I'm not one of *them*! And I loathe them as much as you do. But principles such as Arnoux holds may corrupt the masses. Besides, that kind of thing plays into the hands of the Government; they would not be so strong if they weren't supported by a gang of charlatans like him.'

The painter took up the dealer's defence, for Sénécal's views infuriated him. He went so far as to maintain that Jacques Arnoux had a heart of gold, was loyal to his friends, and devoted to his wife.

'Ho ho! If you offered him enough he wouldn't refuse to let her pose as a model!'

Frederic turned pale.

'Then he must have done you some serious injury, sir?'

'Me? No. I saw him once at a café with a friend—that's all.'

Sénécal was telling the truth. But he was daily exasperated by the advertisements for *Industrial Art*. To him, Arnoux represented a world which he considered disastrous to democracy. An austere Republican, he suspected corruption in all the refinements of life. For he had no need for such things himself, and his integrity was inviolable.

It was difficult to resume the conversation. The painter soon remembered an appointment, the teacher his pupils; their departure was followed by a long silence. Then Deslauriers asked several questions about Arnoux.

'You 'll introduce me to him later on, won't you, old fellow?'

'Of course,' said Frederic.

Then they began to plan their household. Deslauriers had easily secured a position as junior clerk to an advocate; he had enrolled himself at the law school and bought the necessary books, and the life of which they had so often dreamed began.

It was charming, thanks to the beauty of their youth. Deslauriers had not suggested any financial agreement, so Frederic did not raise the point. He paid all the expenses, filled the larder, and took charge of the housekeeping; but if the porter had to be reprimanded, Deslauriers undertook the task, retaining, as at college, his position as elder and protector.

Separated all day long, they met again in the evening. Each took his place by the fireside, and set to work. Interruptions were not slow in coming. There were endless confidences, bursts of sudden gaiety, and occasional arguments over a smoking lamp or a lost book—momentary quarrels, which were quenched by laughter.

They left the door of the wood cupboard open, and chattered from a distance, in bed.

In the morning they strolled on the roof in their shirt sleeves; the sun was rising, light mists floated over the river, they could hear a dog barking in the neighbouring flower market; the smoke of their pipes twirled up into the clear air; their sleepy eyes grew keen; and, breathing deeply, they had a sense of vast and spreading hope.

On fine Sundays they went out for walks; and, arm in arm, they set off through the streets. Nearly always the same thought came to them at the same time, or else they talked, unconscious of their surroundings. Deslauriers longed for wealth, as a means of power over men. He wanted to cut a dash, to make his mark, to have three secretaries at his call, and a big political dinner once a week. Frederic furnished a Moorish palace for himself, and lived stretched on silken divans, beside a murmuring fountain, attended by negro pages; and the objects in these fantasies became so real that in the end they made him miserable, as though he had been deprived of them.

'What's the good of talking about all this,' he used to say, 'since we shall never possess it?'

'You never know,' said Deslauriers.

In spite of his democratic views he urged Frederic to get a footing in the Dambreuses' house. The other referred to his previous failures.

'Nonsense. Go back. They'll invite you.'

About the middle of March they received, among other heavy bills, that of the caterer who supplied their dinner. Frederic, not having enough money, borrowed three hundred francs from Deslauriers; a fortnight later he repeated the request, and the clerk reproached him for his extravagant expenditure at Arnoux's shop.

He had, indeed, abandoned all restraint. Views of Venice, Naples, and Constantinople covered the wall facing the window; there were equestrian studies by Alfred de Dreux all over the place, a group by Pradier on the mantelpiece, old numbers of *Industrial Art* on the piano, and cloth-bound books on the floor in the corners. The flat was so full that there was barely room to put down a book, or move one's elbows. Frederic claimed that all this was necessary for his painting.

He worked in Pellerin's rooms. But Pellerin was often out—for it was his custom to attend any funeral or other event which was likely to be reported in the newspapers—and Frederic spent hours alone in his studio. The quiet of this large room—where nothing could be heard but the scampering of mice—the light that fell from the ceiling, even the wheezing of the stove, filled him at once with a deep intellectual contentment. But soon his eyes, leaving his work, began to stray over the cracked walls, the ornaments on the *étagère*, and the row of plaster casts on which the dust lay thick, like strips of velvet; and, like a traveller lost in the middle of a wood, whom every path leads back to the same place, he always found, behind each thought, the memory of Mme Arnoux.

He made appointments for himself to go and see her; when he reached her door on the second floor he was afraid to ring. Steps approached; the door opened, and at the words, 'Madame is out,' he felt a sense of deliverance, as if there were one less burden on his heart.

Yet he met her. The first time she was with three ladies; another afternoon little Marthe's writing master joined her. He learned that the men who were received by Mme Arnoux never paid her visits. He did not try again, out of discretion.

But he never failed to appear regularly, every Wednesday, at 'Industrial Art,' to secure his invitation to the Thursday dinners; and he stayed after all the rest, longer than Regimbart, until the last minute, pretending to be looking at a print, or reading a newspaper. At last Arnoux would say to him: 'Are you free to-morrow evening?' He would accept before the sentence was finished. Arnoux seemed to have taken a liking to him. He taught him the art of distinguishing wines, of brewing punch, of making salmis of woodcock; Frederic followed his advice with docility—for he was in love with everything connected with Mme Arnoux, her furniture, her servants, her house, her street.

He hardly ever spoke during these dinners; he watched her. On her right temple she had a tiny mole; her side tresses were darker than the rest of her hair, and always seemed a little damp at the edges; she patted them from time to time, with two fingers only. He knew the shape of each of her nails, he loved to hear the rustle of her silk dress when she passed near a doorway, he furtively sniffed the scent on her handkerchief; her comb, her gloves, her rings were objects of special significance for him, as important as works of art, almost as alive as human beings; they caught at his heart and increased his passion.

He had not the strength to hide it from Deslauriers. When he came back from Mme Arnoux's house he would wake him up, as if by accident, so that he could talk about her.

Deslauriers, lying in the wood cupboard, gave a great yawn. Frederic sat down at the foot of his bed. At first he spoke of the dinner; then he described innumerable insignificant details, in which he saw marks of dislike or affection. Once she had refused his arm, to take Dittmer's, and Frederic was miserable.

'Don't be such a fool!' said Deslauriers.

Or she had called him her friend.

'Then cheer up and get on with it!'

'But I dare not,' said Frederic.

'Well, forget about it. Good night.'

Deslauriers turned towards the street and went to sleep.

He did not understand this passion, which he regarded as a final weakness of adolescence; and, since, apparently, his company was no longer enough for Frederic, he had the idea of bringing together their common friends once a week.

The guests used to arrive on Saturday at about nine. The

three curtains of striped cotton would be carefully drawn; the lamp and four candles burned brightly; the tobacco jar, full of pipes, stood in the centre of the table, surrounded by bottles of beer, a tea pot, a flask of rum, and some cakes. They discussed the immortality of the soul, and made comparisons between their professors.

One evening Hussonnet brought in a tall, shy-looking youth, who wore a frock coat with very short sleeves. It was the young man they had tried to rescue from the police station the year before.

He had not been able to restore to his employer the box of lace lost in the struggle; the latter had accused him of theft, and threatened him with proceedings; he was now working for a firm of carriers. Hussonnet had come across him that morning at a street corner; and he had brought him with him, because Dussardier, full of gratitude, wanted to see 'the other.'

He held out the cigar case to Frederic. It was still full, for he had carefully preserved it in the hope of being able to give it back. The young men invited him to come again. He did so.

Every one sympathized. To begin with, their hatred of the Government had the sublimity of an unquestioned dogma. Only Martinon tried to defend Louis-Philippe. They overwhelmed him with facts that could be read in every newspaper—the forts round Paris,[1] the September laws,[2] Pritchard, 'Lord' Guizot.[3] Martinon said nothing, fearing to give offence. During his seven years at college he had not suffered one imposition, and he knew how to please the professors at the law school. He usually wore a large putty-coloured frock coat and galoshes; but one evening he appeared in a bridegroom's costume—velvet shawl waistcoat, white tie, and gold chain.

There was further astonishment when it was learned that he had come from M. Dambreuse's house. As a matter of fact the banker had just bought a large quantity of wood from Martinon's father. The latter had introduced his son to him, and M. Dambreuse had invited them both to dinner.

'Were there plenty of truffles?' asked Deslauriers, 'and did you put your arm round his wife's waist in the passage, in the proper manner?'

Then the conversation turned on women. Pellerin denied that there were any beautiful women (he preferred tigers); besides, the human female took an inferior place in the aesthetic hierarchy.

'The things you find attractive are precisely those which degrade her, as an idea; I mean the breasts, the hair . . .'

54

'All the same,' Frederic protested, 'long black hair, and large, dark eyes . . .'

'Oh! I know,' cried Hussonnet. 'We 've had enough of the Spanish type, thank you! As for Greek and Roman women—they 're all very well; but when all 's said and done a tart is more fun than the Venus of Milo. Let 's be Gallic, for heaven's sake. Let 's be regency rakes, if we can!

Flow free, good wine; and, women, deign to smile!

We must pass from the brunettes to the blondes! Do you agree, Dussardier, old fellow?'

Dussardier did not answer. They all urged him to confess his preferences.

'Well,' he said, blushing, 'I 'd like to love the same woman all the time.'

He said this in such a manner that there was a moment's silence; some were disconcerted by this frank utterance, while others, perhaps, recognized in it the secret desire of their own hearts.

Sénécal put his mug of beer down on the window sill and declared roundly that, as prostitution was tyrannical, and marriage immoral, it was better to abstain. Deslauriers regarded women as a distraction, nothing more. M. de Cisy suffered from every kind of apprehension concerning them.

Brought up under the eye of an adoring grandmother, he found the company of these young men as fascinating as a haunt of vice and as instructive as a university. They did not grudge him his tuition; and he proved to be full of zeal; he even tried to smoke, in spite of the heart attacks which invariably followed each attempt. Frederic was extremely attentive to him. He admired the colour of his cravats, the fur on his jacket, and, above all, his boots, which were as thin as gloves and seemed almost insolent in their spotless elegance. His carriage used to wait for him in the street below.

One snowy evening after he had left, Sénécal began to express pity for his coachman. Then he denounced the Jockey Club and the idle rich. A workman was worth more than all these gentlemen.

'At least, I 'm a worker! I 'm poor!'

'That 's self-evident,' said Frederic at last, losing patience.

Sénécal never forgave him this remark.

As Regimbart had once remarked that he knew Sénécal slightly, Frederic, anxious to be civil to Arnoux's friend, invited him to the Saturday parties. The two patriots enjoyed the encounter.

However, their views differed.

Sénécal—who had a pointed skull—only valued systems. Regimbart, on the other hand, saw nothing in facts but facts. His principal source of anxiety was the Rhine frontier. He claimed to be an artillery expert, and had his clothes made by the tailor of the Polytechnic school.

When he was offered cakes on his first visit, he shrugged his shoulders contemptuously, remarking that such things were more suited to women; and he was scarcely more gracious on subsequent occasions. As soon as the discussion took on a lofty tone, he would murmur: 'No Utopias, no fantasies, please!' On artistic matters—although he often visited studios, where he occasionally condescended to give a fencing lesson—his views were by no means elevated. He compared the style of M. Marast[1] with that of Voltaire, and Mlle Vatnaz to Mme de Staël, on account of an ode on Poland which 'had some feeling in it.' Regimbart ended by boring everybody, and particularly Deslauriers, because he was a member of Arnoux's circle. It was the clerk's ambition to visit this house, where he hoped to make useful acquaintances.

'Well, when are you going to take me there?' he used to say. Arnoux, he was told, was up to his eyes in work, or else was going abroad; then, it was scarcely worth the trouble, as the dinners were coming to an end.

If necessary Frederic would have risked his life for his friend. But he was bent on making the best possible impression; he studied his language, his behaviour, and his dress—when he visited the office of *Industrial Art* his gloves were always immaculate—and he was afraid that Deslauriers, with his old black coat, his attorney's manner, and his aggressive way of talking, would irritate Mme Arnoux, which might reflect on himself, and lower him in her estimation. He did not mind the others, but Deslauriers, somehow, would have embarrassed him enormously. The clerk noticed that he did not intend to keep his promise, and Frederic's silence seemed to add insult to injury.

He would have liked to control Frederic completely, and watch him develop on the lines of their youthful ideal; and his feebleness revolted him—it was mutiny, it was treason. Moreover, Frederic, obsessed with Mme Arnoux, often spoke of her husband, and Deslauriers began a horrible game, which consisted in repeating his name a hundred times a day, at the end of every sentence, like a nervous tic. Whenever there was

56

a knock on the door, he would answer: 'Come in, Arnoux.' At the restaurant, he would ask for Brie cheese 'in the style of Arnoux'; and at night, pretending to have a nightmare, he would awaken his companion with shouts of 'Arnoux! Arnoux!' At last Frederic could bear it no longer, and said to him in a pitiable voice:

'Please stop going on about Arnoux!'

'Never!' replied the clerk.

> 'He's everywhere! Whether in fire or ice,
> The Arnoux image——'

'Shut up!' exclaimed Frederic, raising his fist.

He went on gently:

'You know it's a painful subject.'

'Oh, I beg your pardon, my little fellow,' replied Deslauriers, bowing very low. 'In future we shall make allowances for the young lady's nerves. I'm very sorry indeed. A thousand apologies!'

In this way the joke came to an end.

But three weeks later, Deslauriers said one evening:

'Well, I've just seen Madame Arnoux.'

'Where?'

'At the Palais de Justice, with Balandard, a lawyer; she's a dark woman, isn't she, of medium height?'

Frederic made a gesture of assent. He was waiting for Deslauriers to speak. At the least expression of admiration he would have opened his heart; he was ready to adore his friend. But the other still said nothing; at last he could bear it no longer, and, with an assumed casualness, he asked him what he thought of her.

Deslauriers considered her 'not bad, but not in any way exceptional.'

'Oh, you think so?' said Frederic.

August came, and with it his second examination. The general view was that a fortnight's preparation should be sufficient; Frederic, confident of his ability, swallowed at a gulp the first four books of the Code of Procedure, the first three of the Penal Code, several portions of the Criminal Law and part of the Civil Code, with M. Poncelet's notes. The evening before, Deslauriers went through the subjects with him, the revision lasting until the morning; and, so as not to waste the last quarter of an hour, he continued to ask Frederic questions as they walked along the pavement.

Several examinations were being held that day, and the courtyard was full of people. Hussonnet and Cisy were there, for it was the custom to attend these tests when one's friends were concerned. Frederic assumed the traditional black gown; then he went with three other students into a large room lit by curtainless windows and furnished with benches along the walls. A table with a green cloth stood in the centre surrounded by leather-covered chairs. At this table sat the examiners, in their red robes, with ermine hoods on their shoulder, and gold-braided hats on their heads.

Frederic was last but one in his group—a bad position. The first question was on the difference between a covenant and a contract, and he defined the one for the other; but the professor, a good fellow, said to him: 'Don't be nervous, sir! Take it easy!' Then, after putting two easy questions which received obscure replies, he passed on to the fourth candidate. This unhappy beginning demoralized Frederic. Deslauriers, sitting opposite in the audience, signalled to him that all was not yet lost; and at the second interrogation, on Criminal Law, he did reasonably well. The third concerned the Sealed Testament, and the complete impassivity of the examiner intensified his misery; for Hussonnet had his hands together, as if to applaud, while Deslauriers shrugged his shoulders continuously. At last it was time for the examination on Procedure. They were questioning him about third-party intervention. The professor, annoyed at hearing views contrary to his own, asked him in a brutal tone:

'And is this really your opinion, monsieur? How do you reconcile Article 1351 of the Civil Code with this extraordinary method of approach?'

Frederic, who had not slept all night, felt a terrible pain in his head. A ray of sunlight, passing through a chink in the shutters, shone into his face. Standing behind his chair, he shuffled his feet and tugged at his moustache.

'I'm waiting for your answer,' continued the man in the gold hat.

And, as Frederic's movements seemed to annoy him, he added:
'And you won't find it in your beard, either!'

This sarcastic comment raised a laugh in the audience; the professor, flattered, relented. He asked two more questions about the subpoena and the summary procedure, then inclined his head in a gesture of approval. The oral examination was over. Frederic returned to the ante-room.

While the usher was stripping off his gown, which was immediately passed on to another candidate, his friends surrounded him, and succeeded in bewildering him with their conflicting views on the result of the examination. This was soon declared, in a loud voice, at the door of the hall: 'The third candidate was . . . referred back!'

'Ploughed!' said Hussonnet. 'Let's be off!'

By the porter's lodge they met Martinon, pink-faced and excited, with a smile in his eyes and a halo of triumph round his head. He had just passed his final examination without difficulty. Only the thesis remained. Within a fortnight he would be a qualified lawyer. His parents knew a minister: 'a fine career' was opening before him.

'Whatever you may say, he's put you in your place,' said Deslauriers.

There is nothing more ignominious than seeing fools succeed where one fails oneself. In a fit of pique Frederic said he didn't care. He had loftier ambitions; and, as Hussonnet showed signs of leaving them, he took him aside and said to him:

'Not a word of this to *them*, you understand.'

The secret would be easy to keep; for Arnoux was leaving for Germany the next day.

Returning home that evening, the clerk found a singular change in his friend; he was whistling and pirouetting; and, when he showed surprise at this mood, Frederic declared that he was not going home; he would spend his holidays working.

The news of Arnoux's departure had filled him with joy. He could visit the house freely, without fear of interruption. The certainty of complete security would give him courage. Above all he would not be in exile, separated from Her! He was tied to Paris by a bond stronger than a chain of steel; an inner voice commanded him to stay.

There were difficulties. He overcame them by writing to his mother.

First he confessed his reverse, which was due to changes in the schedule, to bad luck, and to prejudice; besides, all the greatest lawyers—he gave their names—had failed in their examinations. However, he proposed to try again in November. So, as he had no time to lose, he did not intend to come home that year; and, in addition to a term's money, he asked for two hundred and fifty francs, for private coaching in law, which would be of the greatest assistance to him. The letter was embellished with expressions of regret, sympathy, flattery, and filial affection.

Mme Moreau, who was expecting him the following day, was doubly disappointed. She concealed her son's mishap from her friends, and wrote to him 'to come all the same.' Frederic stood firm. A quarrel ensued. Nevertheless, at the end of the week he received a term's allowance, together with the money for his private coaching—which enabled him to purchase a pair of pearl-grey trousers, a white top hat, and a stick with a gold knob.

When he had acquired all this he wondered if his plan might not be in the worst possible taste. And grave qualms assailed him.

He tossed a coin three times into the air to decide if he should go to see Mme Arnoux. Each time the omens were favourable. So it was ordained by fate! He went to the rue de Choiseul in a cab.

He climbed the staircase rapidly, and pulled the bell rope. It did not ring. He felt on the point of fainting.

Then he tugged furiously at the heavy red satin tassel. A deafening peal rang out, and gradually died away. Nothing more was heard. Frederic was frightened.

He glued his ear to the door. Not a sound!

He put his eye to the keyhole; he could see nothing in the hall save the tips of two bulrushes, against the flowered wall paper. He was about to retrace his steps, when he changed his mind. This time he gave a short, gentle ring. The door opened; and there, on the threshold, with tousled hair, a crimson face, and a look of fury, stood Arnoux in person.

'Well! What the devil brings you here? Come in!'

He led him, not into the boudoir, or into his own room, but into the dining-room. There was a bottle of champagne and two glasses on the table. Abruptly he said:

'You've got something to ask me, my dear fellow?'

'No, no! Nothing!' stammered the young man, searching for an excuse for his visit.

At last he said that he had come to get news of him, because he understood from Hussonnet that he was in Germany.

'Nonsense!' said Arnoux. 'It's just like that crack-brained idiot to misunderstand everything!'

To conceal his uneasiness Frederic walked up and down the room. Stumbling against the leg of a chair he knocked down a parasol that was lying on it; the ivory handle broke.

'Good heavens!' he exclaimed. 'I'm most distressed at having broken Madame Arnoux's parasol.'

At these words the dealer raised his head and gave a peculiar smile. Frederic, seizing the opportunity of talking about her, added timidly:

'Could I not see her?'

She was at her old home, with her sick mother.

He dared not inquire how long she would be away. He only asked what district she came from.

'Chartres! Does that surprise you?'

'Me? No! Why? Not in the least!'

After that they found absolutely nothing to say to each other. Arnoux, who had rolled himself a cigarette, walked round the table, puffing. Frederic, standing by the stove, gazed at the walls, the dresser, the floor; and delightful visions passed through his memory, or rather before his eyes. At last he withdrew.

There was a piece of newspaper rolled into a ball on the floor in the hall; Arnoux picked it up and, standing on tiptoe, thrust it into the bell, so that he could continue, as he said, his interrupted siesta. Then, shaking Frederic by the hand, he added:

'Please tell the concierge that I'm not at home.' And he slammed the door behind his back.

Frederic went down the staircase step by step. The failure of his first attempt did not encourage him to try again.

Then began three months of tedium. As he had no occupation, his idleness intensified his melancholy.

He spent hours on his balcony, watching the river flowing between the grey walls of the quays, which were smudged with black here and there from the inflow of a drain; a raft for washerwomen was moored to the bank; sometimes children played in the mud, and amused themselves by bathing a poodle. Leaving on the left the stone bridge of Notre-Dame and the three suspension bridges, his eyes always strayed in the direction of the quai aux Ormes, towards a clump of ancient trees, which reminded him of the limes at Montereau harbour. Facing him, the tower of Saint-Jacques, the Hôtel de Ville, Saint-Gervais, Saint-Louis, and Saint-Paul rose among a labyrinth of roofs—and the statue of Liberty at the Bastille glittered in the east like a great star of gold, while, far away on the other side, the Tuileries reared its heavy blue dome against the sky. Somewhere behind that dome lay the house of Madame Arnoux.

He went back into his room; and lying on his divan, gave himself up to a reverie that mingled schemes of work, plans of action, and dreams for the future. At length, to escape from himself, he went out.

He walked idly up the Latin quarter. The once bustling

streets were deserted, for the students had gone home. The great walls of the colleges looked somehow longer and more gloomy in the silence; all kinds of peaceful sounds could be heard, the beating of wings in bird cages, the whining of a lathe, a cobbler's hammer; while the old-clothes men, in the middle of the road, looked hopefully but in vain at every window. In the depths of deserted cafés the women at the cash desks yawned between untouched decanters; the newspapers lay undisturbed on the reading room tables; in the laundresses' workshops the drying linen flapped in the warm, gusty wind. From time to time he stopped at a bookseller's stall; an omnibus that grazed the pavement as it passed made him turn round; and, having reached the Luxembourg, he turned back.

Sometimes, seeking amusement, he was attracted towards the boulevards. From the damp, cool air of dark alleys he would emerge on to great empty squares, full of dazzling light, where statues threw black jagged shadows on to the edge of the pavement. Soon the traffic and the shops began again; and the crowds made him dizzy, especially on Sundays, when, from the Bastille to the Madeleine, a vast wave of humanity streamed over the asphalt, amid a cloud of dust, in a continuous uproar. He felt utterly nauseated by the vileness of their faces, the stupidity of their talk, the imbecile complacency that glistened on those sweating brows. Yet the knowledge that he was worth more than these men mitigated the fatigue of looking at them.

Every day he went to 'Industrial Art'—and, in order to find out when Mme Arnoux was coming back, he made lengthy inquiries about her mother. Arnoux's answer was always the same: 'the improvement was maintained'; his wife, with the little girl, would be back the following week. The longer she was away the more anxiety Frederic betrayed; so that Arnoux, touched by such constant affection, took him out to dinner at a restaurant five or six times.

During these long meals alone with the dealer, Frederic realized that his friend was not the most amusing of men. Arnoux might notice his diminishing enthusiasm; and, besides, it was time to return some of his hospitality.

Anxious to do things in style, Frederic sold all his new coats to a second-hand shop, for the sum of eighty francs; adding to this a hundred which he had left, he made his way to Arnoux's house to take him out to dinner. Regimbart was there. They went to the 'Trois-Frères-Provençaux.'

The citizen began by undoing his coat, and, confident of the approval of his companions, wrote out the menu. But it was in vain that he visited the kitchen to speak to the chef in person, that he went down to the cellar, where he knew every corner, that he called for the manager, to whom he gave a 'dressing-down'—he was satisfied neither with the food, the wine, nor the service. At every new dish, at every fresh bottle, at the first mouthful, the first sip, he would drop his fork, or push away his glass; then, leaning on the table cloth to the full length of his arm, he would exclaim that one could no longer dine in Paris! At last, not knowing how to please his palate, he ordered beans cooked in oil, 'nothing more,' which, although only partially successful, mollified him slightly. Then he had a conversation with the waiter about former waiters at the 'Trois - Frères.' What had happened to Antoine? And the one called Eugène? And little Théodore, who always worked downstairs? 'In those days they served food of real distinction, and fine Burgundies, the like of which we shall not see again!'

They went and had coffee at a tavern in the passage du Saumon, upstairs. Frederic, standing up, was a spectator of endless games of billiards, washed down with innumerable glasses of beer: and he stayed there until midnight, without knowing why—out of cowardice, out of stupidity, in the vague hope of some occurrence favourable to his passion.

When would he see her again? Frederic was in despair, when one evening, towards the end of November, Arnoux said to him:

'You know my wife came home yesterday.'

The next day, at five, he was at her house. He began by congratulating her on the recovery of her mother, who had been so ill.

'No! no! Who told you?'

'Arnoux.'

She said, 'Oh!' gently; then added that at first she had had serious apprehensions, which were now dispelled.

She was sitting by the fire, in the arm-chair with the tapestry cover. He was on the sofa, his hat between his knees; and their conversation was uncomfortable, as she constantly let it drop; he could find no opening for a reference to his feelings. When he complained that what he was studying was the art of fraud, she replied: 'Yes . . . I can imagine it . . . business . . .' and looked at the ground, suddenly absorbed in her own reflections.

63

He longed to share them and he could think of nothing else. The dusk deepened the shadows around them.

She rose, having an errand to do, then reappeared wearing a velvet bonnet and a black cloak edged with squirrel's fur. Boldly he offered to accompany her.

They could scarcely see their way; the weather was cold, and a heavy, evil-smelling fog lay in the air and blurred the outlines of the houses. Frederic breathed it in with joy, for he could feel, through the thickness of her clothes, the shape of her arm; and her hand, in a chamois leather glove with two buttons— her little hand that he would have liked to cover with kisses— was resting on his sleeve. The slippery pavement made them stagger slightly; it seemed to him as if they were cradled by the wind, in the midst of a cloud.

The blaze of lights on the boulevard brought him back to earth. The opportunity was good; time pressed. He gave himself as far as the rue de Richelieu to declare his passion. But almost at once she stopped short in front of a china-shop, and said to him:

'Here we are, and thank you. We shall see you on Thursday, as usual, shall we not?'

The dinners began again; and the more he saw of Mme Arnoux, the more he pined and languished. To look at this woman took away his strength, like a too powerful perfume. This emotion penetrated the depths of his being; it became a sort of general attitude of mind, a new mode of existence.

The prostitutes whom he met in the gas light, the warbling singers, the galloping horsewomen, the housewives on foot, the courtesans at their windows—every woman reminded him of her, through resemblance or through violent contrast. He looked at the cashmere shawls, the laces, the jewelled pendants in the shops, and imagined them draped about her waist, sewn on her corsage, flaming in her black hair. On the flower-women's trays, the blossoms opened only that she might choose them as she passed; the little satin slippers, edged with swan's-down, in the shoemaker's window, seemed to await her feet; every road led to her house; and the cabs waited in the squares only that they might speed her friends towards her. Paris depended on her person, and the great city, with all its voices, resounded like a vast orchestra about her.

When he went to the Jardin des Plantes, the sight of a palm-tree carried him to far-off lands. They were travelling together on the backs of dromedaries, in the howdahs of elephants, in the cabin of a yacht among blue islets, or side by side on two mules with jingling harness, which stumbled against broken columns in the grass. Sometimes he stopped in front of old pictures at the Louvre; his love embraced her even in vanished ages, and he imagined her in the place of the painted figures. Wearing a wimple, she prayed on her knees behind a leaded casement. Duchess of Castille or Flanders, she sat enthroned, in a starched ruff and a ribbed bodice with puffed sleeves. Now she was descending some great porphyry staircase, surrounded by senators, under a canopy of ostrich feathers, in a gown of brocade. Sometimes he pictured her in yellow silk trousers, on the divans of a harem; and anything beautiful —the glittering of the stars, certain melodies, the turn of a phrase, a curve, brought her suddenly, involuntarily, into his mind.

As for trying to make her his mistress, he was certain that any attempt would be in vain.

One evening Dittmer, coming in, kissed her on the forehead; Lovarias did the same, remarking:

'You don't mind, do you? It's the privilege of friends.'

Frederic stammered:

'I suppose we're all friends here?'

'But not all old friends,' she replied.

Indirectly she had rebuffed him in advance. Then what was he to do? Tell her that he loved her? Of course she would repulse him; or in her anger she might forbid him the house. He preferred any suffering to the hideous possibility of never seeing her again.

He coveted the pianist's talent, the soldier's scars. He longed for a dangerous illness, hoping thus to arouse her interest.

One thing surprised him—that he was not jealous of Arnoux; and he could not imagine her otherwise than clothed—so natural did her modesty appear, withdrawing her sex into a mysterious darkness.

All the time he thought of the happiness of living with her, of talking intimately to her, of passing his hand slowly over her hair, or sitting on the ground, at her knee, with his arms about her waist, while he gazed into her eyes and and drank in her soul! To bring this about, destiny must be overturned; and, incapable of action, cursing God and accusing himself of cowardice, he turned about in his desire, like a prisoner in a dungeon. A permanent anguish stifled him. He would remain motionless for hours, or else burst into tears; and one day, when he had not had the strength to contain himself, Deslauriers said to him:

'God bless my soul! What's the matter with you?' Frederic's nerves were troubling him. Deslauriers did not believe it.

In the face of such suffering, he had felt a re-awakening of his affection, and he comforted Frederic. What folly for a man like him to allow himself to be cast down! In early youth, well and good, but in later life it was a waste of time.

'You're spoiling the Frederic I know. I want my old Frederic back. Same again, waiter! He was the one I liked. Come on. Smoke a pipe, you ass! Pull yourself together; you're making me miserable!'

'It's true,' said Frederic. 'I'm mad.'

The clerk went on:

'Ah, old troubadour, I know what's wrong with you. Heart trouble, isn't it? Own up! What a fool you are! There's as good fish in the sea, you know . . . We console ourselves for virtuous women with the other kind. Would you like me to introduce you to some women? You've only to come to the Alhambra.' This was a public dancing place recently opened at the top of the Champs-Élysées, which went bankrupt in its second season, owing to an extravagance that was premature in this class of establishment. 'I'm told it's good fun there. Let's go! You can bring your friends if you like: I'll even allow you Regimbart!'

Frederic did not invite the citizen. Deslauriers dispensed with Sénécal. They only took Hussonnet, Cisy, and Dussardier; and one cab dropped all five of them at the door of the Alhambra.

Two parallel arcades, in the Moorish style, stretched to right and left. Opposite, the wall of a house took up the whole of the far end, and the fourth side, where the restaurant lay, was in the form of a Gothic cloister with stained-glass windows. The platform on which the musicians played was roofed with a kind of Chinese canopy; the floor all round was covered with asphalt, and Venetian lanterns on poles seemed, in the distance, to surround the dancers with a ring of multi-coloured fire. In the shrubberies plaster statues could be seen, Hebes and Cupids, all sticky with oil paint; and the numerous paths, spread with very yellow sand, carefully raked, made the garden appear much larger than it really was.

Students were strolling about with their mistresses; shop
66

assistants strutted along with walking sticks between their fingers; youths from college smoked cheap cigars; old bachelors drew combs through their dyed beards; there were Englishmen, Russians, South Americans, and three Orientals in fezes. Adventuresses, courtesans, and prostitutes were there, in the hope of finding a protector, a lover, a piece of gold, or simply for the pleasure of the dance; and their dresses, with bodices of sea-green and blue, crimson and mauve, went swaying past among the laburnums and the lilacs. Almost all the men wore check suits; some were in white trousers, in spite of the coolness of the evening. The gas jets were lit.

Hussonnet, through his connections with the fashion papers and the smaller theatres, knew a great many women: he blew them kisses and, from time to time, left his friends to go and talk to them.

This behaviour made Deslauriers jealous. He went boldly up to a tall blonde, dressed in nankeen. After looking at him sourly, she said: 'No! Don't trust you, young man!' and turned on her heel.

He tried again with a big brunette, who was apparently mad, for at his first word she leaped up and threatened to call the police, if he went on. Deslauriers forced a laugh; then, finding a young woman sitting apart under a lantern, he invited her to dance.

The band, perched like monkeys on the platform, scraped and blew with vigour. The conductor, standing up, beat time mechanically. The dancers were jammed together; every one was gay; hat ribbons, flying loose, brushed against cravats; boots vanished under skirts; the whole scene leaped in rhythm; Deslauriers pressed his partner against him, and, carried away by the intoxication of the can-can, capered like a great marionette. Cisy and Dussardier continued their walk; the young nobleman eyed the girls, but, in spite of his friend's encouragement, did not dare speak to them; for he supposed that in the houses of such women there was always 'a man hiding in the cupboard with a pistol, who comes out and forces you to back a bill for him.'

They went and stood near Frederic. Deslauriers was no longer dancing, and they were all wondering how to conclude the evening, when Hussonnet exclaimed:

'Look! The Marquise d'Amaëgui!'

This was a pale, snub-nosed woman, with mittens up to her elbows and large black ear-rings that hung down her cheeks, like the ears of a dog.

67

Hussonnet said to her:

'Let's get up a little party at your house—an Oriental rout. Try and dig up some of your friends for these knights of France. Well, what are you worrying about? Are you waiting for your hidalgo?'

The Spanish girl bowed her head; knowing her friend's frugal habits, she was afraid she might have to pay for the refreshments. At last, at the mention of the word money, Cisy offered five twenty-franc pieces, the whole contents of his purse, and the matter was decided. But Frederic had gone.

Thinking he recognized Arnoux's voice, and catching sight of a woman's hat, he had plunged quickly into the neighbouring thicket.

Mlle Vatnaz was alone with Arnoux.

'I beg your pardon. Do I intrude?'

'Not in the very least,' replied the dealer.

From the last words of their conversation, Frederic understood that he had hurried to the Alhambra to talk to Mlle Vatnaz on an urgent matter; and Arnoux was not completely reassured, for he said to her in an uneasy tone:

'Are you absolutely sure?'

'Absolutely! You are loved! Ah! What a man!' And she pouted at him, thrusting towards him her thick lips, which were so red that they were almost the colour of blood. But she had splendid, wild eyes, with sparks in the pupils, full of wit, love, and sensuality. They lit up her thin yellowish face like lamps. Arnoux seemed to enjoy her archness. He leaned over to her and said:

'How nice you are! Kiss me!'

She took him by the ears and kissed him on the forehead.

At that moment the dancing stopped, and a young man appeared on the conductor's stand; he was handsome, over-corpulent, and pale as wax. He had long black hair arranged after the manner of the Saviour, and a blue velvet waistcoat decorated with large gold palm-leaves; he looked as conceited as a peacock, and as stupid as a turkey. After greeting the public he began to sing a song. A peasant was describing his trip to the capital in his own words; the singer spoke a Norman dialect and played the drunkard; the refrain:

> I laughed until the tears ran down my face!
> Oh, Paris is the devil of a place,

made the audience stamp their feet in their enthusiasm. Delmas, 'the singer with a soul,' was too knowing to allow them to cool down. He was quickly given a guitar and he whined a ballad entitled *The Albanian Woman's Brother*.

The words reminded Frederic of those which the ragged man had sung on the boat, between the paddle boxes. He fastened his eyes involuntarily on the hem of the dress spread out in front of him. After each verse there was a long pause—and the breath of the wind in the trees was like the sound of waves.

Mlle Vatnaz, drawing aside with one hand the branches of a privet that was impeding her view of the stage, gazed fixedly at the singer, her nostrils dilated, her eyes half closed, lost, as it seemed, in a sober delight.

'Excellent!' said Arnoux. 'Now I understand why you're at the Alhambra to-night. Delmas attracts you, my dear!'

She would admit nothing.

'Oh, what shyness!'

And, pointing to Frederic:

'Is it on his account? You're quite wrong! He's the soul of discretion.'

The others, looking for their friend, came into the garden hall. Hussonnet introduced them. Arnoux distributed cigars and entertained the company with ices.

Mlle Vatnaz had blushed at the sight of Dussardier. Soon she got up, and, holding out her hand to him, said:

'Don't you remember me, Monsieur Auguste?'

'How do you know her?' asked Frederic.

'We worked in the same firm,' he replied.

Cisy tugged at his sleeve, and they went away. Scarcely was he out of sight when Mlle Vatnaz began a eulogy of his character. She even added that he was one of 'nature's gentlemen.'

Then they talked about Delmas, who might be successful in the theatre as a mimic; and an argument followed, in which were mingled Shakespeare, the censorship, style, the masses, the receipts of the Porte-Saint-Martin Theatre, Alexandre Dumas, Victor Hugo, and Dumersan. Arnoux had known several celebrated actresses; the young people leaned forward to listen to him. But his words were drowned by the din of the music; and as soon as the quadrille or the polka was over, every one sank down at tables, called the waiter, and laughed; bottles of beer and sparkling lemonade exploded among the shrubberies; women sqawked like hens; two gentlemen tried to fight; a thief was arrested.

When the galop was played, the dancers invaded the paths.

Panting, smiling, flushed, they passed by in a whirlwind with skirts and coat tails flying; the trombones roared louder; the rhythm grew faster; cracklings could be heard behind the medieval cloister, and squibs went off; Catherine wheels began to revolve, the emerald gleam of Bengal lights illuminated the whole garden for a moment; and at the final rocket the crowd gave a great sigh.

The people moved slowly away. A cloud of gunpowder floated in the air. Frederic and Deslauriers were walking slowly with the crowd when they saw something that brought them to a standstill. Martinon was getting change at the cloak room; and with him was a woman of about fifty, ugly, superbly dressed. Her status was problematical.

'That fellow,' said Deslauriers, 'is less simple than one might think. But where has Cisy got to?'

Dussardier pointed to the bar, where they saw the sprig of nobility, with a bowl of punch in front of him, and a pink hat by his side.

Hussonnet, who had been away for five minutes, reappeared at the same moment.

A young girl was leaning on his arm, calling him 'my darling' out loud.

'No, no!' he said to her. 'Not in public! Rather, call me viscount! That has a smack of the cavalier, of Louis the Thirteenth and soft boots, that appeals to me. Yes, my friends, one of the old brigade! Isn't she delightful?' He took her by the chin. 'Greet these gentlemen! They're all sons of peers of France. I'm friends with them so that they'll make me an ambassador!'

'You're quite mad,' sighed Mlle Vatnaz. She asked Dussardier to take her home. Arnoux watched them move away, then, turning to Frederic, said:

'I wonder if the Vatnaz would appeal to you. Anyway, you're not very open about these things. You keep your love affairs dark, don't you?'

Frederic, turning pale, swore that he concealed nothing.

'You see, nobody knows who your mistress is,' Arnoux went on.

Frederic felt inclined to quote a name at random. But the story might be repeated to *her*. He replied that as a matter of fact he had no mistress.

The dealer found this reprehensible.

'To-night you had an excellent opportunity. Why didn't you do as the others? They've each gone off with a woman

'Well, and what about you?' said Frederic, losing patience at this persistence.

'Ah, it's different for me, young man! I'm going home to my wife.'

He called a cab and vanished.

The two friends went away on foot. An east wind blew. Neither spoke. Deslauriers was sorry that he had not 'shone' in front of the owner of a magazine, and Frederic wrapped himself in his melancholy. At last he said that he had found the dance boring.

'Whose fault was that? You shouldn't have left us for your friend Arnoux.'

'Oh, I couldn't have done any good.'

But the clerk had a theory. To get things it was enough to desire them strongly.

'All the same, you yourself, just now . . .'

'I didn't care,' said Deslauriers, cutting the allusion short. 'You won't catch me getting mixed up with women.'

And he denounced their affectation, their stupidity; in short, they did not attract him.

'Don't pose,' said Frederic.

Deslauriers was silent. Then suddenly: 'Will you bet me a hundred francs that I don't "make" the first woman we meet?'

'Yes! Taken.'

The first they met was a hideous beggar-woman; and they were despairing of their luck, when in the middle of the rue de Rivoli they caught sight of a tall prostitute, carrying a small cardboard box in her hand.

Deslauriers accosted her under the arcade. She turned off abruptly in the direction of the Tuileries, and was soon crossing the Place du Carrousel, throwing glances to right and left. She ran after a cab. Deslauriers caught her up. He walked beside her, talking to her with expressive gestures. At last she accepted his arm and they proceeded along the quays. On the hill of the Châtelet they walked up and down the pavement for twenty minutes at least, like two sailors on watch. Suddenly they crossed the Pont au Change, the Flower Market, the quai Napoléon. Frederic entered the house behind them. Deslauriers explained to him that he would be in their way; he had only to follow his example.

'How much have you got left?'

'Two ten-franc pieces.'

'That's plenty. Good night.'

Frederic experienced the kind of surprise that one feels when one sees a practical joke succeed. 'Perhaps he's fooling me,' he thought. 'Shall I go up again?' Deslauriers might think he envied him his affair. 'As if I had not a love of my own, a hundred times purer, nobler, and stronger!' He was driven on by a sort of fury. He arrived at Mme Arnoux's door.

None of the outer windows belonged to her flat. However, he stood with his eyes glued to the front of the house—as though he believed that by gazing thus he might split the walls. Now, doubtless, she was resting, peaceful as a sleeping flower, with her lovely black hair spread over the lace of her pillow, her lips half open, her head on her arm.

Arnoux's face came into view. He hurried away, to escape this apparition.

He remembered Deslauriers's advice. It horrified him. Then he wandered through the streets.

He tried to make out the faces of people walking towards him. From time to time, a beam of light would flash between his legs, describing a wide arc on the pavement; and a man would rise out of the shadows, with a pannier on his back and a lantern in his hand. Now and then the wind shook the iron stack of a chimney; distant sounds arose, mingling with the throbbing in his head; and he seemed to hear the rhythm of the quadrille echoing faintly through the air. The act of walking sustained his trance-like mood; he found himself on the Concorde bridge.

Then he remembered that other winter evening, when, leaving her house for the first time, he had had to stop walking, so fast was his heart beating beneath the pressure of his hopes. They were all dead now!

Dark clouds scurried across the face of the moon. He gazed at it, thinking of the grandeur of space, the misery of life, the nothingness of all things. Dawn broke; his teeth were chattering; half asleep, soaked by the mist, and choked with tears, he asked himself why he should not end it all. He had only to make a single movement. The weight of his head dragged him forward, he saw his corpse floating on the water. Frederic leaned over. The parapet was rather broad, and it was sheer fatigue that prevented him from scaling it.

Panic seized him. He regained the boulevards and sank down on a bench.

Some policemen woke him up; they supposed that he had 'been out on the tiles.'

He began walking again. He felt famished, and, as all the restaurants were closed, he went and had supper in an eating house at Les Halles. After that, imagining that he was still too early, he wandered about the purlieus of the Hôtel de Ville until a quarter past eight.

Deslauriers had long since dismissed his damsel; and he was writing at the table in the middle of the room.

At about four o'clock M. de Cisy came in.

Thanks to Dussardier, he had, the previous evening, made the acquaintance of a lady; and he had even taken her home in a carriage, with her husband, as far as her front door, and there she had given him an assignation, from which he was now returning. And this lady was by no means notorious!

'What do you want me to do?' said Frederic.

Then the nobleman began to digress; he mentioned Mlle Vatnaz, the Spanish girl, and all the others. At length, with many circumlocutions, he explained the object of his visit. Trusting to his friend's discretion, he came to ask his help in a step which would establish him once and for all in his own eyes as a man; and Frederic did not refuse. He told the story to Deslauriers—evasively as regards his own part in it.

The clerk considered that 'he was doing splendidly now.' This deference to his advice increased his good humour.

It was through this good humour that he had seduced, the first day they met, Mlle Clémence Daviou, who was employed as an embroideress for military uniforms. She was the sweetest person in the world—as slim as a reed, with great, wide-open, blue eyes. The clerk took advantage of her simplicity and even persuaded her that he possessed an order; he decorated his coat with a red ribbon when they were alone, but took it off in public, in order, as he said, to avoid humiliating his employer. In general he kept her at a distance; he allowed himself to be fondled like a pasha, and called her 'daughter of the people,' by way of a joke. At each visit she brought him little bunches of violets. Frederic had no desire for an affair of this sort.

Yet when they went out, arm in arm, on their way to a private room at Pinson's or Barillot's, he felt a peculiar sadness. Frederic did not know what suffering he had caused Deslauriers, every Thursday, for a year, when he brushed his nails before going to dine at the rue de Choiseul.

One evening, after he had watched them go off from his lofty balcony, he saw Hussonnet in the distance on the Arcola bridge. The latter waved his arms to attract his attention, and, when Frederic had come down his five flights, he said:

'Here's the point. Next Saturday, the 24th, is Mme Arnoux's feast day.'

'How so? Her name's Marie.'

'Angèle too; it doesn't matter. There's going to be a party at their country house at Saint-Cloud; I've been told to let you know. You'll find a carriage at the office at three. That's settled, then! Sorry to have brought you down. But I've so much to do!'

Frederic had scarcely turned round when the porter handed him a letter.

'Monsieur and Madame Dambreuse request the pleasure of Monsieur F. Moreau's company at dinner on Saturday, the 24th of this month. R.S.V.P.'

'Too late,' he thought.

All the same, he showed the letter to Deslauriers, who exclaimed:

'Ah! At last! But you don't look happy. Why?'

Frederic, after some hesitation, said that he had another invitation for the same day.

'Be good enough to let the rue de Choiseul go hang. Don't be a fool! I shall answer for you, if it embarrasses you.'

And the clerk wrote an acceptance, in the third person.

Deslauriers had never seen society except through the fever of his ambition; consequently he pictured it as an artificial creation, functioning by virtue of mathematical laws. A dinner in town, a meeting with an important personage, the smile of a pretty woman, might, through a series of events in logical succession, produce the most momentous results. There were certain Paris drawing-rooms which resembled those machines that take in material in its raw state and give it out with its value increased a hundredfold. He believed in courtesans advising ambassadors, in rich marriages secured by intrigue, in master criminals, in the submissiveness of fortune to the strong man's hand. In short, he attached so much importance to an association with the Dambreuse family that Frederic did not know how to make up his mind.

In any case, he must give Mme Arnoux a present on her feast day: naturally he thought of a parasol, to make up for his clumsiness. He happened to come upon a shot-silk marquise sunshade, with a little handle of carved ivory, which

74

came from China. But it cost a hundred and seventy-five francs, and he had not a penny; in fact, he was living on credit on his next term's allowance. Nevertheless, he wanted that parasol, he had to have it; and, overcoming his repugnance, he had recourse to Deslauriers.

Deslauriers replied that he had no money.

'I need it,' said Frederic. 'I need it badly.' And as the other repeated the same excuse, he lost his temper. 'I think you might, occasionally . . .'

'What?'

'Nothing.'

The clerk had understood. He took the sum in question out of the reserve, and, after paying it over coin by coin, he said:

'As I 'm living on you, I shan't ask for a receipt.'

Frederic fell on his neck, with countless protestations of affection. Deslauriers remained cold.

The next day, seeing the parasol on the piano, he said:

'Oh, it was for that.'

'Perhaps I shall send it,' said Frederic weakly. He was in luck's way; for in the evening he received a note on black-bordered paper, in which Mme Dambreuse announced the death of an uncle and expressed her regret at having to postpone the pleasure of making his acquaintance.

He was at the office of the magazine by two o'clock. Arnoux had not waited to take him in his carriage. A sudden longing for fresh air had impelled him to start the previous evening. Every year, in early spring, for several days in succession, he used to leave Paris in the morning, walk for miles across the fields, drink milk at farms, joke with the village girls, inquire about the crops, and bring back lettuces in his handkerchief. At last, realizing an old dream, he had bought himself a country house.

While Frederic was talking to the assistant, Mlle Vatnaz came in, and was disappointed at not seeing Arnoux. It appeared that he might be away for another two days. The assistant advised her 'to go down there'; she could not go down there; 'to write a letter'; she was afraid the letter might be lost. Frederic offered to carry it himself. She scribbled a note, and begged him to hand it over in private.

Forty minutes later he alighted at Saint-Cloud.

The house lay half-way up the hill, a hundred yards beyond the bridge. The garden walls were hidden by two rows of

75

limes, and a wide lawn sloped down to the river bank. The gate in the railings was open, and Frederic went in. Arnoux, lying on the grass, was playing with a litter of kittens. He seemed to be deeply immersed in this pastime. The letter from Mlle Vatnaz roused him from his lethargy.

'Damn, damn! It's infuriating. She's right. I must go back.'

Then, thrusting the letter into his pocket, he showed Frederic round the estate. This was one of his chief pleasures.

He showed him everything: the stable, the barn, and even the kitchen. The drawing-room was on the right and, on the Paris side, looked out on to a latticed pergola, covered with clematis. A burst of song rang out above their heads. Mme Arnoux, thinking she was alone, was amusing herself by practising. She sang scales, trills, arpeggios. There were long notes that seemed to be suspended in the air; others tumbled headlong, like the spray of a waterfall; and her voice, passing through the shutter, cleft the deep silence and mounted towards the blue sky.

Suddenly she stopped, for M. and Mme Oudry, two neighbours, had been announced.

Then she herself appeared at the top of the steps; and, as she walked down, he caught sight of her foot. She wore little open-work shoes, of gilded leather, with three cross-straps, that formed a tracery of gold against her stockings.

The guests arrived. Except for Maître Lefaucheur, a lawyer, they consisted of the usual Thursday evening company. Each had brought a gift: Dittmer, a Syrian scarf; Rosenwald, an album of ballads; Sombaz, a caricature of himself; and Pellerin, a charcoal sketch, representing a sort of Dance of Death—a repulsive fantasy, of inferior execution. Hussonnet brought nothing.

Frederic waited until after the others before offering his present. She thanked him warmly for it. Then he said:

'But . . . it's almost a debt. I was so upset . . .'

'What about?' she said. 'I don't understand . . .'

'Dinner time!' said Arnoux, seizing him by the arm; then, in his ear: 'You're not very tactful, are you?'

The dining-room, with its sea-green walls, was perfectly delightful. At one end, a stone nymph dipped her toe into a basin shaped like a shell. Through the open windows the whole garden could be seen, with the long lawn, beside which stood an old Scotch pine, three-quarters bare. The smooth expanse of turf was broken here and there by tall banks of flowers. Beyond the river, in a wide semicircle, stretched the Bois de Boulogne, Neuilly, Sèvres, and Meudon. A sailing dinghy was tacking just in front of the railings.

At first they discussed the view, and then the countryside in general; and an argument was beginning, when Arnoux gave orders to his servant to have the phaeton harnessed by about half-past nine. He had been called back to Paris by a note from his cashier.

'Would you like me to come back with you?' said Mme Arnoux.

'Why, of course.' And, with a deep bow, he added: 'You know quite well, madame, that no one can live without you.'

They all congratulated her on having such an excellent husband.

'Oh, that is because I am not alone,' she replied softly, pointing to her little daughter.

Then the conversation returned to painting; they mentioned a Ruysdael, for which Arnoux expected a considerable sum; and Pellerin asked him if it was true that the celebrated Saul Matthias, of London, had come over the previous month and offered him twenty-five thousand francs for it.

'It's absolutely true,' he said, and, turning to Frederic: 'That was the very gentleman I was walking with the other day at the Alhambra—against my will, I can assure you, for these Englishmen are very poor company.'

Frederic, who suspected that there was some reference to a lady in the letter from Mlle Vatnaz, had admired the facility with which Arnoux had been able to extricate himself honourably; but this new and utterly pointless lie made him open his eyes wide.

The dealer added, in an innocent manner: 'What's the name of that tall young man—your friend?'

'Deslauriers,' said Frederic quickly.

And, to make up for the mischief of which he felt guilty towards him, he lauded him to the skies as a man of exceptional intelligence.

'Oh, indeed? But he didn't look such a fine young fellow as the other—the one who worked for the firm of carriers.'

Frederic cursed Dussardier. She would think he went about with common people.

After that they talked about the improvements in the capital, and the new districts; Oudry mentioned M. Dambreuse as one of the big speculators.

Frederic, seizing the opportunity to show off, said that he knew him. But Pellerin had launched a tirade against the Philistines—he saw no difference between them, whether they dealt in tallow candles or money. Then Rosenwald and Burieu began a conversation about porcelain; Arnoux talked gardening with Mme Oudry; Sombaz, a wag of the old school, amused himself by chaffing her husband; he called him Odry, like the actor, and declared that he must be descended from Oudry, the painter of dogs, for the bump of zoology was visible on his forehead. He even wanted to feel his skull; the other protested on account of his wig, and dessert ended in roars of laughter.

They had coffee and smoked under the limes, walked about the garden, and then went for a stroll along the river bank.

The party stopped beside a fisherman, who was cleaning eels in a sort of lobster pot. Marthe wanted to see them. He emptied his box on to the grass; and the little girl went down on her knees to catch them, laughing with pleasure and screaming with fear. They were all lost. Arnoux paid for them.

Next he thought of going for a row.

The eastern horizon was growing pale, while the whole of the western sky was covered with an orange glow, turning to crimson just above the tops of the hills, which were now quite black. Mme Arnoux was sitting on a big stone, with this fiery light behind her. The others strolled about; Hussonnet, at the foot of the bank, played ducks and drakes.

Arnoux rejoined them with an old skiff, into which, in spite of the protests of the more prudent, he piled his guests. It began to sink; they had to get out.

The candles were already lit in the drawing-room, which was hung with embroidered linen; crystal candelabra stood against the walls. Old Mme Oudry was sleeping peacefully in an arm-chair, while the others listened to M. Lefaucheur, who was discoursing on the glories of the Bar. Mme Arnoux was alone by the window. Frederic went up to her.

They took up the general conversation. She admired orators; he preferred the writer's laurels. But surely, she went on, one should feel a deeper pleasure in moving people directly, by one's own powers; in seeing oneself transmit all the emotions of one's soul into theirs. These triumphs did not tempt Frederic, who lacked ambition.

'But why?' she said. 'You must have a little.'

They were standing close together, in the recess of the window. In front of them the night lay stretched like a huge dark veil, spangled with silver. This was the first time that they had not talked of trivial matters. He even succeeded in finding out her likes and dislikes; certain scents made her feel ill, history books interested her; she believed in dreams.

He broached the subject of sentimental adventures. She pitied the disasters of passion, but was revolted by hypocritical deceit; and this rectitude of mind corresponded so well with the regular beauty of her features that the one seemed to depend on the other.

Sometimes she smiled, fixing her eyes on him for a moment. Then he felt her glance penetrate his soul, like those great sunbeams that go right down to the bottom of water. He loved her without reservation, without hope of return—absolutely; and in those mute raptures, which were like transports of gratitude, he would have liked to cover her forehead with a rain of kisses. All the time, an inward breath seemed to lift him out of himself; it was a longing for self-sacrifice, a yearning for immediate devotion, which was all the stronger because he could not satisfy it.

He did not start back with the others; neither did Hussonnet. They were to return in the carriage; and the phaeton was waiting at the bottom of the steps, when Arnoux went down the garden to pick roses. He had tied his bouquet with a piece of thread; and as the stalks stuck out untidily, he felt in his pocket, which was full of papers, pulled a piece out at random, wrapped the flowers in it, and fastened his handiwork together with a large pin. He then offered it to his wife, not without emotion.

'There, my darling! I'm sorry I forgot you.'

She gave a little scream; the pin, clumsily inserted, had pricked her, and she returned to her room.

They waited nearly a quarter of an hour for her.

At length she reappeared, picked up Marthe, and hurried into the carriage.

'And your bouquet?'

'No, no! It's not worth the trouble.'

Frederic ran to get it; she shouted to him:

'I don't want it!'

He fetched it all the same, remarking that he had had to wrap the flowers up again, for he had found them on the floor.

She thrust them inside the leather apron, against the seat. They set off.

Frederic, sitting next to her, noticed that she was trembling violently. When Arnoux turned to the left, after they had crossed the bridge, she cried:

'No! You 're wrong. It 's the other way—to the right!'

She seemed out of temper; everything irritated her. At length, when Marthe had closed her eyes, she extracted the bouquet and threw it out of the door: then she seized Frederic's arm, signing to him with her other hand never to mention what he had seen.

After that she put her handkerchief to her lips and remained motionless.

The two others, on the box, talked about painting and subscriptions. Arnoux, who was driving carelessly, lost the way in the middle of the Bois de Boulogne. They plunged into narrow lanes. The horse went at a foot's pace; branches scraped the hood. All that Frederic could see of Mme Arnoux was her two eyes in the darkness; Marthe was lying stretched across her, and he supported her head.

'She 's tiring you,' said the mother.

He answered: 'No! Oh, no!'

The dust rose slowly in eddies; they were passing through Auteuil. All the houses were darkened; here and there a street lamp lit up the corner of a wall, then they passed into the shadows again; once he noticed that she was crying.

Was it remorse? Or desire? Or what? This sorrow, of which he knew nothing, absorbed him as if it were his own; now there was a new bond between them, a kind of conspiracy; and he said to her, in his gentlest voice:

'Are you unwell?'

'Yes, a little,' she replied.

The carriage rumbled along; and honeysuckle and syringa, nodding over garden walls, sent whiffs of languorous perfume into the night. The ample folds of her dress covered her feet. It seemed to him that he was in touch with her whole being, through the child's body that lay between them. He leaned over the little girl, and, drawing aside her pretty dark hair, kissed her on the forehead.

'How kind you are!' said Mme Arnoux.

'Why?'

'Because you are fond of children.'

'Not of all children!'

He said no more, but moved his left hand away from his side and left it with the palm wide open—imagining that she might do likewise, and their hands would meet.

Then he felt ashamed, and withdrew it.

Soon they reached the paved road. The carriage went faster, the gas lamps grew more numerous. It was Paris.

At the Garde-Meuble Hussonnet jumped down from the box. Frederic waited until they reached the coach yard before alighting; then he lay in wait at the corner of the rue de Choiseul, and observed Arnoux walking briskly back towards the boulevards.

On the next day he began working with all his might.

He saw himself in a court of assize, on a winter's evening. The pleadings were nearly over, the jury was pale, the breathless crowd was almost bursting the thin walls of the court room. He had been speaking for four hours now; he recapitulated his arguments, discovered new ones, and felt that each phrase, each word, each gesture, was driving back the blade of the guillotine that hung behind him. Now he was an orator on the rostrum in the Chamber, carrying the safety of a whole people on his lips, overwhelming his opponents with invective, crushing them with a retort; there was lightning and music in his voice—he was ironic, pathetic, passionate, and sublime. She was there, somewhere in the crowd, hiding her tears of enthusiasm under her veil; afterwards they met; and slanders, reverses, and insults could not touch him if she said: 'Ah, that was beautiful!' and passed her hands lightly over his forehead.

These pictures blazed like lighthouses on the horizon of his life. Under their stimulus his mind grew brisker and stronger. He shut himself up until August, the date when he was to go up for his final examination. Deslauriers, who had had so much difficulty in pushing him, parrot-wise, through his second examination in December, and his third in February, was astonished at his ardour. The old hopes revived. In ten years, Frederic should be a deputy; in fifteen, a minister; why not? He could begin by starting a newspaper with his father's money, which would soon be in his hands. That would be the first step; after that they would see. His own ambition was still a chair at the law school; and at the oral examination on his thesis for the doctorate, he made so remarkable an impression that he earned the compliments of the professors.

Frederic passed his own examination three days later. Before leaving for his holidays, he conceived the idea of a picnic, to conclude the Saturday parties.

He was in high spirits at the picnic. Mme Arnoux was at present at Chartres with her mother. But they would soon meet again, and eventually he would become her lover.

81

Deslauriers had been elected that very day to the D'Orsay debating society, and he had made a speech which had been enthusiastically received. Although generally abstemious, he got drunk, and said to Dussardier at dessert:

'You're an honest man. When I'm rich, I shall make you my agent.'

They were all cheerful; Cisy was not going to finish his course at the law school; Martinon was to continue his studies in a country district, where he would be appointed deputy prosecutor. Pellerin was working on a large picture representing 'The Genius of the Revolution.' The following week Hussonnet was to read the synopsis of a play to the manager of the Délassement Theatre, and he was confident of success.

'Every one admits,' he said, 'that I'm a master of construction. I know the passions backwards, from personal experience: and characterization is my speciality!'

He did a somersault, landed on his hands, and walked for some time round the table with his legs in the air.

These antics did not dispel the gloom of Sénécal. He had just been turned out of his boarding house for striking the son of an aristocrat. As his poverty increased, he turned his rancour against the social system, and cursed the rich. He opened his heart to Regimbart, who was becoming more and more disillusioned, melancholy, and embittered. The citizen was devoting himself to fiscal questions, and he accused the Camarilla of squandering millions in Algeria.

Since he was unable to sleep without having previously visited the Alexandre tavern, he vanished at eleven o'clock. The others left later; and Frederic, as he said good-bye to Hussonnet, learned that Mme Arnoux had been expected back the previous evening.

He went to the Messageries to change his seat on the coach for the next day, and, at about six, arrived at her house.

The concierge told him that her return had been postponed for a week. Frederic dined alone, then strolled along the boulevards.

Pink clouds, like scarves, floated above the roof tops; the awnings of the shops were being rolled up; water carts poured showers on to the dust; an unaccustomed freshness was blended with the smells of the cafés, where, through the open doors, among the gilt and silver decorations, vases of flowers could be seen reflected in the tall mirrors. The crowd walked slowly. Men chatted in groups in the middle of the pavement; soft-eyed women passed, with that wax-like complexion which the female skin acquires from the fatigue of sultry weather. A sense of vast promise enveloped the houses. Never before had Paris seemed to him so beautiful. The whole future stretched before him as an endless sequence of years filled with love.

He stopped at the Porte-Saint-Martin Theatre to look at the posters; having nothing else to do, he took a ticket.

They were playing an old-fashioned pantomime. The audience was sparse; the casements in the gallery admitted the light in small, sharply defined squares of blue, while the oil lamps of the footlights formed a single line of gleaming yellow. The scene was a slave market in Pekin; there were bells, pointed hats, gongs, *sultanes*, and bad jokes. When the curtain fell, he wandered about the vestibule by himself, and admired a large green landau, with two white horses and a coachman in knee breeches, which was standing in the boulevard at the bottom of the steps.

He was going back to his seat, when a lady and gentleman entered the first stage box, in the circle. The husband had a pale face, with a grey fringe of beard round his chin; he wore the rosette of the Legion of Honour, and that icy look which is supposed to be characteristic of diplomats.

His wife, at least twenty years younger than he, was neither tall nor short, ugly nor pretty; she wore her fair hair in corkscrew curls, in the English fashion; she had a dress with a flat bodice, and carried a large fan of black lace. The presence of people of this class at the theatre at such a season could only be attributed to an accident, or to the tedium of spending an evening alone together. The lady gnawed her fan. The gentleman yawned. Frederic could not remember where he had seen that face before.

During the next interval he met them both in the corridor. He made a vague gesture of greeting, whereupon M. Dambreuse recognized him, went up to him, and immediately apologized for his unpardonable negligence. He was referring to the many visiting cards which Frederic had left, on Deslauriers's advice. He kept mixing up his dates, being under the impression that Frederic was in his second year as a law student. Then he envied his leaving for the country. He needed a rest himself, but business kept him in Paris.

Mme Dambreuse, leaning on his arm, nodded her head gently; and the charm and intelligence of her face contrasted with her sour expression of a moment ago.

'Yet there are admirable amusements here!' she said, at her

husband's last phrase. 'How stupid this piece is! Don't you agree, sir?'

And all three of them stood there in a group, talking about theatres and new plays.

Frederic, accustomed to the simpering of provincial housewives, had never observed such ease of address in any woman, nor that studied simplicity of manner which the inexperienced interpret as a sign of immediate sympathy.

They would expect him, on his return; M. Dambreuse asked to be remembered to old Roque.

Returning to his rooms, Frederic did not forget to tell Deslauriers how he had been greeted.

'Splendid!' said the clerk. 'And don't let your mamma get round you. Come back at once!'

The day following his arrival, after breakfast, Mme Moreau took her son out into the garden.

She said she was happy to know that he had a profession, for they were not so rich as was generally supposed; the land brought in little; the farmers did not pay; she had even had to sell her carriage. Eventually she disclosed their position to him.

During the first difficult months of her widowhood, a shrewd man, M. Roque, had advanced her money, renewing and prolonging the loans against her will. He had suddenly demanded repayment; she had agreed to his terms, handing over the farm of Presles to him at a ridiculous price. Ten years later, her liquid capital had vanished through the failure of a bank at Melun. In her terror of mortgages, and in order to keep up appearances for the sake of her son's future, she had again listened to old Roque when he reappeared. But now, at last, she was free. In short, they had about ten thousand francs a year left, of which two thousand three hundred were his—his entire patrimony!

'It can't be true!' cried Frederic.

His mother indicated by a movement of her head that it was only too true.

Perhaps his uncle would leave him something?

It was extremely doubtful.

And they walked round the garden without speaking. At last she drew him to her breast, and, in a voice choked with tears, said:

'Oh, my poor boy! I have had to give up many a day-dream!'

He sat down on the bench, in the shade of the tall acacia.

Her advice was that he should become clerk to M. Prouharam, an attorney who would pass his practice on to him. If he made the business prosper, he could resell it at a good profit.

Frederic was not listening. He was gazing with unseeing eyes over the hedge, into the garden opposite.

In it, all alone, was a little girl of about twelve, with red hair. She had made herself ear-rings out of sorb apples; her grey holland bodice revealed her slightly sunburned shoulders; her white skirt was stained with spots of jam. Her form had something of the grace of a young wild beast, at once tense and lithe. The presence of a stranger seemed to astonish her, for she stopped abruptly, her watering can in her hand, and flashed on him her clear, blue-green eyes.

'That is Monsieur Roque's daughter,' said Mme Moreau. 'He has just married his servant and made his child legitimate.'

CHAPTER VI

BANKRUPT, robbed, ruined!

He was still sitting on the bench, stunned as if by an earthquake. He cursed fate, he wanted to fight someone; and, to increase his despair, he felt as if a kind of disgrace, a taint, was weighing him down. For Frederic had supposed that his patrimony would one day amount to fifteen thousand francs a year, and he had hinted as much to M. and Mme Arnoux. They would regard him as a boastful scoundrel, a worthless scamp, who had insinuated himself into their house, in the hope of gain. And how was he to see Mme Arnoux again, now?

And, anyway, that was quite out of the question, since he had only three thousand francs a year. He could not always live on the fourth floor, have the porter as his servant, wear a greasy hat and cheap black gloves going blue at the fingers, and keep the same frock coat for a year on end! No, no! Never! Yet life was intolerable without her. Many people managed to live all right without much money—Deslauriers, among others; and he accused himself of cowardice for attaching such importance to trifles. Perhaps poverty would magnify his talents. He became enthusiastic as he thought of great men working in garrets. Such a spectacle would stir a spirit like Mme Arnoux's and might arouse her affection. Thus the disaster was really a piece of luck; like those landslides which bring hidden treasure to light, it had disclosed to him the secret riches of his nature. But there was only one place where he could turn them to account—Paris! For, to his mind, art, learning, and love—those three faces of God, as Pellerin would have said—were centred exclusively in the capital.

That evening he told his mother that he was going back.

Mme Moreau was surprised and indignant. It was absurd, preposterous. He would do better to follow her advice, and stay near her in an office.

Frederic shrugged his shoulders. 'Really, mother!' he said, considering the proposal an insult.

After that the good lady tried another method. In a tender

voice, interspersed with sobs, she began to talk to him of her loneliness, of her old age, of the sacrifices she had made. Now, when she was more wretched than ever before, he was deserting her. Then, referring to her approaching end, she said:

'Can you not be patient a little longer? You will soon be free.'

These lamentations were repeated twenty times a day for three months; and at the same time the luxury of his home corrupted him; he enjoyed having a softer bed, and napkins that were not torn; so that in the end, exhausted, weakened, overcome by the terrible power of comfort, he allowed himself to be led to the office of Maître Prouharam.

There he showed neither knowledge nor skill. Until then he had been regarded as a young man of ample means, who was to be the pride of the district. It was a fraud on the public.

At first he said to himself: 'I must let Mme Arnoux know.' And, for a week, he composed in his head letters of extravagant lyricism, or short notes in a noble lapidary style. He was held back by his reluctance to confess his position.

Then he thought it would be better to write to the husband. Arnoux knew life, and would understand. At last, after a fortnight's hesitation, he said to himself:

'How absurd! I must never see them again. Let them forget me! At least, in her memory I shall not have fallen low. She will think I am dead, and will miss me . . . perhaps.'

The making of highly coloured vows cost him little, and he swore never to return to Paris, and even never to seek news of Mme Arnoux.

Nevertheless he missed his old life, down to the smell of the gas and the noise of the omnibuses. He dreamed of all the words she had said to him, of the sound of her voice, the light in her eyes—and, looking upon himself as a man dead, he ceased to do anything at all.

He used to get up very late, and watch from his window the wagoners' carts going by.

The first six months were particularly hateful. Yet sometimes he was seized with resentment against himself. Then he would go out. He walked over the meadows, which in winter were half flooded by the Seine. Between them stretched lines of poplars, while here and there rose a little bridge. He wandered about until the evening, kicking up the yellow leaves, breathing in the mist, jumping the ditches; as his pulses beat faster, he was overcome by a longing for violent action; he wanted to be a trapper in America, to enter the service of a pasha in the East, to run away to sea; and he poured out his melancholy in long letters to Deslauriers.

The latter was now struggling to make a career. His friend's cowardly behaviour and his eternal jeremiads struck him as ridiculous. Soon their correspondence dwindled to almost nothing.

Frederic had given all his furniture to Deslauriers, who was keeping on his lodgings. His mother spoke to him about the furniture from time to time; one day, at last, he confessed his gift; his mother was scolding him when a letter arrived.

'What is it?' she said. 'You're trembling.'

'I'm all right,' answered Frederic.

Deslauriers had written to tell him that he had taken Sénécal in, and they had been living together for a fortnight. So Sénécal was now sprawling among the things from Arnoux's shop! He might sell them, he might criticize or laugh at them. Frederic was wounded to the depths of his being. He went up to his room. He wanted to die.

His mother called him. She wished to consult him about planting flowers in the garden.

The garden, like an English park, was divided in the middle by a wooden fence. Half of it belonged to old Roque, who also had a kitchen garden by the edge of the river. The neighbours were on bad terms, and avoided appearing there at the same time. But since Frederic's return Roque had been seen there more often; and he was full of civility towards Mme Moreau's son. He pitied him for living in a small town. One day he told him that M. Dambreuse had asked after him. Another time he dilated on the custom of Champagne by which noble rank was inherited through the mother.

'In those days you would have been a *seigneur*, since your mother was a de Fouvens. And you can say what you like—there's something in a name. After all,' he added, giving him a sly glance, 'it only depends on the registrar.'

These aristocratic aspirations were singularly out of keeping with his appearance.

As he was short, his large maroon frock coat exaggerated the length of the upper part of his body. When he took off his cap, he revealed an almost feminine face with an exceedingly pointed nose; his yellow hair was like a wig; he greeted people with a very low bow and walked close to the wall.

Until the age of fifty he had been content with the services of Catherine, a woman from Lorraine of the same age as himself, strongly marked with smallpox. But about 1834 he brought back from Paris a pretty blonde, with a face like a sheep and the airs of a queen. She was soon seen proudly displaying a pair of large ear-rings; and everything was explained at last by the birth of a daughter, who was registered under the name of Élisabeth Olympe Louise Roque.

Catherine, in her jealousy, expected to hate this child. In fact, she adored it. She lavished care, attention, and kisses upon it, in order to take the mother's place and make the child hate her. This was a simple undertaking, for Mme Éléonore completely neglected the baby, preferring to gossip with the tradesmen. The day after her marriage she paid a visit to the sub-prefect, treated the servants as inferiors, and considered it her duty, as a mark of gentility, to be strict with her child. She was present at her lessons; the tutor, an aged bureaucrat from the town hall, did not know how to begin. The pupil rebelled, was slapped, and went and cried at the knee of Catherine, who always took her side. After that the two women quarrelled; M. Roque bade them hold their tongues. He had married out of affection for his daughter, and did not wish her to be treated harshly.

She often wore a tattered white dress, with drawers trimmed with lace; on great feast days she went out robed like a princess, in order to humiliate the townspeople, who would not let their children make friends with her because of her illegitimate birth.

She spent her time by herself in the garden, swung on her swing, chased butterflies, then stopped to watch the beetles swooping on the rose-bushes. It was these pastimes, no doubt, that gave her face an expression at once bold and dreamy. She was about the same height as Marthe, as it happened, and Frederic said to her, the second time they met:

'Will you allow me to kiss you, mademoiselle?'

The little creature raised her head and replied:

'Yes, please!'

But they were separated by the wooden fence.

'I must climb over,' said Frederic.

'No, lift me up!'

He leaned over the fence, pulled her up by the wrists, and kissed her on both cheeks; then he put her back by the same process, which was repeated on subsequent occasions.

She had no more shyness than a child of four. As soon as she heard her friend approaching, she rushed to meet him, or hid behind a tree and barked like a dog, to frighten him.

One day, when Mme Moreau was out, he took her up to his room. She opened all the scent bottles and smeared her hair liberally; then, without the least embarrassment, stretched herself out on the bed and lay there at full length, with her eyes open.

'I'm pretending I'm your wife,' she said.

The next day he saw her in tears. She declared she was 'crying for her sins,' and, when he tried to find out what they were, she hung her head and answered:

'Don't ask me any more!'

Her first communion was at hand; that morning she had been taken to confession.

The sacrament did little to improve her. Sometimes she flew into a real passion of rage; Frederic was sent for to calm her.

He often took her with him on his walks. While he was absorbed in his thoughts, she picked poppies by the edge of the corn fields, and when she saw him more than usually depressed, she tried to console him with cheerful talk. His heart, deprived of love, fell back on the friendship of this child: he drew pictures for her, told her stories, and started reading to her.

He began with *Les Annales romantiques*, a miscellany of verse and poems popular at that time. Then, charmed by her intelligence, he forgot her age, and read to her, in succession, *Atala*, *Cinq-Mars*, *Les Feuilles d'automne*. But one night— she had heard *Macbeth* that evening in Letourneur's simple translation—she woke up, shrieking: 'The spot! The spot!' her teeth chattered, she was trembling, and fixing her terrified eyes on her right hand, she rubbed it, saying: 'Still a spot!' At last the doctor came, and recommended the avoidance of undue excitement.

The townsfolk saw in all this an unhappy augury for her character. It was said that 'young Moreau' intended to make an actress of her later on.

Soon there was another event to discuss—the arrival of Uncle Barthélemy.

Mme Moreau gave up her bedroom to him, and pushed condescension so far as to serve meat on fast days.

The old man was moderately affable. He made continual comparisons between Le Havre and Nogent; at Nogent he found the air heavy, the bread bad, the streets ill-paved, the food mediocre, and the inhabitants lazy. 'And what miserable trade you have here!' He criticized the extravagance of his late brother; he, on the other hand, had amassed an income of twenty-seven thousand francs. He left eventually, at the end of the week, and on the carriage step he let fall these disquieting words:

'I'm relieved to see that you're comfortably off.'

'You'll get nothing!' said Mme Moreau, returning to the drawing-room.

He had only come on her insistence; and for a week she had tried, perhaps too openly, to elicit some declaration from him. She regretted her action and remained sitting in her arm-chair, her head bowed, her lips pursed. Frederic, opposite, watched her; and both were silent, as they had been five years before, when he came back from Montereau. This co-incidence, passing through his mind, reminded him of Mme Arnoux.

At that moment the crack of a whip was heard under the window, and a voice called him.

It was M. Roque, alone in his wagonette. He was off to spend the day at La Fortelle, the house of M. Dambreuse, and warmly invited Frederic to come with him.

'You don't need an invitation if you're with me. Don't be afraid!'

Frederic wanted to accept. But how was he to explain his permanent residence at Nogent? He had no proper summer clothes; and what would his mother say? He refused.

After that their neighbour was less friendly. Louise was growing up; Mme Éléonore fell dangerously ill; and the connection came to an end, to the great relief of Mme Moreau, who feared that the friendship of such people might affect her son's career.

She thought of buying him a post as clerk of the court; Frederic was not entirely opposed to this idea. He now went to mass with her and played his game of all fours in the evening; he became used to country life. He wrapped himself in it—and even his passion took on a sort of embalmed sweetness, an elegiac charm. By pouring his sorrow out in his letters, by mingling it with his reading, by walking with it in the country and scattering it everywhere, he had almost destroyed it. For him Mme Arnoux was a dead woman, and he felt no surprise in the thought that he did not know where her tomb was—so peaceful and resigned had his emotion become.

One day, on the 12th of December, 1845, at about nine o'clock in the morning, the cook brought a letter up to his room. The address, in large letters, was in a strange handwriting; and

Frederic, half asleep, did not hurry to open it. At length he read:

'Court of Conciliation of Le Havre. 3rd arrondissement. Sir, Your uncle M. Moreau having died intestate . . .' He was the heir!

As though a fire had broken out behind the wall, he leaped out of bed, in his night-shirt and bare feet; he passed his hand over his face, not believing his eyes, thinking that he was still dreaming; and, to make sure he was awake, he opened the window wide.

Snow had fallen; the roofs were white; and he even recognized in the yard a wash-tub, over which he had tripped the evening before.

He re-read the letter three times; it was perfectly true. Twenty-seven thousand francs a year! A delirious joy over-whelmed him at the thought of seeing Mme Arnoux again. With the vividness of a hallucination, he saw himself at her side, bringing her a present wrapped in tissue paper, while his tilbury stood at the door—no, a brougham, rather—a black brougham, with a servant in brown livery; he heard his horse snorting, and the rattle of the curb chain mingled with the murmur of their kisses. This scene would be re-enacted, day after day, for ever. He would entertain them at his own house; the dining-room would be hung with red leather, the boudoir in yellow satin; there would be divans everywhere! And what *étagères*! What Chinese vases! What carpets! These pictures flooded his brain in such confusion that he felt his head spinning. Then he remembered his mother; and he went down, with the letter still in his hand.

Mme Moreau tried to hold back her emotion and fainted.

Frederic took her in his arms and kissed her forehead.

'Dear mother, you can buy your carriage back now. Smile, don't cry! Be happy!'

Ten minutes later the news had reached the furthest corners of the town.

Maître Benoist, M. Gamblin, M. Chambrion, all their friends, hurried up. Frederic escaped for a moment to write to Deslauriers. Other visits followed. The afternoon was spent in receiving congratulations. Roque's wife, who was now 'very low,' was forgotten.

In the evening, when they were alone together, Mme Moreau advised her son to become a barrister at Troyes. Being better known in his own district than elsewhere, he would find good clients there more easily.

'Oh, that's a bit thick!' exclaimed Frederic.

His happiness was scarcely in his hands before they wanted to rob him of it. He declared his firm intention of living in Paris.

'What will you do there?'

'Nothing!'

Mme Moreau, surprised at his manner, asked him what he wanted to be.

'A minister!' replied Frederic.

And he assured her that he was not joking; he meant to plunge into politics, for it was towards this career that his reading and his instincts impelled him. To begin with, he would become an official of the Council of State, under the patronage of M. Dambreuse.

'Do you know him, then?'

'Of course. Through Monsieur Roque.'

'That is strange,' said Mme Moreau.

He had reawakened the old ambitious dreams in her heart. She yielded inwardly to them, and did not mention her other plans again.

If Frederic could have obeyed his impatience, he would have started that very instant. But all the seats in the next day's coaches were taken; he fretted until seven o'clock in the evening of the following day.

They were sitting down to dinner, when the church bell rang three times, slowly; the servant, coming in, announced that Mme Éléonore was dead.

This death was not, in point of fact, a calamity for anybody, even for her child. The girl would only be the better for it later on.

As the two houses adjoined, they could hear much bustling and the sound of voices; the idea of the corpse next door cast a certain gloom over their separation. Mme Moreau wiped her eyes two or three times. Frederic's heart was wrung.

The meal over, Catherine stopped him in the passage. Mademoiselle absolutely insisted on seeing him. She was waiting for him in the garden.

He went out, climbed over the fence, and stumbling a little against the trees, made his way towards M. Roque's house. Lights were burning at a window on the second floor; then a shape appeared in the darkness, and a voice whispered:

'It's me.'

She seemed to him taller than usual, probably because of

93

her black dress. Not knowing what to say to her first, he contented himself with taking her hands and sighing:

'My poor Louise!'

She did not answer. For a long time she gazed at him intently. Frederic was afraid of missing the coach; he thought he heard a rumbling in the distance; and to end the interview he said:

'Catherine told me that you had something . . .'

'Yes, it's true. I wanted to tell you . . .'

Her formal manner surprised him, and, as she was silent once more, he said:

'Well, what?'

'I don't know. I've forgotten. Are you really going away?'

'Yes, in a moment.'

She repeated:

'In a moment? And for ever? . . . Shall we never see you again?'

Sobs choked her.

'Good-bye! Good-bye! Kiss me, please.' And she clasped him frantically in her arms.

PART II

CHAPTER I

WHEN he had taken his place on the back seat of the front compartment, and felt the coach quiver under the pull of the five horses plunging forward together, a wild joy swept over him.

Like an architect designing a palace, he planned his future life. He filled it with delights and splendours, until it seemed to touch the sky; he could not count the things that it contained; and his reverie was so deep that the outside world vanished.

At the bottom of the hill of Sourdun, he noticed where they were. They had only done three miles, at the most! He was indignant. He lowered the windows to look at the road. He asked the conductor several times exactly how long it would be before they arrived. However, he calmed down, and stayed in his corner, with his eyes open.

The lantern, hanging from the postilion's seat, lit up the haunches of the wheelers. He could see nothing beyond but the manes of the other horses, swaying to and fro like white waves. Their breath formed a mist on either side of the shafts; the iron chains rattled, the windows shook in their frames; and the heavy coach rumbled along the paved road at an even speed. Now and then the wall of a barn loomed dimly, or a solitary inn. Sometimes, as they passed through a village, a baker's oven would throw out a fiery glow and the gigantic shadows of the horses would race across the opposite house. At the stages, after the team had been unharnessed, there was dead silence for a moment. Someone started stamping about on top of the coach, under the tilt; a woman, standing in a doorway, sheltered her candle with her hand. Then the conductor jumped on to the step and the coach set off again.

At Mormans they heard a quarter past one strike.

'So I shall see her to-day,' he thought; 'to-day, in a little while.'

But gradually his hopes and his memories—Nogent, the rue de Choiseul, Mme Arnoux, his mother—were all merged and intermingled.

He was awakened by the hollow sound of wheels on planks. They were crossing the Charenton bridge; it was Paris. His

97

two companions took off their head-gear—a cap and a silk handkerchief respectively—put on their hats, and began to talk. The first, a stout, red-faced man, in a velvet frock coat, was a merchant, the other was going to Paris to see a doctor—and Frederic, fearing lest he had inconvenienced him during the night, offered a spontaneous apology—to such an extent had his happiness warmed his heart.

The stopping-place was apparently flooded, for they went straight on, and the country began again. Tall factory chimneys were smoking in the distance.

Then they turned into Ivry. They went up a street; suddenly he caught sight of the dome of the Panthéon.

The straggling houses on the plain looked vaguely like a ruined city. Beyond rose the level ridge of the fortifications; on the muddy footpaths fringing the road stood small, branchless trees, protected by wooden frames studded with nails. Chemical factories alternated with timber merchants' sheds. Tall gateways, like those of farms, afforded a view through their open doors of mean yards full of filth and puddles of dirty water. There were long-fronted taverns, painted dark red, displaying between the first-floor windows a pair of crossed billiard cues in a wreath of painted flowers. Here and there a stucco villa had been left half finished. Then the double line of houses became continuous; at rare intervals a huge cigar, marking a tobacconist's shop, relieved the bareness of the long façades. Midwives' signs showed a bonneted matron dandling a baby in a lace-trimmed quilt. Posters covered the corners of walls; half torn off, they flapped in the wind like rags. Workmen in blouses, brewers' drays, laundry vans, and butchers' carts went by; a fine rain fell; it was cold, and the sky was pale, but behind the mist shone two eyes which meant far more than the sun to him.

They stopped at the barrier for a long time, for it was obstructed by poultry farmers, carriers, and a flock of sheep. The sentry, with his hood thrown back, walked up and down in front of his box, trying to get warm. The customs officer climbed on to the top of the coach, and a fanfare on a cornet rang out.

They dashed down the boulevard at a spirited trot, with swingletrees clattering and traces flying. The thong of the long whip cracked in the moist air. The conductor gave his ringing shout: 'Hurry! Hurry! Hallo!' while mud spattered the windows, pedestrians jumped out of the way, and road sweepers stood aside. They swept past wagons, carriages, and omnibuses, and at last reached the iron railings of the Jardin des Plantes.

The Seine, mud-coloured, had risen almost to the keystones of the bridges. A chilly breath came off the river. Frederic sniffed it with all his strength, savouring that delicious Paris air, which seems to be fraught with the redolence of love and the exhalations of the intellect. At the sight of the first cab he felt his heart melt. He was in love with Paris; he even loved the straw-covered floors of the wine shops, the shoe-blacks with their boxes, the grocers' boys shaking out their coffee roasters. Women were hurrying along under umbrellas. He leaned out to examine their faces. Some chance might have brought Mme Arnoux into the street.

The shops flew by, the crowd increased, the noise grew louder. They passed along the quai Saint-Bernard, the quai de la Tournelle and the quai Montebello, and then took the quai Napoléon; he looked out for his own windows; they were a long way off. Crossing the Seine again at the Pont-Neuf, they continued as far as the Louvre; then, taking the rue Saint-Honoré, the rue Croix-des-Petits-Champs, and the rue du Bouloi, they arrived at the rue Coq-Héron, and entered the hotel yard.

To prolong his pleasure, Frederic dressed as slowly as he could. He made his way to the boulevard Montmartre on foot, smiling as he reflected that in a moment he would see once more the beloved name on the marble tablet. He raised his eyes. No shop window, no pictures—nothing!

He ran to the rue de Choiseul. M. and Mme Arnoux no longer lived there, and a neighbour's wife was in the porter's lodge; Frederic waited for the porter; at last he appeared. He was a different porter; and he didn't know their address.

Frederic went into a café and studied the commercial directory over his breakfast. There were three hundred people called Arnoux, but no Jacques Arnoux. Where on earth did they live?

Pellerin would know.

He hurried to his studio, at the very top of the Faubourg Poissonnière. The door had neither bell nor knocker; he hammered on it with his fist, he called and shouted. There was no answer.

Then he thought of Hussonnet. But how was such a man to be found? He had once accompanied him to his mistress's house, in the rue de Fleurus. Arrived at the rue de Fleurus, Frederic realized that he did not know the lady's name.

He betook himself to the police headquarters. He wandered from staircase to staircase, from office to office. The information department was just closing. He was told to come back the next day.

Then he visited all the art dealers he could find, and inquired about Arnoux. M. Arnoux was no longer in the trade.

At last, ill, exhausted, and depressed, he returned to his hotel and went to bed. Just as he was stretching himself between the sheets, an idea made him start up in delight.

'Regimbart! What an idiot I was not to have thought of him!'

The next morning at seven he was at a drinking-place in the rue Notre-Dame-des-Victoires where it had been Regimbart's custom to imbibe white wine. It was still shut; he went for a walk in the neighbourhood, and, half an hour later, returned to the shop. Regimbart had just left. Frederic dashed into the street. He even thought he recognized his hat in the distance; a funeral, with hearse and carriages, came between. When it had passed by, there was no one to be seen.

Luckily, he remembered that the citizen always lunched on the stroke of eleven at a little restaurant in the place Gaillon. He must be patient; and after an interminable stroll from the Bourse to the Madeleine, and from the Madeleine to the Gymnase Theatre, Frederic entered the restaurant in the place Gaillon on the stroke of eleven o'clock, confident that he would find his man there.

'Don't know him,' said the owner in an insolent tone.

Frederic persisted.

'I still don't know him,' the other replied, raising his eyebrows impressively and shaking his head in a manner that suggested some mystery.

The last time they had met, the citizen had mentioned the Alexandre tavern. Frederic swallowed a roll, and, jumping into a fly, asked the coachman if he knew of a certain Café Alexandre somewhere up by Sainte-Geneviève. The coachman drove to a place of that name in the rue des Francs-Bourgeois-Saint-Michel, and to Frederic's inquiry: 'Monsieur Regimbart, please?' the proprietor replied, with a smile of extreme cordiality:

'He has not yet arrived, monsieur,' and threw a meaning glance to his wife, who was sitting behind the counter.

And, turning towards the clock, he continued immediately: 'But I'm expecting him in ten minutes' time, or a quarter of an hour at the most. Célestin, bring the papers! What will monsieur drink?'

Although he did not really want anything, Frederic absorbed a glass of rum, a glass of kirsch, a glass of curaçao, and various punches, both hot and cold. He read the whole of that day's *Siècle*, and read it again; he examined the cartoon in *Charivari* down to the grain of the paper; he ended by knowing the advertisements by heart. From time to time there was a sound of boots on the pavement; it was he! And someone's profile was outlined against the window; but the figure always passed on.

To relieve the tedium, Frederic changed his position; he went and sat at the back of the room, then on the right, then on the left; after that he settled down in the middle of the long wall-sofa, with his arms outstretched. A cat, stepping delicately along the back of the plush seat, terrified him by suddenly jumping down and licking up the drops of syrup on the tray; while the child of the house, an insufferable brat of four, played with a rattle on the steps of the counter. The mother, a sickly little woman with bad teeth, smiled stupidly. What could Regimbart be doing? Frederic waited, in a state of infinite wretchedness.

The rain drummed like hail on the hood of the fly. Through the opening in the muslin curtains he could see the unfortunate horse standing in the street, as still as a horse of wood. The gutter stream, enormously swollen, flowed over the rim of the wheel, and the coachman dozed, sheltering under the apron. From time to time, fearing that his gentleman might slip away, he half opened the door of the café, streaming like a river. If one could wear things out by looking at them, Frederic would have disintegrated the clock by his continuous stare. Nevertheless it did not cease to move. Alexandre walked up and down, repeating: 'He'll come all right. He'll come,' and, to entertain Frederic, aired his opinions and discussed politics. He even unbent so far as to suggest a game of dominoes.

At last, at half-past four, Frederic, having been there since midday, jumped to his feet and declared that he would wait no longer.

'I can't understand it myself,' said the proprietor, frankly. 'This is the first time Monsieur Ledoux has failed us.'

'Monsieur Ledoux?'

'Why, yes, monsieur.'

'I said Regimbart!' shouted Frederic, enraged.

'I beg your pardon, but that is not the case. Madame Alexandre, didn't monsieur say Monsieur Ledoux?'

And, appealing to the waiter:

'Didn't you hear him yourself, the same as I did?'

But the waiter, to score off his master, no doubt, contented himself with grinning.

Frederic drove back to the boulevards, exasperated at the time wasted, furious with the citizen, praying for his presence as if he were a god, and fully resolved to extract him from the most inaccessible of wine cellars. His carriage irritated him; he dismissed it; his mind grew confused; then the names of all the cafés which he had heard that idiot mention flashed through his mind together, like a thousand fireworks: Café Gascard, Café Grimbert, Café Halbout, Bordelais tavern, Havanais, Havrais, Bœuf-à-la-Mode, Brasserie Allemande, Mère-Morel; and he visited them all in succession. At one, Regimbart had just left; at another, he might be coming; at a third, he had not been seen for six months; at a fourth, he had ordered, the day before, a joint for Saturday. At length, at Vautier's bar, Frederic, opening the door, knocked into the waiter.

'Do you know Monsieur Regimbart?'

'Do I know him, monsieur? I myself have the honour of waiting on him. He's upstairs, just finishing his dinner.'

And the proprietor, with a napkin under his arm, came up to him in person:

'Are you looking for Monsieur Regimbart? He was here a moment ago.'

Frederic uttered an oath, but the owner declared that he would find him at Bouttevilain's without fail.

'On my word of honour! He left a little earlier than usual, because he has a business appointment with some gentlemen. But, I repeat, you'll find him at Bouttevilain's, 92 rue Saint-Martin, second staircase, on the left, through the yard, first floor, right-hand door!'

At last, through a haze of tobacco smoke, he caught sight of him, sitting alone at the far end of the back room, behind the billiard table, a glass of beer in front of him, his chin sunk on his chest, in an attitude of contemplation.

'I've been looking for you for ages,' he said.

Regimbart, impassive, offered him two fingers, and, as if he had seen him the previous evening, made a few trivial remarks on the opening of the Chamber.

Frederic interrupted him by inquiring in the most natural tone he could manage:

'How 's Arnoux?'

The reply was long in coming: Regimbart seemed to be gargling his drink.

'He 's all right.'

'Where does he live now?'

'Why . . . in the rue Paradis-Poissonnière,' answered the astonished citizen.

'What number?'

'Thirty-seven, of course. What an odd fellow you are!'

Frederic got up.

'What, are you going?'

'Yes, I have an engagement—a business matter—I 'd forgotten all about it.'

Frederic travelled from the tavern to Arnoux's house as if wafted by a warm wind, with that peculiar ease of motion which is characteristic of dreams. Soon he found himself on a second floor; there was a door in front of him; the bell rang; a maid appeared; a second door opened; Mme Arnoux was sitting beside the fire. Arnoux leapt up, and embraced him.

On her knee was a little boy of about three; her daughter, now as tall as she, was standing on the other side of the fire-place.

'Allow me to introduce this gentleman to you,' said Arnoux, picking up his son by the armpits.

And for some minutes he amused himself by throwing him high into the air and catching him in his outstretched arms.

'You 'll kill him! For heaven's sake, stop!' exclaimed Mme Arnoux.

But Arnoux swore there was no danger and even murmured endearments in Marseilles dialect—his native tongue.

'There, my chicken, there, my poppet . . .' Then he asked Frederic why he had been so long without writing to them, how he had spent his time in the country, and what had brought him back.

'At the moment, my dear fellow, I 'm in the pottery trade. But let 's talk about yourself!'

Frederic spoke of a lengthy lawsuit and of his mother's health; he dilated on the latter subject to make himself appear interesting. In brief, he was settling permanently in Paris; and he said nothing of the legacy, for fear of damaging his past reputation.

The curtains and chair covers were of brown woollen stuff;

two pillows, side by side, leaned against the bolster; a kettle was heating among the coals, and the shaded lamp, standing on the edge of the chest of drawers, cast a dim light over the room. Mme Arnoux wore a dark blue merino dressing-gown. Her eyes were on the fire; she had one hand on the little boy's shoulder, and with the other she was undoing the fastening of his vest; the child, in his shirt, was crying and scratching his head, like M. Alexandre junior.

Frederic had been anticipating paroxysms of joy; but passionate feelings seldom survive a change of atmosphere, and, meeting Mme Arnoux again in an unfamiliar setting, he felt that her stature was somehow diminished, that she had suffered an indefinable deterioration—in short, that she had changed.

He asked after his old friends, including Pellerin.

'I hardly ever see him,' said Arnoux.

She added:

'We no longer entertain as we used to.'

Was that to warn him that he would receive no invitation?

Arnoux, however, continuing his civilities, reproached him for not having dropped in to take pot luck with them; and he explained why he had changed his business.

'What can one do in a decadent period like ours? Real painting is out of fashion. Besides, you can find a place for art in any sphere. You know how fond I am of the beautiful! One of these days I must take you to my factory.'

And he insisted on showing Frederic, there and then, some of his products, which were in his shop on the story below.

The floor was strewn with dishes, soup tureens, plates, and basins. Against the wall stood some large square tiles for bathrooms and lavatories, with designs drawn from mythology, in the Renaissance style; in the middle, a double *étagère* that reached to the ceiling bore ice buckets, flower pots, candelabra, small *jardinières*, and large statuettes in several colours, representing negroes or Pompadour shepherdesses. Arnoux's display bored Frederic, who was cold and hungry. He hurried to the Café Anglais, where he had a splendid supper, and, as he ate, he said to himself:

'What a fool I was in the country, with my melancholy! Why, she scarcely recognized me! What a common woman!'

And, in a sudden burst of health, he resolved to lead a selfish life. He felt that his heart was now as hard as the table on which his elbows rested. Now he could plunge into society without fear. He thought of Dambreuse and his wife; he would make use of them; then he remembered Deslauriers. 'Ah, well, so much the worse for him!' However, he sent him a note by a messenger, asking him to meet him next day at the Palais-Royal, so that they could lunch together.

Fortune had been less kind to Deslauriers.

He had entered for the teachers' examination with a thesis on the right of bequeathing property, in which he maintained that this right should be limited as far as possible. His opponent's arguments had provoked him to make a fool of himself, and he had done so, in good measure; but the examiners had remained impassive. Then he happened to draw by lot, as the subject of his lecture, the Theory of the Statute of Limitations. Deslauriers had indulged in the most unfortunate speculations; old claims should be as valid as new; he asked why an owner should be deprived of his property, merely because his claim happened to be thirty-one years old. This principle places the honest man's security in the hands of the successful robber's heir. Every injustice may be sanctioned by an extension of this right, which is nothing more than tyranny, an abuse of power! He had even exclaimed:

'Abolish it—and the Franks will cease to oppress the Gauls, the English the Irish, the Yankees the Red Indians, the Turks the Arabs, the white men the negroes, Poland . . .'

The chairman had interrupted him:

'That will do, sir. We are not concerned with your political opinions. You will present yourself again at a later date.'

Deslauriers had declined to present himself again. That wretched twentieth article of the third book of the Civil Code had become a regular obsession with him. He began to elaborate a vast work on 'Limitations, viewed as a basis of civil law and of the natural rights of peoples'; and he had lost his way in Dunod, Rogerius, Balbus, Martin, Vazeille, Savigny, Troplong, and other extensive researches. In order to have more leisure for study, he had abandoned his position as chief clerk. He lived by giving lessons and writing theses; and, at the meetings of his debating society, his vitriolic tongue terrified the conservative element, which consisted of youthful doctrinaires of Guizot's school. As a result he had acquired a sort of celebrity in certain quarters, but it was a celebrity mingled with distrust.

When he met Frederic he was wearing a voluminous overcoat lined with red flannel, like the one Sénécal used to have.

Out of deference to the passers-by, they refrained from a lengthy embrace, and they walked to Véfour's, arm in arm, chuckling with pleasure, with unshed tears in their eyes. Then, as soon as they were alone, Deslauriers exclaimed:

'Upon my soul, we're going to take it easy now!'

Frederic did not like the way in which Deslauriers immediately associated himself with his fortune. His friend displayed too much satisfaction for the two of them, and not enough for him alone.

Then Deslauriers mentioned his reverse, and gradually gave a picture of his work and life. He spoke of himself with stoicism, but of others with rancour. He was dissatisfied with everything. There was not a man of position who was not either a fool or a rogue. He stormed at the waiter because of a dirty glass, and to Frederic's mild protest he replied:

'Why should I put myself out for fellows like that? They earn their six or eight thousand francs a year; they've got a vote; they could probably stand for the Chamber. No—not I!'

Then he added, laughingly:

'But I was forgetting that I'm addressing a capitalist, a Croesus; for you are a Croesus now!'

And, going back to the legacy, he expressed the following opinion: that indirect inheritance, being intrinsically unjust—although he was delighted in this particular case—would soon be abolished, in the coming revolution.

'Do you think so?' said Frederic.

'I'm positive of it,' he replied. 'Things can't go on like this. There's too much suffering. When I see men like Sénécal living in poverty——'

Sénécal again! thought Frederic.

'What's the rest of your news? Are you still in love with Madame Arnoux? All over, eh?'

Frederic, not knowing what to answer, closed his eyes and bowed his head.

Talking of Arnoux, Deslauriers informed him that his magazine now belonged to Hussonnet, who had altered it considerably. It was called '*Art*, a literary enterprise, being a company with shares of one hundred francs each; registered capital, forty thousand francs.' Each shareholder had the right to contribute to the paper; for '"the object of the company is to publish the work of new writers and to save authors of talent, or even of genius, from those unhappy reverses which submerge . . ."' and so forth. You know the sort of nonsense!' There was, however, still something to be done; and that was to raise the tone of the magazine, and then suddenly, without changing the staff or interrupting the serial story, to provide the subscribers with a political journal. The sum required was not excessive.

'What do you think of it? Do you want to take an interest?'

Frederic did not reject the proposal. But he had to wait until his affairs were in order.

'Now, if there's anything you need . . .'

'No, thank you, my friend,' said Deslauriers.

Then they smoked cheroots, leaning their elbows on the plush-covered window sill. The sun shone, the air was soft, flocks of birds fluttered down into the garden; the bronze and marble statues glistened after the rain; nurses in aprons sat gossiping on chairs, and the laughter of children could be heard, mingled with the continuous murmur of the fountain.

Frederic had felt a little disturbed by Deslauriers's bitterness; but now, warmed by the wine that flowed through his veins, half dazed, half asleep, with the sun full in his eyes, he felt nothing but a sense of immense, deliciously stupid well-being, like a plant soaked through and through with heat and moisture. Deslauriers, his eyes half closed, was looking vaguely into the distance. His chest heaved and he began to speak:

'Ah, those were the days, when Camille Desmoulins leaped on a table over there and swept the people against the Bastille! Then a man could really feel alive; one could assert oneself and prove one's strength! Mere lawyers ordered generals about, paupers defeated kings, whereas now . . .'

He was silent, then suddenly:

'Never mind! There's promise in the future.'

And, drumming the charge on the window pane, he recited these lines of Barthélemy:

> 'The dread Assembly will appear again,
> That, after forty years, still stirs your heart,
> Fearless Colossus, striding mightily . . .

'I've forgotten the rest. But it's late; shall we go?'

And he went on expounding his theories in the street.

Frederic was not listening. He kept noticing in the shop windows stuffs and furniture suitable for his new home; and he may have been thinking of Mme Arnoux when he stopped at a second-hand dealer's shop, in front of three faience plates. They were decorated with yellow arabesques, with a coppery sheen, and were priced at three hundred francs apiece. He had them put on one side.

'If I were you, I should prefer to buy silver plate,' said

Deslauriers, revealing, by this taste for the sumptuous, the man of humble origin.

As soon as he was alone, Frederic called on the famous Pomadère, from whom he ordered three pairs of trousers, two dress coats, a fur coat, and five waistcoats; then he visited a bootmaker, a shirt-maker, and a hatter, giving instructions that everything was to be ready as soon as possible.

Three days later, in the evening, on his return from Le Havre, he found his wardrobe waiting for him. Impatient to display it, he determined to pay a visit, there and then, to M. and Mme Dambreuse. But it was barely eight o'clock and therefore too early.

'Supposing I went to see the others?' he said to himself.

Arnoux was alone in front of his mirror, shaving.

He offered to take Frederic somewhere where he would have a good time, and, at the mention of M. Dambreuse, he added:

'Ah, that's excellent. You'll meet some friends of his there. Do come! It'll be great fun.'

Frederic excused himself. Mme Arnoux recognized his voice and greeted him through the partition, for her daughter was unwell and she herself indisposed. The clink of a spoon against a glass could be heard, and that light rustling of objects delicately moved which is always associated with a sick-room.

Then Arnoux went out to say good-bye to his wife. He multiplied his excuses:

'It's important, you understand. I simply must go; I'm wanted there; they're expecting me.'

'Go along, my dear! Enjoy yourself!'

Arnoux hailed a cab.

'Palais-Royal. 7 Galerie Montpensier.' And, sinking back on the cushions: 'I'm dying of exhaustion, my dear fellow. Well, I can tell *you*, anyway.'

He leaned over to his ear and whispered mysteriously: 'I'm trying to find the copper-red of the Chinese potters.' And he explained to him about glazing and the slow furnace.

At Chevet's he was handed a large basket, which was placed in the cab. Next he selected grapes, pineapples, and other delicacies 'for his poor wife,' and ordered them to be sent early the next morning.

Then they went to a costumier; for there was a fancy dress ball afoot. Arnoux chose a pair of blue velvet breeches, a waistcoat to match, and a red wig; Frederic a domino; and they alighted at the rue de Laval at a house lit up by coloured lanterns on the second floor.

At the bottom of the stairs they heard the sound of violins.

'Where the devil are you taking me?' said Frederic.

'To see a nice girl! Don't be frightened.'

A groom opened the door to them, and they entered the vestibule, where coats, cloaks, and shawls were piled on chairs. A young woman was passing through, dressed as a Louis Quinze dragoon. It was Mlle Rose-Annette Bron, the mistress of the place.

'Well?' said Arnoux.

'I've done it,' she replied.

'Oh, thank you, my darling!'

And he tried to kiss her.

'Careful, you fool! You'll spoil my make-up!'

Arnoux introduced Frederic.

'Come in and dance! Make yourself at home!'

She drew aside a curtain behind her, and announced with a flourish:

'Mister Arnoux, scullery boy, and his noble friend!'

At first Frederic was dazzled by the lights; he could see nothing but silk, velvet, bare shoulders, a mass of colours swaying to the strains of a band hidden by foliage, between satin-lined walls, hung here and there with pastel portraits and glass sconces in the style of Louis XVI. Tall lamps, whose frosted globes resembled snowballs, rose from among baskets of flowers that stood on small tables in the corners. Opposite, through a second, smaller room, a third apartment could be seen, containing a bed with twisted posts and a Venetian mirror over the pillow.

The dancing stopped, and a roar of acclamation greeted the spectacle of Arnoux advancing, with his basket, heaped high with eatables, on his head. 'Look out for the chandelier!' Frederic raised his eyes; it was the old Dresden china chandelier that used to hang in the shop of 'Industrial Art.' Recollections of the old days flashed through his mind; but an infantryman of the line in undress uniform, with that vacuous expression which tradition attributes to conscripts, barred his way, stretching out his arms to indicate his astonishment; in spite of the disfigurement of a horrible moustache with waxed points, he recognized his old friend Hussonnet. In a droll mixture of Alsatian and nigger talk, the Bohemian overwhelmed him with congratulations and called him 'colonel.' Frederic, embarrassed by the presence of so many strange people, was at a loss for an answer. The rapping of a bow on a music stand recalled the dancers to their places.

There were about sixty of them altogether. Most of the women wore the costumes of peasant girls or countesses, while the men, who were nearly all middle-aged, were dressed as carters, stevedores, or sailors.

Frederic, standing against the wall, watched the quadrille in front of him.

An old buck, dressed as a Doge of Venice in a long cassock of purple silk, was dancing with Mme Rosanette, who wore a green tunic, knitted breeches, and soft top boots with gold spurs. The couple opposite consisted of an Albanian brigand, bristling with scimitars, and a Swiss girl—as white as milk and as plump as a quail—in shirt sleeves and a red bodice. A tall blonde, from the Grand Opera chorus, in order to show off her hair, which came down to her knees, had come as a savage; on top of her brown tights she wore nothing but a leather loin cloth, some glass bangles, and a tinsel tiara, that supported a large spray of peacock's feathers. Opposite her a Pritchard in an absurdly large black coat was beating time on his snuff box with his elbow. A little Watteau shepherd, all blue and silver like a moonlit night, was striking his crook against the wand of a Bacchante, who wore a crown of grapes, a leopard skin on her left side, and tall buskins with red ribbons. On the other side, a Polish girl, in a jacket of orange velvet, was swinging her gauze skirt over stockings of pearl-grey silk and pink boots edged with white fur. She was smiling at a stout man of about forty, disguised as a choir-boy, who was leaping high in the air, lifting his surplice with one hand and holding on to his red skull cap with the other. But the star, the belle of the ball, was Mlle Loulou, a famous music hall dancer. Being temporarily in funds, she wore a broad lace collar over her jacket of plain black velvet; and her wide trousers of poppy-red silk, which were drawn tight round the buttocks and fastened at the waist by a cashmere scarf, were decorated all down the seams with fresh white gardenias. Her pale, rather puffy face, with its turned-up nose, looked more impudent than ever under her tousled wig, which was surmounted by a man's grey felt hat, dented in the crown and cocked over her right ear. When she jumped into the air, the diamond buckles of her shoes nearly touched the nose of her neighbour, who was a tall medieval baron, heavily encumbered by a suit of armour. An angel, with a golden sword in her hand and a pair of swan's wings on her back, threaded the crowd and kept losing her partner, a gorgeous Louis XIV, whose complete ignorance of the quadrille was throwing the dancers opposite into confusion.

Watching these people, Frederic felt neglected and ill at ease. Once more he thought of Mme Arnoux, and it seemed to him as though he were taking part in a kind of conspiracy directed against her.

When the quadrille was over, Mme Rosanette came up to him. She was panting slightly; and her gorget, as bright as a mirror, quivered gently under her chin.

'Well, sir, aren't you dancing?'

Frederic excused himself; he did not dance.

'Really? Not even with me? Are you sure?'

She stood with her weight on one leg, her other knee slightly bent, and stroked the mother-of-pearl hilt of her sword with her left hand. She gazed at him for a moment, with an expression that was half suppliant, half mocking. At length she said 'Good-bye,' did a pirouette, and vanished.

Frederic, dissatisfied with himself and not knowing what to do, began to wander about the place.

He went into the boudoir, which was hung with pale blue silk, embroidered with bunches of wild flowers. On the ceiling, in a gilded wooden frame, cupids sported on pillowy clouds in an azure sky. These refinements—which would seem poor enough to the modern counterparts of Rosanette — dazzled him; and he admired everything: the artificial flowers round the edge of the mirror, the curtains over the fire-place, the Turkish divan, and, in a recess, a kind of tent of white muslin, lined with pink satin. The bedroom had black furniture, inlaid with metal; on a dais covered with swan's-skin rose the great canopied bed, with its spray of ostrich feathers. In the dim light that came from a Bohemian bowl suspended by three slender chains, he could just make out jewelled hairpins in pincushions, rings on trays, gold-framed lockets, and silver caskets. Through a little half-open door a conservatory could be seen; it took up the whole breadth of a terrace and was bounded at the far end by an aviary.

It was indeed a place to delight him. His youth suddenly rebelled; he swore to enjoy it, and took courage; then he made his way back to the door of the drawing-room, where there were now more people. The whole scene seemed to move in a kind of luminous, dusty haze; he stood and watched the dancing, half closing his eyes in order to see better, and sniffing the soft smell of the women, that filled the room like a vast, hovering kiss.

Near him, on the other side of the door, stood Pellerin—Pellerin, in full evening dress, his left arm in his waistcoat, and holding in his right hand his hat and a torn white glove.

'Well, we haven't seen you for a long time! Where on earth have you been? Travelling in Italy? Rather banal, Italy, eh? Not as effective as they say? Never mind! Bring your sketches along one of these days.'

And without waiting for an answer the artist began to talk about himself.

He had made considerable progress, for he had realized once and for all the absurdity of line. In a work of art one should look not for beauty and unity but for character and variety of content.

'Everything exists in nature, therefore you can paint any subject you like. It's a question of striking the right note—that's all. I've discovered the secret.'

And nudging him with his elbow, he repeated several times:

'I've discovered the secret, you see. Look at the little woman with the Egyptian head-dress dancing with the Russian postilion—now that's clear, dry, and sharp—all planes and primary colours. Indigo under the eyes, a dab of scarlet on the cheeks, a little sepia on the temples . . . so . . . and so . . .'

And he drew imaginary brush strokes with his thumb in the air.

'Now—look at that heavy-weight over there,' he went on, pointing to a fishwife in a red dress, with a gold cross on her neck and a knotted lawn kerchief down her back, 'she's entirely a matter of curves. Her nostrils have the same sweep as the wings of her cap. The corners of her mouth turn up, her chin goes down; it's all rich, blended, lush, peaceful, sunny—pure Rubens! And they're perfect of their kind! But where's the ideal?'

He warmed to his subject:

'How do you define a beautiful woman? How do you define the beautiful? Oh, the beautiful! You'll tell me . . .'

Frederic interrupted him to ask about a pierrot with a face like a goat who was at that moment blessing the guests in the middle of a quadrille.

'He's nobody. A widower, with three sons. He lets them go about in rags, while he spends his time at the club, and sleeps with his cook.'

'What about the man dressed as a judge who's talking to the Pompadour marquise in the window?'

'The marquise is Madame Vandaël, who used to act at the Gymnase Theatre; she's the mistress of the doge—he's the Comte de Palazot. They've been together for twenty years; no one knows why. What wonderful eyes that woman had once! The fellow talking to her is known as Captain d'Herbigny—one of the old school. He's got nothing to his name but his medals and his pension. He acts as uncle to chorus girls on formal occasions, arranges duels, and dines out.'

'A rogue?' asked Frederic.

'No, an honest man.'

'Oh!'

The artist pointed out other people to him; then he caught sight of a gentleman dressed, like one of Molière's doctors, in a long black serge gown which he wore wide open in front to show off the trinkets on his watch chain.

'That character,' said Pellerin, 'is Doctor Desrogis. He's furious at not being famous, has written a book of medical pornography, licks every one's boots in society, and can keep a secret; the women here adore him. He and his wife—the thin lady of the manor in grey — trail along together through every public place, and elsewhere. They're not well off; but they have an "at home" day—artistic tea parties with recitations. Careful, now!'

The doctor came up to them; and soon all three were talking in a group at the entrance to the drawing-room. Hussonnet joined them; then the savage woman's lover, a young poet, whose short cloak, in the style of Francis the First, revealed a miserable body underneath; and lastly a young wit, who was dressed as a poor Turkish pedlar. His gold-braided tunic had evidently seen long service with some itinerant dentist; his wide pleated trousers were of the most faded red; his turban, rolled up like a fried eel, presented a lamentable appearance. Indeed, his costume gave so successful an impression of poverty that the women did not conceal their disgust. The doctor consoled him by singing the praises of the *débardeuse*,[1] his mistress. This Turk was a banker's son.

Between two quadrilles, Rosanette made her way to the chimney corner, where a fat little old man in a red coat with gold buttons was sitting in an arm-chair. His sunken cheeks drooped over his high white neck-cloth, but his hair was still blond and curled naturally, like a poodle's coat. This gave him a rather sprightly look.

She listened to him, leaning over his face. Then she brought him a glass of syrup. Her hands were charming, under the lace cuffs that fringed the sleeves of her green tunic. The old man kissed them when he had had his drink.

'Why, that's Monsieur Oudry, Arnoux's neighbour!'

'No longer!' said Pellerin, laughing.

'What do you mean?'

A waltz began, and a postilion of Longjumeau[1] seized her by the waist. Then all the women, who had been sitting on sofas round the room, got up quickly in a line; and their skirts, their scarves, their head-dresses began to revolve.

They came so close to Frederic that he could even see the drops of sweat on their foreheads; and this dizzy, spinning movement, growing ever faster and more rhythmic, aroused a kind of intoxication in his mind, filling it with strange thoughts, while the women swept by him in a single, dazzling whirl; and each, with her special beauty, excited a different desire. The Polish girl's languorous surrender to the dance made him long to hold her to his heart, while they travelled together in a sleigh over a snow-covered plain. The Swiss girl, waltzing with her body upright and her eyelids lowered, opened to him vistas of quiet joy in a chalet beside a lake. Then suddenly the Bacchante, bending her dark head backwards, made him dream of ravenous kisses among groves of oleander, in thundery weather, to the murmur of tabors. The fishwife, out of breath from the speed of the dance, was shrieking with laughter, and he would have liked to go drinking with her at Les Porcherons[2] and to crumple her neckerchief in his hands, as in the good old days. But the *débardeuse*, whose light toes scarcely skimmed the floor, seemed, with her supple limbs and serious face, to suggest all the refinements of modern love, which combines the precision of a science with the restlessness of a bird. Rosanette was dancing with her hand on her hip; her wig bobbed up and down on her collar, scattering powder all around her; and every twirl she almost caught Frederic with her golden spurs.

At the final chord of the waltz, Mlle Vatnaz came in. She wore an Algerian kerchief on her head and numerous coins on her forehead. She had mascara under her eyes and was dressed in a sort of black cashmere jacket, over a thin, silver-spangled skirt. She held a tambourine in her hand.

Behind her walked a tall young man in the classical costume of Dante. He was—she no longer concealed it now—the one-time singer at the Alhambra. His name being Auguste Delamare, he had at first called himself Anténor Dellamarre, then Delmas, then Belmar, and finally Delmar. He had altered and improved his name in this way to correspond with his growing fame; for he had left the music hall for the stage, and had just made a much-heralded first appearance in *Gaspardo le Pêcheur* at the Ambigu Theatre.

Hussonnet scowled at the sight of him. Since the rejection of his play he loathed actors. The vanity of these gentry was inconceivable—and this one was worse than any!

'What an affected ass!' he said.

Delmar, after bowing slightly to Rosanette, had placed himself with his back to the fire-place. He stood there motionless, with one hand on his heart, his left foot advanced, his eyes on the ceiling, and his wreath of gilded laurels on top of his cowl. At the same time he strove to achieve a poetical look in order to fascinate the ladies. A wide circle formed around him from every side.

Mlle Vatnaz enveloped Rosanette in a long embrace, then came up to Hussonnet and begged him to revise the style of an educational book which she wanted to publish—*The Young Persons' Garland*, a literary and moral anthology. The writer promised his collaboration. After that she asked him if he could manage to give her friend a puff in one of the papers to which he had access, and even to offer him a part in a play later on. This made Hussonnet forget to take a glass of punch.

The punch had been brewed by Arnoux; and, followed by the count's groom carrying an empty tray, he handed it round with satisfaction.

When he reached M. Oudry, Rosanette stopped him.

'Well—and the business?'

He blushed slightly; then, turning to the old man:

'Our fair friend,' he said, 'tells me that you might be so kind . . .'

'Come, come, neighbour, I'm at your service.'

The name of M. Dambreuse was mentioned; they conversed in low voices, and Frederic caught only snatches. He moved to the other side of the fire-place, where Rosanette was talking to Delmar.

The actor had a vulgar face, intended, like theatrical scenery, to be viewed from a distance; he had thick hands, large feet, and a heavy jaw. He ran down the most famous actors, spoke patronizingly of the poets, referred to 'my voice, my physique, my resources,' and embellished his conversation with his favourite words which he barely understood himself, such as '*morbidezza*,' 'analogue,' and 'homogeneity.'

Rosanette listened to him with little approving nods of her head. Admiration visibly blossomed under the rouge on her cheeks, and something moist passed like a veil over her pale eyes of indefinable colour. How could she be charmed by such a man? Frederic forced himself inwardly to dislike him still more—in order, perhaps, to banish a kind of envy which he felt for him.

Mlle Vatnaz was now with Arnoux; she was laughing loudly but from time to time cast a glance at Rosanette, whom M. Oudry was watching closely.

Then Arnoux and Mlle Vatnaz disappeared; the old man came and whispered to Rosanette.

'Well, then, it's settled. Leave me alone.'

And she asked Frederic to go and see if M. Arnoux was in the kitchen.

The floor was covered with rows of half-filled glasses; saucepans, casseroles, turbot kettle, and frying-pan bubbled and sizzled. Arnoux was giving instructions to the servants as if they were his friends, stirring the gravy, tasting the sauces, and joking with the cook.

'Right! Tell Rosanette. I'm going to dish up.'

The dancing had stopped, the women were sitting down, the men walked about. In the middle of the room one of the window curtains swelled in the wind, and the sphinx, in spite of comments from all sides, exposed her sweating arms to the draught. Where could Rosanette be? Frederic searched further afield, in the boudoir, the bedroom. Some of the guests had taken refuge there, to be alone, or *tête-à-tête*. The darkness was filled with whisperings. There were glimpses of fans fluttering at the bosoms of dresses—slowly and gently, like the wing-beats of a wounded bird.

Entering the conservatory, he saw, near the fountain, under the broad leaves of a palm, Delmar lying face downwards on the chintz sofa; Rosanette, sitting near him, was passing her hand through his hair; and they were gazing at each other. At the same moment Arnoux came in from the other end, by the aviary. Delmar leaped up, then made a leisurely departure, without turning round. He even stopped by the door to pick a hibiscus flower, which he put in his buttonhole. Rosanette bent her head; Frederic, who saw her side face, noticed that she was crying.

'Hallo! What's the matter?' said Arnoux.

She shrugged her shoulders without answering.

'Is it because of him?' he went on. She flung her arms round his neck, and, kissing him on the forehead, said slowly:

'You know quite well I shall always love you, fatty! Don't let's think about it any more. Let's have supper.'

A copper chandelier with forty candles lit up the dining-room, the walls of which were almost hidden under plates of old majolica. The bright light, shining straight down, intensi-fied the whiteness of a gigantic turbot which took up the middle of the table-cloth, among the side dishes and fruits. Round the table stood plates of shell-fish soup. With a swishing of silk, the women sat down next to each other, crushing their skirts, their sleeves, and their scarves; the men stood in the corners. Pellerin and Oudry took their places near Rosanette. Arnoux was opposite. Palazot and his friend had just left.

'We're off!' said Rosanette. 'Charge!'

And the choir-boy, a humorist, made the sign of the cross with an extravagant gesture and began to recite the *Benedicite*.

The women were horrified, especially the fishwife, who had a daughter whom she was bringing up to be respectable. And Arnoux also 'did not like it,' considering that religion should be treated with reverence.

A German clock, with a crowing cock, struck two, and gave rise to numerous jokes about the cuckoo. Talk of every kind followed; puns, anecdotes, boasts, wagers, plausible lies, un-likely assertions—a stream of words which soon divided into separate conversations. The wine went round, course followed course; the doctor carved. Oranges and corks were thrown from hand to hand; some left their places to talk to friends. Rosanette often turned round to Delmar, who stood motionless behind her; Pellerin was gossiping, M. Oudry smiled. Mlle Vatnaz finished the basket of crayfish almost single-handed; the shells clattered against her long teeth. The angel, perched on the piano stool—the only place where her wings allowed her to sit—munched away placidly without stopping.

'What a trencherwoman!' the astonished choir-boy kept saying. 'What a trencherwoman!'

The sphinx drank brandy, screamed at the top of her voice, and threw herself about like a madwoman. Suddenly her cheeks swelled; she could no longer hold back the blood that choked her. She put her napkin to her lips, then threw it under the table.

Frederic had seen her.

'It's nothing!'

When he urged her to go home and look after herself, she answered slowly:

'Oh, what's the use? If it wasn't this, it would be something else. Life isn't much fun.'

A freezing melancholy seized him, and he shivered. It was as if he had caught sight of whole worlds of misery and despair —the charcoal stove beside the truckle-bed, the corpses at the morgue in their leather aprons, with the cold tap-water trickling over their hair.

Meanwhile Hussonnet, crouching at the feet of the savage woman, was bawling in a husky voice, in imitation of the actor Grassot:

'Be not so cruel, O Celuta! How charming this little family party is! Intoxicate me with rapture, my beloved ones! Let us be gay! Let us be gay!'

And he began to kiss the women on the shoulder. They flinched, pricked by his moustache. Then he had the idea of breaking a plate against his head with a gentle tap. Others copied him; fragments of faience flew about like tiles in a high wind, and the *débardeuse* exclaimed:

'Go ahead! They're free! The old boy who makes them gives them to us.'

All eyes were turned on Arnoux. He replied:

'Ah! Cash on delivery, if you please,' to give the impression, apparently, that he was not, or had ceased to be, Rosanette's lover.

But two voices were raised in anger.

'Idiot!'

'Scoundrel!'

'I'm ready for you, sir!'

'And I for you, sir!'

The medieval knight and the Russian postilion were quarrelling; the latter had maintained that people in armour did not need to be brave; the other had taken this as an insult. He tried to fight; every one interposed; and, in the middle of the uproar, the captain tried to make his voice heard:

'Gentlemen, listen to me! One word! I know what I'm talking about, gentlemen!"

Rosanette, by striking a glass with her knife, at last secured silence; and, turning to the knight, who kept his helmet on, and then to the postilion, who wore a cap of shaggy fur:

' First of all, take off that saucepan—it gives me the vapours!'
she said. 'And you, over there, take off that wolf's head!
Do what I tell you, I say! Don't you see my epaulettes? I
am your marshal!'

They submitted, and every one applauded, crying:

'Long live the marshal! Long live the marshal!'

Then she took a bottle of champagne from the stove and,
lifting it high, poured it into the glasses that were held out to
her. As the table was very wide, the guests, especially the
women, craned over towards her, standing on tiptoe or on the
cross-bars of chairs—so that for a moment one saw a pyramid
of head-dresses, bare shoulders, outstretched arms, and leaning
bodies; and all around flowed long jets of wine, for in the corner
of the room the pierrot and Arnoux had opened a bottle each
and were splashing the faces of the company. The door of the
aviary had been left open, and the little birds invaded the room,
fluttering in terror round the chandelier, and beating their
wings against the window panes and the furniture; some settled
on the heads of the guests, so that they appeared to be wearing
great flowers in their hair.

The band had gone home. The piano was dragged from the
hall into the drawing-room. Mlle Vatnaz sat down at it, and,
accompanied by the choir-boy on the tambourine, she played
a quadrille with furious energy, striking the keys like a prancing
horse, and swaying her hips in time to the music. Rosanette
seized Frederic, Hussonnet turned cart-wheels, the *débardeuse*
performed acrobatics like a clown, the pierrot pretended to be
an orang-outang, while the savage woman, with arms outstretched, imitated the rocking of a skiff. At last they stopped,
tired out; and someone opened a window.

The daylight poured in, with the cool of the morning. There
was an exclamation of astonishment, then a silence. The
yellow flames flickered; sometimes a candle ring cracked; the
floor was strewn with ribbons, flowers, and pearls; the tables
were sticky with drops of punch and syrup. The chair covers
were soiled, costumes were crushed and smeared with powder;
wisps of hair hung down the shoulders of the women; their
paint had run as they perspired, revealing livid faces, with red,
blinking eyelids.

Rosanette, as fresh as if she had come from the bath, had
pink cheeks and sparkling eyes. She flung off her wig; and her
hair fell around her like a fleece, covering all her clothes except
her breeches. The effect was both comic and charming.

The sphinx, whose teeth were chattering with fever, asked for a shawl.

Rosanette ran to fetch it, and when the sphinx followed, shut the door sharply in her face.

The Turk remarked audibly that M. Oudry had not been seen to leave. In the general exhaustion no one took up this innuendo.

Waiting for their carriages, they struggled into hoods and cloaks. Seven o'clock struck. The angel was still in the dining-room, attacking a mixture of butter and sardines; and the fishwife, beside her, smoked cigarettes and gave her advice about life.

At last the cabs arrived and the guests departed. Hussonnet, who was correspondent of a provincial journal, had to read fifty-three newspapers before lunch. The savage woman had a rehearsal at the theatre; Pellerin, a model; the choir-boy three assignations. But the angel, in the grip of the first symptoms of indigestion, could not get up. The medieval baron carried her to the cab.

'Look out for her wings!' cried the *débardeuse* through the window.

On the landing Mlle Vatnaz said to Rosanette:

'Good-bye, my dear! It was a delightful party.'

Then she whispered in her ear:

'Keep him!'

'Until better times,' answered Rosanette slowly, turning away.

Arnoux and Frederic went home together, as they had come. The dealer looked so gloomy that his companion thought he was ill.

'Me? Not at all!'

He bit his moustache and scowled. Frederic asked him if he was worried about business.

'Not in the least.'

Then suddenly:

'You knew old Oudry, didn't you?' he said, adding with a look of bitterness: 'The old scoundrel's rich!'

After that Arnoux talked about an important firing at his factory which was to be finished that day. He wanted to watch it. The train left in an hour.

'But first I must go and give my wife a kiss.'

'His wife!' thought Frederic.

Then he went to bed, with an intolerable pain at the base of his skull; and he drank a decanter of water to quench his thirst.

Another thirst had come upon him—the thirst for women, for luxury, for everything that Parisian life implies. He felt slightly dazed, like a man just disembarked from a ship; and in the clear vision of his first sleep he saw passing and re-passing before him the shoulders of the fishwife, the *débardeuse's* back, the Polish girl's calves, and the hair of the savage woman. Then two great black eyes, which were not at the ball, appeared; light as butterflies, brilliant as torches, they darted to and fro, quivered, climbed to the ceiling, then swooped down to his lips. Frederic struggled to recognize those eyes, without success. But already he was dreaming; he thought he was harnessed beside Arnoux to the shafts of a cab, and Rosanette, sitting astride his back, was disembowelling him with her golden spurs.

CHAPTER II

FREDERIC found a small mansion at the corner of the rue Rumfort, and he bought on a single day a brougham, a horse, furniture, and two flower stands from Arnoux, to put on either side of the drawing-room door. Behind this room were a parlour and a closet. It occurred to him that he might lodge Deslauriers there. But then, how would he be able to entertain *her*—his future mistress? The presence of a friend would be embarrassing. He had the partition removed to lengthen the drawing-room, and turned the closet into a smoking-room.

He bought the works of his favourite poets, as well as books of travel, atlases, and dictionaries; for he had innumerable schemes of work. He hurried the workmen, haunted the shops, and, impatient for possession, took everything away without bargaining.

After studying the tradesmen's bills, Frederic realized that he would shortly have to pay out some forty thousand francs, not including the legacy duties, which would exceed thirty-seven thousand; as his fortune was in land, he wrote to the lawyer at Le Havre to sell a portion so that he could settle his debts and have a certain amount of cash in hand.

Then he felt an inclination to know at last that vague, glittering, indefinable thing called society; he sent a note to M. and Mme Dambreuse to ask if he might visit them. Madame replied that they looked forward to seeing him the following afternoon.

It was their at-home day. Carriages were standing in the courtyard. Two footmen hurried out under the awning, and a third, at the top of the staircase, walked along in front of him.

He crossed a hall, a second room, and then a great reception room with high windows. On the massive mantelpiece stood a spherical clock, flanked by a pair of huge porcelain vases from which sprouted, like golden bushes, two bristling clusters of candlesticks. On the walls hung pictures after Ribera; heavy tapestry door curtains spread their majestic folds. The furniture—arm-chairs, tables, and consoles—was all in the Empire style and had an imposing, almost ambassadorial air. Frederic could not suppress a smile of pleasure.

At length he reached an oval room, panelled in rosewood and packed with tiny pieces of furniture; it was lit by a single window looking out on to a garden. Mme Dambreuse was by the fire, with a group of about a dozen people round her. With a friendly word she motioned to him to sit down; she showed no surprise at not having seen him for so long.

When he came in, they were extolling the eloquence of the Abbé Cœur. Then they deplored the immorality of servants, in connection with a theft committed by a footman; and the gossip continued. Old Mme de Sommery had a cold, Mlle de Turvisot was getting married, the Montcharrons were not returning until the end of January, nor were the Bretancourts —people stayed late in the country nowadays; and the pettiness of the talk seemed to be intensified by the grandeur of the surroundings—although the matter of the conversation was less stupid than the manner, which was aimless, inconsequent, and languid. Although there were men present with experience of life—an ex-minister, the *curé* of a large parish, two or three high Government officials—yet they restricted themselves to the most dreary commonplaces. Some of them looked like exhausted dowagers, others resembled horse dealers; and old men accompanied wives who might have been their granddaughters.

Mme Dambreuse received them with accomplished grace. When they spoke of an invalid, she puckered her brow with concern, while she assumed a joyful look if there was mention of balls or parties. But she would soon have to forgo these pleasures, for she was about to fetch a niece of her husband's, an orphan, from boarding school. They praised her devotion; she was behaving like a true mother.

Frederic watched her. Her lustreless skin seemed to be stretched over her face; it had freshness but no bloom, like a preserved fruit. But her hair, arranged in English corkscrew curls, was finer than silk; her eyes were of a brilliant blue, her movements graceful. Sitting on the settee, at the far end of the room, she was stroking the red tassels of a Japanese screen, in order, as it seemed, to show off her hands, which were long, narrow, and rather thin, with fingers that turned up at the ends. She wore a dress of grey watered silk with a high neck, like a Puritan housewife.

Frederic asked her if she was going to La Fortelle that year. Mme Dambreuse did not know. He could understand that;

she must find Nogent boring. More people arrived. There was a continual rustling of dresses on the carpets; ladies, perched on the edge of their chairs, laughed softly, uttered two or three words, and, after five minutes, went off with their daughters. Soon it was impossible to follow the conversation, and Frederic was just leaving when Mme Dambreuse said to him:

'Every Wednesday, Monsieur Moreau—don't forget.'

By this single phrase she made up for the indifference she had displayed.

He was satisfied. All the same, he drew in a large mouthful of air in the street; and feeling the need for a less artificial environment, he remembered that he owed a visit to Rosanette.

The hall door was open. Two lap-dogs ran up to him. A voice cried:

'Delphine! Delphine! Is that you, Félix?'

He stood where he was; the little dogs went on barking. At last Rosanette appeared, wrapped in a sort of dressing-gown of white muslin trimmed with lace; her bare feet were in slippers.

'Oh! I'm sorry, monsieur. I thought you were the hair-dresser. I'll be back in a minute.'

And he was left alone in the dining-room.

The Venetian shutters were closed. Frederic was glancing round the room, recalling the uproar of the other night, when he noticed, on the table in the centre, a man's top hat—old, battered, greasy, and stained. Whom could this hat belong to? Insolently it displayed its torn lining and seemed to say: 'Well, what do I care? I'm master here!'

Rosanette came in. She took his hand, opened the conservatory, pushed him in, closed the door behind him while other doors opened and closed at the same time, and after leading him through the kitchen, brought him into her dressing-room.

It was obvious at once that this was the most important room, the focal point, as it were, of the house. The walls, the arm-chairs, and the enormous spring divan were covered in chintz, with a bold pattern of leaves; on a white marble table stood two large basins in blue faience; the glass shelves above were loaded with bottles, brushes, combs, sticks of make-up, and powder boxes; a tall cheval glass reflected the fire; a cloth hung over the edge of a bath, and the scents of almond paste and benzoin filled the air.

'I'm sorry the room's in such a mess. I'm dining out this evening.'

And, as she turned round, she almost crushed one of the little dogs. Frederic pronounced them charming. She picked them both up and lifted their black muzzles to his face.

'Smile, please!' she said to them. 'Kiss the gentleman!'

A man dressed in a dirty frock coat with a fur collar came in suddenly.

'My good Félix,' she said, 'that little business of yours will be settled next Sunday, without fail.'

The man began to dress her hair. He told her news of her friends: Mme de Rochegune, Mme de Saint-Florentin, Mme Lombard — they were all aristocrats, as at the Dambreuses' house. Then he talked about the theatre; they were giving a special performance at the Ambigu that evening.

'Are you going?'

'Good heavens, no! I'm staying at home.'

Delphine appeared. She scolded her for going out without permission. Delphine protested that 'she was just back from the market.'

'All right! Bring me your book. You'll excuse me, won't you?'

Rosanette read the book over, half aloud, and made remarks about each item. The addition was wrong.

'Give me back four sous!'

Delphine gave them back, and Rosanette dismissed her.

'Mother of God!' she said. 'These people drive one mad.'

This complaint shocked Frederic. She reminded him too closely of the others, and thus established a sham equality between the two houses that irritated him.

Delphine, returning, went up to Rosanette and whispered a word in her ear.

'No! I won't!'

Delphine appeared again.

'Madame, she insists.'

'What a nuisance! Chuck her out!'

At the same moment an old lady dressed in black pushed open the door. Frederic heard nothing and saw nothing; Rosanette hurried into the bedroom to meet her.

When she reappeared, her cheeks were glowing and she sat down in one of the arm-chairs without speaking. A tear dropped down her cheek, then, turning towards the young man, she said gently:

'What's your Christian name?'

'Frederic.'

'Ah! Federico! You don't mind my calling you that?'

And she looked at him playfully, almost amorously. Suddenly she shrieked with joy at the sight of Mlle Vatnaz.

The latter was in a hurry, for at the stroke of six she had to preside over her boarding house table, and she was breathless with exhaustion. First of all, she took out of her shopping basket a watch chain and a piece of paper, then various things she had purchased.

'In the rue Joubert, you know, they've got splendid suède gloves at three francs sixty. Your cleaner says he'll be another week. I told them to iron the lace. Bugneaux has had the account. I think that's everything. You owe me a hundred and eighty-five francs.'

Rosanette went and took ten napoleons from a drawer. Neither of them had any change, so Frederic offered some.

'I'll pay you back,' said Mlle Vatnaz, thrusting the fifteen francs into her bag. 'But you're a naughty boy, and I don't love you any more. You never asked me to dance once, the other evening. My dear, I've discovered a shop on the quai Voltaire where they've got the most heavenly case of stuffed humming birds. If I were you, I'd have them. And what do you think of this?'

She displayed a piece of old pink silk which she had bought at the Temple market. It was to be a medieval doublet for Delmar.

'He came here to-day, didn't he?'

'No.'

'That's odd.'

And, a minute later:

'Where are you going to-night?'

'To Alphonsine's,' said Rosanette.

This was her third version of how she was going to spend the evening.

Mlle Vatnaz continued:

'Any news of the Old Man of the Mountain?'

But Rosanette, with a rapid wink, bade her be silent; and she went as far as the hall with Frederic, to find out if he was likely to see Arnoux soon.

'Please ask him to come and see me; but look out for his wife, of course!'

An umbrella was standing against the wall at the top of the steps, with a pair of overshoes.

'The galoshes of our Vatnaz,' said Rosanette. 'What a foot! She's a sizable woman, is my friend.'

Then in a melodramatic tone, and rolling the *r*, she added:
'Do not tr-r-r-ust her!'

Emboldened by this confidence, Frederic tried to kiss her on the neck. She said coldly:

'Go on! It's free.'

He left the house in a cheerful mood, for he was certain that Rosanette would shortly be his mistress. This desire awoke another; and he felt a longing to see Mme Arnoux, in spite of the vague grudge he bore her.

He had to go to the house anyway, to deliver Rosanette's message.

Six o'clock was striking. Arnoux, he reflected, would certainly be at home. He put off his visit until the next day.

She was in the same attitude as on the first day; and she was sewing a child's shirt. The little boy was playing with some wooden animals at her feet; further away, Marthe was writing.

He began by complimenting her on her children. She replied without any foolish maternal exaggeration.

The room looked peaceful. Bright sunshine poured through the window-panes and glittered on the corners of the furniture; Mme Arnoux was seated by the window, and a great sunbeam, falling on the little curls at the nape of her neck, flooded her amber skin with liquid gold. Then he said:

'Here's a young lady who's grown in the last three years! Do you remember, mademoiselle, the time when you went to sleep on my knees in the carriage?'

Marthe did not remember.

'One evening, coming back from Saint-Cloud?'

A look of singular sadness crossed Mme Arnoux's face. Was she forbidding him any allusion to the memory they shared?

Her lovely black eyes, with their bright lustre, moved gently under her rather heavy lids and from their depths welled an infinite kindness. A feeling of boundless love, more powerful than ever, possessed him once again; he felt numb as he gazed, but he shook off his torpor. How was he to impress her? By what means? After much thought Frederic decided that money was the best approach. He began to talk of the weather, which was less cold than at Le Havre.

'Have you been there?'

'Yes, on family business. . . . A legacy . . .'

'Oh, I am very glad,' she said, with so sincere a look of pleasure that it touched him like some great service.

Then she asked him what he intended to do; it was a man's

duty to have a definite career. He remembered his lie and said that he hoped to enter the Council of State, through the help of M. Dambreuse, the deputy.

'Perhaps you know him?'

'Only by name.'

Then, in a low voice:

'*He* took you to the ball the other evening, did he not?'

Frederic said nothing.

'Thank you. That is what I wanted to know.'

Then she asked him two or three discreet questions about his family and his home. It was very nice of him not to have forgotten them during his long stay in the country.

'How could I?' he replied. 'Did you think it possible?'

Mme Arnoux rose.

'I think you are a good and loyal friend to us both. Good-bye —until we meet again.'

And she held out her hand to him, in a frank and manly fashion. Was this not a pledge, a promise? Frederic suddenly felt he was glad to be alive; he could hardly keep himself from singing; he felt the need for self-expression, for generous action, for alms-giving. He looked around him for someone to help. No one in need was passing, and his impulse of self-sacrifice faded away, for he was not the man to go out of his way in search of such opportunities.

Then he remembered his friends. First he thought of Hussonnet, next of Pellerin. Dussardier's lowly position had of course to be considered; as for Cisy, he would be delighted to impress him a little with his wealth. So he wrote to all four inviting them to a house-warming party the following Sunday at eleven o'clock precisely, and he told Deslauriers to bring Sénécal.

The teacher had been dismissed from his third school for having opposed the distribution of prizes, a practice which he regarded as fatal to equality. He was now working for a machine manufacturer; he had stopped living with Deslauriers six months before.

There had been nothing painful about their parting. Sénécal had lately been receiving visits from men in blouses; they were all patriots, all workmen, and all staunch fellows; but the lawyer found their company wearisome. Moreover, he disliked certain of his friend's ideas, although they were excellent as propaganda. He said nothing, out of ambition, hoping by the exercise of tact to control Sénécal, for he was impatiently awaiting a great upheaval, through which he expected to find a congenial niche for himself.

Sénécal's convictions were more disinterested. Every evening, when his work was over, he regained his attic and searched in books for a justification for his dreams. He had annotated the *Contrat social*. He devoured the *Revue indépendante*. He was familiar with Mably, Morelly, Fourier, Saint-Simon, Comte, Cabet, Louis Blanc—the whole weighty procession of Socialist writers—those who would like to reduce mankind to the level of the barrack-room, those who would make them find forgetfulness in brothels, or tie them to the bench; and out of this mixture he had evolved for himself an ideally virtuous democracy, combining the characteristics of the farm and the factory—a sort of American Sparta, in which the individual existed solely in order to serve the State, which was more powerful, more absolute, more infallible, and more divine than Nebuchadnezzar or the Grand Lama. He did not doubt that this idea would soon be realized; and, with the logic of a mathematician and the faith of an inquisitor, he bitterly attacked everything that seemed to oppose it. He was shocked by titles, decorations, plumes, liveries—even by excess of fame; for each day his sufferings and his studies revived within him his hatred of every sort of distinction and pre-eminence.

'Why should I make up to this gentleman?' he said. 'If he wanted to see me, he could come here.'

Deslauriers dragged him off.

They found their friend in his bedroom. Roller blinds, double curtains, Venetian glass—there was nothing lacking; and Frederic, in a velvet jacket, was sprawling in an easy-chair, smoking Turkish cigarettes.

Sénécal glowered, like a Puritan at a party. Deslauriers took in everything at a glance; then, bowing low to Frederic:

'My lord,' he said, 'I present my respects.'

Dussardier fell on his neck.

'So you're rich now? So much the better, upon my word, so much the better.'

Cisy appeared with a band of crape round his hat. Since his grandmother's death he enjoyed a considerable fortune; but he placed less value on amusement than on originality, on distinguishing himself from other people, in fact, on 'having style.' That was his expression.

It was now noon and every one was yawning; Frederic was waiting for somebody. At the mention of Arnoux's name,

Pellerin made a face. He regarded him as a renegade since he had deserted the arts.

'Supposing we forget about him? What do you say?'

All approved.

A servant in long leggings opened the door and revealed the dining-room, with its lofty dado of gilded oak and its two dressers loaded with crockery. Bottles of wine were warming on the stove; the blades of the new knives glittered among the oysters; there was a charming softness in the milky tint of the fine glass, and the table was almost hidden under game, fruit, and exotic dishes. These touches were lost on Sénécal.

He began by asking for home-made bread—as hard as possible—and in this connection spoke of the murders at Buzançais and the food crisis.[1]

None of this would have happened if agriculture had been better protected—if everything had not been abandoned to competition, to anarchy, to the deplorable system of laissez-faire and non-interference. It was thus that a newer and even more detestable form of feudalism, the feudalism of money, was being established. But let them beware! In the end the people would lose patience, and avenge their wrongs on the capitalists, either by sanguinary proscriptions, or by looting their mansions.

Frederic had a sudden vision of a flood of men with bare arms invading Mme Dambreuse's grand reception room and breaking the mirrors with their pikes.

In view of the low level of wages, Sénécal continued, the workman was worse off than the helot, the negro, and the pariah—particularly if he had children.

'Must he smother them, as is recommended by some English professor or other of the school of Malthus?'

And turning to Cisy:

'Are we to be reduced,' he said, 'to following the advice of the infamous Malthus?'

Cisy, who did not know of the infamy, or even of the existence of Malthus, replied that, nevertheless, much was done for the poor, and the superior classes . . .

'Oh, the superior classes! To begin with, there are no superior classes—natural worth is the only standard of superiority. You must realize that it isn't charity we want, but equality and a just distribution of goods.'

He asked that the workman should have the opportunity to become a capitalist, in the same way as a private soldier could become a colonel.

The old guild masters, when they limited the number of apprentices, at least prevented a surplus of labour, and the feeling of brotherhood was sustained by festivals and banners.

Hussonnet, as a poet, regretted the banners; so did Pellerin —a taste which he had acquired at the Café Dagneaux when listening to the conversation of some supporters of Fourier. He pronounced Fourier a great man.

'Come, come!' said Deslauriers, 'an old fool, who sees the hand of divine vengeance in the fall of empires! He's like Saint-Simon and his church, with his hatred of the French Revolution: a lot of humbugs who'd like to restore Catholicism.'

M. de Cisy, to clarify his ideas, or else to make a good impression, remarked gently:

'It seems that these two philosophers are not of the same opinion as Voltaire?'

'Voltaire? You can keep him,' answered Sénécal.

'What? Why, I thought . . .'

'No, no. He didn't love the people.'

Then the conversation turned on the events of the day; the Spanish marriages,[1] the Rochefort peculations, the reorganization of the chapter of Saint-Denis, which would result in a doubling of taxation. Taxation was high enough already, according to Sénécal.

'And what's it used for, anyway? To build palaces for the monkeys at the zoo, to send fancy generals parading about our squares, to keep up a feudal etiquette among the servants at court . . .'

'I read in *La Mode*,' said Cisy, 'that at the Tuileries ball on Saint Ferdinand's day every one came in carnival costume.'

'How pathetic!' said the Socialist, shrugging his shoulders in disgust.

'What about the museum at Versailles?' exclaimed Pellerin. 'What about that? Those idiots have cut off part of a Delacroix, and lengthened a Gros! At the Louvre they've made such a terrible mess of the pictures, with all their restoring, scraping, and patching-up, that I don't suppose there'll be one left in ten years' time. A German's written a whole book about the mistakes in the catalogue. Upon my word, the foreigners are laughing at us.'

'Yes—we're the laughing-stock of Europe,' said Sénécal.

'That's because art is in fee to the Crown.'

'So long as you haven't got universal suffrage . . .'

'Excuse me,' said the artist, who, after being rejected at every

Salon for twenty years, had a grievance against authority. 'They should not meddle with us. I don't want anything for myself; all I suggest is that the Chambers should legislate in the interests of art. They should set up a chair of aesthetics: the professor, who would combine theory and practice, might eventually, one hopes, succeed in educating the masses. It wouldn't be a bad idea, Hussonnet, if you said something in your paper about it.'

'As though the press was free! As though we were free!' said Deslauriers passionately. 'When I think that you have to fill in twenty-eight forms before you can even keep a boat on the river, I feel I want to go and live among the cannibals. The Government battens on us! They control everything—philosophy, law, the arts, the air we breathe; and poor exhausted France groans under the policeman's boot and the parson's cassock!'

The future Mirabeau vented his spleen freely in these terms. At last he took his glass, rose to his feet, and with his hand on his hip, his eyes blazing:

'I drink,' he said, 'to the total destruction of the existing order—that is, of everything called privilege, monopoly, authority, hierarchy, power, the State'—and raising his voice —'which I should like to see broken as I now break this'—and he hurled the handsome wineglass on to the table, where it broke into a thousand pieces.

Every one clapped, especially Dussardier.

The spectacle of injustice moved him profoundly. The fate of Barbès[1] filled him with anxiety; for Dussardier was the sort of man who would throw himself under a carriage to help a fallen horse. His learning was limited to two books, one called *Royal Crimes* and the other *Mysteries of the Vatican*. He had listened to the lawyer open-mouthed, in ecstasy. At last he could keep silent no longer.

'What I can't forgive Louis-Philippe,' he said, 'is that he deserted the Poles.'

'One moment,' said Hussonnet. 'To begin with, there's no such thing as Poland; it was an invention of Lafayette's. Most Poles come from the Faubourg Saint-Marceau; the real ones were all drowned with Poniatowski.'

In short, 'he wasn't taken in;' he had 'got over all that.' It was like the sea-serpent, the revocation of the Edict of Nantes, and 'that old cock-and-bull story about Saint Bartholomew.'

Sénécal, without defending the Poles, took up Hussonnet's last words. The papacy had been slandered; and yet, after all, it defended the people; and he described the League as the 'dawn of democracy—a great levelling movement against the individualism of the Protestants.'

Frederic was slightly startled by these views. They appeared to bore Cisy, for he turned the conversation on to the *tableaux vivants* which were then attracting a great many people to the Gymnase Theatre.

Sénécal deplored them. The daughters of the proletariat were corrupted by such spectacles, which offered a display of insolent luxury. He therefore approved of the Bavarian students who had insulted Lola Montez. Like Rousseau, he valued a charcoal burner's wife more highly than a king's mistress.

'That's nothing but sour grapes,' said Hussonnet impressively.

And he took up the defence of these ladies, with special reference to Rosanette. When he mentioned her party and Arnoux's costume, Pellerin remarked:

'They say he's rather shaky, don't they?'

The picture dealer had just had a lawsuit about his property at Belleville, and he was at the moment involved, with other fellows of the same kidney, in a china clay company in western Brittany.

Dussardier knew more; for his employer, M. Moussinot, had made inquiries about Arnoux from Oscar Lefebvre, the banker, who, from his knowledge of some of the bills he had renewed, considered him far from sound.

Dessert was over: they moved into the drawing-room, which, like Rosanette's, was hung with yellow damask, in the style of Louis XVI.

Pellerin blamed Frederic for not having preferred the neo-Grecian style; Sénécal struck matches against the hangings; Deslauriers did not open his mouth. He did so in the library, which he described as a schoolgirl's library. It included most contemporary writers. Discussion of their work was impossible, for Hussonnet at once began to tell personal anecdotes about them, criticizing their faces, their habits, their dress; he extolled the fifth-rate and disparaged the first-class minds, while, of course, deploring the decadence of the age. There was more poetry in this or that folk-song than in all the lyrics of the nineteenth century; Balzac was overrated, Byron discredited, Hugo did not understand the theatre, and so forth.

'Why,' said Sénécal, 'haven't you got the works of our labourer-poets?'

And M. de Cisy, who dabbled in literature, was astonished at not seeing on Frederic's table 'some of these new "physiologies"—"The Physiology of the Smoker, of the Fisherman, of the Customs Official."'

They succeeded in irritating him to such an extent that he felt a desire to take them by the shoulders and push them outside. 'But this is really childish,' he reflected. And drawing Dussardier aside, he asked him if he could be of any service to him.

The good fellow was touched. But he had his position as cashier and he needed nothing.

Then Frederic led Deslauriers to his room and took two thousand francs from his desk.

'There, my friend, put these in your pocket. This settles my old debts to you.'

'But . . . the newspaper?' said the lawyer. 'You know perfectly well I've spoken to Hussonnet about it.'

Frederic replied that 'things were a little difficult' at the moment. The other smiled sourly.

After the liqueurs they drank beer; after the beer, punch; they relighted their pipes. At length, at five in the evening, they all went off; and they were walking side by side, in silence, when Dussardier remarked that Frederic had been a perfect host. Every one agreed.

Hussonnet pronounced the lunch a trifle heavy. Sénécal criticized the absurdity of the interior decoration. Cisy concurred. It was completely devoid of 'style.'

'I think,' said Pellerin, 'that he might at least have commissioned a picture from me.'

Deslauriers said nothing, but held on to the bank notes in the pocket of his trousers.

Frederic was left alone. He thought of his friends; and he felt as if a gulf, wide and dark, separated them from him. He had held out his hand to them; and they had failed to respond to the generous impulse of his heart.

He remembered what Pellerin and Dussardier had said about Arnoux. Of course it was a fabrication, a slander. But why? He saw Mme Arnoux, ruined, in tears, selling her furniture. This vision tormented him all night; the next day he appeared at her house.

Not knowing how to begin to tell her what he knew, he asked her, conversationally, if Arnoux still had his property at Belleville.

'Yes, he's still got it.'

'He's in a china clay company in Brittany now, isn't he?'

'Yes.'

'His factory's doing very well, isn't it?'

'I . . . suppose so.'

He hesitated.

'What's the matter?' she said. 'You frighten me.'

He told her the story of the bills of exchange. She bowed her head, and said:

'I feared as much!'

Arnoux, in fact, hoping to bring off a coup, had refused to sell his property and had borrowed largely on it. Finding no buyers, he had tried to recover his losses by starting a factory. Expenditure had exceeded revenue. She knew no more; he evaded all questions and continually declared that 'things were going very well.'

Frederic tried to reassure her. Perhaps these were temporary difficulties. Meanwhile, he would let her know if he heard anything.

'Oh, you will, won't you?' she said, clasping her hands with a charming look of supplication.

So he could be of use to her. Now he was finding his way into her life, her heart!

Arnoux came in.

'How nice of you to come and take me out to dinner!'

Frederic said nothing.

Arnoux talked of indifferent matters, then warned his wife that he would be coming in very late, as he had an appointment with M. Oudry.

'At his house?'

'Yes, of course—at his house.'

Going down the stairs, he confessed that, as Rosanette was disengaged, they were going to have a little dinner on their own at the Moulin-Rouge; and, since he always needed someone to receive his confidences, he allowed Frederic to see him to her door.

Instead of going in, he walked up and down the pavement, watching the second-floor windows. Suddenly the curtains were drawn aside.

'Splendid! Old Oudry has left. Good night!'

Was old Oudry her protector, then? Frederic did not know what to think, now.

From that day onwards Arnoux was even more friendly than

before; he invited him to dine with his mistress, and soon Frederic frequented both houses at the same time.

Rosanette's amused him. He went there after the club or the theatre; he drank tea and played lotto. On Sunday there were charades—and Rosanette, wilder than the rest, excelled in comic invention: she would go on all fours, or put a cotton night-cap on her head. She wore a suède hat, to watch the passers-by from her window; she smoked Turkish pipes and sang yodelling songs. She passed her idle afternoons cutting the flowers out of a piece of patterned chintz and sticking them on to the window panes; she daubed her two little dogs with rouge, burned incense, or told her own fortune. Unable to resist an impulse, she would fall in love with some trinket she had seen, would lose her sleep, rush to buy it, and then exchange it for another. She wasted her dress materials, lost her jewels, squandered her money, and would have sold her night-gown for a stage box. She often asked Frederic the meaning of a word she had read, but did not stop for his answer; for she would chase after a new idea, and start questioning him anew. Her light-hearted moods were followed by childish rages; or she would sit dreaming on the floor by the fire, her head bowed and her hands clasped round her knee, as still as a torpid lizard. Without thinking she would dress herself in front of him; would slowly draw on her silk stockings, and then sluice her face with water, bending her body backwards, like a shivering naiad; and her white, laughing teeth, her sparkling eyes, her beauty, and her gaiety dazzled Frederic and made his nerves tingle.

He nearly always found Mme Arnoux teaching her little son to read, or standing behind Marthe's stool while she practised scales on the piano. When she sewed, he counted himself happy if he were able to pick up her scissors from time to time. There was a tranquil dignity about all her movements; her little hands seemed made to distribute alms, or to wipe off tears; and her voice, by nature rather husky, had a tender note that seemed to share the lightness of the wind.

She had no enthusiasm for literature, but she showed a charming intelligence in her use of simple, expressive words. She was fond of travelling, of listening to the wind in the woods, of walking bare-headed in the rain. Frederic heard these admissions with delight, thinking he saw in them the beginning of her surrender.

The companionship of the two women made, as it were, two melodies in his life: the one, gay, reckless, amusing—the other

136

serious, almost religious; and the two strains, sounding together, continually swelled and gradually intermingled; for, if Mme Arnoux merely brushed him with her finger, his desire at once evoked the image of the other woman, since, in her case, his hopes were less remote; and if in Rosanette's company his heart should fill with tenderness, he would immediately remember his great love.

This confusion was enhanced by similarities between the two establishments. Of the two chests that used to be seen at the boulevard Montmartre, one now decorated Rosanette's dining-room, the other the drawing-room of Mme Arnoux. There was the same dinner service in both houses; in both the identical velvet skull-cap could be found lying on an arm-chair; a quantity of small gifts—screens, boxes, and fans—came and went between mistress and wife, for Arnoux, without the least embarrassment, often used to take back a present he had given to one, in order to hand it to the other.

Rosanette laughed with Frederic at Arnoux's curious notions of behaviour. One Sunday, after dinner, she took Frederic behind the door and showed him a bag of cakes in his overcoat pocket, which he had just filched off the table, doubtless as a treat for his children. M. Arnoux was addicted to all sorts of tricks that bordered on dishonesty. He regarded it as a duty to defraud the municipal customs; he always went to the theatre without paying, he invariably travelled first-class with a second-class ticket, and used to recount as an excellent joke how it was his custom at the swimming baths to drop a trouser button into the attendant's box instead of a fifty-centime piece. Rosanette loved him all the same.

Talking about him, one day, however, she said:

'When all 's said and done, he gets on my nerves. I 'm tired of him. Well, serve him right—I 'll find someone else.'

Frederic thought she had already found the 'someone else,' and his name was M. Oudry.

'Well,' said Rosanette, 'and what about it?'

Then, with tears in her voice:

'I ask for next to nothing,' she said, 'and even that 's too much for him—beast! He just won't do it! But promises—oh, yes, that 's a different kettle of fish.'

Arnoux had even promised her a quarter of his profits from the celebrated china clay pits; no profit appeared, and neither did the cashmere shawl with which he had been tempting her for the last six months.

At once Frederic thought of giving it to her as a present. This would teach Arnoux a lesson, and annoy him as well.

Yet he was kind-hearted—even his wife said so. But he was so crazy; instead of the daily dinner parties at his house, he now entertained his friends at restaurants. He bought entirely useless objects, such as gold chains, clocks, and household utensils. Mme Arnoux once showed Frederic, in the passage, a vast supply of kettles, foot warmers, and samovars. One day, at last, she confessed her uneasiness; Arnoux had made her sign a bill made out to the order of M. Dambreuse.

Nevertheless Frederic kept his literary projects alive as a sort of private point of honour. He wanted to write a history of aesthetics—a result of his conversations with Pellerin—to put various periods of the French Revolution into dramatic form, and to compose a grand comedy, through the indirect influence of Deslauriers and Hussonnet. Often the face of one or other of the two women passed before his eyes as he worked; he struggled against the desire to see her, to which he soon yielded; and he was more depressed when he came back from Mme Arnoux's house.

One day he was brooding over his melancholy by the fireside, when Deslauriers came in. Sénécal's inflammatory talk had alarmed his employer; and once more he found himself penniless.

'What do you want me to do?' said Frederic.

'Nothing. I know you haven't any money. But I suppose it wouldn't be too much trouble for you to find him a job, either through Monsieur Dambreuse or Arnoux?'

The latter was bound to need engineers in his factory. Frederic had an inspiration; Sénécal could warn him of the husband's absences, could carry letters, and help him to use the innumerable opportunities which would present themselves. Men always did each other good turns of this kind. Besides, he would find a way of using him without his suspecting it. Fortune offered him an ally; it was a good omen, and he must seize the chance. With an assumed casualness he replied that it might perhaps be done and he would see about it.

He saw about it at once. Arnoux was sparing no pains in his manufacture. He was searching for the copper-red of the Chinese; but his colours evaporated in the firing. In order to prevent his faience from cracking, he mixed lime with his clay; but most of the pieces broke. His painting on unbaked clay showed bubbles in the glaze, and his large plates buckled. Attributing his miscalculations to the bad equipment of his factory, he wanted to construct new grinding mills and new drying apparatus. Frederic remembered some of these things; and he went up to Arnoux with the announcement that he had found an excellent man for him, capable of discovering his famous red. Arnoux leaped up, then, after listening to Frederic, replied that he needed nobody.

Frederic extolled Sénécal's enormous knowledge, which combined engineering, chemistry, and accountancy, for he was a first-rate mathematician.

Arnoux agreed to see him.

They quarrelled over terms. Frederic intervened and by the end of the week succeeded in bringing them to agreement.

But as the factory was at Creil, Sénécal could be of no assistance to him. This simple reflection destroyed Frederic's courage like some misfortune.

He thought that the more Arnoux was separated from his wife the better would be his chance with her. So he was always taking up the defence of Rosanette; he reminded Arnoux how badly he had treated her, repeated her recent vague threats, and even mentioned the cashmere shawl, without omitting to say that she had accused him of meanness.

Stung by the word, Arnoux (who was, moreover, beginning to feel uneasy) brought Rosanette the shawl but scolded her for having complained to Frederic. When she pointed out that she had reminded him of his promise a hundred times, he pretended that pressure of business had made him forget about it.

The next day Frederic appeared at her house. Although it was two o'clock, Rosanette was still in bed; and Delmar, sitting at a small table by the bedside, was finishing a slice of *foie gras*. From afar she cried to him:

'I've got it! I've got it!'

Then, taking him by the ears, she kissed him on the forehead, thanked him many times over, was extremely friendly, and even asked him to sit on her bed. Her pretty, soft eyes sparkled, her moist lips smiled, her round arms emerged from her sleeveless night-gown; and from time to time he felt the firm shape of her body under the linen sheet. Meanwhile Delmar kept rolling his eyes.

'Really, my dear,' he said, 'really . . . !'

It was the same the next time, and the next. As soon as Frederic came in she stood on a cushion to kiss him more easily, called him a pet, a darling, put a flower in his buttonhole, and arranged his tie; these attentions were always redoubled when Delmar was there.

Were they advances? Frederic thought so. In his place, Arnoux would not have thought twice about deceiving a friend. Besides, he was entitled to abandon restraint with Arnoux's mistress, since he had always restrained himself with his wife; for he believed that he had restrained himself, or rather, he wanted to make himself believe it, in order to justify his fantastic cowardice.

His conduct was absurd, he concluded, and he decided to make a resolute attack on Rosanette. So one afternoon as she was bending over her chest of drawers he came up to her, and made a movement of so unequivocal a meaning that she started up, crimson in the face. He tried again; then she burst into tears, saying that she was very unhappy, but that was no reason for despising her.

He repeated his attempts. She took another line, which consisted in invariably laughing at him. He thought it clever to reply in the same tone, but with exaggeration. But this made him appear too frivolous to be sincere; and their comradeship hindered the expression of any serious emotion. One day, at last, she said she could not accept someone else's leavings.

'Who else?'

'Oh, yes—go back to Mme Arnoux!'

For Frederic often spoke of her; Arnoux, for his part, had the same habit; in the end Rosanette lost patience at always hearing the praises of this woman; and this insinuation was a kind of revenge.

Frederic resented it.

Besides, he was beginning to find her extremely irritating. Sometimes, posing as a woman of experience, she spoke slightingly of love with a cynical titter that made Frederic itch to slap her. A quarter of an hour later, love was the only thing in the world, and folding her arms across her breast as though embracing a lover, she would murmur: 'Oh, yes. It's wonderful. It's so wonderful,' with her eyes half closed, in a transport of ecstasy. It was impossible to get to know her, to find out, for instance, if she was in love with Arnoux, for she laughed at him and seemed jealous of him as well. It was the same with Mlle Vatnaz, whom she sometimes called a wretch, sometimes her best friend. In every detail of her person, down to the knot at the back of her hair, lay something inexpressible, like a hidden challenge; and he desired her, principally for the pleasure of conquering and dominating her.

What was to be done? Often she sent him unceremoniously away, appearing for a moment in the passage to whisper to him: 'I'm busy—I'll see you to-night'; or he would find her with a dozen people round her; and, when they were alone, there were continuous interruptions; it was as if a wager had been laid against him. He asked her to dinner; she always refused; once she accepted, but did not come.

His brain conceived a Machiavellian plan.

Having heard through Dussardier of Pellerin's complaints against him, he had the idea of commissioning him to paint a portrait of Rosanette—a life-size portrait, which would require many sittings; he would not miss a single one; the artist's habitual unpunctuality would ensure that they were left alone. So he encouraged Rosanette to allow herself to be painted, so that she could offer her likeness to her darling Arnoux. She accepted, for she saw herself in the place of honour in the middle of the Grand Salon, with a crowd in front of her and the newspapers talking about her—which would 'launch her' immediately.

Pellerin, for his part, seized on the proposal with avidity. The portrait would be a masterpiece, and would establish him as a great man.

He thought of all the portraits by old masters that he could remember, and finally decided in favour of a Titian, to which he would add decorations in the style of Veronese. He would execute his composition without artificial shadows, in a clear light, such as would produce a single flesh tone and bring out the lustre of the ornaments.

'Supposing,' he thought, 'I put her in a pink silk dress with an oriental burnous? No—away with the burnous! Perhaps I might dress her in blue velvet, brilliantly coloured, against a grey background? Or she could have a white lace collar, with a black fan and a scarlet curtain behind?'

Meditating thus, he expanded his conception day by day, until its grandeur astonished him.

His heart beat fast when Rosanette, accompanied by Frederic, arrived for the first sitting. He asked her to stand on a sort of platform in the middle of the room; and, while he complained of the light and regretted having left his old studio, he first of all made her lean her elbows on a pedestal, and then sit down in an arm-chair. Now he stepped back, now he came up to her and adjusted the folds of her dress with a flick of his fingers, and as he looked at her with his eyes half closed, he briefly consulted Frederic.

'No, no!' he exclaimed. 'I 'm going back to my first idea. I shall turn you out as a lady of Venice!'

She would wear a dress of poppy-red velvet with a jewelled belt; her broad sleeve, lined with ermine, would reveal her bare arm, which would rest on the balustrade of a staircase mounting behind her. A tall column, rising on her left, would be attached to a mass of architecture forming a curve at the top of the canvas. Below, groups of orange-trees, almost black in colour, would be vaguely visible, framing a blue sky streaked with white clouds. On the balustrade, which would be covered with a carpet, would stand a silver dish containing a nosegay, an amber necklace, a dagger, and an ancient casket of yellow ivory, overflowing with golden sequins; some of the coins would be scattered on the ground and form a series of brilliant splashes, so as to lead the eye towards the point of her foot—for she would be posed on the last step but one, in a natural attitude, full in the light.

He went in search of a packing-case, which he placed on the platform, to be the step; a stool did duty as the balustrade, and, to represent the ornaments, he laid upon it an old jacket, a shield, a box of sardines, a packet of pens, and a knife. Then he threw down a dozen five-centime pieces in front of Rosanette and made her take up her pose.

'You must imagine that these things are all priceless treasures —sumptuous presents! The head a little to the right. Perfect! Don't move! That majestic attitude suits your type of beauty admirably.'

She was wearing a tartan dress with a big muff and was trying hard to prevent herself from laughing.

'The head-dress will consist of a chaplet of pearls; that 's always effective against red hair.'

Rosanette protested that her hair was not red.

'Be quiet! The artist sees quite a different red from the common man.'

He began to sketch in the main outlines; and he was so obsessed with the great Renaissance painters that he began to talk about them. For an hour he dreamed aloud of their splendid lives, full of genius, glory, and magnificence—the triumphal entries into towns, the torchlight feasts, between half-naked women, beautiful as goddesses.

'You ought to have lived in those days! A woman of your type would have merited a prince!'

Rosanette thought these compliments very agreeable. They

fixed a day for the next sitting; Frederic undertook to bring the properties.

The heat of the stove had made her feel a little giddy; so they went home on foot through the rue du Bac, and arrived at the Pont Royal.

The weather was fine, keen and bright. The sun was sinking; the windows of the houses in the Cité glittered in the distance like plates of gold; behind, on the right, the towers of Notre-Dame stood out darkly against the blue sky; and the horizon was bathed in soft, grey mists. The wind blew: Rosanette announced that she was hungry, and they went into the Pâtisserie Anglaise.

Young women with their children were standing eating by the marble counter. There were plates of cakes under glass covers. Rosanette swallowed two cream tarts. The powdered sugar made a moustache at the corner of her mouth. She kept pulling her handkerchief out of her muff to wipe it off; and her face, under her green silk hood, was like a rose in full bloom among its leaves. They set off again; she stopped in the rue de la Paix to look at a bracelet in a jeweller's shop; Frederic wanted to present it to her.

'No,' she said. 'Keep your money.'

He was nettled by this remark.

'What's the matter with the pet? Is he upset?' she inquired.

And when the conversation began again he proceeded, as usual, to declare his love.

'You know perfectly well it's impossible.'

'Why?'

'Oh, because . . .'

They were walking side by side. She was leaning on his arm and the flounces of her dress were flapping against his legs. Then he remembered a winter dusk, when Mme Arnoux walked at his side just so, along this very pavement; and the recollection was so absorbing that he no longer noticed Rosanette and did not think about her.

She was looking vaguely in front of her and allowing herself to be almost dragged along, like a lazy child. The afternoon promenade was over, and carriages were rolling briskly along the dry road. She seemed to be recalling Pellerin's compliments, for she uttered a sigh.

'Oh,' she said, 'there are lucky women in the world. I'm sure I was made for a rich man.'

He replied brutally:

'But you've got one already.' For M. Oudry was said to be worth three millions.

She asked nothing better than to be rid of him.

'What's to prevent you?'

And he indulged in some bitter jokes against this old be-wigged business man, pointing out that such a connection was unworthy of her, and she should break it off.

'Yes,' replied Rosanette, as if talking to herself. 'That's what I shall do in the end, I'm positive.'

Frederic was delighted at her disinterested point of view. She slowed her pace; he thought she was tired. But she firmly refused a carriage and dismissed him at her door, blowing him a kiss.

'What a pity! And to think that some fools think *I*'m a rich man!'

He reached home in a gloomy mood.

Hussonnet and Deslauriers were waiting for him.

Hussonnet, seated at the table, was drawing Turks' heads; Deslauriers, in muddy boots, was dozing on the divan.

'At last!' he exclaimed. 'But what a fierce expression! Can you listen to me?'

His reputation as a tutor was declining, for he crammed his pupils with theories unsuitable for their examinations. He had pleaded in court two or three times and had lost; each fresh disappointment threw him back more violently on his old dream—a newspaper in which he could spread himself, take vengeance, vent his spleen and his opinions. It was with this end in view that he had won over Hussonnet, who owned a magazine.

At the moment he was printing it on pink paper; he made up gossip, composed puzzles, tried to start controversies, and even —in spite of unsuitable premises—attempted to get up concerts. A year's subscription 'entitled the subscriber to a front stall in one of the principal theatres in Paris'; in addition, 'the management undertook to furnish gentlemen from abroad with any information they might require, artistic or otherwise.' But the printer was threatening them, the rent was three quarters in arrear, all sorts of difficulties were arising; and Hussonnet would have allowed *Art* to die but for the encouragement of Deslauriers, who worked on his spirits every day. He had brought the lawyer with him, to add weight to the deputation.

'We've come about the paper,' he said.

'Oh, you're still thinking about that, are you?' replied Frederic absently.

'Of course I'm thinking about it!'

And he explained his plans once more. Their articles about the Bourse would bring them in touch with financiers, and they would thus obtain the essential hundred thousand francs of caution money. However, before the paper could be transformed into a political journal, a large circulation must be secured; and, for this purpose, they must make up their minds to certain expenditure, for paper, printing, and administration- -in short, a sum of fifteen thousand francs.

'I've no money,' said Frederic.

'And what about us?' said Deslauriers, folding his arms.

Frederic, offended by this gesture, replied:

'Can I help that?'

'All right! *They*'ve got wood for their fire, truffles on their table, a comfortable bed, a library, a carriage—every comfort. But if a friend shivers in an attic, dines for two francs, works like a slave, and sinks in poverty—can *they* help that?'

And he went on saying 'Can *they* help that?' with a Ciceronian irony that smacked of the law courts.

'Besides, I quite understand. *They* have certain—well—aristocratic standards; no doubt . . . some woman . . .'

'Well, what of it? I can do as I please, can't I?'

'Oh, yes, you can do as you please!'

There was a moment's silence.

'Promises are so easily made,' he added.

'Good heavens, I don't deny them!'

The lawyer went on:

'At school we make vows; we're going to be a band of brothers, like Balzac's *Thirteen*. Then we meet again; and it's "Good night, my friend. Be off with you!" Because the one who's got the power to help prefers to keep everything for himself.'

'What do you mean?'

'Yes—you haven't even introduced us to Monsieur Dambreuse!'

Frederic looked at him; with his shabby frock coat, his dirty spectacles, and his pallid face, he cut such a miserable figure that he could not prevent a derisive smile from rising to his lips. Deslauriers noticed it and blushed.

He had already picked up his hat to go. Hussonnet, full of anxiety, was trying to sober him by imploring glances; and, as Frederic turned his back:

'Come, my child!' he said. 'Be my Maecenas! Protect the arts!'

With an abrupt gesture of resignation, Frederic took a sheet of paper, scribbled a few lines on it, and held it out to him. Hussonnet's face lit up. Then, passing it to Deslauriers:

'Make your apologies, my lord!' he said.

Their friend had requested his lawyer to send him, with the utmost dispatch, fifteen thousand francs.

'Ah, that's the real Frederic,' said Deslauriers.

'Upon my soul,' said Hussonnet. 'You're a good fellow. We'll put you down on the list of useful men.'

The lawyer continued:

'You won't lose by it. It's an excellent investment.'

'Good heavens,' cried Hussonnet, 'I'd guarantee it with my own head!'

And he said so many ridiculous things and promised so many wonders (which no doubt he believed in), that Frederic did not know if he was laughing at others or at himself.

That evening he received a letter from his mother.

She was surprised that he was not yet a cabinet minister, and teased him a little about it. Then she spoke of her health, and informed him that M. Roque was visiting her again. 'Now that he is a widower, I see no impropriety in receiving him. Louise has greatly improved.' And, as a postscript: 'You tell me nothing about your grand acquaintance, M. Dambreuse. If I were you, I would make use of him.'

Why not? He had given up his intellectual ambitions, and his fortune, as he now saw, was insufficient; for, after settling his debts and paying over the agreed sum to his friends, his income would be diminished by at least four thousand francs. Besides, he felt it necessary to escape from his present existence, and to attach himself to something solid. So the next day, dining with Mme Arnoux, he said that his mother was pestering him to enter some profession.

'But I thought,' she replied, 'that Monsieur Dambreuse was going to get you into the Council of State? That would suit you very well.'

She willed it, then. He obeyed.

As on the first occasion, the banker was seated at his desk; with a gesture he asked him to wait a few minutes, for a gentleman with his back to the door was talking to him on an important matter. It concerned some coal mines, and an amalgamation that was to be brought about between various companies.

A pair of portraits, of General Foy and Louis-Philippe, hung on either side of the mirror; filing cabinets, standing against the panelling, rose to the ceiling; and there were half a dozen straw-bottomed chairs. M. Dambreuse did not require a more sumptuous office for his business; it resembled those dark kitchens in which splendid banquets are prepared. Frederic particularly noticed two gigantic chests in the corners. He wondered how many millions they might hold. The banker opened one; the iron lid swung back, revealing nothing inside but some blue paper note-books.

At last the visitor passed in front of Frederic. It was old Oudry. Both blushed as they exchanged bows, which seemed to surprise M. Dambreuse. For the rest, he was extremely affable. It would be quite a simple matter to recommend his young friend to the Minister of Justice. They would be delighted to have him; and he concluded his civilities by inviting him to an evening party which he was giving in a few days' time.

Frederic was just getting into his brougham to go to this party when a note arrived from Rosanette. By the light of the carriage lamps he read:

'Dearest, I've followed your advice. I've just turned out the old man. After to-morrow night—liberty! How's that for courage?'

Nothing more! But it was a clear invitation to fill the vacant place. He uttered an exclamation, put the note in his pocket, and started off.

Two mounted policemen were posted in the street. A row of fairy lights was burning over the two gates; and servants were shouting in the courtyard, as they called the carriages up to the awning at the bottom of the steps. In the hall the noise ceased suddenly.

Tall trees filled the well of the staircase; the porcelain globes of the lamps shed a quivering light on the walls, like the shimmer of white satin. Frederic climbed the stairs briskly. A footman announced his name: M. Dambreuse held out his hand to him; almost at once, Mme Dambreuse appeared.

She was in a mauve dress trimmed with lace; and her ringlets were more abundant than usual. She wore no jewellery.

She complained of his rare visits, and made conversation for a while. The guests arrived; by way of greeting, they flung their bodies sideways, or bent themselves double, or merely inclined their heads; a married couple went by, then a family;

and every one dispersed into the drawing-room, which was already crowded.

In the middle of the room, under the chandelier, was a vast circular sofa, surrounding a *jardinière* full of flowers, which nodded like plumes and overhung the heads of the women sitting round it. Others were seated in the arm-chairs that formed two lines along the walls—lines which were broken at regular intervals by the long window curtains of orange velvet, and the lofty doorways with their gilded cornices.

The crowd of men standing, hat in hand, on the floor, appeared from a distance as a single mass of black, occasionally relieved by the red flash of a decoration in a buttonhole; the sombre effect was intensified by the monotonous whiteness of their neck-cloths. Apart from some beardless youths of no consequence, they all looked bored; a few dandies with gloomy faces were rocking to and fro on their heels. Grey hair and wigs were plentiful; here and there a bald head glistened, and the faces, either flushed or very pale, betrayed, in their decay, the exhaustion of overwork, for the men present belonged to the world of politics and business. M. Dambreuse had also invited several men of learning, some magistrates, and two or three famous doctors. With deprecatory gestures he protested against the praises of his hospitality and the allusions to his wealth which were addressed to him.

Footmen in gold braid moved about everywhere. The great candelabra, like flaming nosegays, spread their light over the hangings and were reflected in the mirrors; at the far end of the dining-room—the walls of which were lined with a jasmine-covered trellis—stood the buffet, looking like the high altar of a cathedral, or an exhibition of plate, so numerous were the dishes, dish covers, knives, forks, and spoons, in silver and silver-gilt, while the iridescent glitter of cut glass flashed and sparkled above the viands. The three other drawing-rooms were crammed with works of art; there were landscapes by old masters on the walls, porcelain and ivory on the tables, and Chinese curios on pedestals; lacquer screens stood in front of the windows, camellias were banked in masses up the fire-places; and soft music could be heard in the distance, like the hum of bees.

There were not many quadrilles, and the dancers, from the listlessness with which they moved their feet, looked as if they were performing a duty. Frederic overheard this sort of conversation:

'Were you at the Lamberts' last charity ball, mademoiselle?'

'No, monsieur.'

'It's going to be very hot soon.'

'Yes, to be sure—stifling.'

'Whom is this polka by?'

'Indeed, I don't know, madame.'

Behind him, three old bucks, standing in a recess, were whispering obscenities; others talked about railways and free trade; a sportsman told a hunting story; a Legitimist was arguing with an Orleanist.

Wandering from group to group, he reached the card room. There, surrounded by important-looking men, he discovered Martinon, who was now attached to the public prosecutor's office in Paris.

His gross, waxen face fitted snugly into his fur collar, which, with its perfectly even black hairs, was a masterpiece. Keeping a skilful balance between the elegance which his youth desired and the dignity which his profession demanded, he would hook his thumbs into his arm-holes after the fashion of the dandy, and then thrust his arm into his waistcoat in the manner of the doctrinaire. Although his boots were of the brightest patent leather, he had shaved the hair at his temples in order to give himself a thinker's forehead.

After a brief and chilly conversation with Frederic, he returned to his junta. A landowner was saying:

'Those people are longing for social revolution.'

'They're demanding the right to organize labour,' said another. 'Can you imagine it?'

'What can you expect?' said a third, 'when we see Monsieur de Genoude [1] shaking hands with the *Siècle*?'

'And when there are Conservatives who actually call themselves Progressives! . . . Where do they propose to lead us to? To a republic? As though it were possible in France!'

All declared that a republic was impossible in France.

'In any case,' observed a gentleman loudly, 'far too much attention is paid to the revolution; they're publishing quantities of histories and books about it . . .'

'Apart from the fact,' said Martinon, 'that there are perhaps more serious subjects for study.'

A supporter of the Government attacked the scandals of the theatre.

'Take this new play, for instance, *La Reine Margot*—it really goes too far. Why did the author have to mention the Valois?

That sort of thing shows royalty in an unfavourable light. It's the same with the press. The September laws—I've said it over and over again—were a great deal too mild. I'd like to see courts martial set up to keep these journalists quiet! Have them up before a military tribunal for the slightest insubordination! And then we'd see!'

'Oh, be careful, sir, be careful!' said a professor. 'Don't attack our precious gains of 1830! Let us respect our liberties.'

It would be better to decentralize—to spread the surplus population of the towns over the countryside.

'But the towns are rotten with corruption,' exclaimed a Catholic. 'Let us have religion strengthened.'

'Yes, it certainly is a restraining force,' Martinon was careful to say.

The root of the evil was this modern passion for luxury, for rising above one's station.

'All the same,' protested an industrialist, 'luxury is good for trade. I think the Duc de Nemours was quite right to insist on knee breeches at his parties.'

'Monsieur Thiers went in trousers. You know his sally?'

'Yes, yes—delightful. But he's becoming something of a demagogue. His speech on the separation of powers had a good deal to do with the attempt of the 12th of May.'[1]

'Oh, rubbish!'

'Come, come!'

The group was forced to divide to make way for a servant with a tray, who was trying to get in to the cardroom.

Under the green-shaded candles, the tables were covered with cards and pieces of gold. Frederic stopped at one of them, lost the fifteen napoleons that he had in his pocket, turned on his heel, and found himself in the doorway of the boudoir where Mme Dambreuse now was.

It was full of women sitting beside one another on backless seats. Their long skirts, puffed out around them, looked like waves above which their figures emerged, and their low-cut bodices revealed their bosoms to the eye. Almost every one carried a bunch of violets. The dead colour of their gloves intensified the natural whiteness of their arms; ribbons and pearls hung down their shoulders; sometimes, when one shivered, her dress seemed about to fall. But the daring of their costumes was counterbalanced by the respectability of their faces; some wore an expression of almost animal complacency, and this assemblage of half-naked women made him think of the inside of a harem; indeed, an even coarser comparison came into his mind. Every type of beauty was, in fact, represented there: English girls, with picture-book profiles; an Italian with eyes that flashed like Vesuvius; three sisters from Normandy in blue, as fresh as apple-trees in spring; a tall woman with red hair and an amethyst necklace; and the white glint of the diamonds that nodded in the aigrettes in their hair, the sparkle of the jewellery displayed on their bosoms, the soft gleam of the pearls that framed their faces, were mingled with the glitter of gold rings, with lace, powder, feathers, little scarlet mouths, and teeth of mother-of-pearl. The ceiling with its rounded dome gave the boudoir the shape of an inverted basket; and a scented breeze was wafted by the fluttering fans.

Frederic, posted behind them with his monocle in his eye, did not consider all the shoulders beyond reproach; he thought of Rosanette, and this drove away his temptations, or else consoled him for them.

Then he looked at Mme Dambreuse, and he thought her delightful. Although her mouth was a little too long and her nostrils too wide, she had a grace that was all her own. There was a kind of passionate languor about her ringlets; there was, he felt, a powerful mind, and much besides, behind her agate forehead.

Her husband's niece—an ugly girl—was at her side. Mme Dambreuse got up from time to time to greet the women coming in; and the rising murmur of feminine voices was like the chirping of birds.

They were talking about the Tunisian ambassadors and their costumes. A lady had attended the recent reception at the Academy; another mentioned Molière's *Don Juan*, which had just been played at the Comédie française. With a glance at her niece, Mme Dambreuse put her finger to her lips, but a furtive smile gave the lie to her apparent austerity.

Suddenly Martinon appeared in the opposite doorway. She rose. He offered her his arm. To watch him pursue his advances, Frederic crossed the card room, and met them in the big drawing-room; Mme Dambreuse at once left her cavalier and began a friendly conversation.

She understood that he neither played cards nor danced.

'How sad youth is!' she said.

Then, embracing the whole scene in a single glance:

'There's not much pleasure in all this,' she added—'for some people, at any rate.'

She stopped in front of the row of arm-chairs, letting fall a gracious word here and there, while old men in spectacles came up to pay her compliments. She introduced Frederic to some of them. M. Dambreuse touched him gently on the elbow, and led him on to the terrace outside.

He had seen the minister. There were difficulties. Before becoming an auditor to the Council of State, there was an examination to sit for; Frederic, in a burst of extraordinary self-confidence, replied that he knew the subjects required.

The financier was not surprised, considering how highly M. Roque had spoken of him.

This name brought little Louise, his home, and his room into his mind; and he remembered nights just like this one, when he had sat at his window, listening to the wagoners going by. The memory of that gloomy period made him think of Mme Arnoux; and he was silent as he walked up and down the terrace. The windows showed as long patches of red in the darkness; the sound of the ball grew fainter; the carriages were beginning to leave.

'Why,' asked M. Dambreuse, 'are you so keen on the Council of State?'

And, in the manner of a Liberal, he declared that public office led nowhere—he had some experience in the matter; business was more profitable. But business was hard to learn, objected Frederic.

'Nonsense! I could put you up to it in no time.'

Was he offering him an interest in his ventures?

In a flash, the young man saw a huge fortune within his grasp.

'Let's go in,' said the banker. 'You'll have supper with us, won't you?'

It was three o'clock; the guests were leaving. A table had been prepared in the dining-room for the friends of the family.

M. Dambreuse noticed Martinon, and, going up to his wife, he said to her in a low voice:

'Was it you who invited him?'

'Yes,' she answered curtly.

The niece had gone to bed. A good deal was drunk, and there was much loud laughter; and the broadest jokes shocked nobody, since all were experiencing that sense of relief that follows a lengthy period of constraint. Martinon alone appeared serious: he considered it good form to refuse champagne; otherwise he was winning and polite to a degree, for, when M. Dambreuse, who was narrow-chested, complained of breathlessness, he asked after his health several times, and then turned his bluish eyes towards Mme Dambreuse.

She called on Frederic to confess which of the girls he had found most attractive. He had noticed none in particular; in any case, he preferred women of thirty.

'There's something in that, perhaps,' she replied.

While the cloaks and overcoats were being put on, M. Dambreuse said to him:

'Come and see me some morning, and we'll have a talk.'

At the bottom of the staircase, Martinon lit a cigar; and as he pulled at it he displayed so heavy a profile that his companion could not help remarking:

'Upon my word, you've got a head on your shoulders!'

'It's turned a few in its time,' replied the young magistrate, with a mixture of irritation and conviction.

As Frederic went to bed, he reviewed the party in his mind. First of all, his appearance—he had observed himself more than once in the mirrors—had left nothing to be desired, from the cut of his dress coat down to the bows on his pumps; he had talked with influential people, he had seen wealthy women close to; M. Dambreuse had been most cordial, and Mme Dambreuse almost effusive. One by one he weighed her lightest words, her glances, and a hundred other details, intangible yet significant. How splendid it would be to have a mistress like that! And, after all, why not? He was as good as anybody—and perhaps she was not so inaccessible. Then he remembered Martinon, and as he fell asleep he smiled with pity for that excellent youth.

The thought of Rosanette awoke him: the wording of her note —'after to-morrow night'—meant an assignation for that very day. He waited until nine o'clock, then hurried to her house.

Someone, climbing the stairs in front of him, shut the door. He rang the bell: Delphine opened the door, and announced that madame was out.

Frederic begged and threatened. He had something important to tell her—one word only. At length the argument of the five-franc piece succeeded, and the maid left him alone in the hall.

Rosanette appeared. She was in her night-dress, with her hair down: from a distance she shook her head, and made a sweeping gesture with her arms, to indicate that she could not see him.

153

Frederic went slowly down the staircase. This outdid all her other pranks. He could not understand it.

Mlle Vatnaz stopped him opposite the porter's lodge.

'Did she see you?'

'No.'

'You were thrown out!'

'How did you know?'

'It's obvious. Now, come along; let's go out. I'm stifling.'

She led him into the street. She was panting. He felt her thin arm trembling against his. Suddenly she burst out:

'Oh, the wretch!'

'Who?'

'He—he, of course! Delmar!'

This revelation humiliated Frederic.

'Are you absolutely certain?'

'But I tell you I followed him,' exclaimed Mlle Vatnaz. 'I saw him go in. Do you understand now? I only got what was coming to me, anyway. I was idiotic enough to bring him to her house. Good heavens, if you knew . . . I rescued him, I fed him, I clothed him—and then, all the publicity I got for him! A mother couldn't have done more for him.'

Then, with a bitter laugh:

'So the gentleman must have velvet dressing-gowns! She's a fine investment for him, to be sure! And as for her—to think that I knew her when she was selling underclothes. She'd've been in the gutter twenty times, but for me. But I'll drive her there yet—yes, I will! I hope she'll peg out in the work-house! And I shall tell everything I know!'

And, like a surging stream of slop-water full of refuse, she drenched Frederic with the shame of her rival.

'She's slept with Jumillac and Flacourt and little Allard and Bertinaux and Saint-Valéry—the pock-marked one. No, it was the other. They're brothers, it doesn't matter. And when she was in a mess I put everything right. What did I get out of it? She's so mean. I've been much too kind, getting mixed up with someone of her sort. She doesn't belong to my class, after all. Am I a harlot? Do I sell myself? Quite apart from the fact that she's as stupid as they make them. She even spells "catégorie" with a *th*. They are well matched, anyway; they're birds of a feather, though he does call himself an artist and thinks he's a genius. If he wasn't such a blockhead he wouldn't have played me such a filthy trick. To

154

leave an accomplished woman for a bitch—it's just not done. Anyway what do I care! He's getting ugly. I loathe him. If I met him now, mark you, I'd spit in his face!'

She spat.

'Yes, that's what I feel about it now. And what about Arnoux? Isn't it revolting? He's forgiven her so often. You can't imagine what sacrifices he's made! She ought to kiss his feet. He's so good, so generous.'

Frederic was delighted at hearing Delmar attacked. He was resigned to Arnoux's rivalry. Rosanette's treachery seemed to him unnatural, unfair; and under the influence of the old maid's emotion, he began to feel something like affection for him. Suddenly he found himself in front of Arnoux's door; Mlle Vatnaz had led him, without his noticing, down the Faubourg Poissonnière.

'Here we are,' she said. 'I can't go up myself. But there's no reason why you shouldn't.'

'What am I to do?'

'Tell him everything, of course!'

Frederic, as if suddenly awakened, realized the infamous action to which he was being driven.

'Well?' she went on.

He raised his eyes to the second floor. Mme Arnoux's lamp was burning. There was really nothing to stop his going up.

'I shall wait for you here. Go on!'

This peremptory tone damped his sympathy, and he said:

'I'll be a long time up there. You'd better go home. I'll come and see you to-morrow.'

'No, no,' replied Mlle Vatnaz, stamping her foot. 'Bring him down! Take him along with you! Let him catch them.'

'But Delmar will have gone.'

She hung her head.

'Yes—perhaps you're right.'

And she stood silently, in the middle of the road, among the traffic; then, fixing her wild-cat's eyes on him:

'I can count on you, can't I?' she said. 'It's a sacred pledge between the two of us, now. Go on, then. Until to-morrow!'

As Frederic crossed the corridor, he heard two voices arguing. Mme Arnoux was saying:

'Don't lie! Don't lie to me!'

He went in. There was silence.

Arnoux was pacing up and down, and his wife was seated on the little chair by the fire. She was very pale, and her eyes were staring. Frederic moved as if to withdraw. Arnoux seized him by the hand, delighted with the help that had come to him.

'I'm afraid——' began Frederic.

'Please stay!' whispered Arnoux in his ear.

'You must forgive us, Monsieur Moreau,' said Mme Arnoux. 'This is one of those things that one sometimes comes across in married life.'

'You mean, they're put there on purpose,' said Arnoux blithely. 'Every woman has a fad of some sort. Now my wife, for instance, isn't a bad sort. On the contrary. Yet she's been amusing herself for the last hour by pestering me with some ridiculous rigmarole.'

'It's true,' replied Mme Arnoux, losing patience. 'Because, after all, you did buy it.'

'I?'

'Yes, you. At the Persian shop.'

'The shawl,' thought Frederic.

He felt that he was responsible, and was afraid.

She added at once:

'It was last month, on a Saturday—the fourteenth.'

'Exactly! I was at Creil that day. So you see!'

'Not at all. We dined with the Bertins on the fourteenth.'

'The fourteenth?' said Arnoux, raising his eyes as if to work out the date.

'And the assistant who served you had fair hair.'

'As if I could remember the assistant!'

'All the same, he wrote out the address at your dictation. It was 18 rue de Laval.'

'How do you know?' said Arnoux, dumbfounded.

She shrugged her shoulders.

'Oh, it was quite easy: I went in to have my shawl mended, and the shop-walker told me they had just sent a similar one to Mme Arnoux's house.'

'It's not my fault if there's another Mme Arnoux in the same street.'

'Yes, but not Jacques Arnoux,' she replied.

Then he began to digress, protesting his innocence. It was a mistake, a coincidence—one of those extraordinary things that sometimes happen. People should not be condemned on mere suspicion, on vague evidence; and he quoted the example of the unhappy Lesurques.

'In short, I declare you're wrong. Shall I swear it on my word of honour?'

'It's not worth the trouble.'

'Why not?'

She looked him straight in the face, without speaking; then she stretched out her hand, took the silver box from the mantel-piece, and held out to him an open bill.

Arnoux blushed to his ears and his distorted features swelled.

'Well?'

'But . . .' he answered slowly, 'what does that prove?'

'Ah!' she said, with a strange intonation, that suggested both pain and irony. 'Ah!'

Arnoux held the bill in his hands and kept turning it over, not taking his eyes off it, as though he was about to extract the solution of some great problem from it.

'Oh, yes, yes—I remember now,' he said at length. 'It was for somebody else. You must know about it, don't you, Frederic?'

Frederic said nothing.

'Yes . . . it was . . . it was old Oudry who asked me to buy it.'

'And for whom?'

'For his mistress.'

'No, for yours!' cried Mme Arnoux, drawing herself up to her full height.

'I swear to you . . .'

'Don't begin again! I know everything!'

'Oh, very well. So I'm spied on?'

'Does that wound your sense of delicacy?' she answered coldly.

'As soon as people lose their tempers,' said Arnoux, looking for his hat, 'and reasonable discussion becomes impossible . . .'

Then, with a deep sigh:

'Never get married, my poor friend. Believe me, don't do it.'

And he went off in search of fresh air.

A deep silence followed his departure; everything in the room seemed more still than before. There was a circle of white light on the ceiling above the lamp, while the shadows lay in the corners like many thicknesses of black gauze; the ticking of the clock could be heard, and the crackling of the fire.

Mme Arnoux had sat down again in the arm-chair at the other corner of the fire-place; she bit her lip and shivered; she raised her hands; a sob burst from her; she was crying.

He took the little chair; and in a soothing tone, as if he were addressing an invalid:

'Don't imagine,' he said, 'that I don't also feel . . .'

She did not answer, but spoke her thoughts aloud:

'I left him free enough! He need not have lied!'

'No, indeed,' said Frederic.

No doubt it was the result of his way of life, he had been thoughtless, and perhaps, in more important matters . . .

'What could be more important?'

'Oh, nothing!'

Frederic bowed his head, with an obedient smile. All the same, Arnoux possessed certain qualities: he loved his children.

'He does his best to ruin them!'

This was due to his easy-going temperament; for, after all, he was a good fellow.

'What do you mean by "a good fellow"?' she exclaimed.

Thus he defended Arnoux on the vaguest possible grounds, and, as he pitied him, he exulted, he rejoiced to the depths of his soul. Through a desire for revenge or a longing for affection, she would take refuge with him. His hopes, now enormously enhanced, served to strengthen his love.

Never before had she appeared to him so fascinating, so profoundly beautiful. From time to time a deep breath swelled her bosom; her unseeing eyes seemed dilated by an inner vision, and her mouth remained half open, as if to deliver up her soul. Sometimes she pressed her handkerchief hard against her lips; he would have liked to be that little shred of linen, all soaked with tears. In spite of himself, he glanced at the bed in the depths of the alcove, picturing her head on the pillow; and he saw it so clearly that he could scarcely refrain from seizing her in his arms. She closed her eyes, exhausted, inert. Then he came nearer, and, leaning over her, gazed greedily into her face. The noise of boots resounded in the passage; it was Arnoux. They heard him shut the door of his room. He motioned to Mme Arnoux to know if he should follow him.

She signalled 'yes'; and this mute exchange of thoughts was like a surrender, a first step towards adultery.

Arnoux was undoing his frock coat to go to bed.

'Well, how is she?'

'Better,' said Frederic. 'She'll get over it.'

But Arnoux was worried.

'You don't know her. Her nerves are terrible these days. . . . That fool of a shop assistant! See what comes of being generous! I wish I'd never given Rosanette that damned shawl!'

'There's no need for regrets. She's absurdly grateful to you.'

'Do you really think so?'

Frederic was certain of it. The proof was her dismissal ot old Oudry.

'Ah, poor creature!'

And Arnoux, overcome by emotion, wanted to hurry to her house.

'It's not worth it. I've been there. She's ill.'

'All the more reason to go.'

He quickly put his coat on again and seized his candlestick. Frederic cursed himself for his stupidity, and pointed out that it would be only decent to stay with his wife that evening. It would be too bad to desert her now.

'Frankly, you'd be wrong to go. It's not as if there was any hurry. You can go to-morrow. Come now, stay—for my sake!'

Arnoux put down the candlestick, and, as he embraced Frederic:

'How good you are!' he said.

CHAPTER III

FROM that day Frederic's life became wretched. He was the parasite of the house.

If one of the family was ill, he would call for news three times a day; he visited the piano tuner and contrived to perform every kind of service. With a good grace he endured the sulks of little Marthe and the caresses of young Eugène, who invariably ran his dirty hands over his face. He was present at dinners during which the husband and wife sat opposite one another without exchanging a word; or else Arnoux would goad her to fury by his ridiculous remarks. After dinner, Frederic played with the son in the sitting-room, hiding behind the furniture or crawling on all fours with the boy on his back, like Henry IV. At length the husband went out; and immediately she started on the eternal subject of complaint—Arnoux.

It was not his misconduct that she resented. But it seemed that her pride was wounded, and she did not conceal her repugnance for this man, who lacked refinement, dignity, and honour.

'Or more likely he's mad,' she would say.

Skilfully Frederic coaxed her to confide in him. Soon he knew the whole story of her life.

Her parents were small shopkeepers at Chartres. One day, Arnoux, who was sketching beside the river—in those days he thought he was a painter—had caught sight of her coming out of church and had asked for her hand in marriage. Because of his wealth there had been no demur. Besides, he was frantically in love with her.

'Good heavens,' she added, 'he loves me still—in his own way.'

They had spent the first few months travelling in Italy.

In spite of his enthusiasm for the scenery and the old masters, Arnoux had done little except complain about the wine and get up picnics with English tourists, by way of entertainment. A few pictures successfully bought and sold encouraged him to become an art dealer. Then he had set his heart on a faience factory. Now he was tempted by other speculations; and, as his vulgarity grew, he fell into gross and extravagant habits.

She found his vices less reprehensible than his whole way of life. No improvement could be expected, and her unhappiness was beyond remedy.

Frederic declared that his own life, too, had been wasted.

But he was very young. Why despair? And she gave him good advice. 'Work! Get married!' His only reply was a bitter smile; for instead of confessing the real cause of his despondency, he invented another, loftier motive, imitating Antony,[1] the man accursed—a style of expression which was not in fact greatly at variance with his own way of thinking.

Some men find that the very strengthening of desire makes action more difficult. They are hampered by their own diffidence, and by their dread of giving offence; besides, deep feelings of affection are like virtuous women; they are afraid of being found out and spend their lives with downcast eyes.

In spite of the fact that he now knew Mme Arnoux better (or perhaps for that very reason), he was even more cowardly than before. Each morning he vowed to be bold. An unconquerable shyness restrained him; and he could find no example to follow, since she was different from all other women. In his day-dreams he had placed her above all the laws of human nature. Beside her, he felt more insignificant than the scraps of silk that fell from her scissors.

Then he thought of absurd, fantastic devices—such as nocturnal abductions, with drugs and false keys; for anything seemed easier than braving her disdain.

Moreover, the children, the two servants, the arrangement of the rooms, raised insuperable difficulties. He decided that he must have her entirely to himself and live with her far away in some solitary region; he even wondered what lake was blue enough, what shore pleasant enough, whether it should be Spain, Switzerland, or the Orient. Deliberately choosing the days when she seemed most vexed, he would tell her that she must have done with it all, she must seek a solution—and that, for his part, he saw none except a separation. But for her children's sake she would never consent to so extreme a course. Such uprightness increased his reverence for her.

He spent his afternoons in recalling last night's visit, in looking forward to to-day's. When he was not dining at their house, he would take his stand about nine o'clock at the corner of their street; and as soon as Arnoux had closed the outer door, Frederic would hurry up to the second floor and ask the maid in an innocent voice:

'Is monsieur at home?'

And he would pretend to be surprised at not finding him in.

Often Arnoux would return unexpectedly. Then he would have to accompany him to a little café in the rue Sainte-Anne, which was now frequented by Regimbart.

The citizen would begin by stating some new grievance against the monarchy. The subsequent conversation consisted of a friendly exchange of abuse; for Arnoux attributed to Regimbart a brain of a high order; he was irritated at seeing so much talent wasted, and used to chaff him about his laziness. The citizen thought Arnoux full of spirit and imagination, but distinctly too immoral; so he did not show him the least indulgence, and even refused to dine at his house, because 'he could not bear formality.'

Sometimes, as they said good-bye, Arnoux would feel the pangs of hunger. He 'must have' an omelette or some fried potatoes; and as the food was never on the premises he ordered it to be sent out for. They waited. Regimbart did not go home, and finally, with an ill grace, agreed to take something.

Nevertheless, he was a gloomy companion, for he would sit for hours opposite the same half-empty glass. Since providence would not order the world according to his ideas, he turned hypochondriac, refused to read the newspapers, and would utter a roar at the mere mention of England. Once, when the waiter served him badly, he exclaimed:

'Don't we get enough insults from abroad?'

Apart from these outbursts, he was taciturn; he was thinking out 'an infallible plan which would blow up the whole works.'

While he was lost in his reflections, Arnoux, in a monotonous voice and with a tipsy look, would tell incredible stories, in which, thanks to his presence of mind, he was always the hero; and Frederic—no doubt because of some deep resemblance—felt a certain attraction towards him. He blamed himself for this weakness, on the ground that it was his duty to hate him.

Arnoux complained to him about his wife's moods, her obstinacy, her unfair prejudices. She used not to be like that.

'If I were you,' said Frederic, 'I'd make her an allowance and live by myself.'

Arnoux made no answer, and a moment later began to praise her. She was kind, devoted, intelligent, faithful; then, passing on to her physical qualities, he was generous in his revelations, like those careless travellers who display their treasure in inns.

A disaster threw him off his balance

He had gone into a china clay company as a member of the board of trustees. But, believing everything he was told, he had signed inaccurate reports and had approved, without verification, the annual balance sheets which had been fraudulently drawn up by the manager. The company had collapsed, and Arnoux, who was legally liable, had been condemned with the others to pay damages to the extent of about thirty thousand francs—a loss which was aggravated by the circumstances of the case.

Frederic read this in a newspaper, and hurried to the rue de Paradis.

He was shown into madame's room. It was breakfast time. A small table by the fire was covered with bowls of coffee and milk. Old slippers lay on the carpet; there were clothes on the arm-chairs. Arnoux, in drawers and a woollen jacket, had red eyes and tousled hair; Eugène, who had mumps, was crying as he nibbled his bread and butter; his sister was eating quietly; Mme Arnoux, somewhat paler than usual, was waiting on the three of them.

'Well,' said Arnoux, with a heavy sigh, 'you 've heard?'

Frederic made a gesture of sympathy.

'There it is! I 'm a victim of my trusting nature.'

Then he was silent; and his despondency was so deep that he pushed his breakfast away. Mme Arnoux raised her eyes and shrugged her shoulders. He passed his hands over his forehead.

'After all, I 'm not guilty. I 've got nothing on my conscience. It 's just a misfortune. I shall get over it. Ah, well, it serves me right!'

And he began to eat a roll, in obedience to his wife's entreaties.

That evening he wanted to dine alone with her in a private room at the Maison d'Or. Mme Arnoux did not understand this tender impulse and even took offence at being treated as a light woman—although, in fact, as far as Arnoux was concerned, it was a proof of affection. Then, as he was bored, he went to Rosanette's house in search of amusement.

Until then, people had made considerable allowances for him, owing to his reputation as a good fellow. The law case classed him as a shady character. His house was deserted.

As a point of honour, Frederic considered it his duty to see more of them than ever. He hired a box at the Théâtre des Italiens and took them there every week. But they had reached that stage of incompatibility when the mutual concessions of the past produce at length a state of hopeless exhaustion which makes life intolerable. Mme Arnoux could hardly prevent herself from bursting out, while Arnoux glowered; and the sight of these two unhappy beings saddened Frederic.

As he was in Arnoux's confidence, she had given him the task of inquiring into his affairs. But it filled him with shame and embarrassment to eat his dinners while coveting his wife. He continued none the less, on the grounds that it was his duty to protect her and that he might find some opportunity of helping her.

A week after the ball he had gone to see M. Dambreuse. The financier had offered him twenty shares in his coal company; Frederic did not go back. Deslauriers wrote to him; he left his letters unanswered. Pellerin urged him to come and see the portrait; he always excused himself. However, he gave way to Cisy, who had been pressing him for an introduction to Rosanette.

She received him in a very friendly manner, but without falling on his neck, as before. His companion was delighted at finding himself in a courtesan's house, and especially at talking to an actor, for Delmar was there.

A play, in which he had taken the part of a serf who lectures Louis XIV and prophesies the French Revolution, had made him so famous that he was continually being provided with the same part; and it was now his function to chide the monarchs of every country. As an English brewer, he reviled Charles I; as a student of Salamanca, he cursed Philip II; or else as an unhappy father, he denounced the Pompadour—and that was his masterpiece. The street boys waited at the stage door to see him; and his biography, which was on sale in the intervals, described him as tending his aged mother, reading the Bible, and helping the poor; in fact, as a kind of combination of Saint Vincent de Paul, Brutus, and Mirabeau. People spoke of 'our Delmar.' He had a mission; he was becoming a Messiah.

All this fascinated Rosanette; and she had rid herself of old Oudry without thought for the future, for she was not mercenary by nature.

Arnoux, knowing her character, had taken advantage of it and had kept her for a long time at little expense. Oudry had come on the scene, and the three had been careful to avoid direct explanations. Then Arnoux, supposing that she had dismissed the other entirely for his sake, had increased her allowance. But she renewed her demands with a frequency that was surprising considering that she was now living on a more modest scale; she had even sold the cashmere shawl, being determined, as she said, to pay off her old debts; and he always yielded, for she bewitched him and exploited him unmercifully. And now the house was inundated with bills and writs. Frederic felt that a crisis was at hand.

One day he came to see Mme Arnoux. She was out. Monsieur was working in the shop below.

Arnoux, indeed, surrounded by his pots, was trying to 'do' a young middle-class couple from the country. He spoke of 'throwing' and 'turning,' of crackling and glazing; the others, unwilling to betray their ignorance, signified approval and made purchases.

When the customers had left, he confessed that he had had a slight quarrel with his wife that morning. In order to forestall her comments on his expenditure, he had declared that Rosanette was no longer his mistress.

'I even said she was yours.'

Frederic was furious; but reproaches might betray him, so he stammered:

'Oh, you shouldn't have done that—you shouldn't, indeed!'

'What does it matter?' said Arnoux. 'What's the disgrace in being thought her lover? I am her lover, as it happens. Wouldn't you be delighted to be in the same position?'

Had Rosanette spoken of his attempts? Was this an allusion? Frederic replied hastily:

'No—not at all! On the contrary.'

'Well, then?'

'Yes, you're right. It doesn't matter.'

'Why do you never go to see her now?' Arnoux continued.

Frederic promised to go again.

'Oh, I was forgetting . . . when you mention Rosanette to my wife . . . you ought to drop some hint . . . I don't know what, but you'll think of something . . . something to convince her that you really are her lover. You'll do me that good turn, won't you?'

By way of answer, the young man made an equivocal grimace. This slander threatened to undo him. He went to see her that very evening, and swore that Arnoux's alleration was false.

'Really and truly?'

He seemed sincere; she drew a deep breath and said to him: 'I believe you,' with a lovely smile; then she bent her head and, without looking at him, said:

'After all, no one has any claim on you.'

So she guessed nothing, and she despised him, since she did not think he could love her enough to be faithful to her! Forgetting his advances to the other woman, Frederic found this indulgence insulting.

Then she asked him to go and visit 'that woman' occasionally, to find out how things stood.

Arnoux came in, and, five minutes later, tried to take him off to Rosanette's house.

The situation became unbearable.

A distraction was provided by a letter from his lawyer, who was sending him fifteen thousand francs the next day; and to make up for his neglect of Deslauriers he went to tell him the good news without delay. Deslauriers lived in the rue des Trois-Maries, on the fifth floor, looking out over a yard. His study was a small, cold room with a tiled floor and greyish wall paper; its principal decoration was a gold medal, the prize for his doctorate, set in an ebony frame which stood against the mirror. There was a glass-fronted mahogany bookcase which contained about a hundred volumes. A leather-covered desk stood in the middle of the room. Four old green velvet armchairs filled the corners. A fire of shavings blazed in the hearth —there was always a log at hand to be added as soon as the bell rang. It was the hour of his consultations; the lawyer wore a white neck-cloth.

When he heard about the fifteen thousand francs—he had apparently lost hope of them—he chuckled with pleasure.

'That's good, old fellow, that's good. That's very good.

He threw some wood on the fire, sat down again, and at once began to talk about the newspaper. The first thing was to get rid of Hussonnet.

'He's a fool and he bores me. Now, in my opinion, the best and fairest way of discrediting any particular point of view is by not having a point of view oneself.'

Frederic expressed astonishment.

'Why, it stands to reason. It's time to treat politics scientifically. The old men of the eighteenth century were getting on to it, when Rousseau and the literary school brought in philanthropy and poetry and that sort of nonsense, for the greater delight of the Catholics; which in any case was a natural alliance, since our modern reformers, as I can prove, all believe in revealed religion. But if you sing masses for Poland, if you substitute for the God of the Dominicans, who was a butcher, the God of the Romantics, who's an upholsterer—if, in fact, your view of the Absolute is no wider than that of your forefathers, the monarchy will break down your democratic forms, and your cap of liberty will never be anything but a priest's biretta. All that will have happened will be that solitary confinement will have replaced torture; contempt for religion, sacrilege; the concert of Europe, the Holy Alliance; and under this splendid, widely admired regime, composed as it is of relics of Louis XIV and remains of Voltaire, with a coat of Empire whitewash and a few fragments of the British Constitution, you'll find the municipal councils trying to annoy the mayor, the general councils annoying the prefect, the Chambers the king, the press authority, and the Government—every one! There are good souls who go into ecstasies over the Civil Code—which, whatever you may say, was manufactured in a mean, tyrannical spirit; for the legislator, instead of doing his job, which is to regularize tradition, tried to mould society, like Lycurgus. Why does the law interfere with the testamentary rights of fathers? Why does it impede the forced sale of buildings? Why does it punish vagrancy as a crime, when it shouldn't even be a misdemeanour? And there are other examples. I know them. So I'm going to write a little novel to be called *A History of the Idea of Justice*, which will be very amusing indeed. But I'm terribly thirsty. What about you?'

He leaned out of the window and shouted to the porter to go and fetch some punch from the café.

'In brief, I see three parties . . . no, three groups, none of which interests me: the haves, the used-to-haves, and the try-to-haves. But they all agree in their insane veneration for authority. For instance: Mably would like to see the publication of philosophical theories stopped; M. Wronski, the geometer, describes the censorship in his own language as 'the critical repression of speculative spontaneity'; Père Enfantin gives the Hapsburgs his blessing for 'having stretched a weighty hand beyond the Alps to hold Italy in check'; Pierre Leroux would like to force us to listen to an orator; and Louis Blanc favours the worship of the State—such is the passion of our servile race for being governed! But they're none of them correct, in spite of their eternal principles. Now, since *principle* really means *origin*, you must always go back to some revolution, some act of violence, some arbitrary event. The principle of our state is national sovereignty, of which parliament is the expression—although our parliament doesn't admit it. But why should the sovereignty of the people be more sacred than the divine right? They 're both of them fictitious. Away with metaphysics, away with illusions! You don't need religious beliefs to keep the streets clean. I 'll be told that I 'm out to overthrow the social system. Well, what then? Where would be the harm? It 's pretty, isn't it, your social system?'

Frederic might have answered him at length. But, seeing how far his friend had travelled from Sénécal's theories, he was indulgent. He contented himself with protesting that such a method would make them generally hated.

'On the contrary—by giving every party grounds for hating its neighbour, we shall gain the support of all. And you shall join in yourself, and write transcendental criticism for us.'

They must make war on all accepted ideas—the Academy, the École normale, the Conservatoire, the Comédie française—anything which might be described as an institution. In this way they would provide their review with a comprehensive outlook. Then, as soon as it was well established, it would suddenly turn into a daily paper; then they would begin to attack individuals.

'And we shall be respected, you may be sure!'

Deslauriers's old dream was coming true; an editorship, which meant the ineffable joy of controlling other people, of cutting their articles, of commissioning, of refusing their contributions. His eyes glittered under his spectacles, he grew excited, and drank off glass after glass, mechanically.

'You must give a dinner every week. That 's essential, even if it costs you half your income. People will be anxious to come; it will be a centre for them, and a ladder for you; we shall manipulate public opinion by the two handles of politics and literature, and within six months, as you 'll see, we shall have Paris at our feet!'

As Frederic listened, he had a sense of rejuvenation, like a man transported into the open air after long confinement in a room. This enthusiasm was infectious.

'Yes, you 're right. I 've been a lazy idiot!'

'That 's better,' cried Deslauriers. 'I 've found my old Frederic once more!'

And, putting his fist under Frederic's chin:

'When I think how unhappy you 've made me in the past——' he said. 'Never mind! I love you all the same.'

They were standing up, looking at each other, full of tenderness, and on the point of embracing.

A woman's hat appeared at the hall door.

'What are you doing here?' asked Deslauriers.

It was his mistress, Clémence.

Happening to pass his house, she explained, she could not resist her longing to see him; and she had brought some cakes, for a little picnic, which she put down on the table.

'Look out for my papers!' said Deslauriers sharply. 'Anyway, I've told you twice already not to come and see me during my consulting hours.'

She tried to kiss him.

'All right! Be off! Get out!'

He pushed her away; she gave a great sob.

'The fact is, you bore me,' he said.

'It's because I love you!'

'I don't ask to be loved, but to be obliged.'

These hard words stopped Clémence's tears. She took her stand by the window, and stayed there motionless, with her forehead pressed against the glass.

Her attitude and her silence exasperated Deslauriers.

'When you've finished,' he said, 'you'll order your carriage, won't you?'

She swung round on him.

'You're turning me out!'

'Precisely.'

She fastened her big blue eyes on him, as if in a last entreaty, then adjusted the two ends of her plaid, hesitated a moment, and went out.

'You ought to call her back,' said Frederic.

'Oh, nonsense!'

And, as he wanted to go out, Deslauriers moved into his kitchen, which was also his dressing-room. On the stone floor, beside a pair of boots, were the remains of a meagre luncheon; a rolled-up mattress and a blanket lay on the ground in a corner.

'As you observe,' he said, 'I don't entertain many duchesses here. But I don't miss them—nor the others, either. The women you get for nothing take up your time, which is another form of money—and I'm not a rich man. And then they're all so stupid, so stupid. Could you have a real conversation with a woman, Frederic?'

They parted at the corner of the Pont Neuf.

'All right—we've agreed. You'll bring me the money to-morrow, as soon as you get it.'

'Agreed!' said Frederic.

Next morning, when he awoke, the post brought him a bank bond for fifteen thousand francs.

This scrap of paper represented fifteen great sacks of money; with this sum he could run his carriage for three years, instead of selling it, as he would shortly be obliged to do; or he could buy himself two beautiful sets of inlaid armour which he had seen on the quai Voltaire, and countless other things—pictures and books, as well as vast quantities of flowers and presents for Mme Arnoux. Anything would be preferable to risking and losing so much money in this newspaper! Deslauriers struck him as impertinent, for his heartless conduct of yesterday had antagonized Frederic; and he was abandoning himself to these regrets, when he was astonished to see Arnoux come in and sit down heavily on the edge of his bed, like a man crushed.

'What 's the matter?'

'I 'm ruined!'

That very day he had to pay eighteen thousand francs to a certain Vanneroy, at the office of Maître Beauminet, a lawyer in the rue Sainte-Anne.

'It 's an incomprehensible disaster. After all, I gave him a mortgage which ought to have kept him quiet. But he 's threatening me with a writ, if he 's not paid this very afternoon.'

'And then?'

'Why, then, it 's perfectly simple. He 'll sell up my house. The first public notice that appears will finish me—that 's all. If only I could find someone to advance this cursed money, he could take Vanneroy's place and I should be saved. You don't happen to have it, by any chance?'

The bond was still on the night table, beside a book. Frederic lifted the volume and placed it on top of it, as he replied:

'Good Lord, no, my dear fellow!'

But it hurt him to refuse Arnoux.

'But surely you can find someone willing . . .'

'No one! And to think that I shall have money coming in within a week. There 's something like fifty thousand francs due to me at the end of the month . . .'

'Couldn't you ask your debtors to advance . . . ?'

'As though I could!'

'But haven't you any securities, or bills?'

'Nothing!'

'What 's to be done?'

'That 's what I 'm wondering,' said Arnoux.

He was silent and paced up and down the room.

'I 'm not thinking of myself—it 's my children and my poor wife . . .'

Then, articulating each word separately:

'Well . . . I shall be strong-minded,' he said. 'I 'll say good-bye to all this . . . and I 'll go . . . and seek my fortune . . . in some place or other.'

'You can't do that!' exclaimed Frederic.

Arnoux replied calmly:

'How do you expect me to live in Paris, now?'

There was a long silence.

Frederic ventured to speak.

'When would you pay the money back?'

Not that he had it—far from it! But there was no reason why he should not approach his friends and see what he could do. And he rang for his servant to bring his clothes. Arnoux thanked him.

'You need eighteen thousand francs, don't you?'

'Oh, sixteen thousand would do. You see, I could raise two thousand five hundred or three thousand with my silver, provided Vanneroy allows me till to-morrow; and, I repeat, you can promise the lender on oath that the money will be repaid within a week, or even, perhaps, five or six days. And anyway, it 's secured on the mortgage. So it 's quite safe, you understand?'

Frederic assured him that he understood, and that he was going out immediately.

He stayed at home, cursing Deslauriers, for he wanted to keep his word and at the same time help Arnoux.

'Supposing I went to M. Dambreuse? But on what grounds could I ask for money? And if it comes to that I ought to be giving him money for his coal shares. Oh, to hell with him and his coal shares! I don't owe him for them.'

And Frederic congratulated himself on his independence, as if he had refused M. Dambreuse a favour.

'Well, I 'm losing money over that,' he said to himself. 'With my fifteen thousand francs I might have made a hundred thousand. It happens sometimes, on the Bourse. And if I can break my word to Dambreuse I am under no obligation to anybody. And supposing Deslauriers waited . . . No, no, that 's wrong! I must be off.'

He looked at the clock.

'Well, there 's no hurry. The bank doesn't shut till five.'

At half-past four he had drawn his money.

'It 's too late now,' he argued. 'He 'd be out; I 'll go to-night.'

By these means he allowed himself the opportunity of going

back on his decision; for our conscience always retains a trace of the sophisms with which we have drenched it; they leave their after-taste behind them, like a bad liqueur.

He walked about the boulevards and dined at a restaurant by himself. Then, to distract his mind, he looked in for one act at the Vaudeville Theatre. But his bank notes made him uneasy, as if he had stolen them. He would not have been sorry to lose them.

Returning home, he found a letter containing these words:

'What news?

' My wife and I, dear friend, are living in hopes, etc.

'Yours,'

and a scrawled signature.

'His wife—imploring my help!'

At that very moment Arnoux appeared, to find out if he had procured the necessary sum.

'Take it! Here it is!'

And twenty-four hours later he told Deslauriers that nothing had arrived.

Deslauriers came back three days running. He urged him to write to his lawyer. He even offered to go to Le Havre on his own.

'No—there's no point in that. I'm going myself.'

At the end of the week, Frederic timidly asked Arnoux for his fifteen thousand francs.

Arnoux put him off to the next day, and then to the day after. Frederic only ventured out after dark, lest Deslauriers should catch him.

One evening, someone ran into him at the corner of the Madeleine. It was Deslauriers.

'I'm going to get the money,' said Frederic.

Deslauriers accompanied him to the door of a house in the Faubourg Poissonnière.

'Wait for me!'

He waited. At last, forty-three minutes later, Frederic emerged with Arnoux, and signed to him to be patient a little longer. The dealer and his companion went up the rue Hauteville arm in arm, and then took the rue de Chabrol.

The night was dark, with a warm, gusty wind. Arnoux walked slowly, talking continuously about the Galeries du Commerce, a series of arcades intended to link the boulevard Saint-Denis and the Châtelet—a wonderful speculation, which he was most anxious to go in for.   From time to time he stopped, to look at the faces of the prostitutes reflected in the shop windows; then he resumed his conversation.

Frederic heard Deslauriers's steps behind him, like accusing voices, like blows striking his conscience.   But out of false shame he did not dare to claim the money; he feared, too, that it would be useless.   Deslauriers drew nearer.   He made up his mind.

Arnoux replied quite nonchalantly that, as his debtors had failed to pay him, he was unable, at the moment, to give back the fifteen thousand francs.

'I don't suppose you 're in need of them, are you?'

At that moment Deslauriers accosted Frederic and drew him aside.

'Tell me the truth.   Have you got them, or not?'

'Well, no,' said Frederic.   'I 've lost them.'

'Oh—and how?'

'Gambling!'

Deslauriers answered not a word: but bowed very low and went off.   Arnoux had taken the opportunity to light a cigar in a tobacconist's shop.   Coming out, he asked who the young man was.

'No one.   A friend.'

Three minutes later they were at Rosanette's door.

'Come up,' said Arnoux.   'She 'll be delighted to see you. What a bear you are these days!'

A street lamp, opposite, lit up his face.   As he stood there, with his cigar between his white teeth, and his smug look, there was something insufferable about him.

'And—oh, yes—my lawyer 's been to see yours this morning, about registering this mortgage.   My wife reminded me about it.'

'A sensible woman,' said Frederic mechanically.

'I should say so!'

And again Arnoux began to sing her praises.   She hadn't a rival for intelligence, warm-heartedness, and skill in house-keeping: then he added in a low voice, rolling his eyes:

'And in bed . . .'

'Good-bye,' said Frederic.

Arnoux started.

'What!   Why?'

With his hand half stretched towards Frederic, he stared at him, quite disconcerted by the anger in his face.

Frederic answered curtly:

'Good-bye.'

He went down the rue de Bréda like a hurtling stone, furious with Arnoux, vowing never to see either him or her again—heartbroken, despairing. Instead of the expected estrangement, the opposite had happened; and here was Arnoux ready to adore his wife unreservedly, from the hair of her head to the depths of her soul. The vulgarity of the man enraged Frederic. And this fellow had everything! There he was again, on the courtesan's doorstep; the humiliation of a quarrel added to his impotent fury. Besides, there was something mortifying about Arnoux's honesty in offering guarantees for his money; Frederic would have willingly strangled him; and behind his misery there hovered in his conscience, like a fog, the knowledge of his cowardly conduct towards his friend. Tears choked him.

Deslauriers hurried along the rue des Martyrs, swearing out loud in his indignation; for his project, like a fallen obelisk, now seemed to him sublimely lofty. He considered himself robbed, as though he had suffered some serious damage. His friendship for Frederic was dead, and he was glad of it; that was some compensation! He was filled with hatred of the rich. Sénécal's views attracted him, and he vowed he would follow them.

Meanwhile, Arnoux, comfortably seated in an arm-chair by the fire, was sipping his cup of tea, with Rosanette on his knee.

Frederic did not go back to their house; and, to distract his mind from his disastrous passion, he took up the first subject that came to hand, and decided to write a history of the Renaissance. He loaded his desk with a medley of humanists, philosophers, and poets; he visited the print collection, to see the engravings of Marcantonio; he tried to understand Machiavelli. His work gradually tranquillized him. He forgot his own personality by merging it in that of others—which is, perhaps, the only way to avoid suffering.

One day, when he was peacefully taking notes, the door opened, and the servant announced Mme Arnoux.

It was really she! And alone? No! For she was holding little Eugène by the hand, and behind was the nurse in a white apron. She sat down, coughed, and said:

'You haven't been to see us for a long time.'

Frederic could think of no excuse; and she added:

'It's tact on your part.'

'Tact? How?' he said.

'Because of what you did for Arnoux.'

Frederic made a gesture signifying: 'That was nothing. I did it for you.'

She sent the child into the drawing-room, to play with the nurse. They exchanged two or three words about their health; then the conversation dropped.

She was wearing a brown silk dress, the colour of Spanish wine, and a black velvet coat, edged with marten's fur; he longed to stroke this fur, and his lips were drawn towards the broad, smooth loops of her hair. Some qualm disturbed her, and, turning her eyes towards the door:

'It 's rather warm in here,' she said.

Frederic guessed the discreet intention of her glance.

'I beg your pardon. The door is actually ajar.'

'Oh, so it is.'

And she smiled, as if to say: 'I feel perfectly safe.'

At once he asked the object of her visit.

'My husband begged me to come and see you,' she said with some difficulty. 'He did not dare take this step himself.'

'And why?'

'You know Monsieur Dambreuse, don't you?'

'Yes, slightly.'

'Oh, only slightly.'

She was silent.

'Never mind. Go on.'

Then she told him that the day before yesterday Arnoux had been unable to meet four bills of a thousand francs, written to the banker's order, to which he had made her put her signature. She regretted having endangered her children's fortune. But anything was better than dishonour; and if M. Dambreuse refrained from taking action, he would certainly be paid soon, for she was about to sell a little house she had at Chartres.

'Poor woman!' murmured Frederic. 'I 'll go and see him. You can count on me.'

'Thank you.'

And she rose to go.

'Oh, there 's no hurry.'

She remained standing, examining the sheaf of Mongolian arrows fixed to the ceiling, the bookcase, the bindings, the writing utensils; she took up the bronze bowl in which the pens were kept; her feet rested on different spots on the carpet. She had been to see Frederic several times, but always with Arnoux. Now they were alone—alone in his own house; it was an extraordinary event, almost a miracle.

She asked to see his little garden; he offered her his arm to show her his domain—thirty feet of ground, surrounded by houses, laid out with shrubs in the corners and a flower bed in the centre.

It was early in April. The lilac leaves were already green; there was a freshness stirring in the air and little birds were chirping; now and then, the noise of a coach-builder's forge could be heard in the distance.

Frederic went and fetched a fire shovel; and while they strolled side by side, the child built sand castles on the path.

Mme Arnoux did not think he would have much imagination when he grew up; however, he was of an affectionate disposition. But his sister had a natural hardness, which sometimes made her unhappy.

'That will alter,' said Frederic. 'One must never give up hope.'

'One must never give up hope,' she replied. This mechanical repetition of his phrase seemed to him a sort of encouragement; he picked a rose, the only one in the garden.

'Do you remember . . . a certain bunch of roses, one evening in a carriage?'

She blushed a little; then, with a mocking yet compassionate air:

'Ah, I was very young then.'

'And would you do the same with this?' said Frederic in a low voice.

She twisted the stalk round her fingers, like thread round a spindle, and replied:

'No. I shall keep it.'

She beckoned to the nurse, who took the child on her arm: then, on the doorstep, in the street, Mme Arnoux smelled the flower, leaning her head towards her shoulder, with a look as soft as a kiss.

When he was once more in his study, he gazed at the armchair in which she had sat, and at all the things she had touched. Something of her lingered in the air about him. The sweetness of her presence still remained.

'So she came here!' he said to himself.

A wave of infinite tenderness engulfed him.

The next day, at eleven, he was at M. Dambreuse's house. He was shown into the dining-room. The banker was sitting at lunch, opposite his wife. Her niece was beside her and on her other side sat the governess, an Englishwoman, heavily pock-marked.

M. Dambreuse invited his young friend to join them. On his refusing, he asked:

176

'What can I do for you? I am at your service.'

With an assumed indifference, Frederic declared that he came to ask a favour for one Arnoux.

'Oh, yes. The former picture dealer,' said the banker, showing his gums in a silent laugh. 'Oudry used to guarantee him. Every one's sick of him.'

And he began to look through the letters and newspapers lying beside his plate.

Two footmen served the meal, moving noiselessly over the floor; and the lofty room, with its three tapestry door curtains and its two white marble fountains, the glittering spirit lamps, the well-arranged side dishes, even the stiffly folded napkins—all the luxurious comfort of the scene reminded Frederic, by contrast, of a very different meal at Arnoux's house. He did not dare to interrupt M. Dambreuse.

Madame noticed his embarrassment.

'Do you ever see our friend Martinon?' she asked.

'He's coming to-night,' said the girl quickly.

'Oh, you know that?' replied her aunt, throwing her an icy look.

One of the servants whispered in her ear.

'Your dressmaker, my child! . . . Miss John!'

The obedient governess vanished with her pupil.

M. Dambreuse, disturbed by the movement of the chairs, asked what the matter was.

'It's Madame Regimbart.'

'What? Regimbart? I know that name. I've seen the signature.'

At last Frederic broached the question. Arnoux deserved some indulgence; he was even going to sell a house belonging to his wife, with the sole object of fulfilling his obligations.

'They say she's very pretty,' said Mme Dambreuse.

The banker added, in a good-natured tone:

'Are you . . . an intimate friend of theirs?'

Without making a clear reply, Frederic said he would be greatly obliged if he would take into consideration . . .

'Very well—to please you, so be it! I shall wait. I still have time. Suppose we go down to my office?'

Luncheon was over; Mme Dambreuse bowed slightly, with a peculiar smile that combined politeness with irony. Frederic had no time to think about it, for, as soon as they were alone, M. Dambreuse said:

'You never came for your shares.'

Without allowing him to make excuses, he continued:

'Quite right. You're entitled to know a little more about the business.'

He offered him a cigarette and began.

The Amalgamated Coal Company of France had been constituted; they were only waiting for the approval of the court. The mere fact of the merger, by reducing the administrative and working expenses, would increase the profits. In addition, the company envisaged a novel plan—that of giving the workmen an interest in the enterprise. The company would build them houses and healthy tenements; eventually it would become their general purveyor, supplying the employees with everything at cost price.

'And they will gain by it, my dear sir; there's genuine progress for you—a triumphant reply to the croakings of our republicans. On our board we have'—he displayed the prospectus—'a peer of France, a scholar from the Institut, a distinguished ex-engineer—every name is well known. A board of this standing will reassure the timid investor and attract the discerning. The company will secure orders from the State, from the railways, the steamship lines, the metal works, the gas companies, and the kitchens of the middle classes. In this way, by providing heat and light, we shall penetrate to the humblest fireside. You'll ask me how we are to ensure our sales. By means of protective duties, my dear sir, and these we shall obtain; that's up to us. For my part, I'm frankly protectionist. The country comes first!'

He had been appointed a director; but he had not the time to attend to certain details, including the writing of reports.

'I'm not on very good terms with my classics; I've forgotten my Greek! I shall need someone . . . to interpret my ideas.'

Suddenly he added:

'Would you like to be that man—with the title of secretary-general?'

Frederic did not know what to say.

'Well, what's to prevent you?'

His duties would be restricted to writing an annual report for the shareholders. He would find himself in daily contact with the most important men in Paris. As the company's representative among the workmen, he would naturally gain their affection, which would enable him later on to make his way into the Council of the department, and thence to the Chamber.

178

Frederic's ears tingled. What was the reason for this benevolence? He stammered his thanks.

But it was essential that he should not be dependent on any one, said the banker. The best method was to take some shares —'a magnificent investment in any case, for your capital guarantees your position, and your position your capital.'

'About how much should I put in?' asked Frederic.

'Good heavens, anything you like. Between forty and sixty thousand francs, I suppose.'

So exiguous was this sum in the eyes of M. Dambreuse, and so great was his authority, that the young man at once decided to sell a farm. He accepted. M. Dambreuse would fix an appointment in a few days to conclude their arrangements.

'So I can tell Jacques Arnoux . . . ?'

'Anything you like. Poor fellow! Anything you like.'

Frederic wrote to Arnoux and his wife, bidding them set their minds at rest. He sent it round by his servant, who received the reply: 'Excellent!'

But his efforts deserved better than this. He awaited a visit, or at least a letter. He received no visit. No letter arrived.

Was this forgetfulness on their part, or was it intentional? Mme Arnoux had come once; why could she not come again? The sort of hint, the admission she had made—was that nothing but a deliberate, self-interested manœuvre? Were they making a fool of him? Was she in the plot? Although he longed to return to their house, a kind of shyness prevented him.

One morning, three weeks after their interview, M. Dambreuse wrote to say that he expected him that very day, in an hour's time.

He was on his way there, when the thought of M. and Mme Arnoux assailed him once more; he could think of no explanation for their conduct; a pang of anguish, a dreadful presentiment, seized him. To dispel it, he called a cab and drove to the rue Paradis.

Arnoux was away travelling.

'And madame?'

'In the country at the factory.'

'When will monsieur be back?'

'To-morrow, without fail.'

He would find her alone; this was his moment. An imperious voice cried out within him: 'Go to her now!'

But what of M. Dambreuse? 'Well, so much the worse! I'll say I was ill.' He rushed to the station. In the carriage, he thought: 'Perhaps I was wrong. Oh, nonsense! What does it matter?'

Green meadows stretched to right and left; the train rolled on; the little station houses, gliding by, looked like stage scenery, and the puffs of fleecy smoke from the engine, always on the same side, trembled for a moment on the grass, then melted away.

Frederic, alone on the seat, watched this out of boredom, for he was sunk in that torpor which is produced by the very excess of impatience. Cranes and warehouses appeared. It was Creil.

The town was built on the slope of two low hills; one was bare; there was a wood on the summit of the other. With its church tower, its houses of every size, and its stone bridge, Creil gave him an impression of gaiety, neatness, and benevolence. A large flat barge was going down the river, which was lashed into waves by the wind; hens were scratching in the straw at the foot of the calvary; a woman went by with a basket of damp linen on her head.

Past the bridge lay an island, on the right of which was a ruined abbey. A mill wheel turned, blocking the whole width of the second branch of the Oise, above which stood the factory. Frederic was greatly astonished at the size of this building. His respect for Arnoux increased. A few yards further on, he took a pathway that ended in an iron gateway.

He went in. The portress called him back, shouting:

'Have you a pass?'

'What for?'

'For visiting the factory.'

Frederic, in a rough voice, said he had come to see M. Arnoux.

'Who is Monsieur Arnoux?'

'The principal, the master—the owner, in fact.'

'No, sir, this is the factory of Lebœuf and Millet.'

No doubt the good lady was joking. Workmen were arriving; he accosted two or three; their reply was the same.

Frederic left the yard, reeling like a drunken man. He looked so stupefied that a citizen, who was smoking his pipe on the Boucherie bridge, asked him if he was looking for something. This man knew Arnoux's factory. It was at Montataire. Frederic inquired about a carriage. They were only to be found at the station. He went back. A rickety fly, drawn by an old horse with tattered harness that hung down between the shafts, was standing by itself in front of the luggage office.

An urchin offered to find 'old Pilon.' He came back in ten

minutes: old Pilon was having lunch. Frederic, losing patience, set off. But the gates of the level crossing were closed. He had to wait for two trains to pass. At length he hurried into the country.

The monotonous green expanse was like an immense billiard table. Rows of slag heaps stood along each side of the road, like piles of pebbles. A little further on, a group of factory chimneys were smoking. Opposite him, on a rounded hillock, rose a little turreted château, and a square church tower. Beneath, long walls wound their way among the trees; and down below stretched the houses of the village.

These houses had but one story, and staircases of three steps, made of mortarless blocks of stone. Now and then a grocer's bell could be heard. Heavy feet plunged through the black mud, and a thin rain fell, cutting the pale sky with a thousand fine lines.

Frederic kept to the middle of the paved road; then, on his left, at the corner of a turning, he came upon a large wooden arch which bore, in letters of gold, the word FAÏENCES.

Jacques Arnoux's choice of the neighbourhood of Creil had not been accidental; by placing his factory as near as possible to the other, which had a long-standing reputation, he confused the public in a manner favourable to his interests.

The main body of the building was constructed on the very edge of a river which crossed the meadows. The master's house, surrounded by a garden, was distinguished by its flight of steps, which were ornamented with four vases containing prickly cactuses. Piles of white clay were drying in open sheds; there were others out of doors; and in the middle of the yard stood Sénécal, in his everlasting blue overcoat lined with red.

The ex-tutor held out his cold hand.

'Have you come to see the master? He's not here.'

Frederic, disconcerted, replied:

'I knew that.'

But, recovering himself at once:

'My business concerns Madame Arnoux. Can she see me?'

'I haven't set eyes on her for three days,' said Sénécal.

And he embarked on a whole string of complaints. When he had accepted the manufacturer's terms, he had understood that he would live in Paris, not bury himself in the country, away from his friends and deprived of newspapers. No matter! He had risen above that! But Arnoux seemed to take no notice of his merits. He was, moreover, limited, unprogressive.

and incredibly ignorant. It would have been better, instead of searching for artistic perfection, to introduce heating by coal and gas. The merchant was 'going under'; Sénécal emphasized these words. In short, he disliked his occupation, and he more or less commanded Frederic to put in a word for him, so that his salary might be raised.

'Don't worry,' said the other.

He met no one on the stairs. On the first floor he put his head into an empty room; it was the drawing-room. He shouted very loud. There was no answer; the cook and the nurse were doubtless out; at length, reaching the second floor, he pushed open a door. Mme Arnoux was sitting alone, in front of a wardrobe mirror. The cord of her half-open dressing-gown hung down at her thighs. The whole of one side of her hair was spread over her shoulder in a black wave; her arms were raised; she held her chignon in one hand and she was thrusting a pin into it with the other. She uttered a cry, and vanished.

Then she came back fully dressed. Her figure, her eyes, the rustle of her gown enchanted him. Frederic could hardly prevent himself from covering her with kisses.

'I must ask you to forgive me,' she said. 'But I couldn't . . .'

He was bold enough to interrupt:

'All the same . . . you looked splendid . . . just now . . .'

She seemed to find the compliment somewhat coarse, for her cheeks coloured. He was afraid he had offended her. She went on:

'What good wind brings you here?'

He did not know what to answer; and, after a little chuckle, which gave him time to think:

'Would you believe me if I told you?'

'Why not?'

Frederic declared that he had a terrible dream a few nights ago:

'I dreamed that you were seriously ill, almost dying.'

'Neither my husband nor I are ever ill.'

'I only dreamed of you,' he said.

She looked at him calmly.

'Dreams do not always come true.'

Frederic stammered, searched for words, and at length launched into a long discourse on the affinity of souls. There was a force which could bring two people into contact across space, could warn them of each other's feelings and reunite them.

She listened to him with bowed head, smiling her lovely smile.

He watched her out of the corner of his eye, with delight, and poured his love out the more freely, through the medium of a commonplace. She offered to show him the factory; and, as she insisted, he agreed.

In order to begin with something light and entertaining, she showed him the sort of museum which ornamented the staircase. The specimens hanging on the walls or standing on shelves bore witness to the successive efforts and infatuations of Arnoux. After searching for the copper-red of the Chinese, he had tried to make majolica, Faenza, Etruscan, and Oriental ware, and had ended by attempting some of the improvements that were later achieved. In the series one observed huge vases covered with mandarins, iridescent mordoré bowls, pots embossed with Arabic writing, flagons in the Renaissance manner, and large plates decorated with two figures, which looked as if they had been drawn in red chalk, in a vapid and sentimental style. He was now manufacturing signboards and wine labels; but his mind was not elevated enough to attain to art, nor ordinary enough to think solely of profit; so that he was ruining himself without satisfying anybody. They were looking at these things, when little Marthe went by.

'Don't you recognize him?' said her mother to her.

'Oh, yes,' she replied, greeting him, while her clear, suspicious gaze, her virgin gaze, seemed to be murmuring: 'What have you come down here for?' and she went up the steps, turning her head slightly over her shoulder.

Mme Arnoux led Frederic out into the yard, and then explained to him in a serious voice how the clay was crushed, refined, and sifted.

'The important thing is the preparation of the pastes.'

And she led him into a hall full of vats, in which a vertical rod equipped with horizontal arms revolved on its own axis. Frederic was angry with himself for not having declined her proposal straight out, a moment ago.

'These are the drabblers,' she said.

He thought the word grotesque, and somehow unsuited to her lips.

Wide belts moved from one end of the ceiling to the other, and wound themselves round drums. The whole room was in a state of continuous, rhythmical, and maddening movement.

They went out, and passed a derelict hut which had formerly served as a garden tool shed.

'It's no use for anything now,' said Mme Arnoux.

He answered, in a trembling voice:

'Yet happiness might find it sufficient!'

His words were drowned by the din of the fire pump, and they went into the roughing shop.

Men, seated at a narrow table, were laying masses of clay on revolving disks in front of them; with their left hand they scraped out the inside, while their right stroked the surface, and vases could be seen rising, like flowers opening.

Mme Arnoux exhibited the moulds for the more difficult pieces.

In another room, they were decorating the pots with bands, grooves, and embossed lines. On the upper story they were removing flaws, and stopping the holes left by the earlier processes with plaster.

There were rows of pots everywhere—on gratings, in corners, in the middle of corridors.

Frederic was beginning to be bored.

'Perhaps you find this tiring?' she said.

Fearing lest he should have to end his visit there, he feigned great enthusiasm. He even expressed regret at not having devoted himself to this industry.

She seemed surprised.

'Yes, indeed! Then I could have lived near you!'

He tried to catch her eye; to avoid his look, Mme Arnoux laid on a side table some little balls of paste which came from the unsuccessful repairs, pressed them down into a flat cake, and imprinted her hand on them.

'May I take that away?' said Frederic.

'Good heavens, what a child you are!'

He was about to answer when Sénécal came in. From the door, the deputy manager noticed a breach of the regulations. The workshops were supposed to be swept out once a week; as the workmen had not done this, Sénécal informed them that they would have to stay an extra hour—'And serve you right!'

They bent over their work without a murmur; but their anger could be guessed from the harsh sound of their heavy breathing. In any case they were difficult to manage, as they had all been dismissed from the big factory. The Republican ruled them sternly. A man of theory, he thought only in terms of masses, and showed no mercy to the individual.

His presence embarrassed Frederic, who asked Mme Arnoux in a low voice if there was any possibility of seeing the ovens. They went down to the ground floor; and she was just explaining the use of the caskets, when Sénécal, who had followed, placed himself between them.

He continued the demonstration himself, and dilated on the various sorts of fuel, on oven charging, pyroscopes, double furnaces, slip painting, glazes, and metals, with a wealth of chemical terms, like chloride, sulphur, borax, and carbonate. Frederic could make nothing of it, and turned round to Mme Arnoux at every word.

'You're not listening,' she said. 'Yet Monsieur Sénécal is perfectly lucid. He knows much more about all these things than I do.'

Flattered by this eulogy, the mathematician suggested a visit to the colouring department. Frederic threw an anxious glance of inquiry towards Mme Arnoux. She remained impassive, unwilling, as it seemed, either to be alone with him, or yet to leave him. He offered her his arm.

'No, thank you. The staircase is too narrow.'

When they reached the top, Sénécal opened the door of a room full of women.

They were equipped with paint-brushes, small bottles, shells, and glass plates. Along the cornice, against the wall, were rows of engraved blocks; scraps of paper flew about; and an iron stove gave out a sickening heat, mixed with the smell of turpentine.

Almost all the women wore dirty clothes. But there was one in a Madras kerchief and long ear-rings. She was both plump and slender, with great black eyes, and the fleshy lips of a negress. Her ample bosom stood out under her blouse, which was fastened round her waist by the belt of her skirt; one elbow rested on the work-bench, the other arm hung down, and she looked vacantly out into the distant country. Beside her lay a bottle of wine and some sausage meat.

Eating in the workshops was forbidden by the rules, to ensure the cleanliness of the work and the health of the operatives. A sense of duty or a desire to tyrannize made Sénécal point to a notice in a frame and shout from a distance:

'Hi! You, over there—you, from Bordeaux! Read clause 9 aloud to me.'

'Well, and then?'

'And then, mademoiselle? You'll pay a fine of three francs.' She looked him insolently in the face.

'I don't mind. When the master comes back, he'll let me off your fine. You can go to hell, old man!'

Sénécal, who was walking up and down with his hands behind his back, like a master in a class-room, contented himself with smiling.

'Clause 13, insubordination, ten francs.'

The girl from Bordeaux turned back to her task. Out of propriety, Mme Arnoux said nothing, but her brow contracted. Frederic murmured:

'You 're very hard, for a democrat.'

The other replied didactically:

'Democracy does not mean licence for the individual. It means a common level under the law, the division of labour—order!'

'You 've left out humanity,' said Frederic.

Mme Arnoux took his arm; this tacit approbation seemed to offend Sénécal and he went away.

Frederic felt an immense sense of relief. He had been looking for a chance to declare himself since the morning; now it had come. Moreover, Mme Arnoux's spontaneous gesture seemed to contain a promise; and he asked if he might go up to her room, to warm his feet. But as soon as he was seated beside her his difficulties began; he lacked a starting-point. Luckily he thought of Sénécal.

'That punishment was perfectly absurd,' he said.

'Severity is sometimes necessary,' replied Mme Arnoux.

'Fancy your saying that—you, who are so good-natured! Oh, I was forgetting. You sometimes enjoy inflicting pain.'

'I don't understand riddles, my friend.'

And her stern glance checked him, even more than her words. But Frederic was determined to go on. A volume of Musset happened to be lying on the chest of drawers. He turned a few pages, and then began to talk about love—its despairs and its raptures.

According to Mme Arnoux, these things were wicked, or else untrue.

The young man felt hurt by this opposition; and, to overcome it, he cited as proof the suicides described in the newspapers, and praised the great lovers of literature—Phèdre, Dido, Romeo, Desgrieux. He became muddled.

The fire in the hearth was out; the rain lashed against the window panes. Mme Arnoux sat motionless, with her hands on the arms of her chair; the broad ribbons of her cap, hanging down, looked like the head-dress of a sphinx; her classic profile stood out in pale relief among the shadows.

He longed to throw himself at her feet. There was a creaking in the corridor; he dared not.

Besides, he was held back by a kind of religious awe. Her dress, melting into the darkness, seemed to him gigantic, infinite, impossible to lift; and that very conviction intensified his desire. But the dread of going too far, and yet of not going far enough, deprived him of all power of judgment.

'If I don't attract her, let her turn me out! If she wants me, let her encourage me!'

He said, with a sigh:

'Then you refuse to admit that a man can love . . . a woman?'

Mme Arnoux replied:

'If she is free, he may marry her; if she is another's, he must leave her alone.'

'Is happiness, then, impossible?'

'No! But it is never to be found in falsehood, anxiety, and remorse.'

'What does that matter, if exquisite joys are the reward?'

'The experience is too costly.'

He tried to bring irony to the attack.

'So virtue is nothing more than cowardice?'

'I should rather call it clear-sightedness. Some women may forget their duty or their religion; for them, mere common sense should be enough. Self-interest makes a solid foundation for good conduct . . .'

'You 've got all the principles of the middle class!'

'But I don't claim to be a great lady.'

At that moment, the little boy ran up.

'Mamma, are you coming down to dinner?'

'Yes, in a moment.'

Frederic rose; at the same time Marthe appeared. He could not make up his mind to go; and with a look fraught with entreaty he said:

'These women whom you speak of must be very heartless.'

'No, but they are deaf when it is necessary.'

She was standing in the doorway of her room, with her children at her sides. He bowed without a word. In silence she acknowledged his salute.

His first sensation was one of complete stupefaction. This method of making clear to him the vanity of his hopes was crushing. He gave himself up for lost, like a man fallen to the bottom of a chasm, who knows that help will not come and that he must die

Meanwhile, he walked on, unseeing, at random; he stumbled against stones; he lost his way. The noise of clogs sounded at his ear; the workmen were leaving the foundry. Then he saw where he was.

The lamps of the railway drew a line of fire along the horizon. He arrived just as a train was leaving, allowed himself to be pushed into a carriage, and went to sleep.

An hour later he was on the boulevards. The gaiety of Paris by night suddenly banished his journey into a past that was already remote. He tried to steel himself, and salved his wounded heart by vilifying Mme Arnoux:

'She's a fool, a goose. Let's forget her!'

On his return home, he found in his study an eight-page letter on shiny blue paper, signed with the initials 'R. A.'

It began with some friendly reproaches.

'What's happened to you, my dear? I'm bored.'

But the writing was so appalling that Frederic was about to throw the whole missive away when he noticed a postscript.

'I'm expecting you to take me to the races to-morrow.'

What did this invitation mean? Was it another of Rosanette's tricks? But one doesn't make a fool of the same man twice for no good reason at all; and, in a burst of curiosity, he read the letter again carefully.

Frederic made out: 'Misunderstanding . . . taken wrong turning . . . disillusion . . . unhappy children that we are . . . like two rivers reuniting . . .' and so forth.

This style differed from her usual language. What change could have occurred?

For a long time he held the pages between his fingers. There was something about the shape of the letters and the uneven spacing of the lines that disquieted him, like some irregularity of dress.

'Why shouldn't I go?' he said to himself at length. 'But supposing Madame Arnoux found out? Oh, let her find out! So much the better! And let her be jealous—that will give me my revenge!'

CHAPTER IV

Rosanette was ready and waiting for him.

'What a pet you are!' she said, gazing at him with her pretty eyes, that seemed both gay and tender.

When she had tied the ribbons of her bonnet, she sat down on the divan, and was silent.

'Shall we start?' said Frederic.

She looked at the clock.

'Oh, no! Not before half-past one!' as if she had purposely set this limit to her indecision.

At last the half-hour struck.

'Well then, *andiamo, caro mio*!'

She gave her hair a final touch and bestowed her instructions on Delphine.

'Will madame be back to dinner?'

'Why should I? We'll dine together at the Café Anglais, or anywhere you like.'

'All right!'

Her little dogs were barking round her feet.

'We can take them with us, can't we?'

Frederic himself carried them to the conveyance, which was a hired post-chaise, with two horses and a postilion; he had placed his own servant on the rumble. Rosanette seemed satisfied with his arrangements: then, as soon as she was seated, asked him if he had been to see Arnoux lately.

'Not for a month,' said Frederic.

'I met him the day before yesterday: actually he would have come to-day if he weren't in all sorts of difficulties—another lawsuit—I don't know what. What an odd man he is!'

'Yes. Very odd!'

And Frederic added with an assumed indifference:

'Incidentally, do you still see anything of . . . what's his name? . . . that ex-singer . . . Delmar?'

She answered curtly:

'No! It's over.'

Then there was no doubt about their estrangement. Frederic began to hope.

They went through the Bréda district at a walking pace: it being Sunday, the streets were deserted; prosperous faces could be seen behind the windows. The carriage began to move more quickly; the passers-by turned round at the noise of the wheels; the folded leather hood glittered, the servant threw out his chest, and the two little dogs, sitting beside each other, looked like two ermine muffs on the cushions. Frederic let himself be lulled by the rocking of the springs. Rosanette, laughing, turned her head to right and left.

Her hat of pearly straw was trimmed with black lace. The hood of her Arab cloak floated in the breeze, and she sheltered from the sun under a parasol of lilac satin, with an ornate pointed end, like a pagoda.

'What adorable little fingers!' said Frederic, gently taking her free left hand, which bore a gold bracelet in the shape of a horse's curb chain. 'That's nice, I declare. Where did you get it?"

'Oh, I've had it a long time,' said Rosanette.

The young man did not protest against this hypocritical reply. He preferred 'to make the most of the opportunity.' And without letting go of her wrist he pressed his lips to it, between the glove and the sleeve.

'Stop it! Someone'll see us!'

'Nonsense! What does it matter?'

From the Place de la Concorde they took the quai de la Conférence, then the quai de Billy, where a cedar could be seen in a garden. Rosanette thought Lebanon was in China; she laughed at her own ignorance, and asked Frederic to give her lessons in geography. Then, leaving the Trocadéro on their right, they crossed the Jena bridge and at length stopped in the middle of the Champ de Mars, beside other carriages which were already drawn up in the race-course.

The grassy slopes were packed with the proletariat. Spectators could be seen on the balcony of the École militaire; the two tents outside the paddock, the two stands within it, and a third opposite the royal box, were filled with a smartly dressed crowd, whose deportment indicated the reverence they felt for this novel amusement. The racing set of that epoch was more select and less vulgar in appearance than it is to-day; it was the period of foot-straps, velvet collars, and white gloves. The women wore brilliantly coloured dresses with long waists; sitting in rows on the stands, they looked like great banks of flowers, flecked here and there by the dark clothes of the men. But all eyes were turned towards the famous Algerian chieftain, Bou-Maza,[1] who, seated between two staff officers in a private box, betrayed no emotion. The Jockey Club stand was exclusively occupied by serious-looking gentlemen.

The real enthusiasts had stationed themselves below, next to the course, which was enclosed by two lines of posts, linked by ropes. Within the immense oval formed by the track, coco-nut vendors shook their rattles, programmes were being sold, and cigars hawked. A vast hum arose; policemen walked up and down; and a bell which hung from a pole bearing various numbers suddenly rang. Five horses appeared, and every one went back to the stands.

Meanwhile, enormous clouds were rolling up above the tops of the elm-trees opposite. Rosanette was afraid it would rain.

'I have some umbrellas,' said Frederic, 'and everything we need for our entertainment,' he added, opening the boot and revealing a picnic basket full of eatables.

'Bravo! We understand each other.'

'And we'll understand each other better still, eh?'

'Perhaps,' she said, blushing.

The jockeys, in silk jackets, tried to keep their horses in line, reining them in with both hands. A red flag was lowered. Then all five started, bending over their horses' manes. At first they seemed to be bunched together in a solid mass, which soon spread out, and then divided; half-way round the first lap, the jockey in yellow nearly fell; for a long time Filly and Tibi disputed the lead; then Tom Thumb came out ahead; but Clubstick, who had been left at the start, caught them up and came in first, beating Sir Charles by two lengths. This was a surprise: and the crowd shouted and stamped their feet until the wooden stands shook.

'How jolly this is!' said Rosanette. 'Darling, I adore you.'

Frederic no longer doubted his good fortune: Rosanette's last words assured it.

A hundred yards away a lady came into sight in a victoria. She leaned out of the door, then quickly drew back, so that Frederic was unable to make out her face. A suspicion gripped him—it seemed to him that it was Mme Arnoux. But that was impossible! Why should she have come?

He got out of the carriage, saying he was going to stroll in the paddock.

'That's not very polite,' said Rosanette.

Ignoring her, he stepped forward. The victoria, swinging round, moved off at a trot.

At the same moment Frederic was caught by Cisy.

'Good morning, my boy! How are you? Hussonnet's down there. Now, listen to me!'

Frederic tried to disengage himself, so as to catch up the victoria. Rosanette beckoned him back to her side. Cisy noticed her and insisted on greeting her.

Since he had been out of mourning for his grandmother, he had begun to realize his ideal, and was succeeding in acquiring 'style.' His check waistcoat, his short jacket, the big rosettes on his pumps, and the ticket in his hat band all contributed effectively to what he himself described as his 'smartness'—an Anglophile and guardee elegance. He began by complaining of the wretched turf at the Champ de Mars, then spoke of the Chantilly races and the tricks they played there, swore that he could drink twelve glasses of champagne during the twelve strokes of midnight, offered to bet on it with Rosanette, and gently stroked the two dogs. Leaning on the carriage door with his other elbow, he went on talking nonsense with the knob of his stick in his mouth, his legs apart, and his backside sticking out: Frederic was smoking beside him and trying to discover what had happened to the victoria.

The bell rang and Cisy went away, much to the delight of Rosanette, who said she found him very tiresome.

There was nothing special about the second race, nor about the third, apart from a man being carried off on a stretcher. The fourth, in which eight horses competed for the City Stakes, was more interesting.

The onlookers in the stands climbed on to the benches. The other spectators, standing up in their carriages, followed the manœuvres of the jockeys through opera glasses; the riders could be seen as spots of red, yellow, white, and blue, moving against the crowd, which extended all round the circuit of the course. From a distance their speed looked quite moderate; at the far end of the Champ de Mars they even seemed to slow down and to proceed only by a sort of gliding motion, in which the horses appeared to touch the ground with their bellies without bending their outstretched legs. Returning quickly, their size increased; they cut through the air as they passed; the earth trembled; pebbles flew; the wind beat against the jockeys' jackets and made them quiver like sails; they lashed their animals violently with their whips, as they strove towards the winning post. The numbers were taken down, others went up, and, amid cheers, the winning horse dragged itself to the paddock, covered in sweat, with stiff knees and drooping neck, while the rider held his sides, as though he were dying in the saddle.

The start of the last race was held up by a protest. The crowd grew bored and began to scatter. Men chatted in groups at the foot of the stands. The talk was unrestrained; and society ladies went home, shocked at the proximity of loose women.

There were also present the stars of the music hall, and fashionable actresses; nor did mere beauty receive the greatest homage. Here was old Georgine Aubert, whom a wit once called the Louis XI of prostitution. Horribly painted, and from time to time uttering a sort of groan-like laugh, she lay stretched full length in her long barouche, under a fur tippet, as if it were mid-winter. Mme de Remoussot, whose lawsuit had made her the vogue, was holding court in a brake, with a party of Americans; while Thérèse Bachelu, looking, as usual, like a Gothic virgin, had packed the twelve flounces of her dress into a calash, the apron of which had been replaced by a great basket of roses.

Rosanette was jealous of these splendours; and she began to make sweeping gestures and to talk very loud, in order to attract attention.

Some gentlemen recognized her and waved greetings to her. She acknowledged them and told Frederic their names. They were all counts, viscounts, and marquises; and this delighted him, for he could detect in every eye a certain respect for his good luck.

Cisy, surrounded by a group of elderly men, seemed no less contented. They were laughing in their sleeves and seemed to be chaffing him; at last he shook hands vigorously with the eldest of them and advanced towards Rosanette.

She was eating a slice of *foie gras*, pretending to be famished; Frederic, with a bottle of wine on his knees, imitated her faithfully.

The victoria reappeared; it was Mme Arnoux. She turned extraordinarily pale.

'Give me some champagne,' said Rosanette. And lifting her brimming glass as high as she could, she cried:

'Here's to you all down there! Here's to all respectable women—coupled with the name of my protector's wife!'

There were roars of laughter all around her; and the victoria

193

disappeared. Frederic pulled at her dress; he was about to lose his temper. But Cisy was there, in the same attitude as before. In an excess of self-confidence he invited Rosanette to dine with him that very evening.

'Impossible,' she answered. 'We 're going to the Café Anglais together.'

Frederic remained silent, as though he had heard nothing; and Cisy, looking disappointed, left Rosanette.

While Cisy had been leaning against the right-hand door talking to her, Hussonnet had come up on the left, and, catching the words 'Café Anglais,' remarked:

'A nice place! Supposing we had a bite there, eh?'

'As you wish,' said Frederic. He had sunk back in the corner of the carriage and was watching the victoria disappear over the horizon. What had just happened, he felt, was beyond repair; he had lost his great love. And there was the other, at his side—the gay, the easy love! He was tired out, and, torn by conflicting impulses, no longer knowing what he wanted, he felt an infinite melancholy, a longing to die.

A loud noise of footsteps and voices made him raise his head; some street boys, who had climbed over the ropes that enclosed the track, were going to have a look at the stands; the crowd was leaving. Some drops of rain fell. The blockage of carriages grew worse. Hussonnet had vanished.

'Well, so much the better,' said Frederic.

'You mean, it 's nicer to be alone?' said Rosanette, putting her hand on his.

Suddenly, with a flash of brass and steel, there passed in front of them a magnificent landau, with four horses driven, without a coachman, by two jockeys in velvet jackets with gold fringes. Mme Dambreuse was sitting beside her husband. Martinon was on the opposite seat; the faces of all three betrayed astonishment.

'They 've recognized me,' said Frederic to himself.

Rosanette wanted to stop, to get a better view of the parade. But Mme Arnoux might reappear. He shouted to the postilion:

'Drive on! Drive on! straight ahead!'

And the chaise started off towards the Champs-Élysées, surrounded by other carriages. There were barouches, britzkas, wurts, tandems, tilburies, dog-carts, covered wagonettes with leather curtains full of singing workmen on the spree, go-carts carefully driven by the fathers of families. There were victorias, crammed to overflowing, with young men seated on the other passengers' feet and swinging their legs over the side. Tall broughams with cloth-covered cushions carried dozing dowagers; sometimes a superb high-stepper would pass, drawing a curricle, as simple and elegant as a dandy's black coat. Meanwhile the downpour grew heavier. Umbrellas, parasols, and mackintoshes were produced, shouts of 'Good afternoon!—How are you?— Yes—No,' were exchanged from afar; face succeeded face with the rapidity of a magic-lantern show. Frederic and Rosanette did not exchange a word: the sight of so many wheels continuously turning beside them affected them with a kind of numb insensibility.

From time to time the close-packed ranks of vehicles would all halt together in several rows. The passengers, in compulsory proximity, stared at each other. From behind emblazoned panels, indifferent glances were thrown upon the crowd: envious eyes gleamed in the depths of hired cabs: sniggers of disrespect greeted heads too arrogantly poised: gaping mouths expressed fatuous admiration; and here and there a pedestrian, in the middle of the road, would suddenly leap backwards, to avoid a horseman galloping between the carriages and freeing himself at last. Then the whole mass began to move; the coachmen loosened the reins and lowered their long whips; the restive horses, shaking their bits, scattered foam all round them, while their haunches and their damp harness steamed in the watery mist. The setting sun, piercing the vapour, cast through the Arc de Triomphe an almost horizontal beam of reddish light, which glittered on the wheel hubs, the door handles, the butts of the shafts, and the rings of the axle-trees. The great avenue was like a river carrying on its current the bobbing manes of horses and the clothes and heads of men and women. On either side rose the trees, like two green walls, glistening after the rain. Above, patches of blue as soft as satin appeared here and there in the sky.

Then Frederic remembered those days, already distant, when he had coveted the unspeakable delight of riding in one of these carriages, beside one of these women. That delight he now possessed, yet he had no joy in it.

The rain had stopped. Those pedestrians who had taken refuge under the pillars of the Garde-Meubles resumed their walk, while the strollers in the rue Royale began to return towards the boulevard. A few idlers stood in a row on the steps of the Ministry of Foreign Affairs.

Up by the Chinese baths the road was full of holes and the

chaise slowed down. A man in a brown overcoat was walking along the edge of the pavement. A splash of water spurted from under the wheels and flooded his back. The man flung round in a fury. Frederic turned pale; he had recognized Deslauriers.

He dismissed the carriage at the door of the Café Anglais. Rosanette went upstairs ahead of him, while he paid the postilion.

He found her on the staircase, talking to a gentleman. Frederic took her arm. But a second cavalier stopped her in the middle of the corridor.

'Go on,' she said, 'I 'll join you.'

And he entered the private room by himself.

Through the two open casements he could see people at the windows of the houses opposite. Wide puddles rippled on the drying asphalt of the street; a magnolia on the edge of the balcony filled the room with its delicate scent. The fragrance and the freshness relaxed his nerves; and he sank down on the red divan, under the mirror.

Rosanette came back, and kissed him on the forehead.

'Is my poor darling worried?'

'Perhaps,' he replied.

'Well, you 're not the only one!'

This meant: 'Let 's both forget our troubles in a common happiness.'

Then she put the petal of a flower between her lips, and held it out for him to nibble. There was a voluptuous grace, almost a gentleness about this movement, which touched Frederic.

'Why do you make me so unhappy?' he said, thinking of her conduct towards Mme Arnoux.

'I—make you unhappy?'

And standing before him, she looked at him, with her eyes half closed and her hands on his shoulders.

All his virtuous indignation sank into an infinite cowardice. He continued:

'Because you won't love me,' and pulled her down on to his knee.

She did not resist; he put his arms round her waist; the rustling of her silk dress filled him with a burning desire.

'Where are they?' said Hussonnet's voice in the passage.

Rosanette got up abruptly and went and stood at the other end of the room, with her back to the door.

She asked for oysters, and they sat down.

Hussonnet was not amusing. He was compelled to write

daily on all sorts of subjects, to read innumerable newspapers, to listen to countless arguments, and to produce what were supposed to be dazzling paradoxes; in the end his own damp squibs had blinded his eyes and he ceased to be able to see things as they actually were. His once easy life was now full of embarrassments, and his difficulties kept him in a state of continued agitation; while his incapacity, which he would never acknowledge to himself, made him cantankerous and sarcastic.

Talking of a new ballet called *Ozaï*, he launched a violent attack on dancing, and, talking of dancing, on the opera; then, talking of the opera, on the actors at the Théâtre des Italiens who had now been replaced by a troupe of Spanish players, 'as if we weren't sick and tired of Castille!' Frederic, with his romantic love of Spain, was upset; and, to change the subject, asked about the Collège de France, from which Edgar Quinet and Mickiewicz[1] had just been excluded. But Hussonnet, who admired M. de Maistre, declared himself in favour of authority and spiritualism. All the time he never ceased to express doubts of the most positive facts, to deny history, and to argue against the best-founded conclusions. At the mention of geometry he even exclaimed: 'What nonsense geometry is!' His entire conversation was interlarded with imitations of actors, particularly of Sainville.

These extravagances bored Frederic to death. He made a movement of impatience, and kicked one of the dogs under the table.

They both began to bark in an odious manner.

'You ought to send them home,' he said sharply.

Rosanette trusted no one.

Then he turned to the journalist:

'Come, Hussonnet! Be a martyr!'

'Yes, indeed, my friend,' she said, 'it would be charming of you!'

Without waiting to be pressed, Hussonnet departed.

How was he to reward this good turn? Frederic dismissed it from his mind. He was just beginning to enjoy their *tête-à-tête* when a waiter came in.

'Madame, there's someone asking for you.'

'What! Again?'

'All the same, I must go and see,' said Rosanette.

He was mad with longing for her. Her disappearance seemed to him a breach of faith, almost an outrage. What was her purpose? Was she not satisfied with having insulted Mme

Arnoux? So much the worse for Mme Arnoux, anyway! He hated all women now; and tears choked him, for his love had been misunderstood and his lust cheated.

Rosanette came in again, with Cisy. Pointing to him, she said:

'I've invited this gentleman. That was quite right, wasn't it?'

'Why, yes—of course.'

With a tortured smile Frederic motioned to Cisy to sit down.

Rosanette began to read through the menu, pausing at all the most extraordinary dishes.

'Supposing we were to eat a dish of rabbit *à la Richelieu*, and a pudding *à la d'Orléans*?'

'Oh—no Orleans!' exclaimed Cisy, who was a Legitimist and thought he was making a joke.

'Would you prefer a turbot *à la Chambord*?' she continued. Frederic found these civilities offensive.

She decided in favour of a plain steak, some crayfish, truffles, a pineapple salad, and some vanilla ices.

'After that, we'll see. Now, get on with it! Oh, I forgot —bring me a sausage, but not with garlic!'

And she called the waiter 'young man,' struck her glass with her knife, and threw her bread up to the ceiling. She wanted to drink burgundy straight away.

'You don't serve burgundy at the beginning,' said Frederic.

According to the viscount it was occasionally done

'No, no! Never!'

'Yes, yes, I assure you!'

'There, you see?'

The look with which she accompanied this phrase indicated: 'This is a rich man: you should listen to him.'

Meanwhile, the door opened every minute, the waiters yapped, and someone in the room next door strummed a waltz on a frightful piano. After the races, they began to discuss riding, and the two rival schools. Cisy supported Baucher, Frederic the Comte d'Aure, until Rosanette, shrugging her shoulders, said:

'That's enough; good heavens! He knows more about it than you do.'

She was biting into a pomegranate, with her elbow on the table; the candles on the stand in front of her flickered in the draught; the white light steeped her skin with the hues of mother-of-pearl, tinged her eyelids with pink, and made her eyeballs glitter; the red fruit blended its colour with the purple of her lips; her slender nostrils quivered; there was an insolence, an intoxication, a subaqueous quality about her whole person that infuriated Frederic, and yet filled his heart with mad desires.

Then, in a calm tone of voice, she asked who owned that large landau with the men in maroon livery.

'The Countess Dambreuse,' replied Cisy.

'They're very rich, are they not?'

'Yes, very rich—although Madame Dambreuse, who used to be plain Mademoiselle Boutron, the daughter of a prefect, is only moderately well off.'

But her husband had expectations in several directions, which Cisy enumerated; as a frequent visitor, he knew their family history.

To annoy him, Frederic went out of his way to contradict him. He maintained that Mme Dambreuse was a de Boutron, and insisted on her noble origin.

'Never mind! I'd like to have her carriage, anyway!' said Rosanette, throwing herself into the arm-chair.

And the sleeve of her dress, slipping slightly, disclosed a bracelet set with three opals on her left wrist.

Frederic noticed it.

'Hallo! But . . .'

All three looked at one another, and blushed.

The door was discreetly pushed ajar; the brim of a hat appeared, followed by Hussonnet's profile.

'Forgive me if I'm disturbing the love-birds!'

Then he broke off in astonishment when he saw that Cisy was there and had taken his seat.

Dinner was laid for him; and, as he was ravenous, he scavenged haphazard among the remains of the repast. He devoured some meat from a dish, and a piece of fruit from a basket. He drank with one hand and helped himself with the other, while he told the story of his mission.

He had taken the two bow-wows home. No news at the house. He had found the cook with a soldier—an untrue story, invented solely for effect.

Rosanette took her bonnet from its peg. Frederic rushed to the bell and shouted to the waiter in the distance:

'Call a carriage!'

'Mine is here,' said the viscount.

'Excuse me, sir——'

'By your leave, sir——'

And they looked each other in the eye, with pale faces and trembling hands.

At length Rosanette took Cisy's arm, and, pointing to Hussonnet, who was still at the table, she said:

'Look after him! He'll choke himself. I wouldn't like him to die just because he's been kind to my little dogs.'

The door closed behind them.

'Well?' said Hussonnet.

'Well, what?'

'I thought . . .'

'What did you think?'

'Weren't you . . .? that is . . .'

He completed his sentence with a gesture.

'Oh, no! There's never been any question of that!'

Hussonnet did not press the point.

He had had an object in inviting himself to dinner. His paper, the name of which had been changed from *Art* to *The Man about Town*, with the motto: 'Gunners, to your cannon!' was in low water; and he was anxious to transform it into a weekly review, on his own, without the help of Deslauriers. He mentioned the old project again and explained his new plan.

Frederic, who did not seem to understand, made vague replies. Hussonnet grabbed several cigars from the table, said: 'Good-bye, my boy,' and vanished.

Frederic asked for the bill. It was long; and the waiter, his napkin under his arm, was waiting for the money, when another waiter, a pallid individual who looked like Martinon, came and said to him:

'I beg your pardon, but the cashier has forgotten to charge for the cab.'

'What cab?'

'The one that gentleman took just now, for the little dogs.'

And the waiter pulled a long face, as though pitying the poor young man. Frederic could have slapped him. He was given twenty francs change and left it as a tip.

'Thank you, my lord!' said the man with the napkin, bowing very low.

Frederic spent the next day nursing his anger and his humiliation. He blamed himself for not having struck Cisy. As for Rosanette, he swore never to see her again; there were plenty of others, equally beautiful, and, as money was essential for the possession of these women, he would gamble on the Bourse with the price of his farm, he would become rich, and he would crush Rosanette and every one else with his opulence. When evening came he was amazed to find that he had not thought of Mme Arnoux.

'So much the better! What's the use?'

The following morning at eight o'clock Pellerin came to see him. He began by admiring the furniture and otherwise flattering him. Then he said abruptly:

'Were you at the races on Sunday?'

'Yes, unfortunately.'

Then the painter inveighed against the anatomy of English horses, extolling Géricault's horses and the horses of the Parthenon.

'Was Rosanette with you?'

Adroitly, he began to praise her.

Frederic's coldness disconcerted him. He did not know how to introduce the subject of the portrait.

His first ideas had been to produce a Titian. But little by little the varied colouring of his model had fascinated him; and he had worked boldly, building pigment on pigment and light on light. At first Rosanette was delighted; but her assignations with Delmar had interrupted the sittings and allowed Pellerin plenty of time to be dazzled by his own brilliance. Then, as his admiration declined, he began to wonder if his work was not lacking in grandeur. He went to look at the Titians again, saw how far he had travelled from them, and recognized his mistake; and he began to redraw and simplify his outlines. Through this reshaping he sought to create a fusion, a blending of the tones of the head with those of the background; this gave solidity to the face and vigour to the shadows; the whole composition seemed stronger. At last Rosanette came back. She allowed herself to criticize; of course the artist persevered. After some furious outbursts against her stupidity, he admitted to himself that she might be right. Then began the period of doubts—of that anguish of uncertainty which results in stomach-ache, insomnia, fever, and self-contempt. He was courageous enough to retouch the picture, but his heart was not in it and he felt that his work was bad.

He contented himself with complaining that he had been refused by the Salon; then he blamed Frederic for not having been to see Rosanette's portrait.

'I don't care a damn for Rosanette!'

This declaration emboldened the painter.

'Can you believe it?' he said. 'That bitch won't take the picture now!'

He said nothing of the fact that he had asked her for three thousand francs. Rosanette cared little who paid for the portrait; and she had not even mentioned the point to Arnoux, as she preferred to make use of his purse for more urgent matters.

'Well, what about Arnoux?' said Frederic.

She had referred Pellerin to him. The former picture dealer had washed his hands of the portrait.

'He claims that it belongs to Rosanette.'

'That's true—it's hers.'

'What! Why, she's sent me on to you!' answered Pellerin.

If he had really believed in the merits of his work, he would probably not have considered exploiting it. But a price—and a fairly large price—would serve to refute the critics, and provide encouragement for him. To get rid of him, Frederic politely inquired his terms.

The exorbitance of the sum revolted him, and he answered:

'No! Oh, no!'

'But you're her lover! You gave me the order!'

'Excuse me, I was the intermediary.'

'But you can't leave me with this on my hands!'

The artist lost his temper.

'I didn't think you were so grasping.'

'Nor you so mean! Good-bye!'

He had just left when Sénécal appeared.

This disturbed Frederic, who felt a twinge of anxiety.

'What's the matter?'

Sénécal told his story.

'On Saturday, at about nine o'clock, Madame Arnoux received a letter summoning her to Paris. It so happened that there was no one to go and fetch her a carriage from Creil, so she tried to make me go myself. I refused, as this was not part of my duties. She set off, and came back on Sunday evening. Yesterday morning Arnoux turned up at the factory. The girl from Bordeaux complained. I don't know what's going on between them, but he remitted her fine in front of everybody. There were high words between us. In short, he paid me off, and here I am.'

Then, emphasizing each word separately:

'For my part, I've no regret; I've done my duty. Never mind—it was all your fault.'

'What!' exclaimed Frederic, fearing that Sénécal had guessed his secret.

Sénécal had not guessed, for he continued:

'I mean that, but for you, I might have done better for myself.'

Frederic felt a kind of remorse.

'What can I do for you now?'

Sénécal wanted some form of employment—a position.

'It's easy for you. You know so many people, including Monsieur Dambreuse, according to what Deslauriers told me.'

Frederic was not pleased by this reminder of Deslauriers. And he did not care to go back to the Dambreuses' house, after the encounter at the Champ de Mars.

The democrat took this refusal stoically, and, after a moment's silence, he said:

'I'm certain that the girl from Bordeaux is responsible for all this, and so is your Madame Arnoux.'

The word 'your' destroyed the last vestige of goodwill that Frederic felt for him. However, as a gesture of courtesy, he reached for the key of his desk.

Sénécal forestalled him.

'No, thank you!'

Then, forgetting his troubles, he discussed national affairs, the decorations so lavishly bestowed on the king's birthday, a change in the Cabinet, contemporary scandals, such as the cases of Drouillard[1] and Bénier,[2] and he denounced the middle classes and predicted a revolution.

A Japanese kris hanging on the wall caught his eye. He picked it up, tried the haft, then threw it down on the sofa with a look of disgust.

'Well, good-bye! I've got to go to Notre-Dame de Lorette.'

'What on earth for?'

'They're holding the annual memorial service for Godefroy de Cavaignac[3] to-day. There's a man who died in harness! But all is not yet over. . . . Who knows?'

And Sénécal, in a gallant gesture, held out his hand.

'Perhaps we shall never meet again. Good-bye!'

The double repetition of his farewell, the frown with which he gazed at the dagger, and, in particular, his look of solemn resignation, made Frederic thoughtful; but he soon forgot all about it.

The same week his lawyer at Le Havre sent him the price of his farm—a hundred and seventy-four thousand francs. He divided it into two parts; one he put on deposit at the bank, while he took the other to a stockbroker, to gamble with on the Bourse.

He dined at fashionable restaurants, visited the theatres, and tried to amuse himself. Then he received a letter from Hussonnet, describing in a light-hearted vein how Rosanette had dismissed Cisy the day after the races. Frederic was glad to hear it, and did not stop to wonder why Hussonnet should be telling him about this adventure.

It so chanced that he ran into Cisy three days later. The young nobleman showed a bold front, and even asked him to dinner on the following Wednesday.

On the morning of that day Frederic received a sheriff's notice, by which M. Charles-Jean-Baptiste Oudry informed him that, in accordance with the judgment of the court, he had become the purchaser of a property situated at Belleville and belonging to M. Jacques Arnoux, and that he was ready to pay the price of the sale, which amounted to two hundred and twenty-three thousand francs. But by the same instrument the fact was established that the sum of the mortgages taken out on the building exceeded the purchase price, so that Frederic's claim was completely valueless.

The whole trouble arose from the failure to renew the registration of a mortgage at the right time. Arnoux had undertaken to perform this task, and had then forgotten about it. Frederic was furious with him, but his anger soon passed off.

'Well, and what of it? If it's going to help him, so much the better! It won't kill me. I won't think about it.'

But, in shifting the papers on his table, he came across Hussonnet's letter and noticed a postscript which he had not observed the first time. He asked for five thousand francs—no more—to start his newspaper.

'Oh, that fellow annoys me!'

And he refused him bluntly in a curt note. After that, he got dressed to go to the Maison d'Or.

Cisy introduced his guests, beginning with the most respectable, a bulky gentleman with white hair.

'My godfather—the Marquis Gilbert des Aulnays. Monsieur Anselme de Forchambeaux,' he continued. This was a slim, baldish young man with fair hair. Then he pointed to a man of about forty of unpretentious aspect.

'My cousin, Joseph Boffreu; and my former tutor, Monsieur Vezou.' This character looked like a mixture of a seminarist and a carter; he had large whiskers and a long frock coat fastened at the bottom by a single button, so that he appeared to be wearing a shawl across his chest.

Cisy was expecting another guest, the Baron de Comaing, 'who may be coming, but not for certain.' He left the room every minute and seemed uneasy; at length, at eight o'clock, they passed into a superbly illuminated hall, which was too large for the number of guests. Cisy had chosen it on purpose, out of ostentation.

A silver-gilt centre-piece, loaded with flowers and fruit, took up the middle of the table, which was covered with silver platters, after the old French fashion, and surrounded by sweetmeat dishes full of salty and seasoned titbits; at regular intervals stood pitchers of iced wine, perfumed with roses, while five glasses of varying height were drawn up in line beside each plate, together with countless ingenious table utensils, of which the precise purpose was uncertain. For the first course alone there was a sturgeon's head soaked in champagne, a York ham cooked in Tokay, thrushes *au gratin*, roast quail, a *vol-au-vent Béchamel*, a *sauté* of red-legged partridges, and, flanking all this, a garnishing of potatoes mixed with truffles. The room, which was hung with red damask, was lit by a chandelier and candelabra. Four footmen in black coats stood behind the morocco leather arm-chairs. This sight evoked cries of admiration from the guests, particularly from the tutor.

'Upon my word, our Amphitryon has been lavish to the point of folly. This is too magnificent!'

'That?" said the Viscomte de Cisy. 'Come now!'

After the first spoonful he remarked:

'Well, my dear des Aulnays, have you been to see *Père et Portier* at the Palais-Royal?'

'You know I haven't had time,' replied the marquis.

His mornings were taken up by a course in forestry, his evenings by the Cercle Agricole, and all his afternoons by researches in factories where agricultural implements were made. Spending three-quarters of the year at Saintonge, he took advantage of his visits to the capital to acquire knowledge; and his broad-brimmed hat, which lay on a console table, was full of pamphlets.

Then Cisy, noticing that M. Forchambeaux was refusing wine, said:

'Drink up, for heaven's sake! You're not showing much spirit for your last dinner as a bachelor.'

At these words the company all bowed and congratulated him.

'Need we doubt,' said the tutor, 'that the young lady is charming?'

'Of course she is!' exclaimed Cisy. 'All the same, he's wrong; marriage is so stupid.'

'You talk lightly, my friend,' replied M. des Aulnays, while his eyes filled with tears at the recollection of his dear departed. And Forchambeaux, chuckling, said several times in succession:

'You'll come to it yourself, you'll come to it.'

Cisy protested. He preferred to amuse himself, 'to be Regency.' He wanted to learn the *savate* and visit the low haunts of the Cité, like Prince Rodolphe in *Les Mystères de Paris*; he pulled a short clay pipe from his pocket, bullied the servants, drank to excess—and, to gain his guests' esteem, disparaged all the dishes. He even sent back the truffles, and the tutor, who had found them delicious, made the contemptible observation:

'They're not as good as your respected grandmother's *œufs à la neige.*'

Then he began a conversation with his neighbour the agriculturist, who mentioned, among the many advantages of country life, the fact that it enabled him to bring up his daughters with simple tastes. The tutor applauded his sentiments and flattered him; for he supposed that the marquis might have influence on Cisy, whose business adviser he secretly aspired to become.

Frederic had arrived full of resentment towards Cisy; his stupidity had disarmed him. But his gestures, his face, his whole appearance, reminded him of the dinner at the Café Anglais and irritated him more and more; and he was glad to listen to the disrespectful remarks whispered by Cousin Joseph —an excellent fellow, who had not a penny, was fond of hunting, and worked on the Bourse. By way of a joke, Cisy called him 'shark' several times; then suddenly:

'Ah! The baron!'

There entered a young man of thirty. There was a trace of roughness in his expression: his carriage was athletic. He wore his hat over his ear and a flower in his buttonhole. He was the viscount's ideal. Cisy was enchanted at his arrival; and, inspired by his presence, he even attempted a pun, for he remarked, as a *coq de bruyère* [1] was being passed round:

'This is the best of La Bruyère's characters!'

Then he addressed a torrent of questions to M. de Comaing about people unknown to the company; then, as if he had had a sudden idea:

'Tell me! Did you remember me?'

The other shrugged his shoulders.

'You 're too young, my child! It can't be done.'

Cisy had asked him to put him up for his club.

The baron, it seemed, took pity on his wounded pride.

'Oh, I was forgetting. Congratulations on your bet, my dear fellow!'

'What bet?'

'The one you made at the races—that you 'd go home with the lady that night.'

Frederic felt as if he had been struck with a whip. He was immediately calmed by Cisy's crestfallen countenance.

In fact, Rosanette, by the following morning, was beginning to regret the affair. Then Arnoux, her first lover, her man, had come to see her. They had both made it clear to the viscount that he was 'not wanted,' and he had been unceremoniously turned out of the house.

He appeared not to hear. The baron continued: 'What 's happened to good old Rose? Are her legs as pretty as ever?' thus proving that he knew her intimately.

This revelation annoyed Frederic.

'There 's nothing to be ashamed of,' said the baron. 'She 's a good investment.'

Cisy clicked his tongue.

'Pooh! Not as good as all that!'

'Indeed?'

'Why, yes! To begin with, I don't personally see anything particular in her; and then one can pick up plenty more like her, because, after all, she 's for sale.'

'Not to everybody,' said Frederic sharply.

'He thinks he 's different from the others,' answered Cisy. 'What a joke!'

A ripple of laughter went round the table.

Frederic felt stifled by the beating of his heart. He swallowed two glasses of water, one after the other.

The baron had pleasant memories of Rosanette.

'Is she still with that man Arnoux?'

'I don't know,' said Cisy. 'I 've never met the gentleman.'

Nevertheless, he put forward the view that he was a sort of swindler.

'Wait a moment,' cried Frederic.

'But it 's a well-known fact! He 's even been sued.'

'It 's a lie!'

Frederic began to defend Arnoux. He guaranteed his honesty, ended by believing in it, and invented figures to prove it. The viscount, full of rancour, and drunk besides, stuck so obstinately to his point that Frederic said to him seriously:

'Are you trying to offend me, monsieur?'

And he looked at him, with his eyes smouldering like his cigar.

'Oh, not in the least! I'll even grant you that he's got one good thing to his name; his wife.'

'Do you know her?'

'Of course! Sophie Arnoux—why, every one knows about her!'

'Will you repeat that?'

Cisy, who had risen to his feet, stammered once more:

'Every one knows about her!'

'Be quiet! She's not like the women you associate with!'

'No—I've got better taste!'

Frederic hurled his plate at his face.

It crossed the table like a flash of lightning, overturned two bottles, destroyed a fruit dish, broke into three pieces against the table-centre, and struck the viscount in the stomach.

Everybody rose to hold Frederic back. He struggled, shouting, in a sort of frenzy. M. des Aulnays kept saying:

'Calm yourself! Come now, my dear boy!'

'This is awful,' the tutor kept exclaiming.

Forchambeaux, as green as the plums on the table, was trembling; Joseph was roaring with laughter; the waiters were wiping up the wine and picking up the broken glass and crockery; and the baron went and shut the window, for, in spite of the noise of the traffic, the uproar might have been heard in the street.

At the moment when the plate was thrown, every one had been talking at once; it was thus impossible to discover the exact cause of offence, whether it concerned Arnoux, Mme Arnoux, Rosanette, or someone else. The only thing beyond dispute was Frederic's unmitigated barbarity; and he positively refused to express the smallest regret for his conduct.

M. des Aulnays tried to pacify him; so did Cousin Joseph, the tutor, even Forchambeaux. Meanwhile, the baron comforted Cisy, who, yielding to a nervous weakness, had burst into tears; and they would have remained thus until morning if the baron, to conclude the matter, had not said:

'The viscount, sir, will send you his seconds to-morrow.'

'At what time?'

'At noon, if it suits you.'

'Admirably, sir.'

Once in the street, Frederic took a deep breath. For too long he had held his feelings in check. At last he had let himself go; and he felt a sort of overweening virility, an exuberance of inner strength which intoxicated him. He needed two seconds. The first he thought of was Regimbart; and he at once made his way towards a tavern in the rue Saint-Denis. The shutters were down; but there was a gleam from the fanlight over the door. It opened, and he went in, bending very low under the porch.

A tallow candle, on the edge of the counter, lit up the deserted room. The stools were all piled on the tables, with their legs in the air. The owner and his wife, with the waiter, were having supper in the corner by the kitchen; and Regimbart, with his hat on his head, was sharing their meal and getting in the way of the waiter, who was compelled to turn slightly to one side for each mouthful. Frederic gave him a brief account of the affair and demanded his help. At first the citizen made no reply; he rolled his eyes, appeared to reflect, walked several times up and down the room, and eventually said:

'Yes, certainly!'

And his face brightened in a murderous smile when he learned that their opponent was a nobleman.

'We shall give him his marching orders, don't you worry! First of all . . . with your sword . . .'

'But perhaps,' objected Frederic, 'I'm not entitled . . .'

'I tell you, you must choose swords,' said the citizen roughly. 'Do you know how to shoot?'

'A little.'

'Oh, a little! That's what they all say. And they've all got this passion for fencing. As though the fencing schools were any use! Listen to me; keep your distance, guard, enclose yourself in circles, and give ground, give ground! It's perfectly fair. Wear him out! Then thrust straight over his guard. And, above all, no tricks, no finessing. No! Just straightforward lunges—one, two, and disengage! Here, do you see? You turn your wrist as if you were opening a lock. Père Vauthier, give me your stick! Ah, this'll do!'

He seized the wand which was used for lighting the gas, curved his left arm, bent his right, and began lunging against the partition. He stamped his feet, and in his excitement pretended to meet with difficulties. All the time he exclaimed 'Do you follow? Do you follow?' while his shadow, enormously enlarged, was thrown upon the wall, and his hat seemed to touch the ceiling. From time to time the proprietor said: 'Bravo! Excellent!' His wife, in spite of her anxiety, was equally impressed; and Théodore, an old soldier, was rooted to his seat in admiration, for he happened to be a fervent devotee of M. Regimbart.

Early the next morning Frederic hurried to Dussardier's shop. He passed through a series of rooms filled with stuffs arranged on shelves or stretched across tables; here and there shawls were displayed on wooden stands shaped like mushrooms. He caught sight of Dussardier standing at a desk, surrounded by ledgers, in a sort of cage with bars. The good fellow immediately left his work.

The seconds arrived at noon. Frederic thought it good form not to be present at the interview.

The baron and Joseph declared that they would be satisfied with the barest apology. But Regimbart, on principle, never gave way; besides, he meant to defend Arnoux's honour, for Frederic had spoken of nothing else. He therefore demanded that the viscount should apologize. This presumptuous claim disgusted M. de Comaing. The citizen refused to withdraw. Conciliation being thus impossible, the duel would take place.

Further difficulties arose; for Cisy, who had received the affront, was legally entitled to the choice of weapons. But Regimbart maintained that by sending the challenge he automatically became the affronting party. His seconds protested that no affront could be more brutal than a blow. The citizen quibbled, on the ground that there was a distinction between a blow from the hand and a blow from a plate. Eventually they decided to refer the question to the military; and the four seconds set out, to consult the officers at the nearest barracks.

They stopped at the barracks on the quai d'Orsay. M. de Comaing accosted two captains and explained the dispute to them.

The captains did not understand a word of the story, which was complicated by a running commentary from the citizen. In short, they advised the gentlemen to draw up a statement; after that they would give their decision. So the party moved to a café; and, for the sake of discretion, they went so far as to describe Cisy as H. and Frederic as K.

Then they went back to the barracks. The officers had gone

out. Reappearing, they declared that the choice of weapons clearly belonged to Monsieur H. They all went back to Cisy's house. Regimbart and Dussardier remained in the street.

On hearing the result Cisy was so seriously perturbed that he had it repeated to him several times; and, when M. de Comaing told him of Regimbart's demands, he murmured: 'All the same . . .' being inwardly inclined to give in to them. Then he sank into an arm-chair and declared that he would not fight.

'Eh? What?' said the baron.

Then Cisy released an incoherent flow of words. He wanted to fight at point-blank range, or with blunderbusses, or a single pistol.

'Or we could put arsenic in a glass, and draw lots for it. It's sometimes done; I've read about it.'

The baron, who was not over-tolerant by nature, addressed him roughly.

'These gentlemen are waiting for your answer. This is positively indecent. Now, what do you choose? Swords?'

The viscount signified yes with a movement of his head; and the meeting was fixed for the following day, at the Porte Maillot, at seven o'clock precisely.

Dussardier had to return to his business, so Regimbart went to tell Frederic.

He had been left without news all day; his impatience had become unbearable.

'So much the better,' he exclaimed.

The citizen was satisfied with his bearing.

'Would you believe it? They wanted us to apologize. One word would have satisfied them. But I sent them packing! I was right, wasn't I?'

'Oh, yes,' said Frederic, while reflecting that he might have done better to choose a different second.

Then, when he was alone, he said to himself several times, aloud:

'I'm going to fight a duel! Well, I'm going to fight a duel! It's funny, isn't it?'

Walking up and down his room he passed his mirror and noticed that he was pale.

'Am I afraid?'

And a terrible agony gripped him at the thought that he might show fear on the duelling ground.

'But supposing I were killed? My father died in the same way. Yes, I shall be killed.'

Suddenly he saw his mother, in a black dress; and a stream of confused images flowed through his mind. His own cowardice infuriated him. He was seized with a fit of reckless courage, a lust for slaughter. He could have faced an army. When this wild mood had left him he realized, to his joy, that he was unshakable. To distract his mind he went to the Opéra, where they were giving a ballet. He listened to the music, quizzed the dancers, and drank punch in the interval. But when he returned home and saw his study and his furniture, perhaps for the last time, he felt a momentary weakness.

He went down into his garden. The stars were shining; he gazed at them. The idea of fighting a duel for a woman magnified and uplifted him in his own eyes. Then he went quietly to bed.

It was far otherwise with Cisy. After the baron's departure Joseph had been trying to keep up his courage, and, as the viscount was not impressed, he had remarked:

'Of course, if you 'd rather drop the whole thing, my friend, I could go and tell them.'

Cisy dared not reply 'By all means,' but he was annoyed with his cousin for not doing him this service without mentioning it.

He hoped that Frederic would die of apoplexy during the night, or that a revolution would break out, and there would be so many barricades in the streets next day that all the approaches to the Bois de Boulogne would be blocked; or that some accident might keep one of the seconds away, for without seconds the duel could not take place. He wanted to escape by an express train, in any direction. He was sorry that he had not studied medicine, so that he could drink something which, without actually endangering his life, would make him look as if he were dead. He even went so far as to wish to be seriously ill.

In his need for advice and assistance, he sent for M. des Aulnays. This good man had gone back to Saintonge, on receiving a message that one of his daughters was unwell. Cisy thought this a bad omen. Luckily M. Vezou, his tutor, came to see him. Then he opened his heart.

'What 's to be done? For heaven's sake, what 's to be done?'

'If I were you, Monsieur le Comte, I should hire a meat porter to give him a thrashing.'

'He 'd be bound to know who was behind it,' replied Cisy.

From time to time he uttered a groan, then:

'But has one any right to fight a duel?'

'It 's a relic of barbarism—that 's all!'

To please his pupil, the tutor invited himself to dinner. Cisy ate nothing, and, after the meal, felt he needed a short walk.

As they passed a church, he said:

'Shall we go in for a moment . . . just to look round?'

M. Vezou asked nothing better, and even offered him some holy water.

It was the month of the Virgin Mary; the altar was covered with flowers; voices sang; the organ pealed. But he could not pray, for the pomp of religion made him think of funerals; he seemed to hear the distant strains of the *De profundis.*

'Let's go! I'm not feeling well.'

They spent the whole night playing cards. The viscount forced himself to lose, in order to propitiate fortune—an idea of which M. Vezou took advantage. Cisy, exhausted, let his head sink on to the card table and fell into a sleep full of unpleasant dreams.

However, if courage consists in the will to overcome one's weakness, the viscount was courageous. At the sight of his seconds coming to fetch him, he braced himself with all his strength, for his vanity told him that a withdrawal would be his ruin. M. de Comaing congratulated him on his blooming appearance.

But, once started, the movement of the cab and the heat of the morning sun took away his strength. His energy subsided. He no longer noticed where they were.

The baron amused himself by adding to his terror and talking to him of the 'corpse' and how they would bring it back to town in secret. Joseph backed him up; both of them considered the affair ridiculous and were convinced it would be settled amicably.

Cisy's head was sunk on his breast; he raised it slowly and remarked that they had not brought a doctor.

'It's unnecessary,' said the baron.

'Then there's no danger?'

'Let us hope not,' replied Joseph, in a grave voice.

And no one in the carriage said another word.

At ten past seven they reached the Porte Maillot. Frederic and his seconds were there; all three were dressed in black. Instead of a tie, Regimbart wore a horsehair collar, like a soldier; and he carried a kind of long violin case, specially designed for adventures of this kind. A frigid greeting was exchanged. Then, taking the route de Madrid, they plunged into the Bois de Boulogne, in order to find a suitable spot.

Regimbart said to Frederic, who was walking between him and Dussardier:

'Well, you're scared—and what are we going to do about it? If you want anything, don't be ashamed to say so. I know all about it. Fear is natural to man.'

Then in a low voice:

'Don't smoke—it's lowering!'

Frederic threw away his cigar, which was bothering him, and walked on with a firm step. The viscount followed behind, leaning on the arms of his two seconds.

They encountered occasional passers-by. The sky was blue; now and then the scuttling of rabbits could be heard. At the corner of a pathway a woman with a kerchief on her head was talking to a man in a blouse, and, in the grand avenue, grooms in linen coats were exercising horses. Cisy recalled those happy days, when, mounted on his chestnut, with his monocle in his eye, he used to canter up to carriage doors; these memories intensified his anguish; an unbearable thirst parched his throat; the buzzing of the flies blended with the throbbing of his pulses; his feet sank into the sand; he felt as though he had been walking since the beginning of time.

The seconds, without pausing, examined both sides of the road. They debated whether to go to the Croix Catelan, or to stop under the walls of the Bagatelle. At length they turned to the right, and halted in an irregular clearing, among pine-trees.

The place was chosen so as to divide fairly the advantages of the ground. They marked the points where the two adversaries were to stand. Then Regimbart opened his box. It was lined with red leather and contained four exquisite swords, with grooved blades and chased filigree hilts. A ray of sunlight, passing through the leaves, fell upon them, and to Cisy they seemed to glitter like silver vipers in a pool of blood.

The citizen demonstrated that they were of equal length—and he took the third sword himself, so as to separate the combatants in case of need. M. de Comaing held a stick. There was a silence. They looked at each other. Fear or cruelty could be read on every face.

Frederic had removed his coat and waistcoat; Joseph helped Cisy to do the same. When his cravat was taken off he was seen to be wearing a holy medal round his neck. This raised a pitying smile from Regimbart.

Then M. de Comaing (in order to allow Frederic a further moment's reflection) began to raise points of punctilio. He demanded the right to wear a glove, to seize his opponent's sword with his left hand; Regimbart, who was in a hurry, made no objection. At length the baron turned to Frederic.

'It all depends on you, sir. There's nothing dishonourable in acknowledging one's faults.'

Dussardier made a gesture of approval. The citizen was indignant.

'Do you imagine we've come out here to waste our time? On guard!'

The combatants faced each other, with their seconds on each side. He shouted the signal:

'Go!'

Cisy turned terribly pale. The end of his blade quivered like a whip. His head tilted backwards, his arms spread out, and he fell on his back in a faint. Joseph picked him up, held a bottle of smelling-salts to his nose, and shook him sharply. The viscount reopened his eyes, then suddenly leaped on his sword like a madman. Frederic had retained his; and he waited for him, with his guard high and his eyes glaring.

'Stop, stop!' cried a voice from the road, accompanied by the sound of a galloping horse; and the hood of a carriage broke through the branches. A man was leaning out, waving a handkerchief, and shouting continuously: 'Stop, stop!'

M. de Comaing, assuming that the police had intervened, raised his stick.

'Enough! The viscount's bleeding!'

'Me?' said Cisy.

He had, in fact, grazed the thumb of his left hand when he collapsed.

'But that was in falling,' protested the citizen.

The baron pretended not to hear.

Arnoux had leaped out of the carriage.

'I've come too late! No! God be praised!'

He clasped Frederic in his arms, felt him all over, and covered his face with kisses.

'I know your reasons; you wanted to defend your old friend. That was splendid of you—splendid! I shall never forget it! How good you are! Oh, my dear boy!'

He gazed at him and began to cry, chuckling with happiness at the same time.

The baron turned to Joseph.

'I think we're out of place at this little family party. It's all over, isn't it, gentlemen? Viscount, put your arm in a sling; here, take my silk handkerchief.'

Then, with a lordly gesture:

'Come now! No hard feelings! That's your duty.'

The two combatants shook hands gingerly. The viscount, M. de Comaing, and Joseph disappeared in one direction, and Frederic went off in the other, with his friends.

The Restaurant de Madrid being near by, Arnoux suggested going there for a glass of beer.

'Or we could have breakfast,' said Regimbart. But as Dussardier had little time to spare, they restricted themselves to drinking in the garden. They were all feeling that blissful satisfaction that is produced by a happy ending. The citizen, however, was annoyed at the interruption of the duel at the critical moment.

Arnoux had heard of it from a friend of Regimbart's called Compain; and in a burst of emotion he had hurried up to stop it, being, moreover, under the impression that he was the cause of the quarrel. He begged Frederic to tell him the story in detail. Frederic, touched by this proof of Arnoux's affection, was reluctant to add to his illusions.

'Please, please, don't let's talk about it!'

Arnoux thought this reticence very chivalrous. Then, with his usual volatility, he passed on to another subject.

'What news, citizen?'

And they began to talk about bills and maturities. For greater convenience, they went and whispered apart at another table.

Frederic made out the words: 'You'll sign for me.' 'Yes, but you must understand that on your side . . .' 'I got it through for three hundred.' 'Not a bad commission, by Jove!' In fact, it was clear that Arnoux had a somewhat unorthodox business association with the citizen.

Frederic thought of reminding him of his fifteen thousand francs. But his recent intervention forbade even the mildest reproaches. Besides, he felt tired. The place was not suitable. He put it off to another day.

Arnoux, seated in the shade of a privet hedge, was smoking and smiling. He raised his eyes towards the doors of the private rooms, all of which opened on to the garden, and said that he had often come there in the old days.

'And not unaccompanied, I should think,' said the citizen.

'Of course not!'

'What a rogue you are! And a married man, too!'

'Well, and what about you?' said Arnoux. And, with an indulgent smile he added:

'I'm convinced that that rascal has got a room somewhere, where he entertains the girls.'

By merely raising his eyebrows, the citizen confessed that it was true. Then the two men compared their tastes: Arnoux's preference now was for youth, particularly for working girls. Regimbart could not bear affectation and favoured the unsentimental type. The conclusion put forward by Arnoux was that women were not to be taken seriously.

'Yet he loves his wife,' thought Frederic, on his way home; and he decided that Arnoux was dishonest. He bore him a grudge over this duel, as though it had really been for him that he had just risked his life.

But he was grateful to Dussardier for his devotion; and, on his suggestion, the shop assistant soon came to visit him every day.

Frederic lent him books: Thiers, Dulaure, Barante, Lamartine's *Les Girondins*. The good fellow listened to him with deep attention and accepted his opinions as if he were a master.

One evening he arrived in a panic.

That morning a man running at full speed had knocked into him on the boulevard; recognizing him as a friend of Sénécal's, he had said to him:

'He's just been arrested! I'm running for it!'

It was perfectly true. Dussardier had spent the day in inquiries. Sénécal was under lock and key, charged with a grave political crime.

Born at Lyons, the son of a builder's foreman, he had received his education from an old disciple of Chalier. On his arrival in Paris, he had become a member of the Société des Familles;[1] his way of life was known; he was watched by the police. He had fought in the rising of May 1839; after that time he had lain low; but he had grown more and more fanatical, was a great admirer of Alibaud,[2] and confused his own grievances against society with those of the people against the monarchy. Each morning he awoke hoping for a revolution which would alter the world in a fortnight or a month. At last, disgusted by his colleagues' half-heartedness, exasperated by the obstructions placed in the way of his dreams, and despairing of his country, he had joined the incendiary bomb conspiracy as a chemist; and he had been arrested while carrying gunpowder for an attempt at Montmartre, which was to be a supreme effort to establish the republic.

The republic was no less dear to Dussardier, for, to his mind, it signified universal emancipation and happiness. One day, at the age of fifteen, he had seen, in the rue Transnonain, opposite a grocer's shop, soldiers with bayonets red with blood, and human hair sticking to their rifle butts. From that day he had abhorred the Government as being the very incarnation of injustice. He tended to confuse policemen with murderers; a police spy was, in his eyes, as bad as a parricide. Ingenuously, he attributed all the evil on earth to authority, which he hated with an essential, permanent hatred, that possessed his soul and refined his sensibility. He had been dazzled by Sénécal's rhetoric. However guilty he might be, however loathsome his attempt, it did not matter! The moment he became the victim of arbitrary power, it was their duty to help him.

'The peers are bound to condemn him! Then he 'll be taken away in a prison van like a convict and he 'll be shut up at Mont-Saint-Michel, where the Government sees that the prisoners die! Austen went mad! Steuben killed himself! When they put Barbès in a dungeon they dragged him by his legs and his hair! They trampled on his body and his head rebounded against every step on the staircase! What an outrage! What monsters!'

Tears of anger choked him, and he strode about the room as if in the grip of some terrible pain.

'All the same, we must do something. I don't know what. Supposing we try to rescue him? When they 're taking him to the Luxembourg, we could throw ourselves on the escort in the corridor. A dozen resolute men can achieve anything.'

He had so much fire in his eyes that Frederic trembled.

Sénécal seemed a greater man than he had thought him. He remembered his sufferings, his life of self-denial; without sharing Dussardier's enthusiasm for him he felt, nevertheless, the admiration which is inspired by any man who sacrifices himself for an idea; he told himself that Sénécal would not be where he was now, if he had helped him; and the two friends racked their brains to think of some plan to save him.

It was impossible for them to reach him.

Frederic searched the newspapers to find out his fate, and for three weeks haunted the public reading rooms.

One day several numbers of *The Man about Town* fell into his hands. The leading article was invariably devoted to destroying the reputation of some distinguished figure. Then followed notes and gossip of society. After that came passages ridiculing the Odéon, Carpentras, fish-breeding, and any prisoners who had been condemned to death. The sinking of a steamboat furnished humorous matter for a whole year. The third column contained a chronicle of the arts, which, in the form of anecdote or advice, provided advertisements for tailors, combined with descriptions of evening parties, announcements of sales, and summaries of books. The author dealt in precisely the same style with a volume of verse or a pair of boots. The only serious section was devoted to criticism of the smaller theatres, in which two or three managers were savagely attacked; and the interests of art were invoked in connection with the scenery at the Funambules or the heroine at the Délassements.

Frederic was about to throw them all aside when an article entitled 'Three Roosters and One Pullet' met his eye. It was the story of his duel, narrated in a broadly humorous style. He recognized himself without difficulty, for he was designated by a pun which recurred more than once, as 'a young man from the college of Sens, who has no sens-e.' He was even represented as a wretched provincial, an obscure simpleton, trying to rub shoulders with the aristocracy. The viscount was given the hero's role—first, at the supper party, into which he forced his way, then over the bet, when he went off with the lady, and finally on the duelling ground, where he carried himself like a nobleman. Frederic's courage was not exactly denied, but the impression was given that an intermediary—the 'protector' himself—had arrived in the nick of time. The whole was concluded by this phrase, which seemed full of innuendo:

'Whence their affection? There's a problem; and as Basilio says, who the devil is deceiving who?'

There was not the least doubt that this was Hussonnet's revenge on Frederic for refusing the five thousand francs.

What was to be done? If he asked for an explanation, the journalist would protest his innocence, and he could gain nothing. The best thing to do was to swallow the insult in silence. After all, nobody read *The Man about Town*.

As he left the reading room, he noticed a crowd in front of a picture dealer's shop. They were looking at a woman's portrait, which bore the following legend, written at the bottom in black letters:

'Mlle Rose-Annette Bron, the property of M. Frederic Moreau, of Nogent.'

It was indeed she, or something like her. She was viewed front face with her bosom bare, her hair hanging down, and a red velvet purse in her hands. Behind, a peacock thrust its beak over her shoulder, and covered the wall with its great fan-like tail.

Pellerin had arranged this exhibition in order to force Frederic to pay up, for he was convinced that he was famous and that all Paris, rising to his defence, would take up his grievance.

Was it a conspiracy? Had the painter and the journalist prepared their bombshells together?

His duel had been of no help to him. He was becoming ridiculous; every one was laughing at him.

Three days later, at the end of June, there was a rise of fifteen francs in Nord railway shares. He had bought two thousand the month before and he thus found that he had made thirty thousand francs. This favourable turn of fortune restored his confidence. He told himself that he depended on no one, and that all his difficulties were due to his timidity and lack of resolution. He ought to have been brutal with Rosanette from the beginning. He should have refused Hussonnet on the first day, nor should he have compromised himself with Pellerin; and, to demonstrate his freedom from embarrassment, he went to Mme Dambreuse's house, to attend one of the regular evening parties.

Martinon arrived at the same time as he did. He turned round in the hall.

'What—*you* here?' he said, looking surprised and even put out at the sight of him.

'Why not?'

And, wondering what this sort of greeting could signify, Frederic made his way to the drawing-room.

In spite of the lamps that stood in the corners, the light was dim; for the three windows were wide open, and formed three great rectangles of black shadow side by side. The spaces under the pictures were occupied by flower stands at least six feet high; and in the distance a silver tea pot, with a samovar, was reflected in a mirror. A discreet murmur of voices could be heard, and the sound of evening shoes creaking on the carpet.

A few black coats met his eye, in front of a round table lit by a large shaded lamp; beyond, were seven or eight women in summer dresses, and, a little further away, Mme Dambreuse in a rocking-chair. Her lilac taffeta dress had slashed sleeves, lined with puffed muslin; the soft shade of the stuff harmonized with the colour of her hair; and she leaned back a little, with the tip of her foot on a cushion, as calm as some delicate work of art, or a flower of exquisite cultivation.

M. Dambreuse and an old man with white hair were walking up and down the drawing-room. Some of the men had seated themselves on the settees to talk; others, standing up, formed a circle in the centre of the room.

They talked about votes, amendments, and counter-amendments, about M. Grandin's speech and M. Benoist's reply. Unquestionably the Third Party was going too far! The Left Centre should be a little more mindful of their origin! The minister had been severely attacked. However, it was reassuring to reflect that no one saw any possible successor to him. In short, the situation was exactly similar to that of 1834.

As all this bored Frederic, he moved over towards the women. Martinon was standing near them, with his hat under his arm, and his face in half profile. He was so perfectly in place that he looked like a piece of Sèvres porcelain. He picked up a *Revue des Deux Mondes*, which was lying on the table, between an *Imitation of Christ* and an *Almanach de Gotha*, criticized a famous poet in a loud voice, said that he was going to lectures on St Francis, complained of his larynx, and from time to time swallowed a lozenge; in the intervals he talked about music and made light conversation. Mlle Cécile, M. Dambreuse's niece, who was embroidering a pair of cuffs, gazed up at him with her pale blue eyes; Miss John, the flat-nosed governess, had dropped her tapestry work to look at him; and both seemed to be exclaiming inwardly: 'How handsome he is!'

Mme Dambreuse turned towards him.

'Give me my fan; it's on the table over there. No, not that one, the other!'

She rose; and, as he came back, they met in the middle of the room; she spoke a few rapid words to him, in reproach, as it seemed, to judge from his changed expression. Martinon tried to smile, then went and joined the conclave of serious men. Mme Dambreuse sat down again, and, leaning on the arm of her chair, said to Frederic:

'I saw someone the day before yesterday who spoke to me about you—Monsieur de Cisy; you know him, don't you?'

'Yes—a little.'

Suddenly Mme Dambreuse exclaimed:

'Oh, duchess! How delightful!'

And she went over to the door, to meet a little old lady in a brown taffeta dress and a lace bonnet with long ribbons. She was the daughter of a fellow exile of the Comte d'Artois and the widow of a marshal of the Empire, who had been created peer of France in 1830. She was attached as much to the old court as to the new, and her influence was considerable. The men who were standing and talking drew aside, then resumed their conversation.

The subject now was pauperism, the accounts of which, according to these gentlemen, were greatly exaggerated.

'Nevertheless,' protested Martinon, 'we must admit that poverty exists. But the remedy lies in the hands neither of science nor of authority. The question is purely individual.

When the lower classes are willing to discard their vices, they will free themselves from their wants. If the people were more moral, they would be less poor!'

According to M. Dambreuse, no advance could be made without a superfluity of capital. So the only possible plan was to entrust, 'as was suggested, for that matter, by the followers of Saint-Simon (yes, there was some good in them! Give everyone his due!), to entrust, I say, the cause of progress to those who can increase the national wealth.' Imperceptibly the talk turned to the great industrial enterprises, railways, and coal-mining. And M. Dambreuse, turning to Frederic, said to him in a low voice:

'You didn't come for that business of ours.'

Frederic said he had been ill; then, feeling that the excuse was too lame, added:

'Besides, I needed my money.'

'To buy a carriage?' said Mme Dambreuse, who was passing near him, with a cup of tea in her hand. She gazed at him for a moment, turning her head slightly on her shoulder.

She thought he was Rosanette's lover; the allusion was obvious. Frederic was under the impression that all the ladies were looking at him from a distance and whispering together. To find out what they were thinking, he moved over towards them once more.

On the other side of the table, Martinon, sitting beside Mlle Cécile, was turning the leaves of an album. It contained litho-graphs of Spanish costumes. He read the descriptions aloud: 'Woman of Seville' — 'Gardener of Valencia' — 'Andalusian Picador'; once he went on reading down to the bottom of the page, adding, in the same breath:

'Jacques Arnoux, publisher. . . . A friend of yours, isn't he?'

'That 's so,' said Frederic, offended by his tone.

Mme Dambreuse remarked:

'Why, didn't you come here one morning? . . . wasn't it about a house? Yes, a house belonging to his wife?'

This meant: 'She is your mistress.'

He blushed scarlet; and M. Dambreuse, who came up at the same moment, added:

'You seem to be very interested in them.'

These last words succeeded in putting Frederic completely out of countenance. He was just reflecting that his obvious embarrassment must confirm their suspicions, when M. Dambreuse came close to him and said in a grave tone:

'You don't do business together, I trust?'

He shook his head repeatedly. He did not understand the banker's intention, which was to give him a warning.

He wanted to go. He was held back by fear of seeming a coward. A servant was clearing the tea cups away: Mme Dambreuse was talking to a diplomat in a blue coat; two girls, their heads close together, were showing each other a ring; the others, seated in arm-chairs in a half-circle, moved their pale faces, fringed with dark or fair hair, gently from side to side; no one paid any attention to him. Frederic turned on his heel; and by a series of long zigzags had almost gained the door, when he noticed, on a side table, lying between a Chinese vase and the panelling, a folded newspaper. He pulled it out a little, and read the words: *The Man about Town*.

Who had brought it? Cisy! It could be no one else. What did it matter, anyway? They would believe the article; perhaps they all believed it already. Why this hostility? An ironic silence surrounded him. He felt as if he were lost in a desert. But Martinon's voice was raised:

'Talking of Arnoux, I've seen the name of one of his employees, Sénécal, in the list of suspects in the incendiary bomb plot. Is he our Sénécal?'

'The same,' said Frederic.

Martinon repeated at the top of his voice:

'What? Our Sénécal! Our Sénécal!'

At once he was questioned about the plot; being attached to the public prosecutor's office he should have access to information.

He confessed that he had none. As a matter of fact, he scarcely knew the person in question, having seen him only two or three times; to be brief, he considered him an unpleasant rascal. Frederic exclaimed in indignation:

'Not at all! He's a very respectable fellow!'

'Nevertheless, sir,' said a landowner, 'one is scarcely respectable when taking part in a plot!'

Most of the men present had served at least four Governments; and they would have sold France, or the whole human race, to safeguard their fortune, to spare themselves a moment's uneasiness or embarrassment, or else out of sheer servility, through their instinctive reverence for brute strength. They all declared that political crimes were unpardonable. It would be better to forgive the crimes arising from want! And they did not fail to quote the everlasting example of the father of the family, who steals the everlasting piece of bread from the everlasting baker.

A company director even exclaimed:

'For my part, sir, I should denounce my own brother if I found out that he was plotting!'

Frederic invoked the right of resistance; and, recalling some phrases that Deslauriers had used to him, he cited Desolmes, Blackstone, the English Bill of Rights, and Article 2 of the Constitution of 1791. It was in virtue of this right that Napoleon's downfall had been proclaimed; it had been reaffirmed in 1830 and inscribed at the head of the charter.

'Besides, when the sovereign fails to fulfil his contract, justice demands his overthrow.'

'But that's appalling!' exclaimed the wife of a prefect.

All the other women were silent, vaguely alarmed, as though they had heard the sound of bullets. Mme Dambreuse rocked in her chair and listened to him with a smile.

An industrialist, a former *carbonaro*,[1] tried to prove to him that the Orléans family were a splendid lot; no doubt, there were abuses . . .

'Well, what then?'

'But one shouldn't mention them, my dear sir! If you knew how much harm these Opposition complaints do to business!'

'What do I care about business?' said Frederic.

The corruption of these old men infuriated him, and, carried away by the courage that sometimes inspires the most timid, he attacked financiers, deputies, Government, and king, defended the Arabs, and said many foolish things. Some of the men encouraged him ironically, saying: 'Go on! Tell us more!' while others murmured: 'Heavens! What fanaticism!' At last he thought it proper to withdraw; and, as he was leaving, M. Dambreuse said to him in reference to the secretaryship:

'Nothing's settled yet! But you must hurry.'

And Mme Dambreuse said:

'We shall see you soon, shan't we?'

Frederic interpreted this farewell as a final mockery. He was determined never to return to their house, and to abandon this sort of society for ever. He thought that he had offended them, for he did not know what vast reserves of indifference the world possesses. The women, in particular, exasperated him. Not one had supported him, even with a glance. He bore them a grudge because he had failed to move them. As for Mme Dambreuse, he found in her a blend of languor and hardness which prevented him from labelling her definitely. Had she a lover? What lover? Was it the diplomat or someone else? Could it be Martinon? Impossible! Yet he felt a kind of jealousy towards him, and towards her an ill will which he could not explain.

Dussardier, who had arrived that evening as usual, was waiting for him. Frederic's heart was full; he vented his feelings, and his grievances, although vague and hard to understand, distressed the good shop assistant; he even complained of his loneliness. After a little hesitation, Dussardier suggested that they should visit Deslauriers.

On hearing the lawyer's name, Frederic felt an extreme desire to see him again. His mental isolation was complete, and Dussardier's company was insufficient. He told him to make what arrangements he liked.

Since their quarrel, Deslauriers had felt a gap in his life. He welcomed these friendly advances.

They embraced, and then began to talk on indifferent topics.

Deslauriers's guarded manner touched Frederic; and, as a sort of atonement, the following day he told him about his loss of fifteen thousand francs, without saying that these fifteen thousand francs were originally intended for him. Nevertheless, the lawyer had no doubts about it. The misadventure, which justified his prejudices against Arnoux, dispelled his ill-feeling completely, and he made no further mention of the old promise.

Deceived by his silence, Frederic thought he had forgotten it. Some days later he asked Deslauriers if there was any way of recovering his money.

They might dispute the earlier mortgages, or attack Arnoux for fraudulent misrepresentation, or take action against the wife, and sell up her house.

'No, no! Not against her!' cried Frederic.

And, yielding to Deslauriers's questioning, he admitted the truth. Deslauriers was convinced that he was keeping something back, no doubt from chivalrous motives. He was hurt by this lack of trust.

In other respects they were as closely attached as before, and they enjoyed each other's company so much that they began to find Dussardier's presence irksome. By pretending to have appointments they gradually succeeded in getting rid of him. There are some men whose only mission in life is to serve as

225

go-betweens; one crosses them like bridges, and passes beyond them.

Frederic concealed nothing from his old friend. He told him about the coal company, and M. Dambreuse's proposal. The lawyer became thoughtful.

'That's curious. They'd need someone pretty well up in law for that position.'

'But you'll be able to help me?' said Frederic.

'Why . . . yes . . . of course . . . by all means.'

The same week he showed him a letter from his mother.

Mme Moreau accused herself of having misjudged M. Roque, who had given a satisfactory explanation of his conduct. Then she spoke of his fortune, and the possibility of a marriage with Louise later on.

'Perhaps you might do worse,' said Deslauriers.

Frederic would not hear of it; besides, Roque was an old shark. According to the lawyer, that did not matter.

At the end of July an inexplicable slump occurred in Nord railway shares. Frederic had not sold his; and he lost sixty thousand francs at one blow. His income was perceptibly diminished. He must either reduce his expenditure, or take up a profession, or make a wealthy marriage.

Then Deslauriers spoke to him about Mlle Roque. There was no reason why he should not go and see for himself how things were. Frederic was rather tired; the country and his mother's house would restore his energy. He set off.

The sight of the streets of Nogent, through which he passed by moonlight, brought back old memories; and he felt the sort of anguish that is experienced by travellers after long journeys.

At his mother's house were all the usual visitors: M. Gamblin, M. Heudras, and M. Chambrion, the Lebrun family, 'the Auger girls'; and, in addition, there was old Roque, and, opposite Mme Moreau, at a card table, Mlle Louise. She was now a woman. She rose to her feet with a cry. There was general perturbation. She stood there motionless; the four silver candlesticks on the table intensified the pallor of her face. When she began to play again her hand was trembling. Frederic, whose pride was sick, was excessively flattered by these signs of emotion; he said to himself: 'You, at least, shall love me,' and, in revenge for the rebuffs he had suffered there, he began to play the Parisian and the social lion; he gave news of the theatres, told anecdotes culled from the gossip columns about society, and succeeded in dazzling his fellow townsmen.

The next day Mme Moreau dilated on Louise's virtues; then she enumerated the woods and farms which would be hers. M. Roque's fortune was considerable.

He had acquired it by investing money for M. Dambreuse; for he used to lend to people who could offer well-secured mortgages, which enabled him to ask for extras and commissions. Owing to his active supervision the capital was never in danger. Besides, old Roque never scrupled at a foreclosure; then he would buy back the mortgaged property at a low price, and M. Dambreuse, seeing his money thus repaid, thought his business admirably conducted.

But these extra-legal manœuvres compromised the banker with his agent. He could refuse him nothing. It was at M. Roque's request that he had welcomed Frederic so warmly.

As a matter of fact, old Roque nursed one ambition in his heart. He wanted his daughter to be a countess; and Frederic was the only young man he knew through whom he might achieve this without risking the happiness of his child.

Through the influence of M. Dambreuse, he would be granted his ancestor's title, for Mme Moreau was the daughter of a Comte de Fouvens, and was, moreover, related to the oldest families in Champagne—the Lavernades and the d'Étrignys. As regards the Moreau side, a Gothic inscription near the mills of Villeneuve-l'Archevêque mentioned one Jacob Moreau who had restored them in 1576; and the tomb of his son, who was master of the horse to Louis XIV, was to be seen in the chapel of Saint-Nicolas.

Such a pedigree fascinated M. Roque, who was the son of a former footman. If the count's coronet was not forthcoming, he would console himself with other things; for Frederic might succeed in becoming a deputy, when M. Dambreuse was elevated to the peerage; then he could help him in his business and could get him contracts and concessions. He liked the young man personally. In short, he wanted him for a son-in-law; the idea had attracted him for a long time, and its charms were constantly increasing.

He often went to church these days—and he had successfully tempted Mme Moreau with the title. However, she had refrained from giving a definite reply.

So, within a week, without any official engagement, Frederic was looked on as the future husband of Mlle Louise; and old Roque, who had few scruples, sometimes left them alone together.

CHAPTER V

DESLAURIERS had taken from Frederic's house a copy of the deed of subrogation and a power of attorney, correctly drawn up, giving him full authority. But when he had climbed his five flights and was seated in his leather arm-chair, alone, in his dreary study, the sight of the stamped paper nauseated him.

He was tired of it all—tired of cheap restaurants and omnibus rides, of his poverty and his struggles. He took up the papers; there were others beside them; they were the prospectus of the coal company with the list of mines and the details of their capacity. Frederic had left him all this in order to have his opinion on it.

An idea came to him; to go and see M. Dambreuse and ask for the secretaryship for himself. But obviously the position depended on the purchase of a certain number of shares. He realized the folly of all his plan and said to himself:

'Oh, no! That would be wrong.'

Then he racked his brains for a means of recovering the fifteen thousand francs. This sum was nothing to Frederic. But what a lever it would have been for him, if he had had it! And Deslauriers grew indignant because Frederic's fortune was large.

'The use he makes of it is pitiful. He thinks only of himself. Well, what do I care for his fifteen thousand francs?'

Why had he lent them? For love of Mme Arnoux? She was his mistress: Deslauriers was positive of it. 'There's another case where money's useful!' His mind was filled with hatred. Then he began to think of Frederic's appearance, which had always had an almost feminine fascination for him; and soon he came to admire him for a success of which he knew himself incapable.

However, was not the most important part of any enterprise the will to succeed? And since, given that, one could conquer every obstacle——

'Oh! It would be a joke . . .'

But he was ashamed of his treachery: and a minute later:

'Well; am I afraid?'

Mme Arnoux—because he had heard so much about her—-had

228

ended by making an extraordinary impression on his imagination. The long survival of this love worried him like a problem. He was irritated, too, by the slightly theatrical austerity of the affair. Besides, the 'society woman'—or what he imagined as such—was a figure that had always dazzled him, as the symbol, the personification of countless pleasures he had never known. In his poverty he desired luxury in its most obvious form.

'Supposing he's annoyed? Well, after all, it serves him right. He's treated me too badly for me to put myself out for him. I've no proof that she's his mistress. He's denied it. So I'm free!'

His desire persisted: he longed to make the attempt. It was a test of his powers which he was eager to try; so much so that one day, suddenly, he polished his boots himself, bought a pair of white gloves, and started off. He put himself in Frederic's place and was almost persuaded that he was he—by a peculiar mental twist, in which sympathy and vindictiveness, subservience and bravado were strangely mingled.

He had himself announced as 'Doctor Deslauriers.'

Mme Arnoux was surprised, as she had not sent for a doctor.

'Oh, I beg your pardon! I am a Doctor of Laws. I represent Monsieur Moreau.'

The name seemed to disturb her.

'So much the better!' thought Deslauriers. 'Since she wanted him she'll want me!' drawing encouragement from the popular notion that it is easier to supplant a lover than a husband.

He had had the pleasure of meeting her once at the law courts; he even mentioned the date. Mme Arnoux was astonished by his memory. He continued, in an ingratiating tone:

'Even then, you were . . . in difficulties . . . over business matters.' She made no reply; then it was true.

He began to talk about one thing and another, his rooms, the factory; then, observing some miniatures beside the mirror, he said:

'Ah! Family portraits, I suppose?'

He noticed one of an old woman, Mme Arnoux's mother.

'She looks a splendid person—a real southern type.'

It was pointed out that she came from Chartres.

'Chartres! A pretty town!'

He praised its cathedral and its pies; then, returning to the portrait, he found points of resemblance to Mme Arnoux, and paid her compliments, indirectly. This did not shock her. Emboldened, he said that he had known Arnoux for a long time.

'He's a good fellow—but he's always compromising himself. Now take this mortgage: one can't believe that such carelessness . . .'

'Yes! I know,' she said, shrugging her shoulders.

This involuntary evidence of her contempt encouraged Deslauriers to go on.

'Then the china clay affair—perhaps you don't know—it nearly turned out very badly, and even his reputation——'

A frown halted him.

Then, falling back on generalities, he pitied those unfortunate women whose husbands squander their money . . .

'But it's his, sir: I have nothing of my own.'

No matter! One never knew. . . . A man of experience might be of assistance. He offered his devoted service, extolled his own merits; and he looked her in the face, through his glistening spectacles.

A vague languor gripped her. Suddenly she said: 'To business, please!'

He displayed the documents.

'This is Frederic's power of attorney. If this instrument were placed in the hands of an officer of the court, who issued a writ, the rest would be easy; within twenty-four hours . . .' She remained impassive; he changed his tactics. 'For my part, I can't understand what induced him to reclaim this sum; for, after all, he doesn't need it.'

'What! Monsieur Moreau has been extremely kind!'

'Oh, I agree!'

And Deslauriers began singing his praises; and then started, quite gently, to disparage him, describing him as forgetful, selfish, and miserly.

'I thought he was your friend, sir.'

:That doesn't prevent me from seeing his faults. For instance, he's not very grateful for—how shall I put it?—the sympathy——'

Mme Arnoux was turning the leaves of the large portfolio. She interrupted him to ask the meaning of a word.

He leaned over her shoulder, so near her that he brushed her cheek. She blushed; this blush inflamed Deslauriers; he kissed her hand avidly.

'What are you doing, sir?'

And standing against the wall she kept him rooted to the spot, under the angry glance of her great black eyes.

'Listen to me! I love you!'

230

She burst out laughing: her laughter was shrill, desperate, terrible. Rage seized Deslauriers; he could have strangled her. He held himself back; and, with the expression of a victim begging for mercy:

'Oh, you are wrong! I wouldn't be like him . . .'

'Whom are you talking about?'

'Frederic!'

'Indeed! I'm not concerned about Monsieur Moreau, as I've already told you.'

'Oh, I'm sorry . . . I'm sorry . . .'

Then, in a biting voice, he drawled out the following words:

'I did actually think you were sufficiently interested in him to hear with pleasure . . .' She turned very pale. Deslauriers added:

'He's going to get married!'

'He!'

'In a month's time, at latest, to Mademoiselle Roque, the daughter of Monsieur Dambreuse's agent. He's actually gone to Nogent, for that and for nothing else.'

She put her hand to her heart, as if she had been struck a heavy blow: then all at once she pulled the bell. Deslauriers did not wait to be shown out. When she turned round, he had vanished.

Mme Arnoux felt stifled. She went to the window for air.

On the pavement, the other side of the road, a workman in shirt sleeves was nailing up a packing case. Cabs went by. She shut the window and sat down again. The tall houses opposite cut off the sun, and a cold light filled the room. Her children were out—nothing moved around her. She felt utterly deserted.

'He's going to marry! Is it possible?'

And she was seized with a fit of nervous trembling.

'Why am I trembling? Do I love him?'

Then suddenly:

'Yes, yes! I love him! . . . I love him!'

She felt as if she were sinking into a bottomless gulf. The clock struck three. She listened to the sound vibrating and dying away. And she remained sitting on the edge of her arm-chair, gazing in front of her and smiling still.

The same afternoon, at the same hour, Frederic and Louise were walking in M. Roque's garden at the end of the island. Old Catherine was watching them from a distance; they walked side by side; and Frederic was saying:

'Do you remember when I took you into the country?'

'How good you were to me,' she replied. 'You helped me to make mud pies, and filled my water can, and rocked me on the swing.'

'What's become of your dolls? They were all called after queens and countesses.'

'I've really no idea.'

'And your little dog, Nigger?'

'He got drowned—the poor darling!'

'And the *Don Quixote*, with the pictures we coloured?'

'I've still got it!'

He reminded her of the day of her first communion, and how charming she was at vespers, with her white veil and her tall candle, while the children all filed round the choir, and the bell tolled.

These memories had, apparently, little charm for Mlle Roque; she made no answer; and a minute later said:

'It was naughty of you not to write to me once, all the time you were away!'

Frederic pleaded pressure of work.

'What exactly do you do?'

He found the question embarrassing, then said that he was studying politics.

'Oh!'

And without inquiring further:

'That keeps you busy—but as for me! . . .'

Then she told him of the bleakness of her life, without the smallest pleasure, the least distraction. She wanted to ride.

'The priest says it's not proper for a young girl. How silly it is, being proper! They used to let me do whatever I liked: but now—nothing!'

'Still, your father loves you.'

'Yes; but . . .'

She uttered a sigh, which meant: 'That's not enough to make me happy.' Then there was a silence. They could hear nothing but the crunching of the sand under their feet, and the murmur of the weir. The Seine above Nogent is divided into two; and it was here that the stream which turned the water mills discharged its overflow, to rejoin the main current lower down. From the direction of the bridges, a sloping lawn could be seen on the right bank, overlooked by a white house; on the left, in the meadows, stretched a line of poplars, while the horizon opposite was bounded by a bend in the river. The water was as smooth as glass; and large insects skimmed its unruffled surface. Tufts of flags and rushes fringed the banks unevenly; all sorts of plants, springing up there, displayed their golden buds, or trailed their clusters of yellow blossom; others flaunted purple, spindle-shaped flowers, or thrust out scattered spikes of green.

Water lilies floated in an inlet; and a row of ancient willows, concealing spring traps, formed, on this side, the only protection of the garden.

In the middle of the island itself, four walls with a coping of slates enclosed the kitchen garden, with its square patches of newly dug earth. Rows of bell glasses glistened in the narrow melon bed; artichokes, beans, spinach, carrots, and tomatoes grew alternately, and, last of all, came the asparagus bed, which looked like a little forest of feathers.

Under the Directory all this ground had been what was known as a 'folly.' Since that time the trees had grown enormously. The arbours were choked with clematis, the paths covered with moss; everywhere brambles abounded. Crumbling fragments of statues lay under the weeds, and, walking there, one caught one's feet in old pieces of wire netting. Of the pavilion nothing remained but two rooms on the ground floor with some shreds of blue wall paper. In front of the building stretched an Italian pergola; its wooden trellis-work was held up by brick pillars and supported a vine.

They walked underneath it; here and there the sunshine filtered between the leaves, and Frederic, as he turned to talk to Louise, watched the shadows of the foliage on her face.

In the knot at the back of her red hair she had placed a pin with a sham emerald head, made of glass; and, in spite of her mourning (so artless was her bad taste), she wore straw slippers trimmed with pink satin—strange and vulgar objects, bought, no doubt, at some fair.

He noticed them and complimented her on them, ironically.

'Don't make fun of me!' she said.

Then she looked him all over, from his grey felt hat to his silk socks.

'How smart you are!'

After that she asked him to tell her the names of books to read. He mentioned several; and she said:

'What a lot you know!'

When quite small she had been the victim of one of those childish passions which unite the purity of a religion with the violence of an appetite. He had been her comrade, her brother, her master; he had stimulated her mind, made her heart beat, and, unknowing, had filled the depths of her being with a perpetual secret intoxication. Then he had left her at a tragic moment in her life. Her mother had just died. She scarcely distinguished one sorrow from the other. In his absence she had idealized him in memory; he came back wearing a sort of halo, and, without further thought, she gave herself up to the pleasure of looking at him.

For the first time in his life Frederic felt himself loved; and this new pleasure, which was little more than an agreeable sensation, made his heart swell suddenly, so that he stretched out his arms and threw back his head.

A heavy cloud was moving across the sky.

'It's going towards Paris,' said Louise. 'Wouldn't you like to follow it?'

'Me! Why?'

'Who knows?'

And, with a penetrating glance:

'Perhaps you've got some . . .' she searched for the word—'attachment there.'

'No, I've no attachment.'

'Are you sure?'

'Of course, mademoiselle, perfectly sure.'

In less than a year an extraordinary transformation had taken place in the young girl, which astonished Frederic. After a moment's silence, he added:

'We ought to call each other by our Christian names, as we used to. Will you?'

'No.'

'Why not?'

'Because——'

He insisted. She hung her head and answered.

'I don't dare.'

They were now at the end of the garden, on the Livon sandbank. Like a small boy, Frederic began to play ducks and drakes with pebbles. She ordered him to sit down. He obeyed; then, looking at the weir:

'It's like Niagara.'

He began to talk of distant countries and long journeys.

The idea of travelling fascinated her. She would be afraid of nothing—not even of storms or lions.

Sitting beside each other, they scooped up handfuls of sand,

and let it trickle through their fingers as they talked, while the warm wind from the plains wafted the scent of lavender to their nostrils, blended with the smell of tar from a boat moored behind the lock. The sun shone on the falling water, and they saw the green stones of the little wall over which the stream flowed as if through an ever-unrolling veil of silver gauze. At the foot, a long bar of foam leapt in rhythm, then broke into bubbling whirlpools, into a thousand eddying currents, and at last melted into a single limpid pool.

Louise murmured that she envied the way fishes lived.

'It must be so nice to glide about in the water and feel oneself being stroked all over.'

And she shivered, with a movement of voluptuous sensuality.

A voice shouted:

'Where are you?'

'Your maid's calling you,' said Frederic.

'All right! All right!'

Louise did not move.

'She'll be angry,' he went on.

'I don't care! And besides——'

Mlle Roque made a gesture indicating that she had her under her thumb.

However, she got up, then complained of headache. And, as they were passing a huge shed containing faggots:

'Supposing we went inside, under the *égaud*?'

He pretended not to understand this local expression, and even teased her about her accent. Gradually the corners of her mouth turned down, she bit her lips, then moved away to sulk.

Frederic rejoined her, and swore that he had not meant to hurt her; in fact, he was very fond of her.

'Is that true?' she exclaimed looking at him with a smile that lit up her freckled face.

Her utter frankness and the freshness of her youth were irresistible, and he went on:

'Why should I lie to you? You don't believe me, then?' And he put his left arm round her waist.

A cry, as soft as a dove's coo, sprang from her throat; her head fell back, she tottered; he held her up. He did not need to invoke his sense of honour; fear gripped him at the sight of this virgin offering herself to him. Gently he helped her to walk a few steps. His endearments ceased, he tried to speak only of trivial things, and he began talking about the society of Nogent.

Suddenly she pushed him from her, and, in a bitter tone:

'You 'll never have the courage to take me away!'

He remained motionless, with a look of complete bewilderment. She burst out sobbing, and burying her head in his breast:

'As though I could live without you!'

He tried to calm her. She put her hands on his shoulders so that she could look him straight in the face. Then she fixed her green eyes on his. There was something almost ferocious in her moist glance.

'Will you be my husband?' she said.

'But . . .' answered Frederic, searching for words, 'naturally . . . I ask for nothing better.'

At that moment M. Roque's cap appeared behind a lilac bush. He took his 'young friend' on a little two-day tour of his properties in the neighbourhood. On his return, Frederic found three letters at his mother's house.

The first was a note from M. Dambreuse inviting him to dinner on the previous Tuesday. Whence this civility? Perhaps they had forgiven him his outburst.

The second letter was from Rosanette. She thanked him for having risked his life for her; at first Frederic could not understand what she meant; then, after many digressions, she implored his assistance; she invoked his friendship, trusted to his discretion, went down on her knees as if she were begging for a crust of bread—for the need was urgent—in short, could he let her have a little help, to the extent of five hundred francs? He at once decided to comply.

The third letter, from Deslauriers, spoke of the subrogation, and was long and obscure. The lawyer had not yet come to any decision. He urged him to stay where he was. 'There 's no object in your coming back!' He emphasized this point with peculiar insistence.

Frederic lost himself in conjectures of all sorts, and he felt a longing to return to Paris: this attempt to control his movements disgusted him.

Besides, he was beginning to feel homesick for the boulevard; moreover, his mother was so pressing, M. Roque so attentive, and Louise so deeply in love with him, that he could hardly remain longer without declaring himself. He needed time for reflection; he would judge things better from a distance.

He made up a story to explain his journey; and set off, telling every one, and himself believing, that he would be back soon.

CHAPTER VI

His return to Paris afforded him no pleasure. It was an evening in late August; the boulevard seemed empty, and the people in it went by with frowning faces; a few smoking cauldrons of tar stood in the streets; many of the houses were closed and shuttered. He entered his house: dust covered the hangings —and, dining alone, Frederic felt a strange sense of loneliness. Then he thought of Mlle Roque.

The idea of marriage no longer seemed fantastic. They would travel, they would go to Italy, to the East! And he pictured her standing on an eminence, gazing at a landscape, or leaning on his arm in a Florentine gallery, and pausing in front of the pictures. What joy it would be to watch this good little creature blossoming out among the splendours of art and nature! In new surroundings she would soon become a charming companion. Moreover, M. Roque's fortune tempted him. Yet a decision in this sense was somehow repugnant to him: it seemed to him like a weakness, or a degradation.

But, whatever his future was to be, he had resolved to change his way of life, and to cease wasting his emotions on fruitless passions. He even hesitated to carry out the commission with which Louise had entrusted him. This was to purchase from Jacques Arnoux two large coloured statuettes of negroes, like the ones in the prefecture at Troyes. She knew the maker's mark and would have them from no one else. Frederic was afraid of reviving his old love if he went back to *them*.

These reflections took up the whole evening; and he was just going to bed when a woman came in.

'It's me,' said Mlle Vatnaz, laughing. 'I've come from Rosanette.'

So they were reconciled?

'Good Lord, yes! You know, I'm not spiteful. Besides, the poor girl . . . But it's too long a story.'

In short, Rosanette wanted to see him, and was awaiting a reply to her letter, which had travelled from Paris to Nogent; Mlle Vatnaz had no idea what was in it. Then Frederic asked after Rosanette.

237

She was now with a very wealthy Russian, Prince Tzernoukoff, who had seen her at the races at the Champ de Mars, the previous summer.

'She's got three carriages, a saddle horse, servants in livery, a smart English groom. a country house, a box at the Italian opera, and everything else to match. So there you are, my dear.'

And Mlle Vatnaz seemed gayer and more happy, as if she had profited by this change of fortune. She took off her gloves and examined the furniture and ornaments in the room. She put prices on them all, like a dealer. He ought to have consulted her; she could have got them cheaper; and she congratulated him on his good taste.

'Oh, it's charming—extremely nice. For good taste, you're unique.'

Then, noticing a door beside the couch in the recess:

'So that's where you let your lady friends out, eh?'

And, half playfully, she took him by the chin. He shivered at the touch of her long hands, which were both thin and soft. Her cuffs were trimmed with lace, and the bodice of her green dress was frogged with braid, like a hussar's uniform. Her black tulle hat, with its drooping brim, hid part of her forehead; beneath it her eyes glittered, and her hair exhaled an odour of patchouli. The oil lamp, which stood on a table, lit up her face from below, like the footlights of a theatre, making her jaw stand out; and suddenly, in the presence of this ugly woman who yet had the sinuous body of a panther, Frederic felt an overpowering lust, a longing for bestial enjoyment.

She drew three squares of paper from her purse and said to him in an unctuous tone:

'You're going to take these!'

They were three tickets for a performance in Delmar's benefit.

'What! Him?'

'Certainly!'

Without further explanation, Mlle Vatnaz added that she was as much in love with him as ever. The actor, according to her, undoubtedly took his place among 'the giants of the age.' He did not interpret mere individual characters, but the very genius of France, of the People itself. He had 'a philanthropic soul; he understood the sacred duty of the artist.' To put an end to these eulogies, Frederic gave her the money for the seats.

'There's no point in your mentioning this to her. Heavens, how late it is! I must leave you. Oh, I was forgetting the address: it's 14 rue Grange-Batelière.'

And on the doorstep:

'Good-bye, you breaker of hearts!'

Whose heart? wondered Frederic. What a strange character she was!

And he remembered that Dussardier had once said to him, talking of her: 'Oh, there's not much in it,' as if referring to some rather discreditable story.

The next day he went to see Rosanette. She lived in a new house, with window awnings that overhung the street. A mirror stood against the wall on each landing, and there were rustic flower stands under the windows; the stairs were covered with a linen drugget; to the incoming visitor the coolness of the staircase was refreshing.

A manservant opened the door—a footman in a red waistcoat. A woman and two men, who looked like tradespeople, were waiting on the bench in the hall, as if it were a minister's ante-chamber. On the left, the half-open door of the dining-room revealed empty bottles on the sideboards and napkins on the backs of chairs; on the right stretched a gallery, in which a trellis of roses was supported on gilded poles. Below, in the yard, two grooms with bare arms were polishing a landau. Their voices could be heard in the hall, with the occasional sound of a curry comb being knocked against a stone.

The servant returned. 'Madame would receive monsieur'; and he led him through a second hall, and then into a large drawing-room, hung ·with yellow brocade. The rope mould-ings in the corners, extending upwards, met in the middle of the ceiling and appeared to be continued in the branches of the chandelier, which were themselves twisted like cables. There seemed to have been a party the night before. There was still cigar ash on the console tables.

At last he entered a sort of boudoir, with stained-glass windows which let in a diffused light. The wood above the doors had been carved into a trefoil design; behind a balustrade, three purple mattresses formed a divan, on which lay the platinum tube of a hookah. Above the fire-place, instead of a mirror, rose a pyramid of little shelves, bearing a whole collection of curios. There were old silver watches, Bohemian vases, jewelled brooches, jade buttons, enamel ware, Chinese figures, and a tiny Byzantine Virgin with a silver-gilt cope. All this was enveloped in a kind of golden dusk, with which other lights and colours were blended—the cobalt hue of the carpet, the gleam of mother-of-pearl from the inlaid stools, and the fawn tint of the walls, which were hung with brown leather. In the corners there were bronze vases on pedestals containing bunches of flowers, and the air was heavy with their scent.

Rosanette appeared, dressed in a pink satin jacket, white cashmere trousers, a necklace of Eastern coins, and a red smoking cap, round which was twined a spray of jasmine.

Frederic started in surprise; then said that he had brought 'what she had asked for,' and offered her the bank note.

She looked at it in complete bewilderment; he still held the note in his hand, not knowing where to put it down.

'Do take it!'

She seized it and threw it down on the divan.

'You're very kind.'

It was to help pay for a plot of land at Belleville which she was buying by yearly instalments. Her casualness offended Frederic. Apart from that, it was all the better; it would avenge the past.

'Sit down,' she said. 'There—nearer to me.'

And in a serious tone:

'First of all, I must thank you, my dear friend, for having risked your life for me.'

'Oh, that was nothing.'

'Why, it was splendid!'

And Rosanette expressed a gratitude that embarrassed him; for he was sure that she really thought he had fought for Arnoux alone, since Arnoux, who believed it, could not have failed to tell her so.

'Perhaps she's laughing at me,' thought Frederic. His business was over, and, pleading an appointment, he got up.

'No, no! Stay!'

He sat down again and complimented her on her costume.

She answered, in a despondent voice:

'You see, the prince likes me like this. And I have to smoke this sort of contraption,' added Rosanette, pointing to the hookah.

'Shall we try it? Would you care to?'

A light was brought. The zinc furnace was hard to kindle and she began to stamp with impatience. Then suddenly she grew languid; and she lay motionless on the divan, with a cushion under her armpit. Her body was twisted a little; one knee was bent and the other leg outstretched. The long snake of red morocco lay on the floor in rings and coiled about her arm. She pressed the amber mouthpiece to her lips and looked at Frederic with half-closed eyes, through the clouds of smoke that surrounded her. Her breathing made the water gurgle, and she murmured from time to time:

'The poor pet! The poor darling!'

He tried to find a pleasant topic; he remembered the Vatnaz. He said that she had looked very smart.

'No doubt!' said Rosanette. 'It's lucky for her she's got me.' And she said no more—so limited were their subjects of conversation.

They both felt a sense of constraint, a barrier between them. As a matter of fact the duel, of which Rosanette supposed herself the cause, had flattered her vanity. Afterwards she had been very surprised that he had not hurried to take advantage of his action; and she had invented her need for five hundred francs to compel his return. How came it that Frederic did not demand a little love as a reward? His chivalry astonished her, and, in a burst of emotion, she said to him:

'Will you come to the seaside with us?'

'Who do you mean by "us"?'

'Myself and my friend—I'll say you're my cousin, like they do in the old comedies.'

'No, thank you!'

'Very well, then: you can arrange to live near us.'

There was something humiliating in the idea of hiding from a rich man.

'No—it's out of the question.'

'As you wish.'

Rosanette turned away; there were tears on her eye-lashes. Frederic saw them; and to show his interest in her, he said that he was glad to see that she had at length fallen on her feet.

She shrugged her shoulders. Why was she depressed? Was it, by any chance, because nobody loved her?

'Oh, people always love me.'

She added:

'The only point is, how they do it.'

She complained that 'the heat was stifling,' and undid her jacket; with only her silk shift covering her figure, she leaned her head on her shoulder, with a look full of provocation, like a docile slave.

The idea that the viscount or M. de Comaing or someone else might come in would not have occurred to a man less consciously self-centred. But Frederic had been the dupe of these very glances so often that he preferred not to risk a fresh humiliation.

She wanted to know about his friends and his recreations; she even inquired about his finances and offered to lend him money, if he was in need. Frederic could stand it no longer. He took his hat.

'Well, my dear, enjoy yourself at the sea! Good-bye!'

She opened her eyes wide: then answered curtly:

'Good-bye!'

Again he passed through the yellow drawing-room and the second hall. On the table, between a vase full of visiting cards and an inkstand, stood a chased silver box. It was Mme Arnoux's box! Frederic felt a thrill of emotion; at the same time he was horrified, as if by a sacrilege. He wanted to hold it in his hands to open it. He was afraid of being seen, and went away.

Frederic was virtuous. He did not go back to Arnoux's house.

He sent his servant to buy the two negroes, giving him all the necessary instructions; and the package was dispatched to Nogent that very evening. The next day, he was on his way to Deslauriers's room, when, at the corner of the rue Vivienne and the boulevard, he met Mme Arnoux face to face.

Their first instinct was to draw back; then, the same smile came to the lips of both of them and they went up to each other. For a moment neither spoke.

The sunlight surrounded her; and her oval face, her black lace shawl, moulding her shoulders, her shot-silk dress, the bunch of violets in the side of her bonnet, seemed filled with an extraordinary splendour. An infinite sweetness poured from her lovely eyes; he stammered, at random, the first words he could think of:

'How is Arnoux?'

'Very well, thank you.'

'And your children?'

'Very well.'

'Oh . . . oh . . . Beautiful weather, isn't it?'

'Yes, wonderful.'

'You're out shopping?'

'Yes.'

And, with a slight inclination of her head:

'Good-bye!'

She had not held out her hand to him, had not said a single affectionate word, had not even invited him to her house—but it did not matter. He would not have exchanged this meeting for the most glorious of adventures: and he pondered its sweetness as he went on his way.

Deslauriers was surprised to see him, but concealed his resentment; he had not yet abandoned all hope of winning Mme Arnoux, and he had written to Frederic to stay in the country, in order to enjoy more freedom for his own manœuvres.

However, he mentioned that he had been to see her, in order to find out if their marriage settlement stipulated for their property to be held in common, in which case they could proceed against the wife.

'And what an odd face she made when I told her about your marriage!'

'Really! What a story!'

'I had to, to show that you needed your money. She had a sort of heart attack; which proves that she can't be indifferent to you.'

'Are you sure?' exclaimed Frederic.

'Ah, you old dog, you give yourself away. Come now, be frank.'

An immense cowardice overcame Mme Arnoux's adorer.

'No, no . . . I assure you . . . on my word of honour.'

These half-hearted denials succeeded in convincing Deslauriers. He congratulated him. He asked for 'details'; Frederic gave none, and was strong-minded enough not to invent any.

As for the mortgage, he told him to do nothing, to wait. Deslauriers thought he was wrong and was bitter in his protests. In a year's time, unless his luck changed, he would sail for America, or else blow out his brains. In short, he seemed so indignant with everything, and so uncompromising in his Radicalism, that Frederic could not help remarking:

'You're just like Sénécal.'

In this connection, Deslauriers told him that Sénécal had been released from Sainte-Pélagie, as the prosecution, apparently, could not produce sufficient evidence to bring him to trial.

Dussardier was going 'to give a punch party' to celebrate this deliverance, and he asked Frederic 'to come too.' At the same time he warned him that he would meet Hussonnet, who had been very good to Sénécal.

It so happened that *The Man about Town* had opened a department devoted to business enterprise. This was described on the prospectus as 'The Viticultural Agency. Publicity Office. Debt - collecting and Information Bureau.' The journalist was afraid that his commercial activities might injure his literary reputation; so he engaged Sénécal to keep his accounts. The post was worth little, but without it Sénécal would have starved to death. Frederic, not wishing to offend the good fellow, accepted his invitation.

Three days before the party Dussardier himself waxed the red tiles of his attic floor, beat the arm-chair, and dusted the mantelpiece, on which stood an alabaster clock in a glass case between a stalactite and a coco-nut. As his three candle-sticks were insufficient, he borrowed two large ones from the porter: and the five lights glowed on the chest of drawers, the top of which had been decently draped with three napkins, and bore macaroons, biscuits, a *brioche*, and a dozen bottles of beer. Opposite, against the yellow - papered wall, stood a little mahogany bookcase containing Lachambeaudie's *Fables*, the *Mystères de Paris*, and Norvins's *Napoléon*, while in the middle of the bed recess hung the smiling face of Béranger in an ebony frame.

Besides Deslauriers and Sénécal, the guests consisted of a chemist who had just obtained his diploma, but lacked the necessary capital to set up in business; a young man from Dussardier's firm; a traveller in wines; and a gentleman in the insurance business. Regimbart had been unable to come. They expressed regret at his absence.

Frederic was welcomed with exceptional sympathy—for they had all heard, through Dussardier, of the way he had spoken at M. Dambreuse's house. Sénécal contented himself with offering his hand in a dignified manner.

He was standing against the mantelpiece. The others, sitting with their pipes in their mouths, listened to him as he spoke about universal suffrage, which would result in the triumph of democracy and the application of the principles of the Gospel. Morever, the time was drawing near: Reformist banquets were taking place more and more frequently in the provinces; [1] Piedmont, Naples, Tuscany—— [2]

'It's true,' said Deslauriers, cutting him short. 'Things can't go on like this much longer.'

And he began to give a survey of the situation.

Holland had been sacrificed to secure the recognition of Louis-Philippe by England; and the famous English alliance had been lost, thanks to the Spanish marriages. In Switzerland, M. Guizot, under Austria's influence, was supporting the treaties of 1815. Prussia, with its Zollverein, was likely to be trouble-some in the future. The Eastern question was still unsolved.

'There's no reason to trust Russia just because the Grand Duke Constantine sends presents to Monsieur d'Aumale. In home policy, such blindness and stupidity have never been seen before. They can't even keep their majority together. In fact, wherever you look you find nothing, nothing, nothing, as they say. And in the face of all these crying scandals,' continued the lawyer, putting his hands on his hips, 'they declare themselves satisfied.'

This reference to a notorious resolution aroused applause. Dussardier opened a bottle of beer; the foam splashed the curtains; he did not care. He filled pipes, cut the *brioche*, handed it round, went down several times to see if the punch had arrived; and soon every one was stirred to excitement, for all shared the same indignation against authority. It was a violent emotion, and had no other origin than hatred of injustice; and legitimate grievances were mingled with the most inane complaints.

The chemist groaned about the pitiful condition of the fleet. The insurance broker could not tolerate Marshal Soult's two sentries. Deslauriers denounced the Jesuits, who had just installed themselves publicly at Lille. Sénécal found M. Cousin [1] much more detestable, for eclecticism, which taught that truth may be attained through reason, encouraged self-interest, and destroyed mass solidarity. The traveller in wines, who had little knowledge of these matters, remarked loudly that there were many scandals that had not been mentioned.

'The royal coach on the Nord line is going to cost eighty thousand francs! Who's to pay for it?'

'Yes, who's to pay for it?' said Dussardier's colleague, who was as furious as if the money had been stolen from his own pocket.

There followed an outcry against the swindlers of the Bourse and the corruption of the official classes. According to Sénécal, one should go higher and begin by attacking the king's sons, who were reviving the morals of the Regency.

'Did you know that the friends of the Duc de Montpensier, coming back from Vincennes the other day, disturbed the workmen in the Faubourg Saint-Antoine by their singing? I expect they were drunk.'

'Yes, and the workmen shouted: "Down with the robbers,"' said the chemist. 'I was there! I shouted!'

'Excellent! At last the people are waking up, after the Teste-Cubières [2] case.'

'That case distressed me,' said Dussardier, 'because it ended in the disgrace of an old soldier.'

'Do you know,' Sénécal went on, 'that at the Duchesse de Praslin's [1] house they found——'

The door was kicked open. Hussonnet came in.

'Greetings, my lords,' he said, sitting down on the bed.

No reference was made to his article, which in any case he regretted, as Rosanette had trounced him properly for it.

He had just seen *Le Chevalier de Maison-Rouge*, at Dumas's theatre, and found it tiresome.

This criticism amazed the democrats, since the tendencies of the play, and particularly its scenery, favoured their obsession. They protested. To close the argument, Sénécal asked if the piece was helpful to democracy.

'Yes . . . perhaps . . . but the style——'

'In that case, it's good. What does style matter compared with the idea?'

And, without allowing Frederic to speak:

'I was suggesting, with regard to the Praslin case——'

Hussonnet interrupted him.

'Oh, that's another old story. I find it tiresome.'

'You're not the only one,' answered Deslauriers. 'It's caused the suppression of five newspapers! Listen to this note.'

And, pulling it from his pocket-book, he read:

'"Since 'the best of republics' was established, there have been 1,229 prosecutions of the press, as a result of which journalists have been sentenced to 300,041 years' imprisonment and fined the modest sum of 7,110,500 francs." Pretty, isn't it?'

Every one laughed bitterly. Frederic, on fire like the others, continued:

'They've prosecuted *the Démocratie pacifique* for its serial story, a novel called *The Share of Women*.'

'Come, come,' said Hussonnet. 'They're not going to forbid us our share of women.'

'But is there anything that isn't forbidden?' exclaimed Deslauriers. 'We're forbidden to smoke in the Luxembourg, or to sing the hymn to Pius IX.' [2]

'And they've stopped the printers' banquet,' said a hollow voice behind them.

It was the architect, who, concealed in the shadow of the recess, had so far said nothing. He added that last week a man called Rouget had been convicted for insulting the king.

'Rouget[3]'s cooked!' said Hussonnet.

Sénécal thought this joke in such bad taste that he accused Hussonnet of defending 'the conjurer of the Hôtel de Ville,[1] the friend of the traitor Dumouriez.'[2]

'I? On the contrary!'

To his mind, Louis-Philippe was the complete vulgarian, the typical National Guard—a grocer in a cotton nightcap. And, putting his hand on his heart, he recited the ritual phrases: 'It is always with renewed pleasure . . . The Polish nation shall not perish. . . . Our great undertakings will be continued. . . . Give me some money for my poor little family. . . .' Every one laughed a great deal, and pronounced him a capital fellow, and very witty; their joy redoubled at the sight of a bowl of punch brought in by a bar-keeper.

The flames of the brew and those of the candles quickly warmed the room; the light from the attic window, streaming across the yard, illuminated the edge of the roof opposite; a chimney stack stood out black against the night. They talked at the tops of their voices, all at the same time; they took off their coats; they fell over the furniture, they clinked glasses.

Hussonet shouted:

'Great ladies to the fore! 'Sblood, we want more Tour de Nesle,[3] more atmosphere, and a touch of Rembrandt!'

And the chemist, who had not stopped stirring the punch, struck up at the pitch of his lungs:

'I 've two great oxen in my shed,
Two great oxen, white and——'

Sénécal put his hand over his mouth, for he hated disorder; and the tenants appeared at their windows, surprised by the unusual uproar in Dussardier's rooms.

The good fellow was enjoying himself; it reminded him, he said, of their little parties at the quai Napoléon, in the old days: however, many faces were missing; Pellerin, for instance——

'We can do without him,' said Frederic.

And Deslauriers asked after Martinon.

'What 's become of that interesting gentleman?'

At once Frederic gave vent to the grudge he bore him and attacked his intellect, his character, his sham smartness, and everything to do with him. He was a perfect specimen of the peasant who has 'arrived.' The new aristocracy, which was the middle class, was less worthy than the old, which was the nobility. He upheld this view; and the democrats approved, as if they belonged to the latter and were on intimate terms with the former. They were delighted with Frederic. The chemist even compared him with M. d'Alton-Shée, who took the people's side, although a peer of France.

The time had come to go home. They all separated with warm handshakes; out of affection, Dussardier walked back with Frederic and Deslauriers. As soon as they were in the street, the lawyer looked reflective, and, after a moment's silence:

'Are you very annoyed with Pellerin?' he asked.

Frederic did not conceal his rancour.

None the less, the painter had withdrawn the famous picture from exhibition. It wasn't worth quarrelling over trifles! What was the use of making enemies?

'He gave way to a momentary irritation, which is pardonable in a man who hasn't a penny. *You* couldn't understand that!'

And after Deslauriers had gone up to his rooms, Dussardier took up the attack; he even pressed Frederic to buy the portrait. The fact was that Pellerin, having lost hope of intimidating Frederic, had persuaded the two of them to try to influence him to take the picture.

Deslauriers spoke of it again, insistently. The artist's claims were reasonable.

'I 'm sure that for, say, five hundred francs . . .'

'Oh, let him have them! Here they are; take them!' said Frederic.

The picture arrived the same evening. It seemed to him even more repulsive than on the first occasion. Too much re-touching had given a leaden hue to the half-tones and shadows; they seemed too dark in comparison with the high lights, which showed up brilliantly here and there and clashed with the general effect.

Having paid for it, Frederic avenged himself by abusing it mercilessly. Deslauriers believed in his strictures and approved his conduct, for it was still his ambition to collect a group of comrades of which he would be the leader. There are some men who delight in making their friends do things which they dislike.

In the meanwhile, Frederic did not go back to the Dambreuses' house. He lacked the necessary capital; and this would involve endless explanations. He could not make up his mind. Perhaps he was right not to go. Nothing was safe these days—the coal business no more than anything else; he ought to give up society of this kind; finally, Deslauriers was against the enterprise. Through his hatred of the rich, he was turning virtuous; and, besides, he preferred Frederic to be undistinguished. In this way he remained his equal and in closer intimacy with him.

Mlle Roque's commission had been very badly executed. Her father wrote to Frederic, with the most detailed explanations and finished his letter with this piece of wit: 'I hope that the negroes won't give you the *mal de nègre*.'

Frederic had no alternative but to go back to Arnoux's place. He went up into the shop and could see nobody. The business was tottering, and the employees imitated their master's negligence.

He skirted the long *étagère*, loaded with faience ware, that stretched right across the middle of the room, then, reaching the counter at the far end, he began to stamp as he walked, to attract attention.

The door-curtain was lifted: Mme Arnoux came in.

'What! Are you here? You?'

'Yes,' she stammered, a little confused. 'I was looking . . .'

He noticed her handkerchief beside the desk, and guessed that she had come down to her husband's office to verify something, to clear up some matter that was troubling her.

'But . . . perhaps you want something?'

'Nothing of consequence, madame.'

'These assistants are impossible! They 're always away.'

They were not to be blamed. On the contrary, he was delighted with his good luck.

She looked at him ironically.

'Well—and this marriage?'

'What marriage?'

'Yours!'

'Mine? Good heavens, no!'

She made a gesture of denial.

'Well, supposing it were true? One falls back on the second-rate, after losing hope of the ideal one has dreamed of!'

'Yet all your dreams were not so . . . noble.'

'What do you mean?'

'When you went to the races, with . . . certain ladies.'

He cursed Rosanette. Something came back to him.

'But you yourself used to beg me to see her, for Arnoux's sake.'

She tossed her head and replied:

'And you took advantage of that to enjoy yourself!'

'For heaven's sake, don't let 's talk about such absurdities!'

'I quite agree—since you 're getting married.'

And she bit her lips, to hold back a sigh.

Then he exclaimed:

'But I tell you it's not true! Can you believe that someone with intellectual needs and habits like mine could bury himself in the country, and spend his time playing cards, supervising bricklayers, and walking about in clogs? What would be the object of it? I dare say you've been told that she's rich. What do I care about money? I've always desired the perfection of beauty, of love, of enchantment, a sort of paradise in human shape—and now that I've found my ideal at last, now that I can see nothing else but this vision——'

He took her head in his hands and began to kiss her eyelids, saying again and again:

'No! no! no! I shall never marry! Never! never!'

She accepted his caresses, transfixed with surprise and rapture.

The door which led to the shop from the staircase slammed. She leaped up, and stood with one hand outstretched, as if ordering him to be silent. Steps approached. Then someone said outside:

'Is madame there?'

'Come in!'

Mme Arnoux had her elbow on the counter and was calmly rolling a pen between her fingers when the book-keeper opened the door-curtain.

Frederic got up.

'Madame, I am your obedient servant. The dinner service will be ready, will it not? I can count on it, I suppose?'

She made no answer. But her silent complicity made her face glow with all the blushes of a guilty wife.

He went to see her next day, and was admitted. To follow up his advantage he at once began, without more ado, by explaining the encounter at the Champ de Mars. He was with this woman purely by accident. Even allowing that she was pretty—which she was not—how could she occupy his thoughts for a single moment, since he loved another?

'You know that well enough. I told you so.'

Mme Arnoux bowed her head.

'I am sorry that you told me.'

'Why?'

The most elementary propriety now demands that I never see you again.'

He protested that his love was innocent. The past should answer for the future; he had vowed to himself not to disturb her life, nor to deafen her with his complaints.

'But yesterday my heart overflowed.'

'We ought to forget all about that moment, my friend.'

But where would be the harm in two unhappy creatures sharing their sorrows?

'For you are not happy, either! Oh, I know you—you have no one who fulfils your need for affection and devotion; I will do anything you wish! I shan't offend you; I swear it.'

And he fell on his knees, overcome by an inner weight which bore him down.

'Stand up!' she said. 'It is my will!'

And she told him imperiously that if he did not obey he would never see her again.

'Ah! I defy you there!' answered Frederic. 'What have I to do in the world? Others struggle after riches, fame, power. I have no occupation; you are my sole employment, my whole fortune, the end, the centre of my life and thoughts. I can no more live without you than without the air of heaven. Do you not feel the yearning of my spirit mounting towards yours? Do you not feel that our souls must mingle, and that I am dying of desire?'

Mme Arnoux began to tremble in all her limbs.

'Oh, go away, I beg of you!'

The distracted expression of her face halted him. Then he took a step forward. But she drew back, putting her hands together.

'Leave me! In heaven's name! For mercy's sake!'

And Frederic loved her so much that he went out.

Soon he was filled with anger against himself, called himself a fool, and, twenty-four hours later, went back.

Madame was not there. He stood on the landing, numb with rage and indignation. Arnoux appeared and informed him that his wife had left that very morning, to move into a country house they had taken at Auteuil, as the one at Saint-Cloud was no longer theirs.

'It's another of her fads! Well, so much the better—it suits her, and it suits me. Shall we dine together to-night?'

Frederic pleaded urgent business, then hurried to Auteuil.

Mme Arnoux uttered a cry of joy. At once all his anger evaporated.

He did not speak of his love. To give her more confidence he assumed an exaggerated reserve; and when he asked if he might come back, she replied: 'Of course,' giving him her hand, which she withdrew almost immediately.

From that day Frederic was a frequent visitor. He promised the coachman large tips. But he often lost patience with the slowness of the horse and got down: then, panting, climbed on to an omnibus; and how scornfully he scrutinized the faces of his fellow passengers who were not going to see her!

He recognized her house from a distance by a huge honeysuckle which covered one side of the wooden roof. It was a sort of Swiss chalet, painted red, with an outside balcony. In the garden were three old Spanish chestnut-trees, and in the middle a thatched shelter built round the trunk of a tree. Under the slate coping of the walls grew a large vine, which, here and there, had broken from its fastenings and hung down like a rotten rope. The gate bell was rather stiff to pull, and gave a prolonged peal. There was a long wait before any one came. Each time he felt a pang of agony and undefined fear.

Then he heard the maidservant's slippers clopping down the path, or sometimes Mme Arnoux appeared herself. One day he came up behind her when she was crouching on the lawn looking for violets.

Her daughter's waywardness had forced her to send her to a convent. Her little boy spent the afternoons at school, while Arnoux spent hours over luncheon at the Palais-Royal, with Regimbart and his friend Compain. No awkward intruder could surprise them.

It was clearly understood that their passion was not to be consummated. This agreement, which insured them against peril, smoothed the way for confidences.

She told him about her old life at Chartres, in her mother's house; her piety at twelve; then her passion for music, when she sang from morning till night in her little room, which overlooked the ramparts. He told her about his fits of melancholy at college, and of how a woman's face had always shone on the horizon of his imagination, so that, seeing her for the first time, he had immediately recognized her.

Generally these conversations only included the years of their acquaintance. He reminded her of trivial details, the colour of her dress at a certain date, who had come in one day, what she had said another time; and, quite astonished, she would answer:

'Yes, I remember.'

Their tastes, their opinions were the same. Often the one who was listening would exclaim:

'So do I!'

And the other would answer in turn:

'So do I!'

Then came endless complaints against destiny:

'Why was it against the will of heaven? If we had met . . .'

'Oh, if I had been younger!' she would sigh.

'No, if I had been a little older!'

And they imagined a life that would be all love, and yet rich enough to fill the widest deserts; surpassing all joys, defying all sorrows, they would open their hearts to each other for hours on end. It was a life which might have become something splendid and sublime, like the twinkling of the stars.

Almost always they sat out of doors, at the top of the steps; it was autumn, the trees were growing yellow, and their swelling crests rose in broken curves against the pale sky. Sometimes they went down to the end of the avenue, to a pavilion whose sole furniture was a sofa, covered in grey linen. There were black spots on the mirror; a smell of damp came from the walls; and they stayed there enchanted, talking about themselves, about others, about anything in the world. Sometimes sunbeams, streaming through the Venetian blind, would hang from ceiling to floor like the strings of a lyre; motes of dust would float and whirl in these bars of light. She liked to pass her hand through them; Frederic would seize it gently, and gaze at the tracery of her veins, the grain of her skin, the shape of her fingers. For him each of her fingers was a person, not a thing.

She gave him her gloves and, the week after, her handkerchief. She called him Frederic, he called her Marie; he adored that name, for it was, he said, made specially to be sighed in ecstasy; there were clouds of incense in it, and banks of roses.

After a time they fixed the days of his visits in advance; she would go out as if by chance and come to meet him on the road.

She did not do anything to stimulate his love, for she was in that state of carefree unconcern which is the mark of great happiness. During the whole autumn she wore a dressing-gown of brown silk, edged with brown velvet—a loose garment, which suited her yielding attitudes and the soft seriousness of her face. Moreover, she was now approaching the August of a woman's life, a time when reflection and tenderness meet, when the ripeness to come kindles a deeper flame in the eye, when knowledge strengthens the vigour of the heart, and the whole being, in the fullness of its bloom, overflows with richness, harmony, and beauty. She had never been gentler, or more

253

kind. Certain of her safety she gave herself up to an emotion which, she felt, she had earned by her sorrows. Besides, it was so sweet and so new! What a gulf between the coarseness of Arnoux and the tender devotion of Frederic!

He was terrified lest a careless word might lose him all he thought he had gained; a missed opportunity, he used to tell himself, could be recovered, but a foolish act was fatal. He wanted her to give herself, he did not want to take her. The knowledge of her love delighted him, like a foretaste of possession; besides, the charm of her body disturbed his heart more than his senses. It was an ecstasy that could not be defined, an intoxication so deep that it made him forget the very possibility of an absolute happiness. Away from her, furious lusts devoured him.

Soon there were long intervals of silence in their conversation. Sometimes a sort of sexual shyness made them blush in each other's presence. Their passion shone out, through every precaution they took to hide it; the stronger it became, the more restrained was their behaviour. The maintenance of this pretence aggravated their sensibility. They took a delicious pleasure in the smell of damp leaves; the east wind gave them pain; they suffered causeless irritations and dreadful presentiments; the sound of a step, the creaking of a panel, filled them with terror, as if they had been guilty; they felt themselves driven towards an abyss; an atmosphere of storm surrounded them; and when Frederic broke into complaints she blamed herself.

'Yes, I'm doing wrong! I'm behaving like a coquette. Don't come again!'

Then he would repeat the same vows, which she never ceased to listen to with pleasure.

His return to Paris and the fuss and bother of New Year's Day interrupted their meetings a little. When he came back there was a greater boldness in his manner. She kept leaving the room to give orders, and, in spite of his entreaties, let in all the local people who came to visit her. There were long conversations about Léotade,[1] M. Guizot, the Pope, the rising at Palermo [2] and the banquet of the Twelfth Arrondissement,[3] which was arousing anxiety. Frederic consoled himself by inveighing against authority; for, like Deslauriers, he longed for a general upheaval, so embittered had he become. Mme Arnoux, for her part, began to grow melancholy.

Her husband, in an excess of extravagance, was keeping a

woman from his own factory—the one they called 'the girl from Bordeaux.' Mme Arnoux told Frederic about it herself. He tried to use this as an argument. . . . 'Since she was being deceived . . .'

'Oh, that doesn't worry me at all,' she said. This admission seemed to him to establish their relationship once and for all. Did Arnoux suspect him?

'No. Not now.'

She told him how one evening he had left them alone together, and had then come back and listened behind the door. As they were both talking of indifferent matters, he had, from that day on, suffered not the least anxiety.

'And with reason,' said Frederic bitterly.

'Yes, of course.'

She would have done better not to risk a phrase of this sort.

One day she was not at home at the usual hour of his visit. To him it was like a betrayal.

Then he was vexed because she always arranged the flowers he brought her in vases full of water.

'Where would you like me to put them?'

'Oh! not in vases! Yet it's less cold for them there than on your heart!'

Some time later he reproached her with having been to the Théâtre des Italiens the night before, without telling him. Others had seen her, admired her, loved her, perhaps; Frederic clung to his suspicion for the sole purposes of teasing and tormenting her; for he was beginning to hate her, and the least he could do was to make her share his sufferings.

One afternoon, towards the middle of February, he found her deeply disturbed. Eugène had a bad throat. The doctor, however, had said it was nothing; a severe cold or influenza. Frederic was astonished at the child's hectic look. Nevertheless, he reassured the mother, and quoted instances of several children of the same age who had recently had similar complaints and had soon got over them.

'Really and truly?'

'Why, yes, certainly!'

'Oh, how comforting you are!'

And she took his hand. He squeezed it in his own.

'Oh, let me go!'

'What does it matter? You're giving your hand to your consoler! . . . You find me useful for these things, and yet you doubt me . . . when I speak to you about my love.'

'I don't doubt you, my poor friend.'

'Why do you distrust me, as if I were a scoundrel, capable of abusing your confidence?'

'Never!'

'If only I had some proof!'

'What proof?'

'The proof you would give to a stranger, that you once granted to me.'

And he reminded her how they had walked together, one foggy winter dusk. That was a long time ago, now. Why, then, should she not take his arm openly, before the whole world, without fear on her part or ulterior motive on his, with no third person to disturb them?

'So be it,' she said, with a decisive courage which, for a moment, took Frederic by surprise.

But he went on quickly:

'Shall I wait for you at the corner of the rue Tronchet and the rue de la Ferme?'

'Good heavens! my dear . . .' stammered Mme Arnoux.

Without giving her time to reflect, he added:

'Next Tuesday, I suppose?'

'Tuesday?'

'Yes, between two and three o'clock.'

'I shall be there!'

And she turned away her face, in a movement of shame. Frederic pressed his lips to the nape of her neck.

'You shouldn't do that,' she said. 'You'll make me change my mind.'

He drew back, fearing the usual instability of women. Then, on the threshold, he murmured softly, as if it were a matter long agreed between them:

'Till Tuesday!'

She lowered her eyes discreetly and with resignation.

Frederic had a plan.

He hoped that he might persuade her to pause under a doorway, to shelter from the rain or the sun, and that once under the doorway, he could get her into the house. The difficulty was to find a suitable one. He searched and searched, and, towards the middle of the rue Tronchet he read a sign, in the distance, which said: 'Furnished Apartments.'

The servant, understanding his purpose, at once showed him a suite of two rooms, a larger and a smaller, on the first floor, with two entrances. Frederic took it for a month, and paid in advance.

Then he visited three shops, to buy the rarest perfumes; he purchased a piece of imitation lace to replace the appalling red cotton bedspread, he chose a pair of blue satin slippers; only the fear of appearing vulgar limited his expenditure. He brought them back, and, more reverently than a priest decking an altar, he shifted the furniture, draped the curtains, put heather on the mantelpiece and violets on the chest of drawers; he would have liked to pave the whole room with gold. 'It's to-morrow,' he kept telling himself. 'Yes, to-morrow! I'm not dreaming.' And he felt his heart beating wildly, in the delirium of his hopes; then, when all was ready, he carried off the key in his pocket, as if happiness, sleeping there, might have flown away in the night.

A letter from his mother was waiting for him at home.

'Why don't you come back? Your behaviour is beginning to look ridiculous. I quite understand your having some preliminary doubts about this marriage, up to a point; but do think it over!'

And she went into details: forty-five thousands francs a year. Moreover, 'people were beginning to talk'; and M. Roque was expecting a definite reply. Besides, the position of the young person was really embarrassing. 'She is very much in love with you.'

Frederic threw the letter away without finishing it and opened another, a note from Deslauriers:

MY OLD FRIEND,

The pear is ripe. We are relying on you, in accordance with your promise. There's a meeting at dawn to-morrow, at the place du Panthéon. Go to the Café Soufflot. I must speak to you before the demonstration.

'Oh, I know their demonstrations! Thank you very much! I have a pleasanter appointment!'

The next day Frederic was out by eleven o'clock. He wanted to give a final inspection to his preparations; then, who knew? She might, by some accident, be early. As he emerged from the rue Tronchet, he heard a great clamour behind the Madeleine; he went forward; and he saw men in blouses and tradespeople at the far end of the square, on the left.

In fact, all the subscribers to the Reformist banquet had gathered at this spot in response to a manifesto published in the newspapers. The Government had almost immediately posted a proclamation forbidding the banquet. The previous evening the parliamentary Opposition had disowned the manifesto; but the patriots, knowing nothing of their leaders' decision, had come to the meeting-place, followed by great numbers of spectators. A deputation from the schools had just been to the house of Odilon Barrot.[1] It was now at the Foreign Office; and no one knew if the banquet would take place, if the Government would carry out its threat, or if the National Guards[2] would put in an appearance. The deputies were no less unpopular than the authorities. The crowd was growing larger and larger, when suddenly the strains of the *Marseillaise* rang out through the air.

The procession of students was approaching. They marched slowly, in two ranks, in good order. They were unarmed; but there was anger on their faces. At intervals they shouted in unison:

'Reform for ever! Down with Guizot!'

Frederic's friends were bound to be there. They would notice him and drag him off with them. He quickly took refuge in the rue de l'Arcade.

When the students had marched twice round the Madeleine, they went down towards the place de la Concorde. It was full of people: and the dense crowd looked like a black waving cornfield in the distance.

At the same moment the regular soldiers lined up for attack on the left of the church.

Still the people stood their ground. To end the business, plain-clothes policemen began seizing the most unruly and dragging them violently to the police station.

In spite of his indignation, Frederic said nothing; he might have been arrested with the others, and he would have missed Mme Arnoux.

A moment or two later the caps of the Municipal Guards appeared. They struck out in all directions with the flat of their sabres. A horse fell down; people hurried to its aid; and, as soon as the rider was in the saddle, every one made off.

Then a great silence descended. The fine rain, which had made the pavement wet, had ceased. Clouds passed overhead, drifting gently in the west wind.

Frederic began to walk up and down the rue Tronchet, looking in front and behind.

At last two o'clock struck.

'It's now!' he said to himself. 'She's leaving the house,

she's coming nearer,' and, a moment later: 'She could have been here by now.' Until three o'clock he tried to keep calm. 'No, she's not late. Have a little patience!'

And, to pass the time, he examined the few shops in the street: a bookseller, a saddler, a shop that sold mourning. Soon he knew all the books by name, each piece of harness, every roll of stuff. The shopkeepers, seeing him pass by again and again, without stopping, were first astonished and then frightened; they put up their shutters.

No doubt something was keeping her, and she was as anxious as he. But what joy would be theirs in a moment! For she would come; that was certain. 'She promised me!' Nevertheless, an unbearable agony was overcoming him.

Absurdly, he went back into the house, as though she might have been inside. At that very moment, perhaps, she was coming down the street! He dashed out. Nobody! And he began tramping the pavement again.

He stared at the cracks in the paving stones, the mouths of the rain pipes, the street lamps, the numbers on the houses. The smallest objects became companions to him, or rather, ironic spectators; and the unbroken fronts of the houses seemed to be merciless enemies. His feet were cold. He felt that he was falling to pieces in his despair. The echo of his footsteps made his brain reel. When he saw that his watch said four o'clock, he felt a kind of dizziness, a panic. He tried to repeat poetry to himself, to count at random, to make up a story, He could not! The picture of Mme Arnoux haunted him. He longed to run and meet her. But what route should he take so as not to miss her?

He went up to a street porter, put five francs in his hand, and told him to go to the rue Paradis, to the house of Jacques Arnoux, and ask the porter 'if madame was at home.' Then he took his stand at the corner of the rue de la Ferme and the rue Tronchet, in such a position that he could see down both streets at the same time. On the boulevard, at the far end of the vista, confused masses of people were moving to and fro. Sometimes he could make out the crest of a dragoon's helmet or a woman's hat; and he strained his eyes to recognize it. A smiling ragamuffin, who was exhibiting a squirrel in a box, asked him for money.

The street porter, in his velvet jacket, reappeared.

'The porter had not seen her go out.' What was keeping her? If she was ill, they would have said so. Was it a caller? She could easily have refused to see him. He struck his forehead.

'What a fool I am! It's the riot!' This natural explanation comforted him. Then suddenly: 'But there's no trouble in her district.' And he was attacked by an appalling doubt. 'Supposing she isn't coming? Supposing her promise was just a device to get rid of me? No! no!' No doubt what was preventing her was some extraordinary accident—one of those events which defy all foresight. In that case she would have written. And he sent the servant from the house to his home in the rue Rumfort, to find out if there was a letter.

No letter had arrived. This lack of news reassured him.

He drew omens from the number of coins grasped at random in his hand, from the faces of passers-by, from the colour of horses; and, when the augury was unfavourable, he forced himself not to believe it. In his fits of rage against Mme Arnoux, he abused her in a low voice. Sometimes he felt weak to the point of fainting; then suddenly hope would surge up once more. She was coming round the corner. There she was, behind his back. He turned round: nothing! Once, about thirty yards away, he saw a woman of the same height, in the same dress. He went up to her, it was not she! Five o'clock came. Half-past five. Six o'clock. They were lighting the gas. Mme Arnoux had not come.

The night before, she dreamed that she had been standing for hours on the pavement in the rue Tronchet. She was waiting for something indefinite, yet important, and, without knowing why, she was afraid of being seen. But a horrible little dog, which hated her, kept gnawing the bottom of her dress. It would not leave her alone and barked louder and louder. Mme Arnoux awoke. The dog was still barking. She strained her ears. The noise came from her son's room. She hurried there in her bare feet. It was the child coughing. His hands were burning; his face was red and his voice strangely hoarse. Every moment his breathing grew more laboured. She stayed there until daybreak, leaning over his bed, watching him.

At eight o'clock, the drum of the National Guard warned Arnoux that his comrades were waiting for him. He dressed quickly and went off, promising to call immediately at the house of their doctor, M. Colot. At ten o'clock M. Colot had not come. Mme Arnoux sent her maid to inquire: the doctor was away in the country, and the young man who was taking his place was out on his rounds.

Eugène had his head on one side, on the bolster; he kept contracting his brows and dilating his nostrils; his poor little face grew paler than his sheets; and with every intake of breath a sort of whistling, dry and rather metallic, which grew shorter and shorter, emerged from his throat. His cough was like the squeaking of a toy dog.

Mme Arnoux was seized with panic. She flung herself on the bells, calling for help and screaming:

'A doctor! A doctor!'

Ten minutes later there arrived an old gentleman with a white neck-cloth and well-trimmed grey whiskers. He asked many questions about the habits, age, and temperament of the young invalid, then examined his throat, applied his ear to his back, and wrote out a prescription. The man's complacent look was detestable. He made her think of embalmments. She would gladly have struck him. He said he would come back in the evening.

Soon the horrible fits of coughing began again. Sometimes the child sat up suddenly. Spasms shook the muscles of his chest; and when he breathed his stomach contracted, as if he had collapsed from over-exertion. Then he sank back, with his head tilted and his mouth wide open. With infinite precaution Mme Arnoux tried to make him swallow the contents of the bottles, some ipecacuanha syrup, a dose of antimony. But he pushed away the spoon, groaning in a weak voice. When he spoke he seemed to puff out his words.

From time to time she re-read the prescription. Its cryptic appearance terrified her; perhaps the chemist had made a mistake! Her helplessness filled her with despair. M. Colot's pupil arrived.

He was a young man of modest bearing; he was new to his profession, and did not disguise his thoughts. At first he remained undecided, through fear of committing himself, and at last prescribed the application of ice-packs. It was a long time before they could find any ice. The bladder containing the pieces burst. They had to change the child's nightshirt. All this disturbance produced another, more terrible, paroxysm.

The child began tearing the cloths from his throat, as though he were trying to push away the obstruction that was stifling him; and he scrabbled at the wall and seized the curtains of his bed, in his search for some support to aid his breathing. His face was now bluish, and his whole body, which was soaked in a cold sweat, seemed to grow thinner. In terror, he fixed his haggard eyes on his mother. He threw his arms round her neck, and clung to her desperately. Choking back her sobs, she stammered loving words:

'Yes, my precious, my angel, my darling!'

There followed intervals of calm.

She went and fetched toys—a doll, a picture-book—and spread them out on his bed to amuse him. She even tried to sing.

She started a lullaby which she used to sing to him when she was dressing him in his baby-clothes, on that very tapestry chair. But he shivered all over his body, like a wave under a gust of wind; his eyeballs stood out; she thought he was going to die, and turned away so that she should not see.

A moment later she felt strong enough to look at him. He was still alive. The hours passed—leaden, mournful, endless, despairing. She counted the minutes only by the deepening of his agony. The convulsions of his chest threw him forward as if he were breaking in two; at last he vomited a strange object, which looked like a parchment tube. What was it? She supposed he had thrown up a piece of his entrails. But now he was breathing freely and regularly. This apparent improvement frightened her more than anything else; she was standing petrified, her arms hanging at her sides, her eyes staring, when M. Colot came in. He declared the child out of danger.

At first she did not understand, and asked him to repeat what he had said. Was this not the doctor's usual consolation? M. Colot went away looking unperturbed. Then it was as if the cords that had been binding her heart were unloosed.

Saved! Could it be true?

Suddenly the thought of Frederic came into her mind—clearly, inexorably. This was a warning from heaven. But the Lord in His mercy had not wished to punish her completely! How terrible her punishment would be, later on, if she persisted in this passion! No doubt they would insult her son because of her; and Mme Arnoux saw him as a young man —wounded in a duel, carried off on a stretcher, dying. She leaped up and flung herself on the little chair; with all her strength she sent her soul up to the heights, and she sacrificed to God, as a burnt offering, her first love, her solitary weakness.

Frederic had gone home. He sat in his arm-chair, lacking the strength even to curse her. He sank into a kind of sleep; through his nightmare he heard the rain falling, and all the time he thought that he was still out there on the pavement.

The next day, in a final access of cowardice, he sent another messenger to Mme Arnoux's house.

Perhaps the boy did not deliver the message, or perhaps she had so much to say that she could not explain it all in one word. The answer was the same as before. This was intolerable insolence! His injured pride filled him with anger. He swore that he no longer had the least desire for her; and, like a leaf carried away by a hurricane, his love vanished. He felt a sense of relief, a stoic joy, and then a longing for violent action; he went out and walked at random about the streets.

Men from the suburbs were going by, armed with muskets and old sabres; some wore red caps and all were singing the *Marseillaise* or the *Girondins*. Here and there a National Guard was hurrying to his post at the town hall. Drums beat in the distance. They were fighting at the Porte Saint-Martin. There was something brave and martial in the air. Frederic went on walking. The ferment of the great city made him cheerful.

On the hill where Frascati's used to be he caught sight of Rosanette's windows; a mad idea passed through his mind; his youth flared up. He crossed the boulevard.

The outer door was being closed; Delphine, the maid, was writing on it with a piece of charcoal: 'Arms already supplied.'[1] She spoke rapidly:

'Madame is in such a state. She sacked the groom this morning for cheeking her. She thinks there's going to be looting all over the place. She's scared to death—particularly since the gentleman's cleared out!'

'What gentleman?'

'The prince!'

Frederic entered the boudoir. Rosanette appeared, in her petticoat, with her hair down her back, distracted with terror.

'Oh, thank you! You've come to save me. It's the second time! And you never ask for your reward!'

'I beg your pardon,' said Frederic, putting both arms round her waist.

'What! What are you doing?' stammered Rosanette, at once surprised and amused by his behaviour.

He answered:

'I'm in the fashion. I've reformed!'

She allowed herself to be pushed over on to the divan, and went on laughing under his kisses.

They spent the afternoon watching the people in the street from their window. Then he took her to dinner at the Trois-Frères-Provençaux. The meal was long and exquisite. They came back on foot, as there were no carriages.

The news of the change of government [1] had transformed Paris. Every one was celebrating; people were strolling about the streets; there were illuminations on every floor, and the night was as bright as day. The soldiers were slowly returning to their barracks, looking harassed and gloomy. They were greeted with cries of: 'Up the regulars!' They went on their way without answering. On the other hand, the officers of the National Guard, flushed with enthusiasm, were brandishing their sabres and shouting: 'Reform for ever!' and at each repetition of the word the two lovers laughed. Frederic joked and was very gay.

They reached the boulevards through the rue Duphot. Chinese lanterns had been hung from the houses and looked like wreaths of fire. Below, there were confused masses of people moving; here and there a bayonet gleamed white against the dark background. A great hum arose. The crowd was so thick that they could not get straight back; and they were turning into the rue Caumartin when there was a sudden crackling noise behind them, like the tearing of an enormous piece of silk. It was the firing on the boulevard des Capucines.

'Ah! They 're knocking off a few tradesmen,' said Frederic calmly.

For there are times when even the gentlest of men feels so detached from his fellows that he could watch the destruction of the whole human race without a qualm.

Rosanette clasped him tightly by the arm; her teeth were chattering. She declared herself incapable of walking another twenty yards. Then, as a refinement of hatred, as a last private insult to Mme Arnoux, he led Rosanette to the house in the rue Tronchet, to the room prepared for the other.

The flowers had not faded. The lace was still spread on the bed. He drew the little slippers from the cupboard. Rosanette thought these attentions very delicate.

About one o'clock she was awakened by distant rumblings. Looking round she saw that he was sobbing with his head in the pillow.

'What 's the matter, my darling?'

'It 's because I 'm too happy,' said Frederic. 'I 've wanted you for so long!'

PART III

CHAPTER I

A SUDDEN rattle of musketry made him wake with a start; and, in spite of Rosanette's entreaties, Frederic insisted on going to see what was happening. He followed the sound of the firing down the Champs-Élysées. At the corner of the rue Saint-Honoré he was met by a shout from some workmen in blouses:

'No! Not that way! To the Palais-Royal!'

Frederic followed them. The railings of the Church of the Assumption had been pulled down. Further on he noticed three paving stones torn up in the middle of the road, doubtless the foundation of a barricade—then bits of broken bottles, and bundles of wire, to hamper the cavalry. Suddenly, out of an alley, rushed a tall young man, with black hair hanging over his shoulders and wearing a sort of pea-green singlet. He carried a soldier's long musket; there were slippers on his feet and he was running on tiptoe, as lithe as a tiger, yet with the fixed stare of a sleep-walker. Now and then explosions could be heard.

The previous evening the public exhibition of a cart containing five bodies from the boulevard des Capucines had changed the temper of the people. At the Tuileries there was a continuous coming and going of equerries; M. Molé, who was constructing a new Cabinet, did not reappear; M. Thiers tried to form another; the king shuffled, hesitated, gave Bugeaud full authority, then prevented him from making use of it. Meanwhile, as though directed by a single hand, the insurrection grew ever stronger and more menacing. Men addressed crowds at street corners with frantic eloquence; others, in the churches, were sounding the tocsin with all their might; lead was melted, cartridges rolled; trees from the boulevards, public urinals, benches, railings, gas jets were torn down or overturned; by morning Paris was filled with barricades. Resistance was not prolonged; everywhere the National Guard intervened; so that by eight o'clock, through force or by consent, the people were in possession of five barracks, nearly all the town halls, and the most important strategic points. No great exertion was necessary; through its own weakness the monarchy was swiftly tottering to its fall. And now the people were attacking the guard post known as the Château-d'Eau, in order to liberate fifty prisoners who were not there.

Frederic was forced to stop at the edge of the square, which was filled with groups of armed men. The rue Saint-Thomas and the rue Fromanteau were occupied by regular soldiers. A huge barricade blocked the rue de Valois. The smoke that hovered about it melted for a moment; men scaled the parapet with wild gestures, and then vanished; the firing began again. The police station replied, although no one could be seen within; the windows were protected by oak shutters, pierced with loopholes; and the monument, with its two tiers and two wings—with the fountain on the first tier and the little door in the middle—began to show the white marks of bullet pocks. Its flight of three steps was empty.

Next to Frederic a man in a smoking cap, with a cartridge pouch under his woollen jacket, was arguing with a woman with a kerchief on her head.

'Come back! Come back, I say!' she was saying.

'Leave me alone!' replied the husband. 'You can look after the door by yourself. Citizen, I ask you, is it fair? I've always done my duty—in '30, in '32, in '34, in '39. They're fighting to-day. I've got to fight! Go away!'

And in the end the porter's wife yielded to his protests, and to those of a National Guard beside them—a man of about forty, whose good-humoured face was fringed all round with a fair beard. He was loading his piece and firing, while he talked to Frederic, as calm in the midst of the fighting as a gardener among his flowers. A boy in a sackcloth apron was trying to persuade him to give him some caps, so that he could use his gun, a fine sporting carbine which 'a gentleman' had given him.

'Take a handful from my back,' said the guard. 'Then make yourself scarce! You'll be getting killed!'

The drums beat the charge. Shrill cries could be heard, and shouts of triumph. The crowd rocked in a continuous surge. Frederic, wedged between two dense masses, stayed where he was. Fascinated, he was enjoying himself hugely. The wounded falling, and the dead lying stretched out, did not look as if they were really wounded or dead. He felt as though he were watching a play.

Above the heads of the swaying multitude could be seen an old man in a black coat, on a white horse with a velvet saddle.[1] He held a green bough in one hand, and a piece of paper in the

268

other, which he shook persistently. At last he gave up hope of making himself heard and withdrew.

The soldiers had disappeared and only the Municipal Guards remained to defend the guard house. A wave of heroes rushed up the steps; they fell; others followed; the door resounded under heavy blows from iron bars; the guards would not surrender. Then a carriage, stuffed with hay and burning like a giant torch, was pushed up against the walls. Quickly they brought up faggots, straw, a barrel of spirits of wine. The fire leaped up the stone wall; the building began to smoke at every point like a volcano; above, great crackling flames burst out through the balustrade that surrounded the roof. The first floor of the Palais-Royal was packed with National Guards. They were shooting from every window; the bullets whistled, the fountain had burst its basin, and the water, mingled with blood, spread over the ground in puddles. People slipped in the mud on coats, shakos, and muskets; Frederic felt something soft under his foot; it was the hand of a sergeant in a grey overcoat, lying face downwards in the gutter. Fresh crowds kept coming up and pushing the fighters towards the guard house. The firing became more intense. The wine merchants' shops were open; from time to time, men went in to smoke a pipe or drink a glass of beer; then returned to the battle. A lost dog was howling. This made the people laugh.

Frederic staggered back under the weight of a man who fell groaning on his shoulder with a ball in his back. This attack, which was perhaps directed against him, made him furious; and he was dashing forward when a National Guard stopped him.

'It's no use. The king has just left. Well, if you don't believe me, go and see!'

This pronouncement calmed Frederic. The place du Carrousel looked peaceful. The Hôtel de Nantes still stood there, tall and solitary. The houses behind, the dome of the Louvre opposite, the long, wooden gallery on the right, and the sort of sloping no man's land that stretched up to the stall keepers' booths—all seemed steeped in the grey tints of the evening; distant murmurs were heard dimly, as if deadened by the mist. But at the other end of the square, through a gap in the clouds, a hard glaring light fell on the front of the Tuileries, making all its windows stand out in white relief. A dead horse lay stretched out by the Arc de Triomphe. Behind the railings, people were chatting in groups of five or six. The doors of the palace were open, and the servants on the threshold allowed the crowd to go in.

Bowls of coffee were being served in a little room on the ground floor. Some of the visitors sat down to table merrily; others remained standing. A cabman among the latter seized a jar full of soft sugar with both hands, gave an uneasy glance to right and left, and then began to eat voraciously, plunging his nose into the pot. At the foot of the great staircase a man was writing his name in a book. Frederic recognized him from behind.

'Well—Hussonnet!'

'Why, yes,' answered the journalist. 'I'm presenting myself at court. This is a good joke, isn't it?' And they entered the Hall of the Marshals. The portraits of these worthies were intact, except for Bugeaud, who had been pierced through the stomach. The marshals were pictured leaning on their sabres, with gun carriages in the background, in attitudes of menace, little suited to the present juncture. A large clock pointed to twenty past one.

Suddenly the *Marseillaise* rang out. Hussonnet and Frederic leaned over the banisters. It was the people.

The mob surged up the staircase in a swirling stream of bare heads, helmets, caps of liberty, waving bayonets, and heaving shoulders. So violent was their onrush that people vanished in the swarming mass; on and on they climbed, like a spring-tide sweeping up a river, driven forward by an irresistible impulse, with a continuous roar. At the top they scattered and the singing ceased.

Nothing could be heard but the trampling of feet and the babble of voices. The harmless crowd was content to stare. But from time to time an elbow, cramped for space, burst through a window; sometimes a vase or a statuette rolled off a side table on to the ground. The panelling creaked under the pressure of the throng. Sweat trickled down their red faces in large drops; Hussonnet remarked: 'I don't care much for the smell of heroes.'

'Oh, you annoy me,' said Frederic.

Pushed along helplessly, they entered a room in which a red velvet canopy was stretched across the ceiling. On the throne beneath sat a workman with a black beard, his shirt half open, grinning stupidly, like an ape. Others climbed on to the dais to sit in his place.

'What a legend!' said Hussonnet. 'The sovereignty of the people!'

Outstretched arms lifted the arm-chair and passed it, swaying, right across the room.

'Good Lord! See how it rocks! The ship of state is being tossed in a stormy sea! It's dancing a jig! It's dancing a jig!'

It was taken to a window and thrown out, amid hisses.

'Poor old thing!' said Hussonnet, as he watched it fall into the garden, where it was soon picked up to be carried in procession to the Bastille and afterwards burned.

There followed a burst of frantic joy, as though the throne had been replaced by a future of unlimited happiness; and the people, less out of vengeance than from a desire to assert their mastery, broke and tore down mirrors, curtains, chandeliers, sconces, tables, chairs, stools—everything movable, down to albums of drawings and work baskets. They had conquered, therefore they should celebrate. In mockery, the rabble draped themselves in lace and cashmere. Gold fringes were wound about the sleeves of blouses, hats with ostrich plumes decked the heads of blacksmiths, ribbons of the Legion of Honour made sashes for prostitutes. Each man satisfied his whim; some danced, others drank. In the queen's room a woman was greasing her hair with pomade. Two enthusiasts were playing cards behind a screen; Hussonnet pointed out to Frederic a man leaning on a balcony, smoking his clay pipe; and, amid the general fury, the hall re-echoed to the crash of china and the shattering of glass; and the fragments of crystal tinkled as they fell, like the keys of a harmonica.

Then their frenzy took a darker turn. In obscene curiosity they ransacked the cupboards and closets, and turned out all the drawers. Jail-birds thrust their arms into the princesses' bed and rolled on top of it, as a consolation for not being able to rape them. Sinister characters wandered silently about, searching for something to steal; but the crowd was too numerous. Looking through the doorways, down the long series of rooms, one could see nothing but a dark mass of people in a cloud of dust between the gilded walls. They were all out of breath; the heat became more and more stifling; and the two friends went out, to avoid being suffocated.

In the vestibule, on a pile of clothes, stood a prostitute, posed as a statue of Liberty, motionless, with staring eyes—a figure of terror.

They were only just outside when a troop of Municipal Guards in overcoats came towards them. The guards took off their policemen's caps, revealing their somewhat bald heads, and bowed very low to the people. The ragged victors were enchanted with this sign of respect. Nor were Hussonnet and Frederic entirely displeased by the spectacle.

They were burning with excitement. They went back to the Palais-Royal. At the opening of the rue Fromanteau the corpses of soldiers were piled up on straw. They passed them without emotion, and even took a pride in their imperturbability.

The palace was crammed with people. Seven bonfires were blazing in the inner court. Pianos, chests of drawers, and clocks were being flung out of the windows. Fire-pumps were throwing water up to the roof. Some hooligans tried to cut the hoses with their sabres. Frederic urged an artillery cadet to intervene. The cadet did not understand; he seemed to be half-witted. All round, in the two arcades, the mob, having broken open the cellars, were abandoning themselves to a horrible debauch. Wine flowed in streams and wetted their feet; there were ruffians drinking out of the heels of broken bottles, and shouting as they reeled.

'Let's go,' said Hussonnet. 'I find your friends the people revolting.'

All along the Orleans gallery the wounded were lying on mattresses on the ground, with purple curtains for blankets, while the wives of the local tradesmen brought them soup and clean linen.

'No matter!' said Frederic. 'To my mind, the people are sublime!'

The great hall was filled with an angry swarming crowd; some tried to climb to the higher floors to complete the work of destruction; a few National Guards on the steps struggled to hold them back. The boldest of the guards was a bare-headed rifleman, with tousled hair and tattered belt. His shirt was bulging out between his trousers and his coat, and he fought desperately beside his comrades. Hussonnet, who had very long sight, recognized Arnoux in the distance.

Then they went into the Tuileries garden, where they could breathe more freely. They sank down on a bench; and sat for some minutes with their eyes shut, so dead-beat that they had not the strength to speak. Around them passers-by were meeting and talking. The Duchesse d'Orléans had been nominated regent; it was all over; and every one felt that sense of satisfaction that follows the rapid solution of a crisis. Suddenly servants appeared at all the top-floor windows of the palace; they tore up their liveries as a sign of renunciation. The people booed them. They withdrew.

The two friends' attention was distracted by the sight of a tall youth walking briskly through the trees with a musket on his shoulder. He wore a red tunic with a cartridge belt round his waist; a handkerchief was wound round his forehead, under his cap. He turned his head. It was Dussardier. He flung himself into their arms.

'What happiness, my dear old friends!' he said, and could not utter another word; for he was quite breathless with joy and exhaustion.

He had been on his feet for forty-eight hours. He had worked at the barricades in the Latin quarter, fought in the rue Rambuteau, saved the lives of three dragoons, entered the Tuileries with Dunoyer's column, gone to the Chamber, and afterwards to the Hôtel de Ville.

'I'm just back from there. All is well! The people have triumphed. Workmen and shopkeepers are shaking hands! Ah, if you'd seen what I've seen! What wonderful people! How splendid it all is!'

And without noticing that they were unarmed:

'I knew I should find you in the thick of it! Things were warm for a moment—but no matter!'

A drop of blood was trickling down his cheek, and to the others' inquiries he replied:

'It's nothing. A scratch from a bayonet.'

'But you ought to have it seen to.'

'Nonsense! I'm as strong as a horse. What does it matter? The Republic has been proclaimed! We shall be happy now. I heard some journalists talking just now; they said we were going to liberate Poland and Italy. No more kings! Do you understand? The whole world free! The whole world free!'

And, embracing the entire horizon in a glance, he stood with his arms outstretched in an attitude of triumph. Men were running along the terrace, beside the fountains, in a long file.

'Upon my word, I was forgetting. The forts are still occupied. I must go! Good-bye!'

He turned round, and brandishing his musket, shouted to them:

'Long live the republic!'

Great eddies of black smoke, mixed with sparks, were pouring from the chimneys of the palace. The sound of the bells in the distance was like the frightened bleating of sheep. Everywhere, to right and left, the victors were letting off their pieces. Although Frederic was no warrior, he felt his Gallic blood leap. The enthusiasm of the crowd had caught him with its spell. Voluptuously he sniffed the stormy air, which was full of the smell of powder; and at the same time he shivered under the surge of a vast love, a supreme, all-embracing affection, as though the heart of all humanity were beating in his breast.

Hussonnet yawned and said:

'I suppose it's time for me to go and educate the masses.'

Frederic, having followed him to his office on the place de la Bourse, set to work and composed an account of the events in a lyrical style for the newspaper at Troyes; a little work of art, which he signed. Then they dined together at a tavern. Hussonnet was pensive; the eccentricities of the revolution surpassed his own.

After coffee they went to the Hôtel de Ville, in search of news, and there his natural boyishness reasserted itself. He climbed over the barricades like a chamois and answered the sentries' challenge with patriotic pleasantries.

They heard the provisional Government proclaimed by torchlight. At last, at midnight, Frederic returned home, worn out with exhaustion.

'Well,' he said to his servant who was undressing him, 'are you satisfied?'

'Oh, yes, sir. But I don't like to see the people marching in step!'

When he woke up next morning Frederic thought of Deslauriers. He hurried to his house. The lawyer had just left, having been appointed a provincial commissioner. The previous evening he had managed to see Ledru-Rollin,[1] and, by importuning him in the name of the schools, had succeeded in snatching a place and a mission. In any case, said the porter, he would be writing next week, giving his address.

After that, Frederic went to see Rosanette. She received him sourly, for she had not forgiven him for his desertion. Her irritation vanished under his repeated assurances that peace had been restored. All was now quiet; there was no cause for alarm; he kissed her; and she declared herself for the republic. His Grace the Archbishop of Paris had already done this, and he was followed, with marvellous alacrity, by the Magistrature, the Council of State, the Institut, the Marshals of France, Changarnier,[2] M. de Falloux,[3] all the Bonapartists, all the Legitimists, and a considerable number of Orleanists.

The fall of the monarchy had been so sudden that the middle classes, after the first stupefaction, felt a kind of astonishment at finding themselves still alive. The summary execution of some thieves, who were shot without trial, was a reassuring act of justice. For a month Lamartine's[1] remark about the red flag[2] was repeated: 'It had merely paraded round the Champ de Mars, whereas the tricolour flag . . .' and so forth: and they all ranged themselves under the shadow of the tricolour. Of the three colours, each party saw only their own, and each was fully resolved to eliminate the other two as soon as it was strong enough.

Business was at a standstill, and anxiety or idle curiosity drove every one into the streets. The general casualness of dress lessened the distinction between social classes; hatred was concealed, hope spread abroad, and the crowds were full of gentleness. Pride was written on the faces of the people—pride in the rights they had won. There was a carnival spirit abroad, a kind of camp-fire comradeship. Paris was never pleasanter than in those early days.

Frederic took Rosanette on his arm; and they strolled about the streets together. She liked the rosettes that decorated every buttonhole, the flags hanging from every window, the placards of every colour posted on the walls; now and then she threw a few coppers into the box for the wounded, which always stood on a chair in the middle of the road. Then she stopped to look at caricatures showing Louis-Philippe as a confectioner, an acrobat, a dog, a leech. But Caussidière's[3] men, with their sabres and scarves, frightened her a little. Sometimes a tree of liberty was being planted. The clergy, escorted by acolytes in gold braid, took part in the ceremony, to the great delight of the crowd. The commonest sight was the deputations of every kind going to present some petition at the Hôtel de Ville, for each trade and each industry expected the Government to put a final end to its distresses. Some people, it is true, went to tender advice or congratulations, or just for the sake of paying a call on the Government, and seeing the machine at work.

One day, about the middle of March, Frederic was crossing the Arcola bridge, on his way to the Latin quarter on an errand for Rosanette, when he saw coming towards him a column of men with strange hats and long beards. At their head, beating a drum, marched a negro, a former artists' model. Their banner, which floated in the wind, bore the inscription 'Pictorial Artists,' and the man who carried it was none other than Pellerin.

He motioned to Frederic to wait for him, then reappeared five minutes later. He had time to spare, for the Government was at that moment engaged with the stonemasons. He and his colleagues were going to demand the creation of a 'Forum of Art'—a sort of artistic stock exchange where aesthetic matters would be debated; sublime works would be produced, because the genius of all would be shared in common. Soon Paris would be covered with gigantic monuments, which he would decorate; he had already begun a figure of the Republic. One of his comrades hurried to fetch him back, for they were only just ahead of the poulterers' deputation.

'What folly!' grumbled a voice in the crowd. 'All this fancy nonsense! Nothing solid!'

It was Regimbart. He did not greet Frederic; but took advantage of the opportunity to vent his spleen.

The citizen spent his days in wandering about the streets, pulling his moustache, rolling his eyes, and exchanging gloomy forebodings with all and sundry. He only had two phrases: 'Look out! We're going to be outflanked!' and: 'Confound it, they're filching our Republic!' He was dissatisfied with everything, and particularly with the fact that we had not retaken our natural frontiers. The mere mention of Lamartine made him shrug his shoulders. He did not consider that Ledru-Rollin was 'up to the problem.' He regarded Dupont (de l'Eure) as an old stick-in-the-mud, Albert as an idiot, Louis Blanc as a Utopian, and Blanqui[1] as an extremely dangerous man; and when Frederic asked him what ought to be done, he answered, squeezing his arm until he almost crushed it:

'Seize the Rhine, I tell you. Seize the Rhine, damn it!'

Then he denounced the reaction.

This was beginning to show itself. The sack of the castles of Neuilly and Suresne, the fires at Les Batignolles, the riots at Lyons—every excess, every grievance was now exaggerated by the reactionaries, and they added to these Ledru-Rollin's circular letter,[2] the forced issue of bank notes, the fall in Government stock to sixty francs, and finally, as the ultimate iniquity, the last straw, the culmination of horror, the forty-five-centime tax! And on top of that there was Socialism as well! Although these theories were about as novel as the game of chess, and although for forty years they had been attacked and demolished in enough books to fill whole libraries, they were still as terrifying to the middle classes as a shower of meteorites; they aroused that hatred and indignation which any idea produces by its advent, just because it is an idea. This detestation later redounds to the glory of the idea, and, however mediocre it may be, ensures its permanent superiority to its enemies.

Then property, as an object of reverence, was lifted to the level of religion and began to be confused with God. The attacks made on it seemed a form of sacrilege, almost resembling cannibalism. In spite of the unprecedented humanity of the Government's legislation, the spectre of '93 reared its head again, and the blade of the guillotine quivered in every syllable of the word 'Republic.' But this did not prevent people from despising it for its weakness. France, feeling herself without a master, began to cry out in terror, like a blind man without a stick, or a child that has lost its nurse.

Of all the men in France, none trembled more violently than M. Dambreuse. The new condition of things not only threatened his fortune, but, worse still, contradicted his experience. So excellent a system—so good a king! How was it possible? The world was coming to an end!

On the day after the revolution, he dismissed three servants, sold his horses, bought a soft hat to wear in the streets, and even thought of letting his beard grow; and he stayed at home, prostrate, reading and re-reading with bitter feelings those newspapers whose views were most opposed to his own, and so gloomily disposed that even the jokes about Flocon's pipe [1] did not succeed in wringing a smile from him.

As a supporter of the late monarchy, he was afraid that the people would wreak their vengeance on his property in Champagne. Then he came across Frederic's effusion in the Troyes newspaper. He at once concluded that his young friend was a person of great influence, who, if he could not help him, could at least protect him. So one morning M. Dambreuse appeared at Frederic's house, accompanied by Martinon.

The sole object of his visit, he said, was to see Frederic and have a few words with him. All things considered, he was delighted with the turn of events, and welcomed with all his heart 'our glorious motto: Liberty, Equality, Fraternity,' for he had always been a Republican at bottom. If he had voted with the Government, under the old regime, it was only that he might hasten its inevitable downfall. He even attacked M. Guizot, 'who—let 's admit it!—put us in a pretty pickle.' On the other hand, he had a great admiration for Lamartine, who had behaved 'magnificently, upon my soul, when he said about the red flag . . .'

'Yes, I know,' said Frederic.

After that, he declared his sympathy for the workers.

'For, if it comes to that, we 're all workers, more or less.'

And he even went so far in his impartiality as to acknowledge that there was logic in Proudhon. 'Oh, yes, a great deal of logic, upon my soul!' Then, with that detachment which marks an exceptional mind, he talked about the exhibition of painting, in which he had seen Pellerin's picture. He considered it original—very well done.

Martinon supported everything he said with approving comments; he also thought one 'should rally openly to the republic'; he spoke of his working-class father, and played the peasant, the man of the people. Soon they were discussing the elections to the National Assembly,[1] and the candidates in the district of La Fortelle. The Opposition candidate had no chance.

'You ought to take his place!' said M. Dambreuse.

Frederic protested.

But why not? He would gain the votes of the extremists because of his personal opinions, and those of the Conservatives because of his family.

'And perhaps,' added the banker, smiling, 'my influence might be of some assistance.'

Frederic demurred; he would not know how to begin. It was perfectly simple; he must get himself recommended to the patriots of the district of the Aube through a Paris club. His speech should not be one of the usual confessions of faith, but a serious statement of principle.

'Bring it to me; I know what they like down there. And I repeat, you may be able to do great things for your country, for us all, and for me.'

In times like these they must help each other, and if Frederic wanted anything for himself, or for his friends . . .

'No, sir, thank you very much!'

'Of course, you'll do as much for me one day!'

The banker was certainly an excellent fellow. Frederic could not help thinking of his advice; and soon a dazzling ambition made his mind reel.

The great figures of the Convention passed before his eyes. It seemed to him that a magnificent dawn was breaking. Rome, Vienna, and Berlin were in revolt; the Austrians had been driven from Venice; all Europe was in a ferment. Now was the time to throw oneself into the movement, perhaps to hasten its progress; and then he was terribly attracted by the uniform which he understood the deputies would wear. Already he saw himself in a waistcoat with silk facings and a tricolour sash; and this longing, this fantasy became so insistent that he confessed it to Dussardier.

The good fellow's enthusiasm was as strong as ever.

'Certainly—by all means! Put up as a candidate!'

None the less, Frederic consulted Deslauriers as well. The stupid opposition which was hampering the commissioner in his district had increased his Liberalism. He at once sent Frederic some violent exhortations.

However, he needed the approval of a wider circle; and he confided in Rosanette, one day when Mlle Vatnaz was there.

She was one of those Parisian spinsters who, every evening, after they have given their lessons, or tried to sell their sketches or their poor little writings, come back home with mud on their petticoats, cook their dinner, and eat it all alone. Then, with their toes on a foot-warmer, by the light of a dirty lamp, they dream of a sweetheart, a family, a household, a fortune—everything that they have not got. So she, like many others, had welcomed the revolution as the harbinger of her revenge; and she was devoting herself wholeheartedly to Socialist propaganda.

According to Mlle Vatnaz, the emancipation of the proletariat was only possible through the emancipation of women. She wanted to see women admitted to every form of employment; she demanded affiliation rights, a new legal code, and the abolition of marriage, or at least a more intelligent regulation of the practice. Every Frenchwoman should be entitled to marry a Frenchman, or to adopt an old man. Nurses and midwives should become salaried officials of the State; there should be a jury to examine books by women, special publishers for women, a polytechnic school for women, a National Guard for women—everything for women! And since the Government would not recognize their claims, they must overcome force by force. Ten thousand citizenesses, with good muskets, could make the Hôtel de Ville tremble.

Frederic's candidature seemed to favour her ideas. She encouraged him and showed him glory on the horizon. Rosanette was delighted at having a lover who was going to speak in the Chamber.

'And then, perhaps, they'll give you a good position.'

Frederic, the weakest of men, was conquered by the universal madness. He wrote a speech and went to show it to M. Dambreuse.

At the sound of the outer gate closing, a curtain opened slightly behind a window; and a woman appeared. He had not time to see who it was. As he entered the hall, a picture caught his eye and he paused. It was Pellerin's picture, which had been stood on a chair—temporarily, no doubt.

It represented the Republic, or Progress, or Civilization, in the form of Jesus Christ driving a locomotive across a virgin forest. After looking at it for a moment, Frederic exclaimed:

'How disgusting!'

'Yes, indeed,' said M. Dambreuse, who had overheard this remark as he approached and supposed that it referred, not to the painting, but to the doctrine which the picture glorified.

At the same moment Martinon arrived. They went into the study; and Frederic was drawing a piece of paper from his pocket when Mlle Cécile came in suddenly and said with an artless air:

'Is my aunt here?'

'You can see she isn't,' replied the banker. 'Never mind! Make yourself at home, mademoiselle!'

'Oh, no, thank you. I'll leave you.'

Scarcely had she gone out, when Martinon pretended to be looking for his handkerchief.

'I left it in my overcoat. If you don't mind.'

'By all means,' said M. Dambreuse.

He was evidently not deceived by this manœuvre, and even seemed to encourage it. Soon Martinon reappeared, and Frederic began his speech. At the second page, which referred to the predominance of the moneyed interests as a scandal, the banker made a face. Then, touching on the reforms needed, Frederic asked for free trade.

'What! But, excuse me——'

Frederic continued, unhearing. He demanded an income tax, a graduated tax, a federation of Europe, together with universal education and the widest possible encouragement of the fine arts.

'Why should not the country provide men like Delacroix and Victor Hugo with a hundred thousand francs a year?'

The whole concluded with some advice to the upper classes.

'Spare nothing, O men of substance! Give! Give!'

He broke off and remained standing up. The two listeners, who were seated, did not speak; Martinon's eyes were staring, M. Dambreuse was very pale. At last, concealing his emotion under a sour smile, he said:

'Your speech is perfect.'

And he praised the form very highly, so as to avoid expressing himself about the contents.

This virulence on the part of an inoffensive young man terrified him—particularly as a symptom. Martinon tried to reassure him. In a short time the Conservative Party would certainly take its revenge; the commissioners of the provisional Government had already been driven out of several towns; the elections did not take place until the 23rd of April, so there was plenty of time; in short, M. Dambreuse should himself stand for the Aube; and, from that day on, Martinon did not leave him; he became his secretary and surrounded him with filial attentions.

Frederic arrived at Rosanette's well pleased with himself. Delmar was there and informed him that he was 'definitely' standing as a candidate for the Seine elections. In a proclamation addressed 'to the People' (whom he treated with great familiarity) the actor boasted that he was one of the few who understood them; he had, for their sake, been 'crucified on the cross of Art,' so that he was now their incarnation, their ideal. He believed, indeed, that he had an immense influence on the masses. In later years, at a Government office, he offered to quell a riot single-handed, and when asked what means he would employ, he had answered:

'Have no fear! I shall show them my face!'

To annoy him, Frederic told him about his own candidature. As soon as the actor realized that his future colleague had a country district in mind, he placed himself at Frederic's service and offered to sponsor him at the clubs.

He visited them all—the red clubs, the blue clubs, the wild, the peaceful, the austere, the ribald, the mystical, and the drunken—the clubs where they passed the death sentence on kings, the clubs where they denounced the frauds of the grocery trade. Everywhere tenants cursed landlords, blouses attacked frock coats, the rich conspired against the poor. Some demanded compensation, claiming to have been victimized by the police, others begged for money to exploit inventions; plans were put forward for ideal communities, for cantonal bazaars, for systems of universal happiness. Now and then, a flash of intelligence shone out amid the clouds of stupidity—a speaker's appeal, sudden and devastating, a point of law crystallized in an oath, pearls of eloquence on the lips of a ragged workman, wearing his sword belt against the bare skin of his shirtless chest. Sometimes, too, a gentleman would appear—an aristocrat, affecting humility, talking the language of the people and leaving his hands unwashed, so as to make them look horny. A patriot would recognize him; he would be hustled out by the more orthodox; and he would go home with rage in his heart. To gain a reputation for shrewdness, it was essential to abuse the lawyers, and to make the greatest possible use of the following expressions: 'Contribute one's stone to the building — social problem — workshop.'

Delmar never failed to take the platform on these occasions; and when he had nothing more to say, he used to strike an attitude with his hand on his hip, and his other arm in his waistcoat, and turn his head round sharply, so as to show off his profile. This was always followed by a burst of applause— from Mlle Vatnaz at the back of the hall.

In spite of the low standard of oratory, Frederic did not dare to make the attempt. The people all seemed too uncultured or too hostile.

Then Dussardier, who had been making inquiries, informed Frederic that there was a club in the rue Saint-Jacques called the Club de l'Intelligence. Such a name promised well. Besides, he would bring his friends.

He brought along the guests he had invited to his party: the book-keeper, the traveller in wines, and the architect. Even Pellerin came; Hussonnet was expected; and on the pavement, opposite the door, stood Regimbart, with two companions. One was his faithful Compain, a stocky individual, red-eyed and pock-marked; the second was a sort of human ape, excessively hairy, of whom nothing was known except that he was a patriot from Barcelona.

They went down a passage, and were then shown into a large room which was apparently a carpenter's shop. The newly built walls smelt of plaster. Four oil lamps hanging in a row shed an unpleasant light. On a platform at the far end was a desk with a bell; below it stood a table, which did duty as the speakers' rostrum, and on either side of it two lower tables for the use of the secretaries. The audience that filled the benches consisted of elderly art students, poor school teachers, and unsuccessful writers. Among the rows of overcoats with greasy collars could be seen an occasional woman's hat or workman's blouse. Indeed, the back of the hall was full of workmen, some of whom had come out of idle curiosity, while others were there by arrangement with some of the speakers, to provide applause.

Frederic was careful to place himself between Dussardier and Regimbart. As soon as the latter had sat down, he laid his hands on his stick, his chin on his hands, and closed his eyes. At the opposite end of the hall the figure of Delmar towered above the crowd.

Sénécal appeared at the chairman's desk. Dussardier had

supposed that this surprise would give Frederic pleasure; in fact, it annoyed him.

The audience showed great respect for their chairman. He had been among those who had on the 25th of February demanded the immediate organization of labour;[1] the next day, at the Prado, he had urged an attack on the Hôtel de Ville; and, since it was the custom for figures for that period to model themselves after a pattern—some imitating Saint-Just, others Danton, others Marat—Sénécal tried to resemble Blanqui, who was a follower of Robespierre. His black gloves and close-cropped hair gave him a very becoming look of severity.

He opened the meeting with the Declaration of the Rights of Man and the Citizen, a customary act of faith. Then a vigorous voice struck up Béranger's *Recollections of the People*.

Other voices were raised.

'No, no! Not that!'

'*The Cap!*' yelled the patriots at the back. And they sang the verse of the day in chorus:

> 'Off with your hat before my cap!
> On your knees before the workman!'

At a word from the chairman the audience was silent. One of the secretaries proceeded to open the letters.

'Certain young persons inform us that it is their custom to burn a copy of the *Assemblée nationale*[2] every evening in front of the Panthéon. They urge all patriots to follow their example.'

'Bravo! Carried!' answered the crowd.

'Citizen Jean-Jacques Langreneux, printer, rue Dauphine, desires the erection of a monument to the Thermidor martyrs.'

'Michel-Évariste-Népomucène Vincent, ex-professor, expresses the hope that European democracy will adopt a universal language. A dead language might be used, such as Latin of the best period.'

'No! No Latin!' cried the architect.

'Why not?' said a schoolmaster.

And the two of them began an argument in which others joined. Every one tried to show off his knowledge, and the discussion soon became so boring that many went home.

Then a little old man, wearing green spectacles under an enormously high forehead, demanded a hearing for an urgent communication.

This was a memorandum on the assessment of taxation. He poured out statistics; there was no end to them. Losing patience, the crowd began to murmur and talk; then they started hissing and booing. Sénécal reprimanded them; the speaker continued like a machine. He stopped only when taken by the elbow. The good fellow had the appearance of waking from a dream, and, calmly raising his spectacles, he said:

'I'm sorry, citizens, I'm sorry! I'll get down. I beg your pardon!'

The failure of this address disconcerted Frederic. He had his speech in his pocket, but an improvisation would have stood a better chance.

At length the chairman announced that they would pass to the main business of the day—the choice of candidates for the National Assembly. They would not debate the principal Republican lists. But the Club de l'Intelligence was entitled—'with all due respect to the pundits of the Hôtel de Ville'—to form a list of its own, like other institutions. Let those citizens, therefore, who sought the people's mandate put forward their qualifications.

'Go to it, Frederic,' said Dussardier.

A man in a cassock, with crinkly hair and a lively expression, had already raised his hand. Almost inaudibly he declared that his name was Ducretot, priest and agronomist, and that he was the author of a work entitled *Concerning Dung*. He was directed to a horticultural association.

Next, a patriot in a blouse climbed on to the platform. He was a man of the people, with broad shoulders, a plump, very gentle face, and long black hair. He cast an almost voluptuous glance round the audience, threw back his head, and at last, spreading out his arms, began:

'O my brethren, ye have rejected Ducretot and ye have done well! But ye did not do this through contempt for God, for we are all godly.'

Many were listening open-mouthed, like devotees, in ecstatic postures.

'Nor did ye do this because he is a priest, for we too are priests. The workman is a priest, like the founder of Socialism, the Master of us all, Jesus Christ.'

The moment had come to inaugurate the reign of God. The Gospel led straight to 1789. The abolition of slavery would be followed by the abolition of the proletariat. The age of hatred was over; the age of love was about to begin.

'Christianity is the keystone of the arch, and the foundation of the new edifice. . . .'

'Is this some sort of a joke?' cried the traveller in wines. 'Where did they get hold of this damned parson?'

This interruption horrified the audience. Nearly all of them climbed on to the benches, shook their fists and yelled: 'Atheist! Aristocrat! Swine!' while the chairman's bell rang without stopping and shouts of 'Order! Order!' re-echoed. But the interrupter, sustained by three coffees-and-brandy taken beforehand, continued to struggle undismayed.

'What? Me an aristocrat? Go on!'

Permitted at length to explain himself, he declared that there could never be peace with the priests and, since they had just been talking about economy, it would be a splendid saving to suppress the churches, the sacred vessels, and, in due course, all religions.

Someone complained that he was going to extremes.

'Yes! I'm going to extremes! But when a ship is caught in a storm . . .'

Without waiting for the end of the comparison, another voice broke in:

'I agree! But you're destroying everything in one blow, like a stupid builder . . .'

'That's an insult to the building trade!' cried a citizen covered with plaster.

And, insisting that he had been affronted, he stormed and raved, tried to fight, and clung desperately to his seat. Three men were needed to throw him out.

Meanwhile the workman was still on the platform. The two secretaries warned him to get down. He protested against the injustice that was being done to him.

'You will never stop me from uttering this cry: To our beloved France, love eternal! To the republic, love eternal!'

'Citizens!' said Compain, 'citizens!'

By dint of saying 'Citizens!' again and again, he secured comparative quiet. Then he placed his two red hands, that looked like stumps, on the table, thrust his body forward, half-closed his eyes, and began:

'I think we should extend the range of the calf's head.'

All were silent, thinking they had misheard.

'Yes! The calf's head!'

A simultaneous roar of laughter burst from three hundred throats. Compain drew back before these hilarious faces. He continued in a voice of fury:

'What! You've never heard of the calf's head?'

They were convulsed, delirious. They held their sides. Some even fell on to the floor under the seats. Compain, defeated, took refuge beside Regimbart, and tried to get him to leave.

'No, I 'm staying to the end,' said the citizen.

This reply decided Frederic. He was looking to right and left for support among his friends, when he saw Pellerin on the platform in front of him. The artist took a high line with the crowd.

'I wish to know where the candidate for art is to be found. I have painted a picture——'

'We don't want any pictures,' said a thin man with red veins on his cheeks, brutally.

Pellerin protested against the interruption.

The thin man continued in a tragic voice:

'Should not the Government ere now have abolished prostitution and poverty, by decree?'

This remark immediately won him the sympathy of the crowd, and he thundered against the corruption of the great cities.

'Shame and infamy! We ought to seize the rich as they come out of the Maison d'Or and spit in their faces! At least, let the Government not encourage debauchery! Yet our daughters and sisters are vilely maltreated by the officials of the custom houses——'

A distant voice observed:

'That 's a good one!'

'Throw him out!'

'They extort taxes from us to pay for their orgies. For instance, the large emoluments of the actor——'

'My turn!' cried Delmar.

He leapt on to the platform, pushed every one aside and took up his usual pose. Declaring that he despised such mean accusations he dilated on the actor's civilizing mission. Since the theatre was the centre of national education, he was in favour of reforming it. First of all, there should be no more managers and no more privileges.

'That 's right! No more privileges at all!'

The actor's performance inflamed the crowd, and the air was thick with revolutionary proposals.

'Down with academics! Down with the Institut!'

'No more missions!'

'No more matriculation!'

'Down with university degrees!'

'No,' said Sénécal, 'let us preserve them; but let them be

conferred by universal franchise, by the people, the only true judge.'

But this was not the most essential point, he continued. First of all, the rich must be levelled down! And he depicted them wallowing in crime under their gilded ceilings, while the poor, writhing with hunger in their garrets, practised every virtue. The applause grew so loud that he broke off. He stood for some minutes with his eyes closed and his head thrown back—letting himself float, as it were, on the wave of indignation which he had aroused.

Then he began to speak dogmatically, in phrases as peremptory as laws. The State must seize the banks and the insurance companies. Inheritance would be abolished. A public fund would be established for the workers. Other measures would be useful later on. These were enough for the moment; and, returning to the electoral question, he added:

'We need citizens of integrity, men of a new stamp! Who will come forward?'

Frederic rose to his feet. There was a buzz of approval among his friends. But Sénécal, assuming the expression of a Fouquier-Tinville,[1] began to question him about his name, Christian names, antecedents, life, and morals.

Frederic answered briefly, biting his lip. Sénécal asked if any one saw any objection to this candidature.

'No, no!'

But Sénécal did. All leaned forward, straining their ears. The citizen aspirant had failed to pay a certain sum he had promised for the foundation of a democratic paper. Moreover, on the 22nd of February, although sufficiently forewarned, he had failed to appear at the meeting-place on the place du Panthéon.

'I swear he was at the Tuileries!' said Dussardier.

'Can you swear you saw him at the Panthéon?'

Dussardier hung his head. Frederic said nothing; his friends, shocked, looked at him with uneasiness.

'At least,' Sénécal continued, 'you must know some patriot who will answer for your principles.'

'I will,' said Dussardier.

'That's not enough. Another!'

Frederic turned towards Pellerin. The artist replied by an abundance of gestures as if to say:

'My dear fellow, they have rejected me. Well, what can you expect?'

Then Frederic nudged Regimbart.

'Yes. You 're right, it 's time. Well, here goes!'

And Regimbart climbed on to the platform; then, pointing to the Spaniard, who had followed him:

'Allow me, citizens,' he said, 'to present to you a patriot from Barcelona.'

The patriot bowed low, rolled his silver eyes like a mechanical toy, and placing his hand on his heart, began:

'Ciudadanos! Mucho aprecio el honor que me dispensáis, y si grande es vuestra bondad mayor es vuestra atención.'

'I demand a hearing!' cried Frederic.

'Desde que se proclamó la constitución de Cadiz, ese pacto fundamental de las libertades españolas hasta la última revolución, nuestra patria cuenta numerosos y heroicos martires.'

Yet once more Frederic tried to make his voice heard:

'But, citizens——'

The Spaniard continued:

'El martes próximo tendrá lugar en la iglesia de la Magdalena un servicio funebre.'

'Why, this is ridiculous. No one can understand a word.'

This remark infuriated the crowd.

'Throw him out! Throw him out!'

'Who? Me?' asked Frederic.

'Yes, you!' said Sénécal imperiously. 'Get out!'

He rose to leave; and the voice of the Spaniard pursued him:

'Y todos los Españoles desearían ver allí reunidas las deputaciones de los clubs y de la milicia nacional. Un oración funebre en honor de la libertad española y del mundo entero será pronunciada por un miembro del clero de Paris en la sala Bonne-Nouvelle. Honor al pueblo francés, que llamaría yo el primero pueblo del mundo, sino fuese ciudadano de otra nación!'

'Aristo!' snarled a ragged tramp, shaking his fist at Frederic. He hurried indignantly into the street.

He blamed himself for his public spirit, without reflecting that the charges brought against him were, after all, perfectly justified. What a fatal plan this candidature had been! But what dolts, what morons! He compared himself to these men and soothed his wounded pride with the thought of their stupidity.

Then he felt a desire to see Rosanette. After so much ugliness, and so much pomposity, her gentleness would be refreshing. She knew that he had been due to make his appearance at a club that evening. However, when he came in, she did not ask him a single question about it.

She was sitting by the fire, unpicking the lining of a dress. This task surprised him.

'Hallo! What are you doing?'

'You can see for yourself,' she said dryly. 'I'm doing up my old clothes. That's your republic!'

'How—my republic?'

'Perhaps it's mine, then?'

And she started blaming him for everything that had happened in France in the last two months; he was responsible for the revolution, for every one being ruined, for the rich people leaving Paris, and for her dying, later on, in the workhouse.

'It's easy for you to talk with your income. Not that you'll have that much longer, the way things are going.'

'That's possible,' said Frederic. 'Public-spirited men are always misunderstood; and if it was not for one's conscience, the brutishness of the people one has to deal with would soon sicken one of self-sacrifice.'

Rosanette looked at him with half-closed eyes.

'Eh? What? What self-sacrifice? It looks as if our Frederic has made a mess of it! Serve you right! That'll teach you to make patriotic contributions. Oh, don't lie to me! I know you gave them three hundred francs; for your republic's an expensive mistress. Well, go and have a good time with your republic, my fine friend!'

This idiotic outburst made Frederic forget his recent disappointment in a more grievous disillusion.

He withdrew to the far end of the room. She came up to him.

'Come on! Put two and two together! A country has to have a master, like a house; otherwise every one will just do as he damn well pleases. To begin with, everybody knows that Ledru-Rollin's up to his ears in debt. Then, look at Lamartine—what can a poet know about politics? Oh, it's no use your looking sulky and thinking you're cleverer than other people—it's true, all the same. But you're always quibbling—one can't get a word in edgeways. Now take Fournier-Fontaine, of the Saint-Roch stores—do you know how much of the cash is missing? Only eight hundred thousand francs! And what about Gomer, the furniture remover opposite? There's another Republican for you. Broke the tongs over his old woman's head, and he's boozed so much absinthe that they're taking him to the madhouse. That's the Republicans all over! A republic at bargain prices! Oh, yes! Go on! Boast about it!'

Frederic went away. The stupidity of the woman, suddenly

revealed in these vulgar phrases, disgusted him. He even felt a slight resurgence of patriotism.

Rosanette's ill humour grew worse and worse. The enthusiasm of Mlle Vatnaz annoyed her. For Mlle Vatnaz, believing she had a mission, insisted on holding forth to Rosanette and cross-questioning her; with her wider knowledge, she overwhelmed her friend with her arguments.

One day she arrived full of indignation against Hussonnet, who had been indulging in bawdy jokes at the women's club. Rosanette approved of his conduct and declared that she would put on men's clothes herself and go and tell them what she thought of them, and give them a whipping. Frederic came in at the same moment.

'You'll come with me, won't you?'

And in spite of his presence they started to squabble, one taking the housewife's part, the other the philosopher's.

According to Rosanette, the only purpose for which women were born was to make love, or else to bring up children and manage a household.

Mlle Vatnaz contended that woman should have a place in the State. The ancient Gallic women made laws, and so did the Anglo-Saxons; the wives of the Hurons took their part in the national council. The work of civilization was common to both sexes. All should contribute to it, and eventually replace egotism by fraternity, individualism by co-operation, and small holdings by collective farms.

'Oh, very good! So now you're a farming expert!'

'Why shouldn't I be? Besides, it's a question of the future of humanity.'

'Think of your own!'

'That's my affair!'

They were getting angry. Frederic intervened. In her excitement, Mlle Vatnaz went so far as to argue in favour of Communism.

'What nonsense!' said Rosanette. 'As though it could ever happen!'

As evidence the other referred to the Essenes, the Moravian Brethren, the Jesuits of Paraguay, the Pingon family, near Thiers in Auvergne: and in her wild gesticulations her watch-chain got caught upon a little gold sheep which was hanging in her bunch of charms.

Suddenly Rosanette turned extraordinarily pale.

Mlle Vatnaz went on trying to disentangle the ornament.

'Don't trouble yourself,' said Rosanette. 'I know all about your political opinions now.'

'What?' said Mlle Vatnaz, blushing like a virgin.

'Oh—you know what I mean.'

Frederic did not understand. Clearly, something more important and more personal than Socialism had come up between them. 'Well, supposing I 've got it,' said Mlle Vatnaz, drawing herself up boldly. 'It 's a loan, my dear—a debt for a debt!'

'I 'm not denying my debts. But somehow I don't see you taking that in exchange for several thousand francs. At least, I borrow: I 'm not a thief!'

Mlle Vatnaz forced a laugh.

'If I 'm not telling the truth, I 'll put my hand in the fire!'

'Take care! It 's dry enough to burn!'

The old maid held out her right hand, and kept it raised just opposite Rosanette's face.

'But there are some of your friends who find my hand to their liking!'

'Oh, Spaniards, no doubt—to use for castanets!'

'Harlot!'

Rosanette bowed very low.

'Calling names won't make you any prettier!'

Mlle Vatnaz did not reply. Drops of sweat appeared on her temples. Her eyes were fixed on the carpet. She was panting. At last she reached the door, and slamming it vigorously, she said:

'Good night! You 'll hear from me!'

'Delighted!' said Rosanette.

Her self-restraint had shattered her. She fell on to the divan trembling all over, stammering insults, in tears. Was she disturbed by this threat of Mlle Vatnaz? No—she had never been frightened of her. Or, again, perhaps the other owed her money? No, it was the gold sheep, a present; and through her tears the name of Delmar slipped out. So she loved the actor!

'Then why has she chosen me?' Frederic wondered. 'How did he manage to get back into favour? What makes her keep me? What 's the meaning of all this?'

Rosanette's little sobs continued. She was still lying on her side, with her right cheek in her hands, and seemed so charming, so unself-conscious, and so unhappy a creature that he came up to her and kissed her gently on the forehead.

Then she assured him of her love for him; the prince had just gone away; they would be free. But for the moment she found herself . . . embarrassed. 'You saw it yourself the other day, when I was using up my old linings.' No more carriages now! And that was not all; the upholsterers were threatening to take away the furniture from the bedroom and the big drawing-room. She did not know what to do.

Frederic had an impulse to reply: 'Don't worry! I'll pay.' But the lady might be lying. He contented himself with merely consoling her.

Rosanette's fears were well grounded; she had to give back the furniture and leave the fine apartment in the rue Drouot. She took another, in the boulevard Poissonière, on the fourth floor. The ornaments from her old boudoir sufficed to make the three rooms look smart. They had Chinese blinds and a tent on the terrace, a brand-new card table and red silk footstools in the drawing-room. Frederic had contributed largely to these acquisitions; he was experiencing the pleasures of a newly married man, who at last has his own house and his own wife. Enjoying the sensation, he came and slept there almost every night.

One morning, as he was coming out of the hall, he saw the shako of a National Guard on the stairs. He was approaching the third floor. Where was he going? Frederic waited. The man continued to mount, with his head slightly bowed. He raised his eyes. It was Arnoux. The situation was obvious. Both blushed at the same time, suffering the same embarrassment.

Arnoux was the first to find a way out.

'She's better, isn't she?' he said, as if Rosanette were ill and he had come to inquire after her.

Frederic took advantage of this opening.

'Yes, to be sure! That is to say, her maid told me so,' he replied, wishing to give the impression that he had not been admitted.

Then they stood there, face to face, irresolute, and watching each other. Who was going to stay? Yet again, Arnoux solved the dilemma.

'Oh, well! I'll come back later! Where were you going to? I'll come with you.'

And, when they were in the street, he talked as naturally as ever. Evidently, jealousy was not in his character, or else he was too good-natured to be angry.

Besides, his duty to his country preoccupied him. He never

took off his uniform these days. He had defended the offices of the *Presse* on the 29th of March.[1] When the Chamber was invaded[2] he distinguished himself by his courage, and he was at the banquet given to the National Guard at Amiens.

Hussonnet, who was always on duty with him, took particular advantage of his distributions of wine and cigars; but, irreverent by nature, he amused himself by contradicting him. He mocked the incorrect style of the decrees, the Luxembourg conferences [3] the Vesuvian Society,[4] the Tyrolese Club, and everything else, including the Car of Agriculture, which was drawn by horses instead of oxen and escorted by hideous young women. Arnoux, on the other hand, defended authority and dreamed of the fusion of the parties. Meanwhile, his business affairs took a turn for the worse. He found this only moderately disturbing. The relations between Frederic and Rosanette did not make him unhappy, for his discovery enabled him, with a clear conscience, to cut off the allowance which he had restored to her after the departure of the prince. He pleaded his financial difficulties and groaned a great deal. Rosanette was generous. After that M. Arnoux looked on himself as the lover of her choice, which flattered his vanity, and made him feel younger. Positive that Frederic was keeping Rosanette, he supposed that he was playing an excellent trick; he went so far as to hide from Frederic, and left him a clear field when they met.

This joint possession distressed Frederic; and his rival's civilities seemed to him a joke that was liable to become tedious. But an angry scene would have deprived him of all chance of going back to Mme Arnoux, and this was the only way he could get news of her. According to his custom, or perhaps out of malice, Arnoux often mentioned her in conversation, and even asked him why he never came to see her.

After exhausting all his excuses, Frederic declared that he had been to see Mme Arnoux several times, without success. Arnoux was convinced, for he often expressed to her his extreme delight at the absence of their friend, and she always replied that she had missed his visit; so that the two lies confirmed instead of contradicting one another.

The young man's forbearance and the pleasure of duping him increased Arnoux's affection for him. He went to extreme lengths of familiarity, not because he despised Frederic, but because he trusted him. One day he wrote to him that he had been called to the country for twenty-four hours on urgent business, and begged him to take his place on guard. Frederic, not daring to refuse, went to the guard post at the place du Carrousel.

So he had to endure the company of the National Guards! Apart from a Government spy, a facetious individual who drank to excess, they all seemed to him as brainless as their knapsacks. The chief subject of conversation was the replacement of leather equipment by sword belts. Several of them talked bitterly against the National Workshops.[1] Someone remarked: 'Where will it all end?' The man who had been thus appealed to opened his eyes wide in horror, as if he had suddenly found himself on the edge of a precipice, and replied: 'Where will it all end?' Then a bolder spirit exclaimed: 'We can't go on like this! It's got to be stopped!' And the same topics were repeated until the evening, so that Frederic grew mortally bored.

He was greatly surprised when, at eleven o'clock, Arnoux appeared. The latter at once told him that, his business being completed, he had hurried to his relief.

There had been no business. He had invented the story so as to be able to spend twenty-four hours alone with Rosanette. But Arnoux had overtaxed his strength, and in his exhaustion had been seized with remorse. He came and thanked Frederic and offered him supper.

'Thank you very much—but I'm not hungry. I want nothing but my bed.'

'That's a good reason why we should breakfast together, to-morrow! What a milksop you are! You can't go home at this hour! It's too late. It would be dangerous.'

Once again Frederic gave way. Arnoux, who had not been expected, was welcomed by his comrades in arms, particularly the Government spy. They all adored him, and he was in such good form that he even regretted Hussonnet's absence. Then he felt the need for a nap—forty winks, no more.

'Stay beside me,' he said to Frederic, as he stretched himself on his camp bed, without taking off his equipment.

Through fear of an alarm, he kept his musket near him, although this was against the rules; he murmured a few words: 'My darling! My little angel!' and quickly went to sleep.

The conversation died away; and, little by little, silence descended on the guard post. Frederic, who was tormented by fleas, looked around him. Half-way up the yellow-painted wall was a long shelf, on which the packs were lined up, like a row of little humps. Below, the lead-coloured muskets were ranged one beside another. Snores arose from the National Guards, whose stomachs were dimly outlined in the darkness. An empty bottle and some plates littered the stove. There were three straw-bottomed chairs round the table, on which was spread a pack of cards. A drum stood on the bench, its strap dangling. The warm wind blew through the door and made the oil lamp smoke. Arnoux was sleeping with his arms outstretched; his musket was resting on its butt at a slight angle, so that the muzzle was under his armpit. Frederic noticed it and was afraid.

'No, no! I'm wrong. There's nothing to be afraid of. But supposing he were to die. . . .' And suddenly an endless series of pictures streamed through his mind. He saw himself at Her side at night in a post chaise; then beside a river on a summer evening; at home, in their own house, in the dim light of a lamp. Thinking of his happiness, already savouring it, he lingered over domestic calculations and the details of his household; and all that was needed to realize his dream was the pulling of the trigger. He could push it with the tip of his toe; it would be a pure accident.

Frederic brooded over this idea like a dramatist over the plot of a play. Suddenly he felt that it was really going to happen, that he was going to take part in it, that he longed to do so; then panic gripped him. In the midst of his anguish he felt a strange delight, which became more and more powerful; he realized with terror that his scruples were fading; in his wild reverie, the outer world vanished; and he was no longer conscious of himself, save through a dreadful agony in his heart.

'Shall we have some white wine?' said the spy, waking up.

Arnoux jumped off his bed; after the white wine had been drunk, he insisted on taking Frederic's guard.

Then he carried him off to lunch at Parly's in the rue de Chartres; and, as he needed restoring, he ordered two dishes of meat, a lobster, a rum omelette, a salad, and so forth, washing down the whole with a bottle of 1819 Sauterne and a '42 Romanée in addition to the champagne at dessert, and liqueurs. Frederic did not oppose him. He was uneasy, as if Arnoux could have guessed his thoughts from the expression on his face.

With his elbows on the edge of the table, Arnoux leaned right forward, and, staring relentlessly at Frederic, confided his ideas to him.

He wanted to take a lease of all the embankments on the Nord railway and sow them with potatoes; or to organize a monster procession along the boulevards, which would include all 'the celebrities of the age.' He proposed to hire all the windows, and to relet them at an average of three francs a seat, thus securing a fine profit. In short, he was hoping to corner something and so make his fortune quickly. At the same time, he had strict moral scruples; he was against excesses or misconduct, spoke of his 'poor father,' and confessed that he examined his conscience every evening, before offering his soul to God.

'What about a drop of curaçao?'

'If you like.'

As for the republic, everything would be all right; the long and the short of it was, he was the happiest man on earth; and, forgetting himself, he extolled the qualities of Rosanette, and even contrasted her with his wife. That was quite a different matter! Her thighs were really incomparable.

'Your health!'

Frederic clinked glasses. Out of politeness, he had drunk a little too much; moreover, he was dazzled by the bright sunshine; and, as they walked up the rue Vivienne together, their epaulettes were in fraternal contact.

At home once more, Frederic slept until seven o'clock. Then he went to call on Rosanette. She had gone out with someone. Could it be Arnoux? Not knowing what to do, he went on walking down the boulevard, but could not get beyond the Porte Saint-Martin, so thick was the crowd.

Numbers of workmen had been abandoned to destitution; and they used to gather there every evening for a sort of parade; it seemed that they were awaiting a signal. In spite of the new Riot Act, these 'clubs of despair' were increasing in an alarming manner; and many of the better-off people used to go there every day, through bravado, or because it was the fashion.

Suddenly Frederic caught sight of M. Dambreuse with Martinon; he turned his head away, for he bore a grudge against the banker since he had become a member of the Assembly. But M. Dambreuse stopped him.

'One moment, my dear sir! I owe you an explanation.'

'I don't want one.'

'Please! Listen to me!'

It was not his fault at all. He had been importuned, almost compelled to stand. Martinon at once supported his remarks; the people of Nogent had come to him in a deputation.

'Besides, I assumed I was at liberty, since——'

A rush of people on to the pavement forced M. Dambreuse to step aside. A moment later he reappeared and said to Martinon:

That was a real good turn you did me. You won't regret it.'

All three stood with their backs against a shop, so as to talk more easily.

From time to time shouts were raised of 'Long live Napoleon!'[1] 'Long live Barbès!' 'Down with Marie!'[2] Every one in the vast multitude was talking very loud; and these countless voices, reverberating from the houses, sounded like the continual roar of waves in a harbour. At moments there was silence; then the *Marseillaise* rang out. Under gateways, mysterious-looking figures hawked sword sticks. Sometimes two people would wink as they passed each other, and then separate briskly. Groups of idlers filled the pavements: a dense throng swarmed in the roadway. Whole companies of policemen were swallowed up in the crowd as soon as they emerged from the side streets. Here and there little red flags showed up like flames; the coachmen on their boxes made expressive gestures and then turned back. The shifting scene made a most diverting spectacle.

'How Mademoiselle Cécile would have enjoyed this!' said Martinon.

'You know my wife doesn't like my niece to come with us,' answered M. Dambreuse smiling.

He had changed beyond recognition. He had been shouting 'Long live the Republic!' for the last three months; he had even voted for the exile of the Orléans family. But there must be no more concessions. So strongly did he feel on this point that he carried a life-preserver in his pocket.

Martinon had one too. Now that judicial offices were no longer bestowed for life, he had retired from the department of public prosecutions, and he even exceeded M. Dambreuse in the violence of his opinions.

The banker particularly hated Lamartine because he had supported Ledru - Rollin; he also detested Pierre Leroux, Proudhon, Considérant, Lamennais, all the extremists, and all the Socialists.

'When all 's said and done, what are they after? They 've abolished the tax on meat and imprisonment for debt; now they 're working on a plan for a mortgage bank; the other day it was a national bank! And there 's five millions on the budget for the workmen! But I 'm glad to say that 's over now, thanks to Monsieur de Falloux.[3] Good riddance, I say! Let them go!'

In fact, the Minister for Public Works, at his wits' end how to feed the 130,000 workmen in the National Workshops, had, that very day, signed a decree inviting all citizens between the ages of eighteen and twenty to take service in the army, or else to go and till the land in the country.

This offer infuriated the people, who were convinced that it was an attempt to destroy the republic. Life away from the capital would be as painful as an exile; they saw themselves dying of fever in barbarous regions. Many, too, who were accustomed to highly skilled work, looked on agriculture as a degrading occupation; it was evidently a trap, a mockery, a public denial of all the promises made to them. If they resisted, force would be used against them; they had no doubt of that, and they prepared to forestall it.

About nine o'clock the mob that had gathered at the Bastille and the Châtelet streamed back along the boulevard. From the Porte Saint-Denis to the Porte Saint-Martin there stretched a single vast swarming throng—a solid mass of dark blue, verging on black. One caught glimpses of men with burning eyes and pale skins; their faces were drawn with hunger, and exalted by their wrongs. Meanwhile, clouds were rolling up; the thundery sky seemed to electrify the crowd; they swayed irresolutely, eddying this way and that; in those swirling depths a terrible strength seemed to lie, an elemental vigour. Then they all began to chant: 'Light up! Light up!' Several windows were not illuminated; stones were hurled through them. M. Dambreuse considered it prudent to retire. The two young men saw him home.

He foretold grave calamities. Once again the people might invade the Chamber, and, in this connection, he described how he would have been killed on the 15th of May, but for the devotion of a National Guard.

'Why, I was forgetting—it was your friend! Your friend, Jacques Arnoux, the crockery manufacturer!'

He had been almost crushed by the rioters; this brave citizen had taken him in his arms and put him in a place of safety. Since then a kind of attachment had sprung up between them.

'We must all dine together one of these days, and, since you see a great deal of him, you must tell him I'm very fond of him. He's an excellent fellow—as I think, unfairly abused; and he's got wit too, the old dog! Once more, my compliments, and a very good evening to you!'

After leaving M. Dambreuse, Frederic went back to Rosanette's; and, very gloomily, told her that she must choose between him and Arnoux. She answered mildly that she did not understand 'that sort of tittle-tattle'; she was not in love with Arnoux and was in no way attached to him. Frederic felt a longing to leave Paris. She did not oppose this whim, and they started for Fontainebleau the next day.

The hotel where they stayed was distinguished from the others by a fountain splashing in the middle of the yard. The doors of the rooms opened on a corridor as in a monastery. Theirs was large, well furnished, and hung with chintz; it was quiet, since travellers were few and far between. Well-to-do citizens with nothing to do strolled about the streets; towards evening, children played touch-last in the road under their windows; after the turbulence of Paris this tranquillity both surprised and soothed them.

Early in the morning they went to visit the palace. Entering by the main gateway, they saw the whole façade—the five towers with their pointed roofs, the horse-shoe staircase sweeping down into the courtyard, and the two lower wings, to right and left. In the distance, the lichened flagstones seemed to blend their tints with the red-gold hue of the bricks; and the whole palace, rust-coloured like old armour, gave an impression of royal dignity, of gloomy, military grandeur.

At length a servant appeared, bearing a bunch of keys. First he showed them the apartments of the queens, the pope's oratory, the gallery of Francis I, the little mahogany table on which Napoleon signed his abdication, and, in one of the rooms into which the old Hunting Gallery had been divided, the spot where Christina had had Monaldeschi murdered. Rosanette listened to this story attentively; then, turning to Frederic:

'It was jealousy, I suppose? Look out for yourself!'

Then they crossed the Council Hall, the Hall of the Guard, the Throne Room, the saloon of Louis XIII. A pale light poured through the high, curtainless casements; a thin layer of dust dimmed the brightness of the window fastenings and the brass feet of the console tables; everywhere, the arm-chairs were hidden under thick linen sheets; above the doors were pictures of Louis XV hunting, and, here and there, tapestries representing the gods of Olympus, Psyche, or the battles of Alexander.

Passing in front of the mirrors, Rosanette would stop for a moment to smooth her hair.

They passed through the Oval Court and the Chapel of Saint Saturninus and reached the Banqueting Hall.

They were dazzled by the splendour of the roof, which was divided into octagonal compartments in gold and silver relief, more elaborately worked than a piece of jewellery, and by the innumerable pictures which covered the walls, from the gigantic chimney-piece, bearing the arms of France surrounded by crescents and quivers, to the musicians' gallery, at the other end, in the widest part of the hall. The ten arched windows were wide open; the sun made the paintings glitter, the blue sky seemed to prolong to infinity the ultramarine of the arches; and, from the depths of the forest, which filled the horizon with its misty tree tops, there seemed to come an echo of the hunting calls once blown on horns of ivory, an echo of those antique ballets, when princesses and noblemen, disguised as nymphs and sylvans, assembled for the dance beneath the leaves—an echo of those days of primitive science, violent passions, and sumptuous art, when it was man's ideal to dissolve the whole world in a dream of the Golden Isles, and when the mistresses of kings took their place among the constellations. The most beautiful of these famous women was shown in a picture on the right, in the character of Diana the huntress, and even of Diana of the infernal regions, to indicate, apparently, her power beyond the grave. All these symbols asserted her glory; and something of her remained there yet—a dim voice, a still perceptible exhalation.

Frederic was seized with a strange frenzy of desire, directed towards the past. To divert his longing, he began to gaze tenderly at Rosanette and asked her if she would like to have been this woman.

'What woman?'

'Diane de Poitiers!'

He repeated:

'Diane de Poitiers, the mistress of Henry II.'

She said 'Oh,' briefly. That was all.

Her silence clearly proved that she knew and understood nothing; so that he said to her out of kindness:

'Perhaps you 're bored?'

'No, no—not at all. On the contrary.'

And with her chin in the air, gazing vaguely round her, Rosanette remarked:

'It brings back memories!'

Yet her face betrayed an effort, a strained look of respect; and as this serious expression made her look prettier, Frederic forgave her.

The carp pond amused her more. For a quarter of an hour she threw pieces of bread into the water to watch the fishes leap.

Frederic sat down beside her, under the lime-trees. He

thought of all the people who had haunted these walls; Charles V, the Valois, Henry IV, Peter the Great, Jean-Jacques Rousseau, 'the lovely weeping women in the stage boxes,'[1] Voltaire, Napoleon, Pius VII, Louis-Philippe. He felt himself surrounded, jostled by the tumultuous dead; and all these pictures passing through his mind dazzled yet fascinated him.

At last they went down into the flower garden.

This was a vast rectangle; in a single glance the eye embraced its broad yellow paths, its squares of turf, its thin box hedges, its conical yews, its low shrubberies, and its narrow flower beds in which scattered blooms made spots of colour against the grey earth. At the far end of the garden was a spreading park, along the side of which stretched a long canal.

There is a peculiar melancholy about royal residences, which is probably due to their inordinate size, compared with the number of their inhabitants, or to their silence, which is somehow surprising after the trumpets that have sounded there, or it may be because of their fixed and motionless splendour, which proves by its antiquity the transience of dynasties, the inevitable decay of all things; and this emanation of the centuries, numbing and deathly as the smell of a mummy, affects even the shallowest mind. Rosanette was yawning vastly. They went back to their hotel.

After lunch an open carriage came for them. They left Fontainebleau by a broad cross-roads; then, at a foot's pace, drove up a sandy road through a wood of small pines; from time to time the coachman said: 'Here are the Siamese Twins, the Pharamond, the Royal Bouquet,' omitting none of the beauty spots, and occasionally even stopping for his passengers to admire them.

They entered the Forest of Franchard. The carriage glided over the turf like a sleigh; invisible pigeons cooed; suddenly a waiter appeared; and they got down at the gate of a garden full of round tables. Then, leaving the walls of a ruined abbey on the left, they walked over some big rocks and soon reached the lowest part of the gorge.

One side is covered with a confusion of junipers and sandstone boulders; the almost bare surface of the other slopes down to the bottom of the valley, where the footpath stands out white against the purple of the heather; in the distance, the top of a hill can be seen, like a flattened cone, with a telegraph tower behind.

The road zigzags up between dwarf pines, under rocks with jagged outlines; there is a curious sense of muffled quiet, of solitude, of other-worldliness about this part of the forest. It makes one think of hermits, having as their companions great deer with fiery crosses between their horns, and greeting with paternal smiles the good kings of France as they kneel before their caves. A smell of resin filled the warm air; tree roots stretched across the ground in a vein-like network. Rosanette tripped over them, was in despair, and wanted to cry.

But on gaining the summit, she was made happy once more by the discovery of a sort of kiosk with a roof made of branches, where there were wood carvings for sale. She drank a bottle of lemonade, and bought herself a stick made of holly wood; and, without glancing at the landscape which is to be seen from the plateau, went into the Brigands' Cave, preceded by a small boy carrying a torch.

The carriage was waiting for them in the Bas-Bréau.

A painter in a blue blouse was working at the foot of an oak with his colour box on his knees. He raised his head and watched them pass.

When they were in the middle of the Chailly slope, there was a sudden downpour of rain and they had to put up the hood. The shower stopped almost immediately; and the stones of the roadway were glittering in the sun as they re-entered the town.

Some travellers, just arrived, told them that a terrible and bloody battle was taking place in Paris. Rosanette and her lover were not surprised. Then they all went away, the hotel was quiet once more, the gas was put out, and they went to sleep to the murmur of the fountain in the yard.

The next day they visited the Gorge of the Wolves, the Fairies' Pool, the Long Rock, and La Marlotte; the day after, they went off at random wherever their coachman took them, without asking where they were; often they failed to visit even the most celebrated beauty spots.

They were very comfortable in their old landau, with its low, sofa-like seat, covered with faded striped chintz. They watched the ditches, full of brushwood, gliding past with a gentle, continuous motion. White sunbeams, like arrows, pierced the tall bracken; sometimes, straight in front of them, a disused road came into view, carpeted here and there with scattered plants. Where four roads met a sign-post stretched out its four arms; now and then stakes could be seen leaning obliquely, like dead trees; little curving paths, that lost themselves under the leaves, made them long to follow them; at that very moment the horse turned off; on they went, sinking into the mud; further on, moss had grown up to the very edge of the deep ruts.

They felt completely alone, far away from other people. But suddenly they would see a keeper going by with his gun, or a band of ragged women carrying great bundles of faggots on their backs.

When the carriage stopped there was silence everywhere; all that could be heard was the panting of the horse in the shafts, and the faint, repeated cry of a bird.

In some places the sun lit up the skirt of the woods, leaving the inner parts in gloom; or else the light, dwindling to a kind of dusk among the nearer trees, spread a veil of misty purple, a pallid brightness, over the deeper recesses.

At midday, the sun, blazing down from overhead, splashed the spreading verdure with brilliant light, hung drops of silver on the tips of the branches, streaked the grass with trails of emeralds, and threw spots of gold on to the banks of dead leaves. Bending backwards, one saw the sky through the top-most twigs of the trees. Some of these, immensely tall, had the air of patriarchs or emperors; some, with their lofty trunks and interlacing boughs, looked like triumphal arches; others, crooked from the roots, leaned sideways, like columns about to fall.

Then there would come an opening in the endless ranks of tall, upright stems. Huge waves of green swept down in broken curves to the bottom of valleys, or other hills thrust their ridges forward, disclosing a view of yellow plains, which stretched away until they vanished in a pale and shadowy distance.

Standing side by side, on some hillock, breathing in the wind, they felt enter their hearts a thrill of pride in a freer life—an exuberance of strength, a causeless joy.

The different trees afforded a varied spectacle. The beeches, with their white, smooth bark, intertwined their foliage; ashes gently curved their grey-green boughs; among the hornbeam copses, prickly holly-trees stood out like bronze; then came a line of slender birches, leaning in elegiac poses, and the pines, straight and regular as organ pipes, swayed continuously and seemed to sing. Huge gnarled oaks reared their writhing boles from the earth, and met in tortuous embraces; firm-set on their trunks, like headless bodies, they threw out desperate appeals and furious threats with their bare arms, like a group of Titans struck motionless in their anger. A sense of oppression, a noxious torpor hovered over the pools, which spread their calm waters among thickets of thorn-bushes; the lichens on their banks, where the wolves came to drink, were sulphur-coloured, as though they had been scorched by witches' footsteps, and the incessant croaking of the frogs echoed the cawing of the wheeling rooks. Then they crossed monotonous clearings, planted with an occasional sapling. The sound of iron, a rapid, repeated hammering, reached their ears; some quarrymen were striking the rocks. These rocks grew more and more numerous, and at last filled the whole landscape; square as houses, flat as paving stones, piled together, overhanging, jumbled in heaps, they lay like the monstrous and chaotic ruins of some vanished city. The very wildness of their confusion called up thoughts of volcanoes, deluges, and vast unknown cataclysms. Frederic said they had been there since the beginning of the world, and would stay there until its end. Rosanette turned away her head, saying that it would send her mad, and went off to pick heather. The little, close-packed purple flowers grew in irregular patches, and the dark soil that oozed from under their roots formed a black fringe to the quartz-spangled sand.

One day they had climbed half way up a sand hill. Its untrodden surface was ribbed in even undulations; here and there, like promontories on the dried-up bed of an ocean, rose rocks that vaguely resembled the shapes of animals—tortoises thrusting their heads forward, crawling seals, hippopotamuses, and bears. No one. Not a sound. The sand was dazzling in the sunshine, and suddenly, in this quivering light, the beasts seemed to move. They turned back, pursued by vertigo, almost panic-stricken.

The solemnity of the forest overcame them; and there were hours of silence when they let themselves be lulled by the gentle rocking of the springs, and lay there as if entranced in some serene intoxication. With his arm round her waist, he listened to her talking, while the birds twittered; in a single glance he could see the black grapes on her bonnet and the berries on the junipers, the folds of her veil and the curves of the clouds; and, when he leaned over her, the freshness of her skin mingled with the all-pervading scent of the woods. They took pleasure in everything; they pointed out, for each other's admiration, gossamer hanging from bushes, holes full of water in stones, a squirrel on the branches of a tree, two butterflies flying after each other; sometimes, twenty yards away, under the trees, a doe would be walking peacefully along, with a gentle, dignified air, her fawn at her side. Rosanette would have liked to run after it and give it a kiss.

She was very frightened once when a man, suddenly appearing, showed her three adders in a box. She threw herself into

Frederic's arms at once; and he was glad to feel that she was weak, and that he was strong enough to protect her.

That evening they dined in an inn by the edge of the Seine. Their table was near the window; Rosanette was opposite him; and he gazed at her delicate little white nose, her pouting lips, her clear eyes, her chestnut hair with its swelling tresses, her pretty oval face. Her dress of undyed silk clung round her slightly sloping shoulders; and he watched her hands, emerging from her turned-back cuffs, cutting up her food, pouring out her wine, moving over the table cloth. They were given a spread-eagled chicken, an eel stew in a pipe-clay fruit dish, sour wine, hard bread, and jagged knives. This increased their pleasure, and their illusion. They almost came to believe that they were travelling in Italy on their honeymoon.

Before starting again they went for a walk along the river bank.

The soft blue sky, rounded like a dome, rested at the horizon on the jagged outline of the forest. Opposite, at the end of the meadow, there was a bell tower in a village; further away, on the left, the roof of a house stood out red against the river, which seemed to show no movement over all its curves and reaches. Only the reeds were bending, and the water gently shook the sticks that had been fixed on the bank to hold nets; there was an eel pot there and two or three old boats. Near the inn a girl in a straw hat was drawing buckets of water from a well; each time the bucket came up Frederic listened to the grinding of the chain with inexpressible delight.

He was certain that he would be happy for the rest of his days, so natural did his contentment appear, so much a part of his life and so inseparable from this woman. He felt the need to say loving words to her. She answered him by gentle endearments, by softly patting his shoulder, by charming movements, made sweeter by their unexpectedness. He was, in fact, revealing to her a beauty which she had never known, a beauty that was, perhaps, only a reflection of their environment, a beauty created by the secret powers of the things about them.

When they were resting in the open country, he used to stretch himself out with his head on her knees, in the shade of her parasol; or they would throw themselves on the grass, face to face, and stare long and deeply into each other's eyes, with a thirst that was constantly slaked and rekindled, and then with half-closed lids they would lie there in silence.

Sometimes they heard the roll of drums in the distance. They were beating the call to arms in the villages for the defence of Paris.

'Oh, of course! The rising!' Frederic would say with pitying contempt, for all this excitement seemed petty to him compared with their love, and nature, the eternal.

They would talk of nothing in particular, of things they already knew perfectly, of people who did not interest them, of countless absurd trifles. She told him about her maid and her hairdresser. One day, she forgot herself and told him her age —twenty-nine; she was growing old.

Several times, without meaning to, she told him things about herself. She had been a shop girl, had travelled to England, had begun training as an actress; but all this was recounted without sequence, so that he could not piece together a connected story. She told him more one day when they were sitting under a plane-tree at the edge of a meadow. Below, by the roadside, a little girl, barefooted in the dust, was pasturing a cow. When she saw them she came up to beg from them. Holding her ragged petticoat in one hand she used the other to scratch her black hair, that stood out like a Louis XIV wig all round her brown face, which was lit up by a pair of splendid eyes.

'She'll be very pretty one day,' said Frederic.

'What luck for her if she hasn't got a mother!' said Rosanette.

'Eh? What?'

'Yes, if I had not had a mother . . .'

She sighed and began to speak of her childhood. Her parents had been silk weavers at Croix-Rousse.[1] She helped her father as apprentice. The poor man worked himself to the bone, but in vain; his wife nagged at him incessantly, and sold everything to buy drink. Rosanette could still picture their room, with the looms standing all along the windows, the stew pan on the stove, the bed painted to look like mahogany; the cupboard opposite, and the dark loft where she slept until she was fifteen. At length a gentleman had arrived, a fat man, dressed in black, with a face the colour of boxwood and a sanctimonious manner. He and her mother had had a talk together; and three days later—— Rosanette broke off, and with a brazen, bitter look, said:

'It was settled!'

Then, answering Frederic's gesture:

'He was married, and didn't want to compromise himself in his own house. So I was taken to a private room at a restaurant, and told that I would be happy and would be given a lovely present.

'When the door was opened, the first thing that struck my eyes was a silver-gilt candelabrum, on a table laid for two. The table was reflected in a mirror on the ceiling, and the blue silk hangings on the walls made the whole room look like an alcove. I was astonished. You can imagine the effect on a poor creature who'd never been anywhere! But although I was dazzled, I was also afraid. I wanted to go away. All the same, I stayed.

'The only seat was a divan drawn up to the table. It gave softly under me; I felt a gust of hot air from the heater in the carpet, and I sat there without eating or drinking anything. The waiter who was standing there urged me to eat. Suddenly he poured me out a large glass of wine; my head swam, I wanted to open the window; he said to me: 'No, mademoiselle, that's not allowed.' And he went away. The table was covered with masses of things I had never seen before. I did not like any of them. I fell back on a pot of jam, and still I waited. I don't know what was keeping him. It was very late—at least midnight; I was tired out; I moved aside one of the pillows so as to lie down more comfortably, and I found a kind of album, a portfolio, under my hand; it was full of obscene pictures . . . I was asleep on top of it when he came in.'

She bent her head and remained pensive.

The leaves whispered around them; a tall foxglove nodded among a tangle of weeds; the sunlight flooded the grass like a wave; and the silence was broken at frequent intervals by the browsing of the cow, which was now out of sight.

Rosanette was staring fixedly at the ground a few yards away from her; her nostrils quivered; she was absorbed in her thoughts.

'My poor darling, how you've suffered!'

'Yes,' she said, 'more than you think. I even wanted to end it all. They fished me out of the river.'

'How did that happen?'

'Oh, don't let's think about it. I love you! Kiss me!' And one by one she extracted the sprigs of thistles that had attached themselves to the hem of her skirt.

Frederic was thinking particularly of what she had left unsaid. By what steps had she succeeded in emerging from poverty? What lover had given her her education? What was the story of her life up to the day when he had first been to see her? Her last avowal forbade further questioning. He only asked her how she had got to know Arnoux.

'Through the Vatnaz woman.'

'Didn't I once see you at the Palais-Royal, with the two of them?'

He mentioned the exact date. Rosanette made an effort.

'Yes, that's right. I wasn't exactly gay in those days.'

But Arnoux had been very kind. Frederic did not doubt it; nevertheless, their friend was a queer customer, full of faults; he took pains to remind her of them. She agreed with him.

'Never mind! I'm still fond of the old goat!'

'Even now?' asked Frederic.

She began to blush, half laughing, half angry.

'No, no! That's ancient history. I don't keep anything from you. And even if it were true, it's different with him. Anyway, you're not being very kind to your victim!'

'My victim?'

Rosanette took him by the chin.

'Of course!'

And, talking baby talk like a nurse:

'Baby hasn't always been good boy. Baby's gone bye-bye with his wife.'

'Me! Never!'

Rosanette smiled. This smile distressed him; it seemed a sign of indifference. But she went on gently, with one of those looks that implore a false reply:

'Quite sure?'

'Certainly.'

Frederic swore on his word of honour that he had never given a thought to Mme Arnoux; he was too much in love with someone else.

'Who?'

'Why, you, my sweetheart!'

'Oh, don't try and fool me! I'm fed up with you.'

He thought it prudent to invent a love-story. He made up circumstantial details. But the person in question had made him very unhappy.

'You're certainly not very lucky,' said Rosanette.

'Perhaps, perhaps,' he replied. He wished to give the impression of several successful affairs in order to enhance his reputation. In the same way Rosanette did not confess to all her lovers, so that he should think more highly of her. For even in the midst of the most intimate confidences, false shame, delicacy, or pity always imposes some restraint. We come across precipices or quagmires in ourselves, or in the other person, which prevent pursuit; or we feel that we would not be understood; it is hard to define the obstacle exactly; but because of it, complete relationships are uncommon.

Poor Rosanette had known nothing better than this. Often, tears came into her eyes when she contemplated Frederic; then she would look up, or gaze at the horizon, as if she had caught sight of some splendid dawn, an endless vista of happiness; so that one day she confessed that she wanted to have a mass said 'to bring luck to our love.'

How was it, then, that she had held out against him so long? She did not know herself. He asked her this again and again; and she would answer, as she strained him in her arms:

'I was afraid of loving you too much, my darling!'

On Sunday morning Frederic read Dussardier's name in a newspaper among a list of wounded. He uttered an exclamation, and, showing the paper to Rosanette, declared that he was going to leave immediately.

'What for?'

'Why, to see him, to look after him.'

'I suppose you 're not going to leave me here alone?'

'Come with me!'

'Do you think I 'm going to get myself mixed up in this row? Not likely!'

'All the same, I can't . . .'

'Nonsense! As if there weren't enough nurses in the hospitals! And, anyway, why did he have to join in? Every one for himself!'

This selfishness made him indignant; and he reproached himself for not being in Paris with his friends. There was something mean and petty in his indifference to the sufferings of his country. His love suddenly began to weigh on his conscience like a crime. They sulked at each other for an hour.

Then she implored him to wait and not to endanger himself.

'Supposing you were killed!'

'I should only have done my duty!'

Rosanette leapt up. His first duty was to love her. He was tired of her, she supposed. There was no sense in it! It was madness!

Frederic rang for the bill. But it was not easy to get back to Paris. The conveyance of Leloir, the carrier, had just left; Lecomte's carriages were not running; the coach from the Bourbonnais would not pass until late at night and might be full—it was impossible to tell. After wasting a great deal of time in these inquiries, he thought of hiring a post chaise.

The owner of the stables refused to give him horses, as Frederic had no passport. At last he hired a landau—the one which had taken them on their excursions—and at five o'clock they reached the Hôtel du Commerce at Melun.

The market square was covered with piles of arms. The prefect had forbidden the National Guards to go to Paris. The guards who did not belong to his department wanted to go on. There was much shouting. The inn was in an uproar.

Rosanette, terrified, declared that she would go no further, and once more begged him to stay. The innkeeper and his wife supported her. A friendly diner took Frederic's side, declaring that the battle would soon be over; besides, one must do one's duty. This made Rosanette cry all the harder. Frederic was exasperated. He gave her his purse, kissed her quickly, and vanished.

When he reached the station at Corbeil, he was told that the rebels had cut the rails in several places; and the coachman refused to drive him any further; he said his horses were 'done.'

However, through his influence, Frederic secured a wretched fly, the driver of which agreed to take him as far as the Barrière d'Italie for sixty francs, exclusive of tip. The coachman set him down a hundred yards from the barrier and turned back. Frederic was walking along the road, when suddenly a sentry put his bayonet across his path. Four men seized him, shouting:

'Here's one! Take care! Search him! Thief! Scum!'

And so intense was his bewilderment that he allowed himself to be dragged to the guard post at the barrier, which was set up at the cross roads where the boulevard des Gobelins and the boulevard de l'Hôpital meet the rue Godefroy and rue Mouffetard. Four great ramparts of paving stones formed barricades in the mouth of each street. Through clouds of dust, he could distinguish infantrymen of the line and National Guards, all with black faces, dishevelled and haggard. They had just taken the square, and had shot several men; their anger was not yet appeased. Frederic said that he had come from Fontainebleau to succour a wounded comrade; at first no one would believe him; they examined his hands, they even sniffed his ears, to make sure that he did not smell of powder.

However, by dint of repeating the same thing over and over again, he finally convinced a captain, who ordered two fusiliers to escort him to the guard post at the Jardin des Plantes.

They went down the boulevard de l'Hôpital. A strong breeze was blowing. This revived him.

Then they turned down the rue du Marché-aux-Chevaux. A heavy black mass on the right was the Jardin des Plantes; on the left, the Hôpital de la Pitié was lit up in every window; the whole façade was blazing as if it were on fire, while shadows flitted to and fro behind the panes.

Frederic's two men left him. Another accompanied him as far as the Polytechnic School.

The rue Saint-Victor was in complete darkness—not a gas jet, not a light in any of the houses.

Every ten minutes one heard the words:

'Sentries, alert!'

And this cry, breaking the silence, went echoing on, like the reverberation of a stone falling into a chasm.

Sometimes the tramp of heavy footsteps could be heard approaching. This was a patrol of a hundred men at least; whispers, the vague clinking of steel came from the half-seen mass; and, marching by with a rhythmical swing, they melted into the gloom.

In the centre of the cross roads stood a mounted dragoon, motionless. From time to time a dispatch-rider went galloping by; then there was silence once more. Then came the muffled, menacing rumble of guns moving along the road in the distance; and these sounds, so different from the sounds of every day, brought a pang to the heart. They even seemed to intensify the silence, which was profound and complete—a black silence. Men in white blouses would come up to the soldiers, say a word to them, and vanish like ghosts.

The guard post at the Polytechnic School was packed to overflowing. The doorway was blocked by women asking to see their sons or husbands. They were sent on to the Panthéon, which had been transformed into a mortuary; no one listened to Frederic. He persisted, swearing that his friend Dussardier was expecting him, was on the point of death. At length he was given a corporal who led him to the top of the rue Saint-Jacques, to the town hall of the Twelfth Arrondissement.

The place du Panthéon was full of soldiers lying on straw. Day was breaking. The camp fires were going out.

The rising had left impressive traces in this district. The surface of the streets was broken from end to end into lumps and hummocks. Omnibuses, gas pipes, and cart wheels were still lying on the ruined barricades; there were little black smears in certain places, which could only be blood. The houses were riddled with bullets, and their inner framework could be seen through the splintered plaster. Blinds, hanging from a single nail, flapped like rags. Doors opened on to a void, where the staircase had fallen in. The inside of rooms could be seen, with their wall-paper in shreds; sometimes fragile objects had been preserved. Frederic noticed a clock, a parrot's perch, some prints.

When he entered the town hall, the National Guards were gossiping inexhaustibly about the death of Bréa and Négrier, of Charbonnel, the deputy, and of the Archbishop of Paris. It was said that the Duc d'Aumale had landed at Boulogne, that Barbès had escaped from Vincennes; that artillery was coming up from Bourges, that help was pouring in from the provinces. About three o'clock good news arrived; the rebel spokesmen were with the President of the Assembly.

Then there was rejoicing; and Frederic, who still had twelve francs, sent for a dozen bottles of wine, hoping thereby to hasten his release. Suddenly they thought they heard firing. The libations ceased; and they looked at the stranger with mistrustful eyes; he might be Henry V.

So as to avoid all responsibility, they transferred him to the town hall of the Ninth Arrondissement, which he was forbidden to leave before nine o'clock in the morning.

He ran as far as the quai Voltaire. An old man in shirt sleeves was weeping at an open window, with his eyes uplifted. The Seine was flowing peacefully. The sky was blue; birds were singing in the trees of the Tuileries.

Frederic was crossing the place du Carrousel when a bier passed. At once the guard presented arms, and the officer, saluting, said:

'All honour to our unhappy heroes!'

This phrase had become almost compulsory; whoever pronounced it always appeared profoundly moved. A group of angry people escorted the bier, shouting: 'Revenge! Revenge!'

Carriages were moving down the boulevard, and women in front of doorways were making lint. But the rebellion was conquered, or nearly so; so declared a proclamation by Cavaignac which had just been posted. A company of Mobile Guards appeared at the top of the rue Vivienne. The wealthier citizens shouted with enthusiasm; they raised their hats, clapped their hands, tried to kiss the soldiers, and offered them drinks, while women threw flowers down from the balconies.

At length, at ten o'clock, at the moment when the guns were roaring for the storming of the Faubourg Saint-Antoine, Frederic reached Dussardier's house. He found him in his attic, stretched on his back, asleep. A woman emerged silently from the neighbouring room. It was Mlle Vatnaz.

She took Frederic aside and told him how Dussardier had received his wound.

On the Saturday, a boy, wrapped in a tricolour flag, had climbed on top of a barricade in the rue Lafayette and shouted to the National Guards: 'Are you going to shoot your brothers?' As they advanced Dussardier had thrown down his musket, pushed aside the others, leapt on to the barricade, kicked the rebel over, and snatched the flag from him. He had been found under the debris, his thigh pierced by a copper slug. They had had to incise the wound and remove the bullet. Mlle Vatnaz had arrived the same evening and had been with him ever since.

She skilfully made all the preparations for the dressings, helped him to drink, anticipated his least wish, came and went as quietly as a mouse, and gazed at him with loving eyes.

Frederic came in every morning for a fortnight. One day he was talking of Mlle Vatnaz's devotion, when Dussardier shrugged his shoulders.

'No, no! She does it from self-interest.'

'Do you think so?'

'I'm positive,' he answered, without wishing to explain further.

She overwhelmed him with attentions, even bringing him newspapers in which his brave deed was extolled. This homage seemed to annoy him. He even confessed the scruples of his conscience to Frederic.

Perhaps he ought to have been on the other side, with the workers; for, after all, they had been promised quantities of things which had not been given them. Their conquerors loathed the republic; and then, they had been so brutally treated! They were wrong, perhaps, but not completely; and the good fellow was tortured by the idea that he might have been fighting against a just cause.

Sénécal, shut in the Tuileries, below the terrace by the water, did not share these torments.

There they were—nine hundred men, packed together pell-mell in the filth, black with powder and caked blood, trembling with fever and shouting with rage; and there was no one to carry away those who died. Sometimes, at the sound of a sudden explosion, they believed that they were all going to be shot; they flung themselves against the walls and then fell back to their old positions, so numbed by suffering that they seemed to be living in a nightmare, a dismal trance. The lamp, hanging from the vaulted ceiling, looked like a smear of blood; and the vapours of the dungeon produced little green and yellow flames that flickered to and fro. Fear of epidemics had led to the appointment of a commission of inquiry. At the top of the steps the chairman had leapt backwards, terrified by the smell of excrement and corpses. When the prisoners approached one of the gratings, the National Guards, who had been posted there to see that the iron bars were not torn down, thrust their bayonets at random into the mass.

For the most part the National Guards were merciless. Those who had not fought were anxious to distinguish themselves. Panic drove them to excesses. They exacted a simultaneous vengeance for the newspapers, the clubs, the demonstrations, the doctrines—everything which had been infuriating them for the last six months; and in spite of this victory, equality—as if for the chastisement of its defenders and the mockery of its enemies—displayed itself in triumph; an equality of brute beasts, a single level of bloodthirsty degradation; for the bigotry of the rich rivalled the frenzy of the starving; the aristocracy shared the madness of the rabble, and the cotton nightcap was no less savage than the cap of liberty. The public reason was deranged as if by some great upheaval of nature. Intelligent men were driven mad by it for the rest of their lives.

Old Roque had become very brave, almost reckless. He had arrived in Paris on the 26th with the men of Nogent; but instead of going back with them, he had joined the National Guards who had encamped at the Tuileries; and he was delighted at being put on sentry duty on the terrace by the edge of the water. There at least, he had the ruffians under him! He rejoiced in their defeat, in their abjection, and could not refrain from taunting them.

One of them, a youth with long fair hair, put his face to the bars and asked for bread. M. Roque ordered him to be silent. But the young man went on repeating in a lamentable voice:

'Bread!'

'Do you think I've got any?'

Other prisoners appeared at the grating, with bristling beards and blazing eyes, all pushing each other and howling:

'Bread!'

Old Roque was furious at seeing his authority flouted. He pointed his musket at them to frighten them; and the young man, swept up to the roof by the heaving crowd behind him, flung back his head and cried once more:

314

'Bread!'

'All right! Here you are!' said old Roque. And he fired.

There was one terrific yell, then nothing. Something white remained on the iron bars.

After which M. Roque went home; for he owned a house in the rue Saint-Martin, in which he kept a little flat for himself; and the damage caused to the front of the house by the rising had contributed not a little to his anger. On his return, he felt he had exaggerated the mischief. His recent action had soothed him. It was as if he had been granted compensation.

His own daughter opened the door to him. She told him straight away that his long absence had made her uneasy; she was afraid he had had an accident or been wounded.

This mark of filial love touched old Roque's heart. He was surprised that she had come from Nogent without Catherine.

'She's here, but I sent her on an errand,' answered Louise.

And she asked after his health, about this and that; then, with an assumed indifference, she inquired if he had met Frederic.

'No—not a sign of him.'

It was entirely for his sake that she had made the journey.

Steps were heard in the passage.

'Excuse me——'

And she vanished.

Catherine had not found Frederic. He had been away for some days, and his intimate friend, M. Deslauriers, now lived in the country.

Louise returned, trembling all over, unable to speak. She leaned against the furniture.

'What is it? What's the matter?' asked her father.

She made a sign that it was nothing, and by a great effort of will pulled herself together.

The caterer opposite brought the soup. But old Roque had suffered too violent an emotional disturbance. 'He could not get it down,' and at dessert he almost fainted. A doctor was quickly sent for; he prescribed a draught. Once in bed, M. Roque asked for the greatest possible number of blankets to make him sweat. He sighed and groaned.

'Thank you, my good Catherine! Kiss your father, my precious! Oh, these revolutions!'

His daughter scolded him; he had made himself ill, worrying about her. He answered:

'Yes, you're right! But I can't help it. I'm much too sensitive!'

CHAPTER II

MADAME DAMBREUSE was seated in her boudoir, between her niece and Miss John, listening to M. Roque, who was describing the hardships of his military life. She bit her lips and seemed to be in pain.

'Oh, it's nothing! It'll pass off.'

And in a gracious tone:

'We have one of your acquaintances, Monsieur Moreau, coming to dinner.'

Louise trembled.

'Otherwise, just a few of our closest friends—Alfred de Cisy, among others.'

And she praised his manners, his appearance, and, most of all, his morals.

Regarding his morals Mme Dambreuse was more accurate than she knew; for the viscount was contemplating marriage. He had said so to Martinon, adding that he was sure to please Mlle Cécile and that his family would accept her.

Cisy would not have risked this confidence, thought Martinon, unless he had favourable information about the dowry. Now Martinon suspected Cécile of being M. Dambreuse's natural daughter; and it would probably have been well worth while to take the risk and ask for her hand himself. But this bold stroke had its dangers; and, up till now, Martinon had regulated his conduct so as to avoid compromising himself; besides, he did not know how to free himself from Mme Dambreuse. Cisy's remark decided him; and he made his proposal to the banker, who, seeing no objection, had just informed his wife of it. Cisy appeared. She rose and said:

'You're quite a stranger.' Then, in English: 'Cécile, shake hands.'

At the same moment Frederic came in.

'Ah! At last we've found you,' exclaimed old Roque. 'I've been to your house with Louise three times this week.'

Frederic had carefully avoided them. He explained that he spent all his days at the bedside of a wounded friend. In addition, he had been heavily occupied with various matters for a long time; and he racked his brains for a story to tell. Luckily, the guests arrived, led by M. Paul de Grémonville, the diplomat whom he had seen for a moment at the ball; then came Fumichon, the industrialist who had shocked Frederic one evening by his Conservative zeal; and next the old Duchesse de Montreuil-Nantua.

Suddenly two voices were heard in the hall.

'I'm positive of it,' said one.

'Dear lady! dear lady!' replied the other, 'I beg you to calm yourself.'

It was M. de Nonancourt, an elderly buck, who looked as if he had been embalmed in cold cream, and Mme de Larsillois, the wife of a prefect of Louis-Philippe's reign. She was trembling violently, for she had just heard, on an organ, a polka which was a pre-arranged signal among the rebels. Many of the richer people nursed similar fantasies: there were men in the catacombs who were planning to blow up the Faubourg Saint-Germain; peculiar noises escaped from cellars; strange things were seen through windows.

For the moment, they all devoted themselves to the task of soothing Mme de Larsillois. Order had been restored. There was nothing to fear any more. 'Cavaignac has saved us!' As though the horrors of the rebellion were insufficient, they exaggerated them. There had been no fewer than twenty-three thousand convicts fighting for the Socialists!

They believed implicitly the tales of poisoned food, of Mobile Guards sawn in half between two planks, of flags bearing inscriptions inciting to pillage and arson.

'And there's something more!' added the ex-prefect's wife.

'My dear!' interrupted Mme Dambreuse, out of propriety, with a glance at the three young girls.

M. Dambreuse emerged from his study with Martinon. She turned her head away and answered the greetings of Pellerin, who was coming in. The artist was looking uneasily round the walls. The banker took him aside and explained to him that he had had to conceal his revolutionary picture for the time being. 'Of course,' said Pellerin, whose opinions had been modified by his reverse at the Club de l'Intelligence.

M. Dambreuse hinted very civilly that he would commission other works from him.

'Excuse me! . . . Ah, my dear fellow! How delightful!'

Arnoux and Mme Arnoux stood before Frederic.

He felt a kind of dizziness. Rosanette's admiration for the soldiers had annoyed him all the afternoon. The old love awoke again.

The butler announced that dinner was served. Mme Dambreuse ordered Cisy, with a glance, to take Cécile's arm. To Martinon she whispered: 'Traitor!' and they moved into the dining-room.

In the middle of the table cloth, under the green leaves of a pineapple, lay a dolphin, with its head pointing to a haunch of venison and its tail towards a pyramid of crayfish. Figs, huge cherries, pears, and grapes—all forced in Paris—were piled high on baskets of old Dresden china; vases of flowers alternated here and there with the gleaming silver; the white silk blinds, drawn over the windows, filled the room with a soft light; two fountains containing pieces of ice cooled the air; and tall servants in knee-breeches waited on the guests. The scene was all the pleasanter for the excitement of the last few days. They had feared that they had lost these things, and now their enjoyment was restored; and Nonancourt expressed the general sentiment when he said:

'Let us hope that our friends the Republicans will allow us to have our dinner!'

'In spite of their fraternity,' added M. Roque, wittily.

These two worthies were sitting to the right and left of Mme Dambreuse. Her husband was opposite to her, between Mme de Larsillois, who had the diplomat next to her, and the duchess, beside whom sat Fumichon. Next came Pellerin, Arnoux, and Mlle Louise. Martinon had taken Frederic's place so as to be near Cécile, so that Frederic found himself next to Mme Arnoux.

She was wearing a dress of black barège, with a gold bracelet at her wrist, and she had, as on the first evening he had dined with them, something red in her hair—a spray of fuchsia twined in her chignon. He could not help saying to her:

'It 's a long time since we last met.'

'Ah,' she replied, coldly.

He went on, with a gentleness in his voice that mitigated the impertinence of his question:

'Did you ever think about me?'

'Why should I think about you?'

Frederic was hurt by this phrase.

'Perhaps you 're right, after all.'

But, repenting quickly, he swore that he had not spent a single day without being tormented by her memory.

318

'I don't believe a word of it, sir.'

'All the same, you know I love you.'

Mme Arnoux made no reply.

'You know I love you.'

She was still silent.

'All right, go to the devil!' said Frederic to himself. And, raising his eyes, he caught sight of Mlle Roque at the other end of the table.

She had thought it smart to dress all in green, a colour which clashed hideously with her red hair. The buckle of her belt was too high; her embroidered collar did not fit her; and this lack of elegance probably contributed to the coolness of Frederic's greeting. She watched him with curiosity, from a distance; and Arnoux's lavish gallantries were all in vain; he could not get a word out of her, so he stopped trying to please and listened to the conversation, which was now concerned with the pine-apple puddings at the Luxembourg.

According to Fumichon, Louis Blanc owned a mansion in the rue Saint-Dominique which he refused to let to the workmen.

'What makes me laugh,' said Nonancourt, 'is Ledru-Rollin hunting on the royal estates.'

'He owes a jeweller twenty thousand francs,' added Cisy, 'and they even say——'

Mme Dambreuse interrupted:

'It's very bad manners to get excited about politics. A young man, too—you should know better! Why don't you talk to your neighbour?'

Then the more serious-minded began to attack the news-papers.

Arnoux took up their defence; Frederic took the other side and declared that they were just like any other enterprise—run for profit. Those who wrote for them were generally either fools or humbugs; he claimed to know them well, and countered his friend's generous sentiments with sarcastic comments. Mme Arnoux did not realize that this was a revenge against her.

Meanwhile, the viscount was desperately racking his brains for a way to conquer Cécile. He began by displaying his aesthetic taste, and criticized the shape of the decanters and the chasing on the knives. Then he spoke of his stable, his tailor, his shirt maker; at length he broached the subject of religion and found an opportunity of explaining that he was extremely regular in his devotions.

Martinon did better. Talking at a steady pace and not taking his eyes off her, he extolled her bird-like profile, her faded fair hair, and her stumpy hands. The ugly girl was delighted with this shower of compliments.

Every one was talking at the top of his voice: nothing could be heard. M. Roque wanted 'an iron hand' to govern France. Nonancourt even regretted the abolition of the death penalty for political crimes. All these rogues ought to be wiped out in a body!

'They 're cowards, too,' said Fumichon. 'I don't see anything very brave in skulking behind a barricade!'

'Talking of that, tell us about Dussardier,' said M. Dambreuse, turning towards Frederic.

The gallant shop assistant was now a hero, like Sallesse, the brothers Jeanson, the woman Péquillet, and the rest.

Without waiting to be pressed, Frederic told the story of his friend; and he gained a kind of reflected glory from it.

Quite naturally, they turned to discussing different forms of courage. According to the diplomat, it was not difficult to face death—as was shown by the people who fought duels.

'We can take the viscount's word for that,' said Martinon.

The viscount went very red.

The guests stared at him; and Louise, more surprised than the others, murmured:

'What is it?'

'He funked it against Frederic,' whispered Arnoux.

'Do you know something about it, mademoiselle?' asked Nonancourt, immediately.

And he repeated her reply to Mme Dambreuse, who leaned forward a little and began to look at Frederic.

Martinon did not wait for Cécile's questions. He told her that the other party concerned was a complete outsider. The young girl drew back a little on her chair, as if to shun contact with this libertine.

The conversation had begun again. Choice clarets were served, and the party grew livelier. Pellerin could not forgive the revolution for the final destruction of the Spanish museum. It was that that distressed him most, as a painter. At this remark, M. Roque turned to him:

'Aren't you the artist who painted a very remarkable picture?'

'Possibly. Which one?'

'It represents a lady in a . . . well . . . in a rather scanty costume, carrying a purse, with a peacock behind.'

Frederic went crimson in his turn. Pellerin pretended not to hear.

'But I assure you it's by you. For your name's written at the bottom, and there's a line on the frame to say it belongs to Monsieur Moreau.'

M. Roque and his daughter had seen Rosanette's portrait one day, when they were waiting for Frederic at his house. The old man had even taken it for 'a Gothic picture.'

'No!' said Pellerin, with some heat. 'It's the portrait of a woman.'

Martinon added:

'And of a woman who's very much alive! Isn't she, Cisy?'

'I don't know anything about it.'

'I thought you knew her. But I seem to have upset you; I beg your pardon!'

Cisy lowered his eyes, proving by his embarrassment that he had played a pitiful role in connection with the portrait. As for Frederic, the model could only be his mistress. It was one of those sudden, universal convictions, and it was clearly reflected in the faces of the company.

'How he lied to me!' said Mme Arnoux to herself.

'So that was why he left me!' thought Louise.

Frederic supposed that these two stories might injure his reputation, so he attacked Martinon about it as soon as they were in the garden.

Cécile's suitor laughed in his face.

'No, not at all! They'll do you good! Go straight ahead!'

What did he mean? And why this unusual benevolence? Without explanation, Martinon went over to the far end of the garden where the ladies were sitting. The men were standing up, and Pellerin, in the midst of them, was expounding his views. A monarchy was unquestionably the form of government most favourable to the arts. The present times disgusted him—'if only because of the National Guard'; he regretted the Middle Ages and Louis XIV. M. Roque congratulated him on his opinions, confessing that they had removed all his prejudices against artists. But he went off almost immediately, attracted by Fumichon's voice. Arnoux was trying to prove that there were two sorts of Socialism, a good and a bad. The industrialist did not see the difference, for the word 'property' made him wild with righteous indignation.

'It's a law upheld by nature! Children cling to their toys; every tribe, every animal, supports my view; if the lion could speak, he would say he was in favour of property! Look at me, gentlemen—I began with fifteen thousand francs capital. Do you know, I got up regularly at four o'clock in the morning every day? I've had the devil's own job making my fortune. And then they come and tell me that it doesn't belong to me—that my money isn't my money—in fact, that property is theft!'

'But Proudhon——'

'Don't talk to me about your Proudhon! If he was here, I should strangle him!'

He would have strangled him. After the liqueurs, Fumichon was scarcely himself; and his apoplectic face seemed on the point of exploding like a bomb.

'Good day, Arnoux,' said Hussonnet, passing briskly across the lawn.

He was bringing M. Dambreuse the first sheet of a pamphlet called *The Hydra*, in which he defended the interests of a reactionary club, and it was in this capacity that the banker introduced him to his guests.

Hussonnet amused them, first by maintaining that the candle makers were in the habit of hiring three hundred and ninety-two small boys to shout 'Light up!' every evening, and then by mocking the principles of '89, the emancipation of the negroes, and the orators of the Left. Perhaps from a simple-minded jealousy of these prosperous people who had dined so well, he went so far as to attempt a take-off of 'John Citizen on a Barricade.' The burlesque was not very successful. Their faces grew longer.

Besides, this was not time for joking, as Nonancourt remarked, recalling the death of Monsignor Affre and that of General de Bréa. These deaths were always being recalled; arguments were based on them. M. Roque declared that the archibishop's demise was 'incomparably sublime'; Fumichon awarded the palm to the soldier; and, instead of merely deploring the two murders, a discussion arose as to which ought to excite the stronger indignation. A second parallel followed; that of Lamoricière and Cavaignac;[1] M. Dambreuse extolled Cavaignac and Nonancourt Lamoricière. Except for Arnoux no one present could have seen them at work. None the less, everybody passed an irrevocable judgment on their activities. Frederic declined to do so, confessing that he had not taken up arms. The diplomat and M. Dambreuse gave him an approving nod. In fact, those who had combated the rising had actually been defending the republic, and although the result was favourable, the republic was strengthened by it. Now that they were rid of the conquered, they wanted to free themselves from the conquerors.

Scarcely were they in the garden when Mme Dambreuse took Cisy aside and scolded him for his awkwardness; at the sight of Martinon she dismissed him and asked her future nephew the reason for his jokes against the viscount.

'There is none.'

'And all this for Monsieur Moreau's glory! With what object?'

'None. Frederic is a charming boy. I'm very fond of him.'

'So am I. Send him here! Go and look for him!'

After a few commonplace phrases, she began by quietly criticizing her guests, which made him feel superior to them. He did not fail to disparage the other women a little—a skilful method of paying her compliments. From time to time she left him; it was an 'at home' evening; ladies kept arriving; then she came back to her place, and the chance arrangement of the seats prevented them from being overheard.

She appeared to be lively, serious, melancholy, and reasonable. The problems of the day interested her little; there was another world of less transitory emotions. She complained of poets who distort the truth; then she raised her eyes to the sky and asked him the name of a star.

Two or three Chinese lanterns hung among the trees; they swayed in the wind, and a ray of coloured light quivered on her white dress. As usual, she was leaning back a little in her arm-chair, with a stool in front of her; the point of a black satin shoe could be seen; from time to time Mme Dambreuse spoke a word in a louder voice or laughed.

This flirtation was unnoticed by Martinon, who was busy with Cécile, but it struck the eye of Louise, who was talking to Mme Arnoux. Of all these women, she was the only one whose manner did not seem supercilious. She had taken a seat beside her; then, feeling the need to express her feelings, she said:

'Doesn't Frederic Moreau talk well?'

'Do you know him?'

'Oh, very well! We're neighbours. He played with me when I was quite small.'

Mme Arnoux shot her a long glance, signifiying: 'I suppose you're not in love with him?'

The young girl's look answered without embarrassment·
'Yes, I am!'

'Then you see a great deal of him?'

'Oh, no! Only when he comes to stay with his mother. He hasn't been down for ten months now—although he promised to be more regular.'

'My child, you shouldn't put too much faith in the promises of men.'

'But he hasn't deceived me!'

'He's deceived others!'

Louise shivered. 'Could he, by chance, have promised her something, too?'—and her face was contracted with mistrust and hatred.

Mme Arnoux was almost afraid; she would have liked to take back what she had said. Then the two were silent.

Frederic was sitting opposite them, on a folding chair, and they looked at him—the one modestly, out of the corner of her eye, the other openly, with her mouth gaping; so that Mme Dambreuse said to him:

'Turn round and let her see you!'

'Who?'

'Why, Monsieur Roque's daughter!'

And she teased him about the young country girl's love for him. He denied it and tried to laugh.

'Is it conceivable? I ask you! With a face like that!'

At the same time he felt the intense pleasure of gratified vanity. He remembered that other evening party, which he had left with his heart full of humiliation. He felt that he was now in his true surroundings, almost in his own estate, as though everything there, including the Dambreuse mansion, were his property. The ladies formed a half-circle as they listened to him; and, in order to shine, he declared himself in favour of the re-establishment of divorce, which should be made so easy that people could separate and come together in complete freedom. The women protested in horror. Some were whispering; there were little bursts of conversation in the shadow, at the foot of the creeper-covered wall. It was like the merry clucking of hens; and he developed his theory, with the self-assurance that springs from the consciousness of success. A servant brought a tray full of glasses into the arbour. The gentlemen came up. They were talking about the arrests.

Then Frederic avenged himself on the viscount by persuading him that he might be in danger as a Legitimist. Cisy protested that he had not moved from his room; his enemy enlarged on the chances against him; even M. Dambreuse and M. de Grémonville were amused. Then they complimented Frederic, and expressed their regret that he did not use his talents in the defence of law and order; and their handshake was cordial; he could rely on them in the future.   At last, as every one was leaving, the viscount bowed very low to Cécile:

'Mademoiselle, I have the honour to wish you a very good night!'

'Good night,' she answered curtly.

But she had a smile for Martinon.

Old Roque, in order to continue his discussion with Arnoux, suggested seeing him home. 'And madame, too,' as they were going in the same direction.   Louise and Frederic walked ahead. She had seized his arm; and when they were a little way from the others, she said:

'At last! At last! Haven't I been through enough the whole evening? How wicked those women are! What haughty airs!'

He tried to defend them.

'First of all, you might have spoken to me when you came in, considering you haven't been back for a year!'

'It's not a year,' said Frederic, who was glad to take her up on this detail, so as to avoid the rest.

'All right! It seemed a long time to me, that's all! But all through that frightful dinner you looked as though you were ashamed of me. Oh, I understand. I haven't got what they've got to attract you.'

'You're wrong,' said Frederic.

'Really? Swear you're not in love with any of them?'

He swore.

'And you're not in love with any one but me?'

'Of course not!'

This assurance cheered her up. She would gladly have got lost in the streets so that they could walk about together all night.

'I was so worried at home! They talked about nothing but barricades! I saw you lying on your back, covered with blood! Your mother was in bed with her rheumatism; she knew nothing about it. I had to keep quiet. I couldn't stand it. So I took Catherine and set off.'

And she told him all about her departure, her journey, and the lie she had told her father.

'He's taking me back in two days' time. Come in to-morrow evening, as if by chance; take your opportunity, and ask for me in marriage.'

Frederic had never felt less inclined for marriage. Moreover, Mlle Roque seemed to him a rather ridiculous little creature. What a contrast between her and a woman like Mme Dambreuse! A very different future awaited him! He had had the proof of it that night; so now was scarcely the moment to involve himself, on an emotional impulse, in a decision of such importance. It was the time for realism; and, besides, he had seen Mme Arnoux again. Yet Louise's candour embarrassed him. He answered:

'Have you thought the matter over carefully?'

'What!' she exclaimed, frozen with surprise and indignation. He said it would be madness to marry at the present moment.

'So you don't want me?'

'But you don't understand what I mean!'

And he began a very complicated speech, explaining that he was held back by major considerations, that he had endless business on hand, that even his fortune was in danger—she should not jump to conclusions about his motives—and lastly that the political situation was unfavourable. So the most sensible course was to be patient for a time. All would, no doubt, come right in the end; at least, he hoped so; and, having come to the end of his excuses, he pretended suddenly to remember that he should have been at Dussardier's two hours ago.

Then, having said good-bye to the others, he plunged into the rue Hauteville, went round the Gymnase Theatre, struck the boulevard again, and climbed Rosanette's four flights of stairs at a run.

M. and Mme Arnoux left old Roque and his daughter at the entrance of the rue Saint-Denis. They went home without speaking a word; for he was exhausted with chattering, and she felt extraordinarily tired; she even leant her head on his shoulder. He was the only man who had spoken honestly the whole evening. She felt full of indulgence towards him. For his part, he still felt some resentment against Frederic.

'Did you see his expression when they were talking about the portrait? You wouldn't believe me when I told you he was her lover!'

'Yes, I was wrong.'

Arnoux, enjoying his triumph, continued.

'I'll even wager that he went straight back to her when he left us. He's with her now! He's spending the night there!'

Mme Arnoux had pulled down her hood very low.

'But you're trembling!'

'It's because I'm cold,' she answered.

As soon as her father was asleep, Louise came into Catherine's room and shook her by the shoulder.

'Get up! . . . quickly! quicker! And go and get me a cab.'

Catherine told her there were none to be had at that hour.

'Then you'll come with me yourself, won't you?'

'Where to?'

'To Frederic's house.'

'You can't mean it! Why?'

She wanted to talk to him. She could not wait. She had to see him immediately.

'But think what you're doing! Going to a house, like that, in the middle of the night! Besides, he'll be asleep now.'

'I shall wake him up!'

'But it's not proper for a young girl.'

'I'm not a young girl! I'm his wife! I love him! Come on, put on your shawl!'

Catherine stood beside her bed, thinking. At last she said: 'No! I won't!'

'Well then, stay behind! I'm going anyhow!'

Louise slipped down the staircase like a snake. Catherine dashed down behind her and joined her on the pavement. Her expostulations were in vain; and, still fastening up her jacket, she followed Louise. The journey seemed extremely long. She complained of her old legs.

'After all, I've got nothing to make me go fast, like you!'

Then she was softened.

'Poor darling! You've got no one but your old Cathy now!'

From time to time she was seized with misgivings.

'Ah! this is a nice thing you're making me do. If your father wakes up—God above! I hope nothing dreadful will happen!'

In front of the Variétés Theatre a patrol of National Guards stopped them. At once Louise said that she and her maid were going to the rue Rumfort to fetch a doctor. They were allowed to pass.

At the corner of the Madeleine they met a second patrol, and, when Louise gave the same explanation, one of the citizens replied:

'Is it for a nine-months' illness, my pretty one?'

'Gougibaud!' exclaimed the captain. 'No foul talk in the ranks! Ladies, proceed!'

In spite of this order, the display of wit continued.

'Enjoy yourselves!'

'My compliments to the doctor!'

'Look out for the wolf!'

'They like a laugh,' said Catherine loudly. 'They 're young.'

At length they reached Frederic's door. Louise pulled the bell several times vigorously. The door half-opened and the porter answered her question:

'No!'

'But he must be in bed?'

'I tell you, no! He hasn't slept at home for the last three months!'

And the little square window of the porter's lodge fell to with a slam, like a guillotine. They were left in the passage, in the darkness. A furious voice shouted at them:

'Get out!'

The door opened again; they went out.

Louise felt obliged to sit down on a milestone, and with her head in her hands, she wept copiously, with all her heart. Day was breaking; some carts went by.

Catherine supported her home, kissing her and telling her all sorts of good things, drawn from her own experience. She shouldn't worry so much about a sweetheart. If this one failed her she would find plenty of others!

*

CHAPTER III

WHEN Rosanette's enthusiasm for the Mobile Guards had waned, she was more captivating than ever, and Frederic gradually fell into the habit of living continously at her apartment.

The best part of the day was the morning on the terrace. In a loose cambric jacket, with slippers over her bare feet, she pottered about round his chair, cleaning the canaries' cage, changing the goldfishes' water, gardening with a fire shovel in the window box, from which a trellis of nasturtiums grew up the wall. Then, leaning on the balcony, side by side, they would watch the carriages and the passers-by; they warmed themselves in the sun and made plans for the evening. He was never away for more than two hours in the day; on his return they would go to the theatre, in a stage box; and Rosanette, with a huge bouquet of flowers in her hand, would listen to the music, while Frederic whispered jokes or compliments into her ear. Or, again, they would take a carriage for a drive into the Bois de Boulogne, and walk about until midnight. At length they would come back by the Arc de Triomphe and the grand avenue, sniffing the air, with the stars above their heads, while all the gas jets stretched in line right down the vista, like a double string of luminous pearls.

Frederic always had to wait for her when they were going out; she was hours arranging the ribbons of her bonnet round her chin; and she smiled at herself in her wardrobe mirror. Then she put her arm on his and made him stand in front of the glass beside her.

'We look nice like that—the two of us, side by side. My poor darling, I could eat you!'

He was now her chattel, her property. It was this that gave a continued radiance on her face, while her movements now seemed more languorous, her contours more rounded; at the same time he found a change in her which he could not define.

One day, she told him, as an important piece of news, that Arnoux had just opened a linen shop for a woman who used to work at his factory; he went there every evening, and spent a great deal. 'Why, only last week he gave her a lot of ebony furniture.'

'How do you know that?' said Frederic.

'Oh, I'm certain of it.'

On her instructions Delphine had made inquiries. She must be very fond of Arnoux to take such an interest in him! He contented himself with saying:

'What's it got to do with you?'

Rosanette looked surprised at this question.

'Why, he owes me money, the swine! It makes me sick to see him spending it on whores!'

Then, with an expression of triumphant hatred:

'But she makes a pretty good fool out of him! She's got three other men. Serve him right! And I'd be glad to see her sting him for his last farthing.'

Arnoux was, in fact, allowing the girl from Bordeaux to exploit him, with all the indulgence of an old man in love.

His factory was no longer working; his affairs, in general, were in a pitiful condition; his first idea, to recoup himself, was to set up a musical café, where nothing but patriotic songs would be sung: the Government would grant him a subsidy, and his establishment would become both a centre of propaganda and a source of profit. Authority had changed its course, and the plan was impracticable. He was now thinking of setting up an enormous military hat shop. He lacked the capital to begin.

He was no more fortunate in his domestic life. Mme Arnoux was now less gentle with him and was even, at times, a little harsh. Marthe always took her father's side. This increased the discord, and the house became unbearable. He often went out in the morning, spent the day in protracted activities, to tire himself out, and then dined at a country inn alone with his thoughts.

Frederic's prolonged absence interfered with his usual life. One afternoon he appeared at Frederic's, begged him to come and call as in the old days, and extracted a promise from him.

Frederic did not dare go and see Mme Arnoux again. He felt that he had betrayed her. But this was pure cowardice. He had no excuse for further delay. The thing must be put an end to; and, one evening, he set off.

Rain was falling, so he sought the shelter of the passage Jouffroy. In the light of the shop windows, a short, fat man in a cap came up to him. Frederic had no difficulty in recognizing Compain, the orator whose motion had aroused so much laughter at the club. He was leaning on the arm of a person whose head was wrapped in a long zouave cap. His upper lip was inordinately long, his complexion was as yellow as an orange, he wore a short beard, and he was gazing at Compain with eyes glistening with admiration.

Compain seemed to be proud of him, for he said:

'Let me introduce this good fellow! He's a friend of mine, a bootmaker and a patriot. Shall we have a drink?'

Frederic having politely declined, Compain at once thundered against Rateau's proposal,[1] which was a manœuvre of the aristocracy. They needed a second '93 to put a stop to that! Then he asked after Regimbart and some others, equally famous, such as Masselin, Sanson, Lecornu, Maréchal, and one Deslauriers who was involved in the matter of the carbines recently intercepted at Troyes.

This was all news to Frederic. Compain knew no further details. He left him, saying:

'We'll meet again soon, because, of course, you belong.'

'To what?'

'To the calf's head!'

'What calf's head?'

'Ah, you humorist!' answered Compain, digging him in the ribs.

And the two Terrorists took refuge in a café.

Ten minutes later Frederic had forgotten Deslauriers. He was on the pavement of the rue Paradis, in front of a house; and he was gazing at the light of a lamp behind the curtains on the second floor.

At last he climbed the stairs.

'Is Arnoux in?'

The maid answered:

'No! But come in, all the same.'

And, suddenly opening a door:

'Madame, it's Monsieur Moreau!'

She rose, paler than her lace collar. She was trembling.

'To what do I owe the honour . . . of this . . . unexpected visit?'

'Nothing! Just the pleasure of seeing old friends again.'

And as he sat down:

'How is my friend Arnoux?'

'Very well. He's out.'

'Oh, I understand. The same old nocturnal habits—a little fun.'

331

'Why not? A man's brain needs a rest after a day's hard work.'

She even praised her husband's industry. This eulogy annoyed Frederic; and pointing to a piece of black cloth, with blue braid, which she had on her knees:

'What are you working at?'

'It's a jacket I'm making for my daughter.'

'Incidentally, I haven't seen her. Where is she?'

'At boarding school,' said Mme Arnoux.

Tears came into her eyes; she held them back, plying her needle vigorously. Out of tact he picked up a number of *L'Illustration* from the table beside her.

'These caricatures by Cham are very funny, aren't they?'

'Yes.'

Then silence fell once more.

A gust of wind suddenly shook the window panes.

'What weather!' said Frederic.

'It was really very good of you to come in this dreadful rain.'

'Oh, I don't care about the rain. Some people might let it keep them from their appointments, but I'm not that sort of person.'

'What appointments?' she asked innocently.

'Don't you remember?'

She shivered and hung her head.

He put his hand gently on her arm.

'You made me very unhappy, I can assure you.'

She answered, in a voice that was like a cry of anguish:

'But I was afraid for my child!'

She told him about little Eugène's illness and all the agonies of that day.

'Thank you! Thank you! I have no more doubts. I love you as I have always done.'

'No, no! It isn't true!'

'Why not?'

She looked at him coldly.

'You forget the other woman! The one you took to the races with you! The woman whose portrait you own—your mistress!'

'Yes, I admit it!' exclaimed Frederic. 'I deny nothing! I'm a brute! Listen to me!'

He had taken her out of despair, as men commit suicide. Moreover, he had made her very unhappy, to avenge his own shame upon her.

'What torture! Don't you understand?'

Mme Arnoux turned her lovely face towards him, holding out her hand; and they shut their eyes, lulled in a sweet and boundless intoxication. Then, standing nearer, they gazed at each other, face to face.

'Could you believe that I no longer loved you?'

She answered him in a low voice, full of tenderness:

'No. In spite of everything, I felt at the bottom of my heart that it could not be so, and that one day the barrier between us would melt away.'

'So did I! And I nearly died, longing to see you again!'

'Once,' she said, 'I passed quite near you in the Palais-Royal.'

'Really?'

And he told her how happy he had been to find her at the Dambreuses' house.

'But how I hated you that evening, when I left!'

'Poor boy!'

'My life is so sad.'

'So is mine. I could bear my disappointments, my anxieties, my humiliations—everything I endure as wife and mother—without complaining, since every one must die. But what is so terrible is my loneliness—not a soul——'

'But I am here.'

'Oh, yes!'

Her breast heaved with a passionate sob. She stretched out her arms; and, standing up, they clasped each other in a long kiss.

The floor creaked. A woman was beside them—Rosanette. Mme Arnoux recognized her; and she stared at her with wide-open eyes, full of surprise and indignation. At length Rosanette said:

'I want to speak to Monsieur Arnoux on business.'

'He's not here—as you can see.'

'That's true,' said Rosanette. 'Your maid was right. A thousand apologies!'

And turning to Frederic:

'So you're here, darling?'

This familiarity in her presence made Mme Arnoux blush, like a blow in the face.

'I repeat, he's not here.'

Then Rosanette, who was looking about her, said calmly:

'Shall we go home? I've a cab waiting.'

He pretended not to hear.

'Come along, now!'

'Yes. Yes! Now is your chance! Go! Go!' said Mme Arnoux.

They went out. She leant over the banisters, for a last look at them, and a laugh, shrill and terrible, came to their ears from the top of the staircase. Frederic pushed Rosanette into the cab, sat down opposite her, and did not utter a word during the entire journey.

He was himself the cause of this horrible scene, with its disastrous consequences for him. He felt the shame of a crushing humiliation; he also regretted his lost happiness. At the very moment when he was about to win her at last, she had become inaccessible for ever! And all because of that woman, that harlot, that trollop! He would have gladly strangled her; he was choking. When they got home, he flung his hat on a table and tore off his tie.

'This is a nice thing you 've done, you must admit!'

She took her stand proudly in front of him.

'Well, what about it? Where 's the harm in it?'

'What! Have you been spying on me?'

'Is that my fault? Why should you go and amuse yourself with respectable women?'

'That 's got nothing to do with it. I won't have you insulting them!'

'How did I insult her?'

He could find no answer; and, in a more bitter tone:

'That other time, at the Champ du Mars . . .'

'Oh, I 'm sick and tired of your old stories.'

'Wretch!'

He raised his fist.

'Don't kill me! I 'm pregnant!'

'You 're lying!'

'Look at me!'

She took a candlestick and, pointing to her face said:

'Can't you tell?'

Her skin was strangely puffy, and flecked with yellow spots. Frederic could not deny the evidence. He went and opened the window, walked up and down the room a few times, and then sank into an arm-chair.

This event was a disaster; first of all, it postponed their separation, and secondly, it destroyed all his plans. Besides, the idea of being a father seemed to him grotesque, inconceivable. But why? If, instead of Rosanette . . .? And his reverie was so profound that he had a sort of hallucination.

There, on the carpet, in front of the fire, he saw a little girl. She was like Mme Arnoux, and a little like him; dark-haired and pale-skinned. She had black eyes, heavy eyebrows, and a pink ribbon in her curly hair. How he would have loved her! And he seemed to hear her voice saying: 'Papa! Papa!'

Rosanette, who had just undressed, came up to him and saw a tear on his eyelashes. She kissed him gravely on the forehead. He got up, saying:

'All right! We'll let the poor little brute live!'

Then she started chattering endlessly. It was sure to be a boy! They would call him Frederic. She must begin getting his clothes ready; and, seeing her so happy, he was moved to pity. His anger had vanished, and he was able to ask her why she had done what she had done just now.

The reason was that Mlle Vatnaz had sent her, that very day, a bill which matured long ago; and she had rushed to Arnoux's house to get the money.

'I would have given it you,' said Frederic.

'It was simpler to get my just dues from Arnoux, and give Vatnaz back her thousand francs.'

'I suppose that's all you owe her?'

She answered:

'Of course!'

The next day, at nine o'clock in the evening, Frederic went to Mlle Vatnaz's house.

He stumbled over the crowded furniture in the hall. The sound of voices and music guided him. He opened a door and found himself in the middle of a 'rout.' In front of the piano, which was being played by a young lady in spectacles, stood Delmar, earnest as a high priest, reciting a humanitarian poem about prostitution: his hollow voice, supported by sustained chords, echoed round the room. Against the wall sat a row of women, dressed for the most part in dark colours, without either collars or cuffs. Five or six men—all intellectuals—were seated on chairs here and there. In an arm-chair was a one-time fabulist,[1] a wreck of a man; and the acrid smell of the two lamps mingled with the aroma of chocolate, which filled the bowls on the card table.

Mlle Vatnaz, with an Oriental scarf round her waist, was standing at one corner of the mantelpiece; Dussardier was at the other corner, opposite her; he looked slightly embarrassed by his position. Besides, he was intimidated by his artistic environment.

Had the Vatnaz finished with Delmar? It seemed not. Yet she seemed jealous of the shop assistant; and when Frederic asked for a few words with her, she motioned to Dussardier to join them in her room. When the thousand francs were displayed before her she asked for the interest as well.

'It's not worth bothering about!' said Dussardier.

'Hold your tongue!'

This lack of courage in so brave a man pleased Frederic; it somehow justified his own cowardice. He brought back the receipted bill, and never referred to the scene with Mme Arnoux again. But from that time all Rosanette's defects became apparent to him.

Her taste was hopelessly bad; she was extraordinarily lazy; she was as ignorant as a savage, and even thought Doctor Desrogis a great celebrity; and she was proud to entertain him and his wife because they were 'a married couple.' She exercised a despotic sway over the life of Mlle Irma, a poor little thing with a tiny voice, who was kept by a 'very gentlemanly' man, a former customs official, who excelled at card tricks— Rosanette called him 'ducky.' Nor could he endure the repetitions of her stupid phrases, such as: 'I'm not having any!' 'Dry up!' 'You never can tell!'; and she insisted on dusting the ornaments in her room with a pair of old white gloves. He was particularly revolted by her behaviour towards her servant, whose wages were always in arrears and who even lent her money. The days when they settled their accounts, they squabbled like a pair of fishwives; then kissed and made friends. It was a relief when Mme Dambreuse's parties began again.

At least, Mme Dambreuse was amusing! She could tell him about society intrigues, movements of ambassadors, and who was who in the fashion houses; if she made a commonplace remark, she emphasized its banality in such a way that she might be either deferring to convention or mocking it. She was at her best in a group of twenty people, talking—forgetting nobody, provoking the replies she wanted, avoiding dangerous subjects. The simplest story, told by her, seemed like a confidence; her least smile opened vistas; indeed, her charm, like the exquisite perfume she always wore, was complex and indefinable. In her company, Frederic always felt the excitement of a voyage of discovery; yet, whenever he saw her, she always displayed the same calm serenity, like the shimmer of clear water. But why was her manner towards her niece so cold? Sometimes she threw very strange glances in her direction.

336

As soon as the question of marriage was mooted, she had raised objections on the ground of the 'poor child's' health, and she had immediately taken her to the baths at Balaruc. On their return, new difficulties had arisen: the young man had no position; this grand passion did not seem serious; there was no harm in waiting. Martinon said he would wait. He behaved magnificently. He sang Frederic's praises. He did more: he told him exactly how to attract Mme Dambreuse, hinting, even, that he knew the aunt's feelings through the niece.

M. Dambreuse, so far from showing jealousy, lavished attentions on his young friend, consulted him on various matters, even concerned himself about his future, so that one day, when old Roque was mentioned, he whispered slyly in his ear:

'You did well!'

Cécile, Miss John, the servants, the porter—every one in the house was charming to him. He went round every evening, deserting Rosanette. Her approaching confinement made her more serious, even a little melancholy; she seemed to be tormented by anxiety. To all his inquiries she replied:

'You're wrong! I'm perfectly all right.'

She was thinking of the five bills she had signed long ago; not daring to confess to Frederic after he had paid the first, she went back to Arnoux, who promised her, in writing, a third of the profits in his company for providing gaslight for the towns of Languedoc—a wonderful enterprise!—at the same time advising her not to use the letter until the shareholders' meeting; the meeting was put off from week to week.

Meanwhile, Rosanette needed money. She would have died rather than ask Frederic. She did not want his money. It would have spoiled their love. He provided amply for the household expenses: but a little carriage, hired by the month, and other sacrifices which had become necessary since his friendship with the Dambreuse family, prevented him from doing more for his mistress. Two or three times, coming in at unexpected hours, he thought he saw masculine backs vanishing; and she often went out, refusing to tell him where she was going. Frederic did not attempt to press the question. One of these days he would take up a definite attitude. He was dreaming of another life, grander and more amusing. This ideal made him lenient towards the Dambreuse mansion.

It was an intimate annexe to the rue de Poitiers. There he met the great Monsieur A, the famous B, the learned C, the eloquent Z, the terrific Y, the ageing heroes of the Left Centre, the knights-errant of the Right, the old buffers of the Centre Party—the stock figures of comedy. He was astonished at their appalling conversation, their meanness, their spite, their bad faith; for all these men who had voted for the Constitution were now struggling to destroy it; they warmed to their task, publishing manifestoes, pamphlets, and biographies; the life of Fumichon by Hussonnet was a masterpiece. Nonancourt busied himself with propaganda in the country, M. de Grémonville worked on the clergy, Martinon rallied the youth of the middle classes. Every one took up some activity, according to his capacities; even Cisy himself. He was now absorbed in serious matters, and all day long he drove about in a cab, on party business.

M. Dambreuse, like a barometer, always expressed the latest political variation. Lamartine could not be mentioned without his quoting the workman's remark: 'We 've had enough poetry!' To his mind, Cavaignac was no more than a traitor. The President,[1] whom he had admired for three months, was beginning to go down in his estimation; he did not think he had 'the necessary energy.' And as he always had to have a saviour, his gratitude was now offered to Changarnier, since the Conservatoire[2] affair. 'Thank God for Changarnier. . . . Let us hope that Changarnier . . . There 's nothing to be afraid of so long as Changarnier . . .'

M. Thiers received particular praise for his volume against Socialism, in which he showed himself to be a thinker as well as a writer. They laughed immoderately at Pierre Leroux, who quoted passages from Diderot and his school in the Chamber. They made jokes about the remnants of Fourier's party. They went to see the *Foire aux Idées*,[3] and applauded it, comparing the authors to Aristophanes. Frederic went with the others.

Good food and political verbiage were deadening his moral sense. However second-rate these people might seem, he was proud to know them, and inwardly longed to be esteemed by the rich. A mistress like Mme Dambreuse would establish his position.

He set out to do all that was necessary.

He stationed himself in her path when she went out walking, he never failed to go and greet her in her box at the theatre; he found out the times when she usually went to church, and took his stand behind a pillar, in an attitude of romantic melancholy. There was a continued exchange of little notes, details about a concert or a curiosity, loans of books and magazines. Apart from his evening visit, he often paid her another in the late afternoon; and he experienced an ascending scale of pleasures as he passed in succession through the front door, the hall, and the two drawing-rooms. At length he reached her boudoir, which was quiet as a tomb, and warm as an alcove. One stumbled against padded furniture among a whole medley of objects; there were cabinets, screens, cups, and trays in lacquer, tortoise-shell, ivory, and malachite—expensive trifles, frequently replaced. There were simple things as well: a paper-weight consisting of three pebbles from the beach at Étretat, a Frisian cap hanging on a Chinese screen; and the general effect, curiously enough, was one of grandeur—perhaps because of the height of the ceiling, the richness of the door curtains, and the long silk fringes which drooped round the gilded legs of the stools.

She was nearly always on a little settee, beside the flower stand in the window recess. Seated on the edge of a large *pouf* on castors, he paid her the most nicely calculated compliments; and she looked at him with her head a little on one side, and a smile on her lips.

He read her pages of poetry, putting his whole soul into his voice, in order to move her heart and excite her admiration. She would interrupt him with a disparaging remark or a practical observation; and their conversation would invariably return to the eternal question of love. They asked each other what caused it, if women felt it more than men, in what way their own views about it differed. Frederic tried to express his opinion without being either coarse or vapid. It became a kind of battle, which was sometimes pleasant and occasionally tedious. With her he did not feel that all-embracing rapture which impelled him towards Mme Arnoux, or the happy turmoil of the emotions into which Rosanette had flung him at first. But he desired her as a singular, almost unattainable object, because she was noble, because she was rich, because she was devout. He attributed to her a refinement of feeling as exquisite as her lace; he felt she would wear holy medals next her skin, and turn modest suddenly in the midst of debauchery.

He turned his old love to account. He told her of all the emotions which Mme Arnoux had formerly made him feel, as though she had inspired them—his pining, his fears, his dreams. She listened to this like a woman accustomed to such things; she neither rebuffed him directly nor yielded an inch; and he was no more successful in seducing her than Martinon in getting married. In order to get rid of her niece's admirer once and for all, she accused him of trying to marry for money, and asked her husband to test him on the point. So M. Dambreuse announced to the young man that Cécile, being the orphan daughter of poor parents, had neither dowry nor 'expectations.'

Either because he did not believe it, or because he had gone too far to draw back, or in one of those fits of crazy obstinacy which are often strokes of genius, Martinon replied that his own income of fifteen thousand francs a year would be enough for them both. The banker was touched by this disinterested attitude; he had not expected it. He undertook to secure him a post in the Inland Revenue, promising to put up the necessary caution money; and, in May 1850, Martinon married Mlle Cécile. There was no ball. The young people left for Italy the same evening. On the next day Frederic called on Mme Dambreuse. She seemed to be paler than usual. She contradicted him sharply on two or three trivial matters. In any case men were all egotists.

There were some—if only himself—who were unselfish by nature.

'Nonsense! You're as bad as the rest!'

Her eyes were red; she was crying. Then, forcing herself to laugh:

'I beg your pardon. I was wrong. It was an idea that crossed my mind and made me sad.'

He did not understand.

'Never mind,' he thought to himself. 'She's weaker than I thought.'

She rang for a glass of water, swallowed a mouthful, and sent it back; then she complained that she was abominably looked after. To divert her he offered his services to the household, maintaining that he could wait at table, dust the furniture, and announce the guests; he could be a flunkey, or rather a footboy; although these were out of fashion. He would have liked to stand at the back of her carriage, wearing a hat trimmed with cock's feathers.

'And I should look most impressive, walking behind you carrying a little dog on my arm!'

'You're very cheerful,' said Mme Dambreuse.

But wasn't it absurd, he answered, to take everything seriously? There were enough troubles in the world, without creating one's own. It was not worth while making oneself miserable over anything. Mme Dambreuse raised her eyebrows, in a manner that seemed to signify approval.

This similarity of views encouraged Frederic to greater

boldness. His previous mistakes now made him clear-sighted. He went on:

'Our grandfathers knew better than we do how to live. Why shouldn't we yield to the impulse that 's driving us on?'

After all, love was not in itself such an important matter.

'But what you 're saying is immoral!'

She sank on to the settee once more. He sat down on the edge, against her feet.

'Don't you realize that I 'm lying? To please a woman one has to play either the careless buffoon or the frenzied tragedian. Women laugh at us when we tell them we love them, and nothing more! To me the flights of fancy they enjoy are a sacrilege against true love; so that one doesn't know how to express oneself, particularly to a woman . . . who is . . . very intelligent.'

She gazed at him with her eyes half closed. He lowered his voice and leant over her face.

'Yes! You frighten me! Perhaps I 've offended you? I 'm sorry! . . . I didn't mean to say all that. It 's not my fault. You 're so beautiful!'

Mme Dambreuse closed her eyes and he was astonished at the ease of his conquest. The tall trees in the garden ceased to rustle and were still. Motionless clouds painted long streaks of red on the sky; the whole universe seemed held in suspense. Then there crossed his mind, indistinctly, memories of similar evenings and silences like this one. Where could it have been?

He went down on his knees, took her hand, and swore eternal devotion to her. When he left, she beckoned him back and whispered to him:

'Come back to dinner! We shall be alone.'

As Frederic went down the staircase, he felt that he had become a different man, that the heavily perfumed air of conservatories surrounded him, that he had finally made his way into the higher world of patrician liaisons and aristocratic intrigues. With a woman like Mme Dambreuse behind him, he could force his way to the front. Greedy for power and activity, married to a second-rate husband whom she had served to the utmost, she doubtless felt the need for a strong man to guide her. Anything was possible, now! He felt capable of travelling five hundred miles on horseback, of working for several nights on end, without fatigue; his heart was overflowing with pride.

A man in an old overcoat was walking along the pavement

in front of him. His head was bowed and he looked so dejected that Frederic turned round to look at him. He raised his eyes. It was Deslauriers. He hesitated. Frederic fell on his neck.

'My dear fellow! Is it really you?'

And he carried him off to his house, asking him all sorts of questions at the same time.

The ex-commissioner of the provisional Government began by telling him all that he had suffered. He had preached fraternity to the Conservatives and respect for the laws to the Socialists: the former had turned their muskets on him, the latter had brought a rope to hang him. After the events of June he had been brusquely dismissed. He had taken part in the plot in connection with the arms that had been seized at Troyes. He had been released, for lack of evidence. The committee of action had sent him to London, where he had come to blows with his colleagues in the middle of a banquet. Back to Paris . . .

'Why didn't you come to see me?'

'You were always away. Your porter had a mysterious manner; I didn't know what to think. Besides, I didn't want to come back as a failure.'

He had knocked at the gates of Democracy, had offered his pen, his oratory, his energy, for her service; everywhere he had been rejected. Nobody trusted him; and he had sold his watch, his library, his linen.

'It would be better to die, like Sénécal, in the hulks of Belle-Isle!'

Frederic, who happened to be arranging his neck-cloth, did not seem particularly upset by this news.

'So friend Sénécal has been transported?'

Deslauriers, glancing round the walls with an envious eye, replied:

'Every one hasn't got your luck.'

'You must forgive me,' said Frederic, without noticing the allusion, 'but I'm dining out. They'll get you something to eat; order anything you want. Take my bed, if you like!'

This unstinting hospitality banished Deslauriers's bitterness.

'Your bed? But . . . that would put you out!'

'Not at all. I've got others!'

'Excellent,' said the lawyer, laughing. 'Where are you dining?'

'With Madame Dambreuse.'

'Is it . . . by any chance . . .?'

342

'You 're too inquisitive,' said Frederic with a smile that confirmed this conjecture.

Then, looking at the clock, he sat down again.

'Life is like that. You must never lose heart, my old defender of the people!'

'Damn it! I 'm sick of bothering about the people!'

The lawyer loathed the workers; he had suffered from them in his district, a coal-mining area. Each mine had appointed a provisional government of its own to order him about.

'And they 've behaved charmingly everywhere — Lyons, Lille, Le Havre, Paris. These gentlemen have followed the example of the manufacturers who want to exclude foreign products, and they demand the expulsion of all workers from England, Belgium, Germany, and Savoy. As for their intelligence, what good did their famous guilds do them under the restoration? In 1830 they joined the National Guard, without even having the sense to get control of it! And, just after '48, the trade unions appeared again with their own private banners! They even wanted their own representatives in Parliament, to speak for them alone! Just like the beetroot deputies, who never bother about anything but beetroot. Oh, I 've had enough of these fellows! First they bowed down before Robespierre's scaffold, then it was the emperor's boots, and then Louis-Philippe's umbrella. That scum will always worship any one who thrusts bread down their gullets! People are always blaming Talleyrand and Mirabeau for taking bribes; but the porter downstairs would sell his country for fifty centimes if he was promised a regular three francs for his errands! What a fiasco! And we might have set the four corners of Europe on fire!'

Frederic replied:

'The spark was lacking. You were all small tradesmen at heart; the best of you were only theorists. The workers have a right to complain; apart from a million out of the civil list, which you handed over to them with the vilest flattery, you 've given them nothing but empty phrases. The bank book remains in the hands of the master; and, even in the sight of the law, the employee is inferior to his employer, because his word is never believed. The fact is the republic 's out of date. Who knows? It may be that we can only achieve progress through an aristocracy or a single man. The impulse always comes from above. The people don't count, whatever you may say!'

'Perhaps you 're right,' said Deslauriers.

343

According to Frederic, the great mass of the people only wanted to be left in peace—he had profited from what he had heard at the Dambreuses' house—and all the odds were in favour of the Conservatives. But this party needed new men.

'If you put yourself forward, I 'm certain——'

He broke off. Deslauriers understood and passed his hands over his forehead; then, suddenly:

'But what about you? You 're not tied. Why shouldn't you be a deputy?'

Through a double election, there was a vacant seat in the Aube department. M. Dambreuse, who had been re-elected to the Legislative Assembly, belonged to another district.

'Shall I see what I can do?'

He knew numerous innkeepers, schoolmasters, doctors, lawyers' clerks, and their employers.

'Besides, one can make the peasants believe anything one likes.'

Frederic felt his ambition rekindled.

Deslauriers added:

'You ought to be able to find me a job in Paris.'

'It won't be difficult, through Monsieur Dambreuse.'

'Talking of coal,' said the lawyer, 'what 's happened to his great company? That 's the sort of employment I need. And I could be useful to them, while keeping my independence.'

Frederic promised to introduce him to the banker within three days.

His meal alone with Mme Dambreuse was an exquisite experience. She smiled at him from the other side of the table, over the flowers in their basket, in the light of a hanging lamp. Through the open window the stars could be seen. They talked very little, no doubt, because they did not trust themselves; but, as soon as the servants turned their backs, they blew each other a kiss. He told her his idea of becoming a candidate. She approved, and even promised to get M. Dambreuse to work for him.

After dinner some friends appeared to congratulate and sympathize with her; she must miss her niece a great deal. It was a good thing that the young couple had gone abroad; later there would be children and other obstacles. But Italy did not come up to one's preconceived idea of it. However, they were at the age of illusions! And besides, everything seems beautiful on a honeymoon. The last to go were M. de Grémonville and Frederic. The diplomat did not want to leave. At last, at midnight, he rose. Mme Dambreuse motioned to Frederic to leave with him, and thanked him for his obedience by pressing his hand, which set the seal on his happiness.

Rosanette uttered a cry of joy at seeing him again. She had been waiting for him since five o'clock. He excused himself on the ground that he had had to do something for Deslauriers. His face had an air of triumph, a halo, which dazzled Rosanette.

'It may be because of your black coat suiting you so well, but I've never seen you look so handsome before. How handsome you are!' In a transport of love, she swore inwardly that she would never give herself to another man — whatever happened, even if she had to die of hunger!

Her pretty, moist eyes glistened with so deep a passion that Frederic drew her on to his knees. 'What a brute I am!' he said to himself, and gloried in his wickedness.

CHAPTER IV

WHEN Deslauriers came to see M. Dambreuse the banker was thinking of reviving his great coal business. But his idea of merging all the companies into one was not viewed with favour; he would be attacked as a monopolist, although it was well known that abundant capital was needed for enterprises of this kind!

Deslauriers, who had carefully read Gobet's work and M. Chappe's articles in the *Journal des Mines*, knew the subject thoroughly. He demonstrated that by the law of 1810 the owner of a concession had an inalienable right to the profits from it. Besides, they could give a democratic colour to the venture, by claiming that any restriction of coal amalgamations was a blow against the right of combination.

M. Dambreuse gave him notes from which to draw up a memorandum. As to payment for his work, he made him promises which were all the more enticing for being vague.

Deslauriers came back to Frederic's house with a report of his interview. Moreover, he had seen Mme Dambreuse at the foot of the stairs on his way out.

'Upon my word, I congratulate you!'

Then they talked about the election. There was a plan to think over.

Three days later, Deslauriers reappeared with a sheet of writing intended for publication in the press. It was a friendly letter in which M. Dambreuse expressed approval of his young friend's candidature. Supported by a Conservative and aided by a Radical, he was bound to succeed. But how was the banker to be persuaded to sign such a document? Without the least embarrassment the lawyer had, on his own initiative, shown it to Mme Dambreuse, who thought it very good and undertook the rest of the task.

This bold step surprised Frederic. Nevertheless, he approved of it: and then, as Deslauriers was in touch with Mlle Roque, he told him how he stood towards Louise.

'Tell them anything you like; that I'm in financial difficulties —that I shall get things straight; she's young enough to wait.'

Deslauriers set out; and Frederic regarded himself as a man of strong character. Moreover, he had a sense of contentment, of profound satisfaction. No contrast spoiled his delight in the possession of a rich woman: his feelings were at one with his environment. His life, nowadays, was full of pleasures.

The most delicious, perhaps, was watching Mme Dambreuse in her drawing-room, in a group of several people. The propriety of her manners made him think of some very different postures: as she talked in chilly phrases, he recalled her stammered words of love: the respect paid to her virtue seemed a kind of homage offered indirectly to him; and he sometimes longed to exclaim: 'But I know her better than you! She's mine!'

Their relationship soon became a thing accepted and acknowledged. Throughout the whole winter, Mme Dambreuse took Frederic into society.

Nearly always he arrived ahead of her, and he watched her come in, with her arms bare, her fan in her hand, and pearls in her hair. She paused on the threshold; the doorway surrounded her like a frame, and she made a slight movement of indecision, half-closing her eyes to find out if he was there. She brought him back in her carriage; the rain lashed the windows; the passers-by flitted through the mud like shadows; and pressed against one another, they observed this indistinctly, with a calm disdain. On various pretexts he used to stay an extra hour in her room.

Mme Dambreuse had yielded largely out of boredom. But this final experiment was not to be wasted. She wanted a grand passion, and she began to load him with flattering attentions.

She sent him flowers; she made him a tapestry chair; she gave him a cigar case, an inkstand, countless small objects of daily use, so that his every action should evoke her memory. These kindnesses charmed him at first; soon he took them for granted.

She hired a cab, dismissed it at the entrance to an alley, and came out at the other end; then, with a double veil over her face, she slipped along the walls until she reached the street where Frederic was watching for her. He quickly took her arm and led her to his house. His two servants were out, the porter was on an errand; she cast her eyes all round; there was no danger. And she sighed like an exile returning to his country. Their good luck made them bold. They met more often. One night she appeared in full evening dress. He reproached her for her rashness—these surprise visits might be dangerous;

besides, she looked particularly unattractive. Her open bodice showed too much of her meagre bosom.

Then he acknowledged what he had until then refused to admit—the disillusion of his senses. This did not prevent his simulating the most passionate ardour; but in order to feel it, he had to call up the image of Rosanette or Mme Arnoux.

This atrophy of the heart left his head completely clear; and he was more eager than ever for a high position in the world. Having this lever, the least he could do was to make use of it.

Towards the middle of January, Sénécal came into his study; and, on his exclamation of astonishment, said that he was Deslauriers's secretary. He brought Frederic a letter. It contained good news, and at the same time blamed him for his negligence: he ought to go down to his constituency.

The future deputy said he would set out next day.

Sénécal expressed no opinion on this candidature. He spoke about himself, and conditions in the country.

Bad though they were, he rejoiced at them; for things were moving towards Communism. First of all, the administration was tending in that direction, for every day more things were placed under Government control. The constitution of '48, in spite of its weaknesses, had been uncompromising in regard to property; in the name of the common weal, the State could take over whatever it considered useful. Sénécal declared that he was for authority; Frederic noticed in his conversation an exaggerated version of his own remarks to Deslauriers. The Republican even thundered against the inadequacy of the masses.

'By defending the right of the minority, Robespierre brought Louis XVI before the National Convention, and saved the people. The end justifies the means. Dictatorship is sometimes necessary. Provided the tyrant does good—long live tyranny!'

Their discussion was protracted, and, as he was leaving, Sénécal said—this was, perhaps, the object of his visit—that M. Dambreuse's silence had made Deslauriers very impatient.

But M. Dambreuse was ill. Frederic saw him every day; as an intimate friend, he was always admitted to his presence.

The dismissal of General Changarnier had upset the banker very much. That same evening, he had had an attack of heartburn, with a tightness of the chest that prevented his lying down. The application of leeches gave immediate relief. The dry cough vanished, the breathing became more regular; and a week later, as he swallowed some soup, he remarked:

'Well, I'm better now. But I nearly passed over!'

'Not without me,' exclaimed Mme Dambreuse, thus indicating that she would have been unable to survive him.

Instead of answering he looked at her and her lover with a peculiar smile, at once indulgent, resigned, and ironic—which yet contained a sort of hint or suggestion of a private joke.

Frederic was anxious to leave for Nogent; Mme Dambreuse was against it; and he kept on packing and unpacking his luggage, according to the fluctuations of the illness.

Suddenly M. Dambreuse began spitting blood freely. The leading doctors, when consulted, had no fresh advice to give. His limbs swelled up and his weakness increased. He had several times shown a desire to see Cécile, who was at the other end of France with her husband; for Martinon had been appointed to the Department of Inland Revenue some months before. He expressly ordered her to be sent for. Mme Dambreuse wrote three letters which she showed him.

She did not even trust the nun who was nursing him; she never left him for a second, never went to bed. The callers who wrote their names at the porter's lodge asked after her admiringly; and the passers-by were deeply impressed by the amount of straw in the street, under the windows.

On the 12th of February, a most alarming haemoptysis took place. The doctor on duty explained the danger. A priest was hurriedly sent for.

During M. Dambreuse's confession, his wife watched him with curiosity from a distance. After that, the doctor applied a blister and waited.

The lamps, masked by the furniture, shed an uneven light over the room. Frederic and Mme Dambreuse, at the foot of the bed, watched the dying man. In the recess of a window the priest and the doctor were talking in low voices; the nun, on her knees, was mumbling prayers.

At last the death rattle was heard. The hands grew cold, the face began to turn pale. Sometimes he suddenly drew in a huge gulp of air; but this happened more and more rarely. He muttered two or three incoherent words; as he turned his eyes about, he exhaled gently, and his head, a little on one side, fell back on the pillow.

For a moment nobody moved.

Mme Dambreuse came up to the bed and without hesitation, quite simply, as an act of duty to be done, closed his eyes.

Then she stretched out her arms, and twisted her body as if

349

in a paroxysm of controlled despair, and left the room, supported by the doctor and the priest. A quarter of an hour later Frederic came up to her room.

An indefinable odour was perceptible there, an emanation of the delicate things which filled the place. A black dress was spread out in the middle of the bed, contrasting with the pink coverlet.

Mme Dambreuse stood at the corner of the mantelpiece. Without attributing any violent grief to her, he supposed she would be rather cast down; and, in a doleful voice, he said:

'Are you unhappy?'

'I? Not in the least!'

Turning round, she saw the dress and examined it; then she told him to make himself at home.

'Smoke, if you like. You're in my house now.'

And with a heavy sigh:

'Heavens above! What a relief!'

Frederic was astonished at this exclamation. He kissed her hand and replied:

'Yet we were free enough!'

This reference to the easy circumstances of their affair seemed to wound Mme Dambreuse.

'Oh, you don't know what I did for him, or what agonies I lived in!'

'What?'

'Of course! Do you think I could feel safe with that bastard girl always near me? The child was brought into the house after we'd been married five years, and she would certainly have made him do something foolish, but for me.'

Then she explained her financial position. They had married under the system of separation of fortunes. Her own amounted to three hundred thousand francs. By their contract, M. Dambreuse guaranteed her an income of fifteen thousand francs a year, together with the ownership of the mansion if she survived him. But a little later he made a will in which he left her his entire fortune; which she valued, as far as she could calculate at the moment, at more than three millions.

Frederic opened his eyes wide.

'It was worth the trouble, wasn't it? Besides, I helped to make it. I was defending my own property; Cécile would have robbed me of it, unjustly.'

'Why did she not come to see her father?' said Frederic.

At this inquiry, Mme Dambreuse looked at him; then she answered dryly:

'I don't know. Heartlessness, I should think. Oh, I know her! And she won't get a penny from me!'

But she had been very little trouble, at least since her marriage.

'Ah! Her marriage!' said Mme Dambreuse derisively.

And she blamed herself for having been too good to this jealous, hypocritical, self-interested creature.

'All her father's faults!' And she decried him more and more. He was profoundly deceitful, ruthless, and hard as stone—'a bad man! a bad man!'

Even the cleverest people sometimes make mistakes. Mme Dambreuse had made one now in giving vent to her hatred. Frederic, in an arm-chair opposite her, was shocked and thoughtful.

She rose and sat down gently on his knee.

'You're the only one who's good at heart. I love you—and you alone!'

As she looked at him her heart softened; a nervous reaction brought tears to her eyes and she murmured:

'Will you marry me?'

At first he thought he had misheard. Such wealth made his brain reel. She repeated louder:

'Will you marry me?'

At last, with a smile, he answered:

'Do you doubt it?'

Then he felt suddenly ashamed, and as a kind of reparation to the dead man, he offered to watch over him himself. He did not like to confess this pious impulse, so he added casually:

'Perhaps it would look better if I did.'

'Yes, you may be right,' she said, 'on account of the servants.'

The bed had been pulled right out of its recess. The nun was at the foot; and at the head stood a priest. This time it was a tall, thin, fanatical-looking man, who might have been a Spaniard. Three candlesticks burned on the night table, which was covered with a white napkin.

Frederic took a chair and looked at the dead man.

His face was a yellow as straw: there were flecks of blood-streaked foam at the corners of his mouth. A silk handkerchief had been placed round his head: he wore a woollen waistcoat, and had a silver crucifix on his breast, between his folded arms.

So his life, with all its excitement, was over! How many times had he hurried from office to office, studied figures, launched deals, and listened to reports! How often had he flattered, smiled, and bowed the knee! For he had acclaimed Napoleon, the Russians, Louis XVIII, 1830, the workers; he had welcomed every government. He worshipped authority with so complete a veneration that he would have paid for the privilege of selling himself.

But he left the estate of La Fortelle, three factories in Picardy, the wood of Crancé in the district of the Yonne, a farm near Orleans, and considerable liquid assets.

Thus Frederic assessed his fortune; and it was going to belong to him! First he thought of 'what people would say,' then of a present for his mother, of the carriages he was going to have, of an old family coachman whom he would like to engage as porter. Of course, the livery would be changed. He would turn the big drawing-room into his study. By knocking down three walls, he could easily arrange a picture gallery on the second floor. It might also be possible to fit up some Turkish baths in the basement. But what could he do with that unpleasant room, M. Dambreuse's office?

His flights of fancy were rudely interrupted by the priest blowing his nose or the nun making up the fire. But the external world confirmed them; the body was still there. The eyes had opened again, the pupils, although obscured by the thick darkness, wore an inscrutable expression, which Frederic could not bear. He thought he saw in it a kind of judgment passed on him: and he almost felt remorseful, for this man had never done him any harm; on the contrary, he—— 'Come, come. He was an old scoundrel!'; and he took a closer look at him to reassure himself. Silently he shouted at him:

'Well, what is it? Do you think I killed you?'

Meanwhile the priest read his breviary; the nun dozed and did not move; the wicks of the candles lengthened.

For two hours they listened to the muffled rumbling of the carts on their way to the market. The windows grew whiter; a cab passed by, a troop of she-asses trotted along the road. There followed a noise of hammering, the cries of street hawkers, bugle calls: and already these sounds were beginning to melt into the great voice of awakening Paris.

Frederic set to work. First he visited the town hall to announce the death; then, after the official doctor had given him a certificate, he returned to the town hall again to tell them which cemetery the family had chosen, and to make arrangements at the undertaking department.

The clerk showed him a drawing and a programme. The programme described the different classes of funeral, the drawing showed the trappings in detail. Did he want a hearse with a rail round the roof, or a hearse with plumes? Were the horses to have plaits, and the footmen to wear cockades? Initials or a coat of arms? Funeral lamps? A man to carry the decorations of the deceased? And how many carriages? Frederic was lavish; for Mme Dambreuse was determined to spare no expense.

Then he went to the church.

The curate who dealt with funerals began by complaining of the undertakers' extravagance. For instance, the man to carry the decorations was quite unnecessary; it would be much better to spend the money on candles. They agreed on a low mass with music. Frederic signed the agreement, including a binding guarantee to pay all the expenses.

Then he went to the Hôtel de Ville to buy a piece of ground. A plot two yards by one cost five hundred francs. Was the lease to be for fifty years or in perpetuity?

'Oh, in perpetuity,' said Frederic.

He took the matter seriously and went to considerable pains about it.

A stonemason was waiting for him in the courtyard of the mansion, to show him plans and estimates for Greek, Egyptian, and Moorish tombs; but the house architect had already been talking to madame about it; while on the hall table were all sorts of advertisements for cleaning mattresses, disinfecting rooms, and for various forms of embalmment.

After dinner, he went back to the tailor to see about the servants' mourning; and he had one last errand to do, for he had ordered beaver gloves, whereas floss silk gloves were correct.

When he arrived next day at ten o'clock the big drawing-room was filling up with people. Almost all of them addressed each other in melancholy tones, remarking:

'And I saw him only a month ago! Well, well—it's the fate of all of us!'

'Yes, but let's try and put it off as long as possible!'

This was followed by a titter of satisfaction; and they even embarked on conversations which had nothing whatever to do with the funeral. At length, the master of the ceremonies, dressed in a black coat, knee breeches, cloak, and weepers, with his sword at his side and his three-cornered hat under his arm, bowed, and uttered the customary words:

'Gentlemen, when you are ready.'

They set out.

It was the day of the flower market at the place de la Madeleine. The weather was fine and warm; the breeze gently shook the canvas booths and swelled the edges of the immense black cloth draped over the porch. M. Dambreuse's arms, in a black frame, appeared on it three times. They were sable, with sinister arm or, with clenched fist gauntleted argent, with a count's coronet and the device: 'By every path.'

The bearers carried the heavy coffin on the top of the stairs, and the party went in.

The six chapels, the apse, and the chairs were hung with black. The catafalque at the bottom of the choir, with its tall candles, formed a single centre of yellow light. From some candelabra in the corner flames of spirits of wine were rising.

The most important mourners sat in the sanctuary, the others in the nave; and the service began.

With few exceptions the company showed so deep an ignorance of religion that the master of the ceremonies motioned to them from time to time to stand, kneel, and sit; the voices alternated with the organ and the two double basses; in the intervals of silence, the priest could be heard muttering at the altar; then the music and the singing began again.

A dull light fell from the three domes; but the open door let in a horizontal stream of white radiance, which struck the bare heads of the worshippers. In the air, midway between the roof and floor, hovered a shadow, through which glimmered the gilded tracery of the arches and the carved foliage of the capitals.

To beguile the time, Frederic listened to the *Dies irae*; he stared at the people round him, and tried to look at the pictures of, the life of Mary Magdalene, which were hung too high. Luckily Pellerin came and sat beside him, and at once began a long dissertation on the frescoes. The bell tolled. They left the church.

The hearse, decked with hanging draperies and tall plumes, set out towards Père-Lachaise. It was drawn by four black horses, with knots in their manes and plumes on their heads, wearing great capes embroidered with silver which stretched down to their hoofs. The coachman wore top boots and a three-cornered hat with a long crape streamer. The ropes were held by four people; a treasurer of the Chamber of Deputies, a member of the General Council of the Aube department, a representative of the coal industry, and Fumichon, as a friend. The barouche of the deceased and twelve mourning carriages followed. Behind came the guests, filling the middle of the boulevard.

The passers-by stopped to watch; women, their babies in their arms, climbed on to chairs, and men drinking beer in cafés appeared at windows with billiard cues in their hands.

It was a long way; and, just as at official dinners reserve soon gives way to expansiveness, the social atmosphere rapidly relaxed. They could talk about nothing but the Chamber's refusal of supply to the President.[1] M. Piscatory had been too severe: Montalambert, 'superb, as usual': and M. Chambolle, M. Pidoux, M. Creton—the whole commission, in fact—should have followed the advice of M. Quentin-Bauchard and M. Dufour.

This conversation continued down the rue de la Roquette, with its double line of shops. These shops contain nothing but coloured glass chains and black patterned disks covered with gold lettering, which made them look like grottoes full of stalactites, or china warehouses. But when they reached the gate of the cemetery, every one was immediately silent.

Among the trees rose the tombs. There were broken columns, pyramids, temples, cromlechs, obelisks, and Etruscan vaults with bronze doors. Some contained a form of funerary parlour, with rustic arm-chairs and folding seats; cobwebs hung in shreds from the chains of the urns; the bunches of satin ribbon and the crucifixes were thick with dust. Everywhere, between the pillars of balustrades, on the tombs themselves, were wreaths of immortelles, candlesticks, vases, flowers, black disks embossed with gold lettering, and plaster statuettes. There were little boys and girls and little angels, suspended in the air by brass wire; some were even sheltered by tiny roofs of zinc. Vast ropes of spun glass, in black, white, and blue, hung coiled like pythons from the top of the headstones to the bottom. The sun fell on them and made them glitter among the black wooden crosses; while the hearse proceeded along the wide pathways, which were paved like the streets of a town. From time to time the axles creaked. Kneeling women, their dresses trailing on the grass, talked softly to the dead. Puffs of white smoke rose among the green yew-trees. They were burning up some old, abandoned offerings.

M. Dambreuse's grave was not far from those of Manuel and Benjamin Constant. Here the ground slopes steeply down. There are tree tops under one's feet; beyond, some fire engines showed their funnels, and in the distance could be seen all Paris.

Frederic could admire the landscape while the speeches were being made.

The first was on behalf of the Chamber of Deputies, the second for the General Council of the Aube district, the third for the Saône-et-Loire coal company, the fourth for the Agricultural Society of the Yonne; and there was another on behalf of a philanthropic association. Finally, as they were going away, a stranger began to read a sixth speech in the name of the Amiens Society of Antiquaries.

They all took the opportunity to thunder against Socialism, of which M. Dambreuse had died a victim. The spectacle of anarchy, and his own devotion to law and order, had cut short his days. They lauded his intelligence, his honesty, his generosity, and even his silence in Parliament, for, if he was no orator, he was endowed with compensating virtues—those solid virtues which are infinitely preferable—and so forth. They included all the necessary phrases: 'Premature end—everlasting regret—that other homeland—good-bye, or rather, till we meet again!'

The earth and pebbles fell into place; and the world had finished with M. Dambreuse.

They did talk about him a little on their way back through the cemetery: and they did not scruple to express their opinions of him. Hussonnet, who had to write a description of the burial for the newspapers, even burlesqued all the speeches; for the fact was that old Dambreuse had been one of the most distinguished 'palm-greasers' of the previous reign. Then the funeral carriages took the men of affairs back to their business; the ceremony had not been too long; and this was a matter for congratulation.

Frederic went home tired out.

Next day, on arriving at the Dambreuse mansion, he was told that madame was working in the office downstairs. Files and drawers were lying open all over the place; account books were scattered to right and left; a roll of documents entitled 'Bad debts' was on the ground; he nearly fell over it, and picked it up. Mme Dambreuse, buried beneath a mass of papers, was almost invisible in the arm-chair.

'Well? What are you doing? What's the matter?'

She leapt to her feet.

'The matter? I'm ruined! Ruined—do you understand?'

M. Adolphe Langlois, the lawyer, had called her to his office, and had shown her a will drawn up by her husband, before they married; he left everything to Cécile; and the other will was lost. Frederic turned very pale. Perhaps she had not looked thoroughly?

'See for yourself!' said Mme Dambreuse, pointing round the room.

The two strong boxes were wide open: they had been forced with an axe. She had ransacked the desk, searched the wall cupboards, and shaken the door mats; suddenly, with a shrill cry she dashed into a corner where she had just caught sight of a little box with a brass lock; she opened it. Nothing!

'Oh, the villain! And I looked after him with such devotion!' Then she burst out crying.

'Perhaps it's somewhere else,' said Frederic.

'No, no! It was there—in that strong box. I saw it quite recently. It's burnt. I'm sure of it.'

One day, at the beginning of his illness, M. Dambreuse had gone downstairs to sign some papers.

'It was then that he must have done it.'

And she fell back on to a chair, prostrate. A mourning mother beside an empty cradle could not have been more pitiful than Mme Dambreuse before the gaping strong boxes. Indeed, her grief, however base its motive, seemed so profound that he tried to console her by telling her that she was not, after all, reduced to penury.

'But it is penury, since I haven't a large fortune to offer you!'

She had no more than thirty thousand francs a year, not counting the house, which might possibly bring in another eighteen to twenty.

Although this represented riches for Frederic, he felt, none the less, a sense of disappointment. Good-bye to his dreams and the grand life he would have led! He was in honour bound to marry Mme Dambreuse. He thought for a moment; and then, in loving tones:

'I shall always have you.'

She flung herself into his arms; and he pressed her to his breast, with a feeling of tenderness not unmixed with admiration for himself. Mme Dambreuse, who had stopped crying, lifted her face, which was beaming with happiness, and took his hand.

'Oh, I never doubted you! I was certain of it.'

The young man was not pleased by her premature confidence concerning something which he regarded as a noble action.

Then she took him to her room and they made plans. Frederic must now concentrate on his career. She even gave him some excellent advice about his candidature.

The first thing was to learn two or three phrases of political economy. He should specialize in some subject—say, horse-breeding; write one or two articles on questions of local interest; always have some post office jobs and tobacco concessions at his disposal; and be prepared to render small services of every kind. M. Dambreuse had been ideal in this respect. For instance, in the country, he had once stopped his brake, full of friends, in front of a cobbler's workshop, bought a dozen pairs of shoes for his guests, and an appalling pair of boots for himself, which he wore like a hero for the next fortnight. This anecdote amused them. She told others; and her charm, her youth, and her wit sprang into new life.

She approved of his idea of an immediate journey to Nogent. Their farewells were tender; then, on the doorstep, she murmured yet again:

'You do love me, don't you?'

'For ever,' he replied.

A messenger was waiting for him at home with a pencilled note informing him that Rosanette was about to be confined. He had been so busy for the last few days that he had not given her a thought. She was in a private home at Chaillot.

Frederic took a cab and set out.

At the corner of the rue de Marbeuf stood a notice board, announcing in large letters: 'Nursing and Maternity Home. Principal, Mme Alessandri, first-class midwife, former student at the Maternity Hospital, author of various works, etc.' The sign reappeared half-way up the road, on the small, single-leaf front door. It said: 'Mme Allesandri's Nursing Home,' omitting the word 'maternity' but adding all her qualifications.

Frederic knocked on the door.

A maid, looking like a soubrette, showed him into the drawing-room, which contained a mahogany table, some red velvet armchairs, and a clock in a glass case.

Almost at once madame came in. She was a tall, dark woman of forty, with a slender figure, fine eyes, and a well-bred manner. She informed Frederic that the mother was happily delivered and took him up to her room.

Rosanette gave a smile of unutterable joy, and, as though submerged beneath the waves of an almost suffocating love, she said in a low voice:

'A boy. Over there,' pointing to a bassinette beside her bed.

He drew aside the curtains, and saw, among the bedclothes, a yellowish-red object, excessively wrinkled, that smelt unpleasant and was crying.

'Kiss him!'

To hide his repugnance, he answered:

'But I may hurt him.'

'No, no!'

Then he gave his child a gingerly kiss.

'How like you he is!'

And, with her weak arms she hung round his neck. He had never seen such a demonstration of emotion.

He remembered Mme Dambreuse. He thought himself a monster of guilt in betraying this poor creature, who loved and suffered with all the openness of her nature. For several days he kept her company until nightfall.

She was happy in this quiet house: the shutters of the front windows were always discreetly closed: her room, hung with bright chintz, overlooked a large garden: Mme Alessandri, whose only fault was her habit of referring to famous doctors as her intimate friends, surrounded her with attentions; her fellow patients—nearly all country girls—were extremely bored, as they had no visitors; Rosanette noticed that she was envied; she mentioned this to Frederic with pride. But they had to whisper; for the partitions were thin, and every one did their best to overhear, in spite of the continual din of pianos.

At length he was about to start for Nogent, when he received a letter from Deslauriers.

Two new candidates had appeared—one Conservative, the other Red; a third would have no chance whoever he was. It was Frederic's own fault; he had missed his opportunity; he ought to have come sooner; he should have bestirred himself. 'You didn't even appear at the agricultural show.' The lawyer criticized him for having no connections in the newspapers. 'Oh, if only you'd taken my advice long ago! If only we had a paper of our own!' He emphasized this point. Besides, many people who would have voted for him out of deference to M. Dambreuse would now desert him. Deslauriers was one of these. Having nothing more to hope for from the banker, he was abandoning his *protégé*.

Frederic took the letter to Mme Dambreuse.

'So you didn't go to Nogent?' she said.

'Why do you say that?'

'I saw Deslauriers three days ago.'

Hearing of her husband's death the lawyer had come with some notes on coal, and had offered his services as business adviser. This seemed strange to Frederic; and what had his friend been doing at Nogent?

Mme Dambreuse wanted to know how he had spent his time since their separation.

'I was ill,' he answered.

'You might at least have told me.'

'Oh, it wasn't worth while.'

Besides, he had had countless preoccupations—people to see and visits to pay.

From that day he led a double life, spending the night conscientiously with Rosanette, and passing his afternoons with Mme Dambreuse, so that he had a bare hour to himself, in the middle of the day.

The child was at Andilly, in the country. They went to see it every week.

The nurse's house was in the highest part of the village, at the back of a little yard which was as dark as a tunnel. There was straw on the ground, a few chickens, and a vegetable cart in the shed. Rosanette began by kissing her baby frantically; she rushed about in a sort of frenzy, tried to milk the she-goat, ate the farm bread, sniffed the dung heap, and wanted to put a little of it in her handkerchief.

Then they went for long walks; she trespassed in nursery gardens, pulled branches of lilac down from walls; shouted 'Hey, Neddy!' at donkey carts, and stopped to admire beautiful gardens through the railings. Sometimes the nurse took the child and put it under a walnut-tree in the shade; and for hours the two women would keep up an idle and excessively tedious conversation.

From where he sat beside them, Frederic could look down on the square vineyards that covered the sloping ground, with a tree top here and there; he could see dusty paths like grey ribbons, and houses flecking the green background with red and white. Sometimes, at the foot of the wooded hills, the smoke of an engine appeared, streaming out in a level line, like an enormous feathery ostrich plume, the end of which was always blowing away.

Then his eyes fell once more on his son. He pictured him as a young man; he would make him his companion; but perhaps he would turn out a fool; he would certainly be a failure. His doubtful birth would always weigh on him; it would have been better if he had not been born—and Frederic murmured: 'Poor child!' his heart swelling with an inexplicable sadness.

They often missed the last train home. Then Mme Dambreuse would scold him for his unpunctuality. He invented a story for her.

He had to invent one for Rosanette as well. She did not understand how he spent all his evenings and why he was never in when she sent a message to his house. One day, he was at home when they both appeared almost simultaneously. He got

Rosanette out of the house and hid Mme Dambreuse, telling her that he was expecting his mother.

Soon he began to derive amusement from his lies; he repeated to one the vow he had just made to the other; he sent them two similar bouquets, wrote to them both at the same time, then made comparisons between them; and there was a third woman who was never absent from his thoughts. The fact that she was beyond his reach seemed to justify his deception, which sharpened his pleasure by providing contrast; the more he deceived one of the pair, the more she loved him, as if the two passions were kept reciprocally alight by interaction, and each mistress, out of a kind of rivalry, were striving to make him forget the other.

'Admire my confidence in you!' said Mme Dambreuse to him one day, unfolding a note which informed her that M. Moreau was living with a certain Rose Bron. 'Is she the lady you went racing with, by any chance?'

'How ridiculous!' he answered. 'Let me see it.'

The letter, which was written in capitals, was unsigned. At first Mme Dambreuse had tolerated this mistress, as a cover to their intrigue. But as her passion grew, she had insisted on his breaking with her; which, according to Frederic, he had done long ago. When he had finished his protestations, she half-closed her eyes, which glittered like the points of stilettos seen through muslin.

'Well, and the other?' she said.

'Which other?'

'The crockery dealer's wife!'

He shrugged his shoulders contemptuously. Mme Dambreuse did not press him.

A month later, they were discussing honour and loyalty, and he was praising his own in a casual manner, by way of precaution. Suddenly she said to him:

'Yes, it's true. You're a man of your word. You've never been back there.'

Frederic, who was thinking of Rosanette, stammered:

'Where?'

'To see Madame Arnoux.'

He begged her to tell him where she had obtained this information. It was through Mme Regimbart, her sewing woman.

So she was familiar with his life and he knew nothing of hers!

However, he had found in her dressing-room a miniature of a gentleman with a long moustache. Was this the man about whom he had once heard a vague story that ended in a suicide? But there was no way of learning more! And anyhow, what was the use? Women's hearts are like those little secret boxes, full of drawers fitting one inside another; you struggle with them, you break your nails, and you find at the bottom a withered flower, a little dust, or nothing at all! Besides, he was perhaps afraid of finding out too much.

She made him refuse invitations to places to which she could not accompany him; she kept him at her side, in dread of losing him; and, in spite of their daily closer relationship, rifts kept opening between them, over trivial matters—the appreciation of a work of art, or of a person's character.

She had a hard, correct manner of playing the piano. Her spiritualism—she believed in the transmigration of souls into the stars—did not prevent her from managing her money with great skill. She was haughty with her servants; the misery of the poor left her dry-eyed. Her naïve selfishness came to light in her habitual turns of speech: 'What does it matter to me? I'd be a fool. Why should I?'—and there was something indefinably loathsome about many of her actions. She was the sort of woman who would listen behind doors and lie to her confessor. Her domineering nature made her demand Frederic's company at church on Sunday. He obeyed and carried the prayer book.

The loss of her inheritance had altered her considerably. The marks of grief which were attributed to her husband's death made her look interesting; and, as before, she gave large parties. Since Frederic's failure in the elections, she was aiming to secure allegation in Germany for the two of them; the first step towards this was to fall in with the prevailing ideas.

Some were for the empire, some for the Orléans family, some for the Comte de Chambord; but all were at one on the pressing need for decentralization, and several methods were proposed. Paris ought to be divided into innumerable high streets, which should form centres for villages; the seat of administration should be transferred to Versailles; the schools should be moved to Bourges; the libraries should be suppressed; there should be a government of lieutenant-generals; and they praised the military, since men without education were naturally more sensible than any one else! Hatred abounded: hatred of the elementary school teachers, of the wine merchants, of the classes in philosophy, the lectures in history, of novels, red waistcoats, and long beards, hatred of all independence, of any symptom of individuality; for it was essential 'to restore the principle of authority': it did not matter in whose name it was wielded, or whence it came, so long as it was power — authority! The Conservatives were now talking like Sénécal. Frederic was baffled; and at Rosanette's apartment he found the same topics discussed by the same men.

The courtesans' drawing-rooms—their importance dates from this period—formed a neutral territory, where reactionaries of different shades could meet. Hussonnet, who spent his time crying down the triumphs of the day—a useful step, this, towards the restoration of order—inspired her with a longing to have her own evening parties, like everybody else. Hussonnet would write descriptions of them; and he began by bringing along Fumichon, a serious-minded man: than came Nonancourt, M. de Grémonville, M. de Larsillois, the former prefect, and Cisy, who was now a farmer in western Brittany, and more religious than ever.

Some of Rosanette's former lovers also appeared; the Baron de Comaing, the Comte de Jumillac, and a few others; Frederic was distressed by the familiarity of their manners.

To prove that he was master in his own house, he increased the scale of the establishment. They engaged a groom, changed their address, and bought new furniture. This expenditure had the advantage of making his marriage appear less out of proportion to his fortune, which, indeed, was dwindling alarmingly; and this was a thing that Rosanette could never understand!

Belonging by instinct to the middle class, she adored domestic life—the snug, the peaceful interior. She enjoyed having an 'at home' day, and described her sort as 'those women'; longed to be 'a lady in society' and came to believe that she was one. She asked Frederic not to smoke in the drawing-room, and tried to make him keep fast days for good form's sake.

But she belied her new role, for she was becoming serious. She was always rather melancholy before going to bed. It was like finding a cypress-tree by the door of a tavern.

He found out the reason; she, too, was dreaming of marriage. Frederic was furious. Besides, he remembered her sudden appearance at Mme Arnoux's, nor had he yet forgiven her for resisting him so long.

He was always trying to discover the names of her old lovers. She denied them all. He was attacked by a kind of jealousy. He was annoyed about the presents she had received and was still receiving; and, while he was becoming more and more exasperated by her whole personality, a sensual urge, bestial and violent, would sometimes impel him towards her—a momentary illusion, which soon dissolved into hatred.

Her voice, her smile, the words she used—everything about her now disgusted him and, above all, the look in her eye—that limpid, empty, feminine look. Sometimes he found her so irritating that he could have watched her die unmoved. But how could he show his anger? The sweetness of her temper baffled him.

Deslauriers reappeared and explained his stay at Nogent on the grounds that he had been trying to purchase a lawyer's practice. Frederic was glad to see him again; it was someone to talk to. He made him the third partner in their company.

The lawyer dined with them from time to time, and whenever small arguments arose he always took Rosanette's side, so that Frederic said to him once:

'Well, sleep with her if it amuses you!'

So anxious was he for some accident to rid him of her.

Towards the middle of June, she received a summons in which Maître Athanase Gautherot, officer of the court, instructed her to pay four thousand francs to the demoiselle Clémence Vatnaz; otherwise, he would come next day and seize her belongings.

The fact was that only one of the four bills which she had previously signed had been paid, and such money as she might have used for this purpose had been spent on other things.

She hurried to Arnoux's house. He was now living in the Faubourg Saint-Germain, and the porter did not know his address. She visited several friends, found no one at home, and came back in despair. She did not want to breathe a word to Frederic, as she feared that this fresh mishap might affect her marriage.

The next morning, Maître Athanase Gautherot appeared, accompanied by two minions. One, with a pale, cunning face, appeared to be devoured with envy; the other wore a detachable collar, very tight foot-straps, and a black silk finger stall. Both of them were horribly dirty; their coat collars were greasy and their sleeves too short.

Their master, on the other hand, was extremely handsome, and he began by apologizing for his painful mission, while he looked round the room, which was 'full of pretty things, upon my word!' He added, 'quite apart from the ones that can't be seized.' At a sign from him the two bailiffs vanished.

He became even more complimentary. Was it possible that

so . . . charming a person should not have some responsible friend? A sale by order of the court was a real disaster. One never recovered from it. He tried to frighten her; then, seeing that she was upset, suddenly adopted a paternal tone. He knew the world, he had had to deal with all these ladies; and, as he gave their names, he examined the pictures on the walls. These had belonged to Arnoux; there were sketches by Sombaz, watercolours by Burieu, three landscapes by Dittmer. Rosanette obviously did not know their value. Maître Gautherot turned to her and said: .

'I say! To prove I 'm a good sort, let 's do a deal. Give me those Dittmers and I 'll pay your debt. Is it agreed?'

At that moment Frederic, who had been enlightened by Delphine in the hall and had caught sight of the two assistants, came in with his hat on his head, and a scowl on his face. Maître Gautherot resumed his dignity, and, as the door had been left open, he shouted through:

'Come, gentlemen, take this down. In the second room, we put down: one oak table, with two leaves; two sideboards——'

Frederic interrupted him and asked if there were no way of preventing the seizure.

'Oh, naturally. Who paid for the furniture?'

'I did.'

'Very well; make an application for recovery; you 've got plenty of time.'

Maître Gautherot hurriedly finished his writing, and in his report summoned Mlle Bron before a court of summary jurisdiction. Then he left.

Frederic uttered no word of reproach. He gazed at the muddy footprints of the bailiffs on the carpet; and, talking to himself, said:

'I must go and find some money.'

'Good heavens, what a fool I am!' said Rosanette.

She rummaged in a drawer, took out a letter and hurried off to the offices of the Languedoc Lighting Company, to get her shares.

She came back an hour later. The shares had been sold to someone else! The clerk, having examined the paper, which was Arnoux's written promise, had replied:

'This document doesn't make you a shareholder. It isn't recognized by the company.'

In short, he had sent her away; it was killing her; and Frederic must go and see Arnoux at once, to clear the matter up.

But Arnoux might believe that the indirect object of his

365

visit was to recover the fifteen thousand francs of his lost mortgage. Besides, there was something ignoble about making a claim on the man who had been his mistress's lover. Taking a middle course, he visited the Dambreuse mansion, where he found out Mme Regimbart's address, sent a messenger to her, and thus discovered the café which was then frequented by the citizen.

It was a little café in the place de la Bastille, where he used to spend the whole day at the back of the room, in the right-hand corner, as immobile as if he had been part of the furniture. Having passed through the successive stages of coffee, grog, punch, mulled wine, and even wine and water, he had fallen back on beer; and every half-hour he uttered the word 'Bock!'; for he had reduced his conversation to a minimum. Frederic asked him if he ever saw Arnoux.

'No.'

'Why on earth not?'

'A fool!'

Politics might be the cause of the rift, and Frederic thought it advisable to ask after Compain.

'What a nincompoop!' said Regimbart.

'How do you mean?'

'His calf's head!'

'Do tell me what the calf's head means.'

Regimbart gave a pitying smile.

'All nonsense!'

After a long silence Frederic continued:

'So he's changed his address?'

'Who?'

'Arnoux.'

'Yes; rue de Fleurus.'

'What number?'

'Do you think I go about with Jesuits?'

'How, Jesuits?'

The citizen answered in a fury:

'The swine has taken the money of a patriot I introduced him to, and set up as a dealer in rosaries!'

'I don't believe it!'

'Go and see!'

It was, indeed, true; Arnoux, weakened by an attack of illness, had turned to religion; he 'had always been religious at heart'—and with his natural combination of business instinct and sincerity, he had become a dealer in religious supplies, thus, as he hoped, securing both his salvation and his fortune

Frederic had little difficulty in finding his establishment, the signboard of which read: 'The Gothick House'—Restoration of Worship—Church Ornaments—Polychrome Sculpture—Incense of the Magi' and so forth.

On either side of the shop window rose two wooden statues, painted in blue, vermilion, and gold: a John the Baptist with his sheepskin, and a Saint Geneviève with roses in her apron and a distaff under her arm; there were also groups in plaster: a nun teaching a little girl, a mother on her knees beside a cot, three schoolboys at the communion table. The prettiest was a kind of chalet representing the stable at Bethlehem, with the donkey, the ox, and the Infant Jesus lying on real straw. The rows of shelves were covered from top to bottom with innumerable medals, rosaries of every kind, stoups for holy water in the shape of shells, and portraits of luminaries of the Church, among which shone the smiling faces of Archbishop Affre and the Pope.

Arnoux was dozing at his counter with his head bowed. He had aged enormously; he had a ring of red pimples round his forehead, on which the gold crosses, glittering in the sun, cast their reflection.

The sight of this decline filled Frederic with sudden pity. But out of loyalty to Rosanette he hardened his heart and stepped forward; Mme Arnoux appeared at the back of the shop, and he turned on his heel.

'I couldn't find him,' he said, when he reached home.

And although he went on to say that he was going to write to his Le Havre lawyer for money immediately, Rosanette lost her temper with him. A weaker, more spineless man had never existed; she had to put up with every sort of privation, while others lived in luxury.

Frederic thought of poor Mme Arnoux, and pictured to himself the appalling dreariness of her home. He sat down at the writing table: Rosanette's shrill voice was still uplifted.

'For heaven's sake, be quiet!'

'You're not going to take their side, by any chance?'

'Yes, I am!' he exclaimed. 'I don't see why you should be so set against them.'

'But why don't you want them to pay? You're afraid of making your old love unhappy—you might as well admit it!'

He felt like braining her with the clock; words failed him. He was silent. Rosanette walked up and down the room, then added:

'I'm going to have the law on your friend Arnoux. Oh, I don't need your help.'

367

And, pursing her lips:

'I 'll get advice.'

Three days later Delphine came in suddenly.

'Madame, madame, there 's a man here with a pot of paste. I 'm afraid of him!'

Rosanette went into the kitchen; and saw a heavily pock-marked ruffian, who was paralysed in one arm, three-quarters drunk, and muttering.

This was Maître Gautherot's bill sticker. As the objection to the seizure had been overruled, the sale followed inevitably.

First, he asked for a little drink, for his pains in coming upstairs; then he begged another favour—some theatre tickets, for he imagined that madame was an actress. Then he spent several minutes winking unintelligibly; at last he announced that for four francs he would tear off the corners of the placard which had already been posted on the door below. Rosanette found herself mentioned by name—an exceptional severity which indicated the depth of her persecutor's hatred.

Mlle Vatnaz had been sensitive in her youth; once, when crossed in love she had written to Béranger for advice. But the storms of life had embittered her; she had, successively, given piano lessons, kept a boarding-house, contributed to the fashion papers, let lodgings, and traded in lace among the women of the town—a sphere where her connections enabled her to be of service to many people, including Arnoux. Earlier still, she had worked in a business house.

One of her duties was to pay the salaries of the girls who worked there. There were two account-books for each girl, one of which was always in the possession of Mlle Vatnaz. Dussardier, as a kindness to her, used to keep the account of a girl called Hortense Baslin. One day he happened to be at the cashier's desk just as Mlle Vatnaz was giving in this girl's account. It was for 1,682 francs. The cashier paid it. Now Dussardier remembered having written out this very account the previous evening: the figure had been 1,082 francs. He asked for the book back on some pretext; and, as he wished to obliterate the story of this theft, he told the girl he had lost it. Hortense Baslin innocently repeated his falsehood to Mlle Vatnaz; and she, to clear the matter, asked Dussardier about it, with an assumed casualness. He merely replied: 'I 've burnt it'; nothing more. She left the firm soon after; she did not believe that the book had been destroyed and supposed that Dussardier still had it.

When she heard he had been wounded she hastened to his house to get it back. She found nothing in spite of the most exhaustive search; and she was filled with respect, which soon became love, for this loyal, gentle, heroic, stout-hearted youth. Such good fortune, at her age, was quite unexpected. She fell on him with the appetite of an ogress; for him, she abandoned literature, Socialism, 'the soothing doctrine and the happier State,' the lectures she was giving on 'The De-subordination of Women'—everything, Delmar included; and she ended by making Dussardier a proposal of marriage.

Although she was his mistress, he was not in love with her. Besides, he had not forgotten her theft. And then she was too rich. He refused her. Then she told him, through her tears, of the plan she had dreamed of—to run a ready-made dress shop between them. She had the preliminary capital, which would be increased the following week by four thousand francs; and she told him about the action she had taken against Rosanette.

Dussardier was sorry because of his friend. He remembered the cigar case at the police station, the evenings at the quai Napoléon, the good talk, the books lent—the manifold kindnesses of Frederic. He begged Mlle Vatnaz to refrain.

She laughed at his good nature; she betrayed an extraordinary loathing for Rosanette; indeed, she longed for wealth only in order that she might one day crush her under her carriage wheels.

These dark depths alarmed Dussardier; and, as soon as he knew the day of the sale for certain he went out. The next morning he called on Frederic looking sheepish.

'I owe you an apology——'

'What on earth for?'

'You must think me very ungrateful, considering she's my——' He stammered. 'Oh, I'll never see her again! I won't be her accomplice!' Frederic looked at him in complete bewilderment. 'Aren't they going to sell up your mistress's furniture in three day's time?'

'Who told you that?'

'The Vatnaz herself! But I'm afraid of offending you——'

'You couldn't, my dear fellow!'

'Yes, that's true. You're so good-hearted!'

And, with a discreet gesture, he held out to him a little red leather pocket-book.

It contained four thousand francs—the whole of his savings.

'What! Oh, no—I couldn't . . .'

'I knew I should hurt your feelings,' answered Dussardier, with a tear in the corner of his eye.

Frederic clasped his hand; and the good fellow continued in a mournful voice:

'Take them! Give me that pleasure! I'm in such despair. And anyway, isn't everything over now? I thought we'd be happy when the revolution came. You remember how splendid it was—how freely we breathed. But here we are, worse off than ever.'

He fixed his eyes on the ground.

'They're murdering our republic now, just as they murdered the Roman republic long ago. Poor Venice! Poor Poland! Poor Hungary![1] What villainy! To begin with, they've cut down the trees of liberty, then they've restricted the suffrage, closed the clubs, started the censorship again, and put education into the hands of the priests until the Inquisition's ready. What's to stop them? Some of the Conservatives would like to see the Cossacks in Paris again.[2] They punish the newspapers for writing against the death penalty; Paris is crammed with soldiers; sixteen departments are in a state of siege, and they've refused an amnesty again!'

He put both hands to his forehead; then, stretching out his arms as if he were in agony:

'If only people would try . . . with good faith, an understanding could be reached. But it's no good. You see, the workers are no better than the middle classes. Just now, at Elbeuf, they refused to help to put out a fire. There are some swine who look on Barbès as an aristocrat. And just to make the people look ridiculous, they're trying to put up Nadaud for the presidency. A bricklayer—I ask you! And there's no way out—no remedy. Every one's against us. I've never done anybody any harm, myself; and yet it's like a weight on my stomach. I shall go mad if this goes on! I'd like to kill myself! I tell you I don't need my money! You'll give it me back, I know. I'll lend it you.'

Frederic, compelled by necessity, ended by taking his four thousand francs. So, as far as Mlle Vatnaz was concerned, they could set their minds at rest.

But shortly afterwards Rosanette lost her case against Arnoux. She wanted to appeal, out of obstinacy. Deslauriers did his best to explain to her that Arnoux's promise represented neither a gift nor a proper transfer; she would not listen, and thought the law unfair; it was because she was a woman: men always stuck together. However, she followed his advice in the end.

He had made himself so at home in the house that he brought Sénécal in to dinner several times. This casualness annoyed Frederic, who had been lending him money and even ordering clothes for him from his own tailor; and the lawyer passed on his old frock coats to the Socialist, whose means of livelihood were unknown. But Deslauriers would have been glad to help Rosanette. One day she showed him twelve shares in the china clay company—the one that had involved Arnoux in a fine of thirty thousand francs.

'Here's something shady,' he said to her. 'This is a stroke of luck!'

She was entitled to prosecute him for the repayment of her claim. First, she could prove that he had guaranteed to pay all the company's liabilities, since he had declared that personal debts would be regarded as collective debts, and also that he had misappropriated several of the company's assets.

'All this makes him guilty of fraudulent bankruptcy, by Articles 586 and 587 of the Commercial Code; and we'll send him packing and no mistake about it, my angel.'

Rosanette fell on his neck. Next day he recommended her to his former employer; he could not take up the case himself, since he had to go to Nogent; Sénécal would write to him, if necessary.

His negotiations for the purchase of a practice were a blind. He spent his time at M. Roque's house, where he had begun not only by praising Frederic, but also by imitating his manner and address as far as he could. In this way he had won the confidence of Louise, while he secured that of her father by inveighing against Ledru-Rollin.

The reason why Frederic did not come back was because he was moving in high society; and gradually Deslauriers informed them that he was in love with someone, that he had a child, and that he kept a mistress.

Louise's despair was extreme; equally strong was the indignation of Mme Moreau. She saw her son being whirled into the depths of a mysterious abyss: her sense of propriety, always deep, was affronted: it was like a personal disgrace. Suddenly her expression changed. When asked about Frederic, she would reply, with a cunning look:

'He's doing well—very well.'

She knew of his coming marriage with Mme Dambreuse.

The date was fixed; and he was wondering how he was to reconcile Rosanette to the idea.

Towards the middle of the autumn, she won her case about the china clay shares. Frederic found this out by meeting Sénécal on his doorstep. The Socialist was on his way back from the court.

It had been shown that Arnoux was involved in all the fraudulent transactions; and Sénécal looked so gleeful that Frederic prevented his going any further, by assuring him that he would deliver his message to Rosanette himself. He came into her room looking angry.

'Well—now you 're happy, I suppose!'

She paid no attention.

'Look!' she said.

And she pointed to the child, who was lying in a cradle by the fire. She had found him looking so poorly at the nurse's that morning that she had brought him back to Paris.

His limbs had all grown extraordinarily thin, and his lips were encrusted with white spots; the inside of his mouth looked as if it were covered with clots of milk.

'What did the doctor say?'

'Oh, the doctor! He thinks the journey has increased his . . . I don't know—some word ending in *itis*—that he 's got thrush, in fact. Do you know about it?'

Frederic unhesitatingly replied in the affirmative, and went on to say that it was nothing.

But when evening came he was terrified by the debilitated appearance of the child, and by the spreading of the white mildew-like rash. It was as if life had already abandoned the poor little body, leaving only dead matter, a spawning ground for vegetation. His hands were cold; he could no longer drink, and the nurse, a new one, engaged at random by the porter from an agency, kept repeating:

'He looks very low, very low.'

Rosanette was up all night.

Next morning she went to look for Frederic.

'Come and see. He 's not moving.'

The child was dead. She picked him up, shook him, squeezed him, called him all the dearest names, covered him with kisses and tears; then, in her frenzy, she turned on herself, screaming and tearing her hair. She sank down on the edge of the divan, where she sat with her mouth open, while a flood of tears poured from her unseeing eyes. Then a torpor overcame her and all was quiet in the room. The furniture had been overturned Two or three napkins lay on the ground. Six o'clock struck. The night-light went out.

Frederic, looking about him, almost believed that he was dreaming. Anguish gripped his heart. He felt that this death was only a beginning, that close behind it would follow some heavier misfortune.

Suddenly, Rosanette said, in a voice full of tenderness:

'We'll keep him, won't we?'

She wanted to have him embalmed. There were many objections. The most cogent, according to Frederic, was that it was impracticable in the case of such young children. A portrait would be better. She took up this idea. He wrote a line to Pellerin and Delphine hurried off with it.

Pellerin arrived promptly; by his alacrity he intended to efface all memories of his previous conduct. At first he said:

'Poor little darling! Heavens! what a dreadful thing to happen!'

But gradually he was carried away by his artistic soul and he declared that he could do nothing with those blistered eyes, that livid face; it was a veritable still-life, demanding great skill; and he kept murmuring:

'Awkward; very awkward!'

'So long as it's a good likeness . . .' said Rosanette.

'What do I care about a good likeness? Down with realism! I paint the spirit! Now let me try and work out what to make of it.'

With his left hand on his forehead and his right hand on his left elbow he remained in thought. Suddenly he said:

'Ah, an idea! A pastel! I'll work up the half-tones and make them almost flat, which will bring up the outlines in relief.'

He sent the maid for his colour box; then with his feet on one chair and another at his side he began to sketch the broad outlines as coolly as if he were copying a cast. He praised Correggio's little 'Saint John,' the 'Infanta Margarita' of Velasquez, the milky tones of Reynolds, the distinction of Lawrence, with special reference to the long-haired child on Lady Gower's knee.

'And what could be more charming than those brats? The essence of the sublime, as Raphael's Madonnas show, is, perhaps, a mother with her child.'

Rosanette, who was stifling her tears, went out: and Pellerin said immediately:

'Well, and Arnoux . . . You've heard what's going on?'

'No. What?'

'Anyway, it was bound to end like that.'

'What is it?'

'Perhaps at this moment he's . . . Excuse me one moment.'

The painter got up to raise the little corpse's head.

'You were saying . . .?' Frederic continued.

And Pellerin, as he half-closed his eyes to take the measurements, added:

'I was saying that our friend Arnoux is quite possibly at this moment under lock and key!'

Then, in a tone of satisfaction:

'Look here a moment! Have I got it?'

'Yes, admirably. But Arnoux?'

Pellerin put down his pencil.

'As I understand it he's being prosecuted by a man called Mignot, a crony of Regimbart's. There's a brain for you! What a fool! Can you imagine it? One day——'

'But we're not talking about Regimbart!'

'That's true. Well, yesterday evening Arnoux had to find twelve thousand francs. Otherwise he was ruined.'

'Perhaps it's not really as bad as that.'

'On the contrary. It looked serious, very serious indeed.'

At this moment Rosanette came in again with red marks under her eyes, as bright as patches of rouge. She sat down beside the drawing-book and looked at it. Pellerin indicated by a gesture that he would say no more, on her account. But Frederic paid no attention.

'All the same, I can't believe——'

'I tell you, I met him yesterday,' said the artist, 'at seven o'clock in the evening, in the rue Jacob. He even had his passport with him, just in case; and he was talking of taking ship at Le Havre with the whole bag of tricks.'

'What! With his wife?'

'Naturally. He's too good a family man to live on his own.'

'And are you positive?'

'Of course. Where do you think he could get hold of twelve thousand francs?'

Frederic walked up and down the room two or three times. He was breathing heavily and biting his lips; then he seized his hat.

'Where are you off to?' said Rosanette.

He made no reply and vanished.

CHAPTER V

HE must have twelve thousand francs or else he would never see Mme Arnoux again; and up to now he had never allowed his hopes to die. Was she not made of the stuff of his heart, the very foundation of his life? For some moments he stood tottering on the pavement in desperate agony; yet he was glad to have got away from Rosanette.

Where was he to find the money? Frederic knew from his own experience how difficult it was to get cash at short notice, whatever price he might offer. Only one person could help him —Mme Dambreuse. She always kept some bank notes in her writing table. He went to see her and addressed her boldly:

'Have you got twelve thousand francs you could lend me?'

'What for?'

It was another's secret. She wanted to know what it was. He refused to tell. Both of them stood firm. At last she declared she would give him nothing unless she knew the purpose of the loan. Frederic went very red. One of his friends had committed a theft. The money had to be given back that very day.

'What's he called? His name? Come, his name?'

'Dussardier!'

And he threw himself at her feet, imploring her to tell no one.

'What do you take me for?' said Mme Dambreuse. 'Any one would think you'd done it yourself! Do stop pretending to be tragic! Here's the money! And much good may it do him!'

He rushed to Arnoux's place. The dealer was not in his shop. But he was still living in the rue Paradis, for he had two residences.

The porter at the rue Paradis swore that M. Arnoux had been away since the previous evening; as regards madame, he would not like to say. Frederic climbed the stairs like an arrow from a bow, and pressed his ear to the keyhole. At last the door opened. Madame had left with monsieur. The maid did not know when they would be back; her wages had been paid; she was leaving herself.

Suddenly he heard a door creak.

375

'There's somebody here!'

'Oh, no, sir! It's the wind.'

Then he withdrew. Whatever might have happened there was something inexplicable about so sudden a disappearance.

Perhaps Regimbart, being Mignot's friend, could shed some light on the matter. And Frederic drove to his home in the rue de l'Empereur, in Montmartre.

His house had a small garden beside it, enclosed by railings which were backed with sheets of iron. A flight of three steps projected from the white front of the house; passing along the pavement, one could see into the two ground-floor rooms. The first was a drawing-room, with dresses strewn all over the furniture, and the second the place where Mme Regimbart's seamstresses worked.

These were all convinced that monsieur had an important position and distinguished connections—that he was, in fact, a very remarkable personage. When he crossed the passage, in his hat with the turned-up brim, with his long, earnest face and his green frock coat, they broke off their work to look. Besides, he invariably gave them a word of encouragement, a brief, courteous phrase; and later, when they got home, they were discontented because they had come to regard him as their ideal.

Yet none of them was as fond of him as Mme Regimbart, a small, intelligent creature, who kept him by her trade.

As soon as M. Moreau mentioned his name, she hurried out to greet him, for she knew of his relationship with Mme Dambreuse through the servants. Her husband 'would be back in half a moment'; and Frederic, as he followed her, admired the way the house was kept and the quantities of oilcloth everywhere. Then he waited for a few minutes in a sort of study, to which the citizen would retire for meditation.

His greeting was less surly than usual.

He told the story of Arnoux. He had got round Mignot, a patriot who owned a hundred shares in the *Siècle*, by proving to him that it was necessary, in the interests of democracy, to change the management and the editorship of the paper; and, on the ground that he would carry this point at the next shareholders' meeting, Arnoux had asked him for fifty shares, telling him that he would pass them on to reliable friends, who would support his vote: Mignot would have no responsibility, and would make no enemies; then, when they had succeeded, he would get him a good position on the staff, worth five or six thousand francs a year at least. The shares were handed over.

But Arnoux had sold them on the spot, and used the money to go into partnership with a vendor of devotional objects. There followed complaints from Mignot, and equivocations from Arnoux; eventually, the patriot had threatened to prosecute him for fraud, if he did not give him back his shares or an equivalent sum of money; to wit, fifty thousand francs.

Despair was written on Frederic's face.

'That's not all,' said the citizen. 'Mignot, who's a good fellow, reduced his demands to a quarter. More promises from Arnoux—more moonshine, of course. In short, the day before yesterday, in the morning, Mignot insisted on his paying back twelve thousand francs within twenty-four hours, without prejudice to the remainder of the debt.'

'But I've got the money!' said Frederic.

The citizen turned round slowly.

'Liar!'

'On the contrary! It's in my pocket. I was bringing it to Arnoux.'

'You do go the pace, upon my word! But it's too late; the case has been brought and Arnoux has gone.'

'Alone?'

'No, with his wife. They were seen at the Le Havre station.'

Frederic turned extraordinarily pale. Mme Regimbart thought he was going to faint. He controlled himself and even had the strength to ask one or two questions about the affair. Regimbart was depressed about it, for such things, when all was said and done, did democracy no good. Arnoux had always been reckless and irresponsible.

'A feather-brained fellow! He burned the candle at both ends. The women did for him. I'm not sorry for him so much as for his poor wife.'

For the citizen admired virtuous women and was deeply concerned about Mme Arnoux.

'She must have suffered a lot.'

Frederic was grateful to him for this sympathy; and he clasped his hand with emotion, as if he had done him a good turn.

'Did you make all the arrangements?' said Rosanette when she saw him again.

He had not had the heart to do so, he replied. He had walked about the streets at random, to numb his senses.

At eight o'clock they went into the dining-room, but they sat facing each other in silence; they sighed from time to time and pushed their plates away. Frederic drank brandy. He felt utterly shattered, crushed, prostrate; he was conscious of nothing but extreme exhaustion.

She went to fetch the portrait. Red, yellow, green, and indigo clashed in glaring streaks; the thing was hideous, almost laughable.

Moreover, the dead baby was now unrecognizable. The mauve tint of his lips enhanced the pallor of his skin; his nostrils were thinner, his eyes more hollow; and his head rested on a blue taffeta pillow, among petals of camellia, autumn roses, and violets. This was the maid's idea; and the two of them had posed him thus, with devotion. On the mantelpiece, with its lace cover, stood silver - gilt candlesticks, alternating with bunches of holy box; incense was burning in the two vases at either end; all this, with the cradle, made a kind of lying in state; and Frederic remembered his vigil beside M. Dambreuse.

Almost every quarter of an hour, Rosanette drew aside the curtains to look at her child. She could see him, in a few months' time, learning to walk, then in the yard at school playing touch-last; then as a young man of twenty; and these varying pictures made her feel that she had lost as many sons. It was as if the very excess of her grief had made her a mother many times over.

Frederic, motionless in the other arm-chair, thought of Mme Arnoux.

Doubtless she was in the train, with her face at the carriage window, watching the country-side slip by behind her, back to Paris; or she was on the deck of a steamer, as she had been the first day that he met her; but this ship was sailing inexorably towards lands whence she would never return. Then she saw her in a room at an inn; her luggage lay on the floor and the wall paper hung in tatters; the door rattled in the wind. And afterwards? What would become of her? Would she be a schoolmistress, a companion, or even a lady's maid? She had been abandoned to all the perils of poverty. His ignorance of her fate tormented him. He should have prevented her flight, or else followed her. Was he not her real husband? And when he realized that he would never see her again, that it was all over, he felt his whole being torn in two; his tears, which had been gathering since the morning, overflowed.

Rosanette noticed it.

'So you're crying, like me? You're unhappy?'

'Yes, yes, I am!'

He clasped her to his breast, and they sobbed in each other's arms.

Mme Dambreuse was crying, too, as she lay face downwards on her bed, with her head in her hands.

Mme Regimbart, who had come that evening to try on her first coloured dress, had told her of Frederic's visit, and of how he had brought twelve thousand francs for M. Arnoux.

So this money—her money—was to be used to prevent the departure of her rival, to preserve his mistress!

Her first reaction was a fit of fury; and she had made up her mind to dismiss him like a lackey. Her flowing tears calmed her. It would be better to hide all and say nothing.

Next day, Frederic brought back the twelve thousand francs.

She begged him to keep them for his friend, in case of need, and she asked him many questions about this gentleman. What could have induced him to commit this breach of trust? A woman, doubtless! Women lead men on to every crime. This mocking tone disconcerted Frederic. He felt deeply repentant about his slander. But he was reassured by the thought that Mme Dambreuse could not know the truth.

But she would not drop the subject; two days later, she asked after his young comrade yet again, and then after another friend, Deslauriers.

'Is he a trustworthy, intelligent man?'

Frederic praised him highly.

'Ask him to call here one of these mornings; I'd like to consult him on business.'

Among a mass of documents she had found some of Arnoux's bills of exchange, correctly drawn up and bearing the signature of Mme Arnoux. They were the very bills on account of which Frederic had once visited M. Dambreuse at lunch time; and although the banker had decided not to recover the money by prosecution, he had secured a formal judgment of the civil courts, not only against Arnoux but against his wife as well. Mme Arnoux was unaware of this as her husband had not thought fit to tell her.

This was a weapon, indeed!—Mme Dambreuse had no doubt of it. But her own lawyer might advise her to refrain; she would rather employ a less prominent agent; and she had remembered this lanky fellow with the impudent face, who had once offered her his services.

Frederic innocently delivered the message.

The lawyer was delighted at being put in touch with so great a lady.

He hurried to her home.

* N 9⁶9

She told him that the estate had gone to her niece, and this was a further reason for getting these outstanding debts settled. She would pay the money over to the heiress, hoping by these friendly services to win the gratitude of Martinon and his wife.

Deslauriers realized that there was some secret behind all this; and he examined the bills meditatively. Mme Arnoux's name, in her own handwriting, brought her whole figure before his eyes, and the affront he had received from her. Why should he not seize this opportunity for revenge?

He advised Mme Dambreuse to sell the bad debts belonging to the estate by auction. A nominee would buy them back surreptitiously and would carry out the prosecution. He undertook to provide the nominee.

Towards the end of November, Frederic was walking down Mme Arnoux's street when he raised his eyes to her windows and noticed a placard on the door, announcing, in large letters:

'Sale of handsome furniture and household effects. Kitchen utensils, personal and table linen, chemises, laces, petticoats, drawers, French and Indian cashmere shawls, Erard piano, pair of Renaissance oak cupboards, Venetian mirrors, Chinese and Japanese porcelain.'

'It's their furniture!' said Frederic to himself; and the porter confirmed his suspicions. He did not know the name of the person who was having the goods sold. But Maître Berthelmot, the chief auctioneer, might be able to give him some information.

At first the official refused to tell him which creditor was responsible for the sale. Frederic persisted. It was a certain Sénécal, a business agent; and Maître Berthelmot was kind enough to lend him his copy of the *Petites-Affiches*.

When Frederic reached Rosanette's apartment, he threw it down open on the table.

'Read this!'

'Well, what is it?' she said, with such a placid expression on her face that he was disgusted.

'All right! Pretend to look innocent!'

'I don't understand.'

'You're selling up Madame Arnoux!'

She re-read the advertisement.

'Where's her name?'

'It's her furniture! You know that better than I do.'

'What's it got to do with me?' Rosanette said, shrugging her shoulders.

'To do with you? You're taking your revenge, that's all. You're going on with your persecution. Didn't you insult her enough, when you came to her house? A worthless harlot like you, and the holiest, the loveliest, the best woman in the world! Why are you so determined to ruin her?'

'I tell you, you're wrong!'

'Come, now! As though you didn't put Sénécal up to it!'

'What nonsense!'

Then a fit of wild rage swept over him.

'You're lying! You're lying, you wretch! You're jealous of her. You've got a judgment of the court against her husband! Sénécal's meddled in your affairs before now! He loathes Arnoux, and, in your hatred, you've come to an agreement together. I saw how pleased he was when you won your case over the china clay. You won't deny what you've done with him?'

'I give you my word . . .'

'Your word! I know what that means!'

And Frederic gave a list of her lovers, with names and circumstantial details. Rosanette, turning quite pale, drew back.

'You're surprised! You thought I was blind because I shut my eyes. To-day I've finished. Men don't break their hearts when they're betrayed by women of your class. If they're too grossly unfaithful one steps aside; it's beneath one's dignity to punish them.'

She flung out her arms in agony.

'My God, what can have changed you?'

'You—only you!'

'And all this for Madame Arnoux!' cried Rosanette, in tears.

He answered coldly:

'I've never loved any one but her.'

This insult stopped her tears.

'That shows your good taste! A middle-aged woman, with a complexion like liquorice, a dumpy figure, and eyes as big as man-holes and about as empty! If that's what you like, go and join her!'

'I was waiting for that! Thank you!'

Rosanette stood motionless, stupefied by this extraordinary behaviour. She even let him shut the door behind him, then, leaping up, caught him in the hall. She put her arms round him.

'But you're mad, you're mad! This is ridiculous! I love you!'

She implored him:

381

'For heaven's sake—in the name of our little child!'

'Confess that this was your doing!' said Frederic.

She protested her innocence once more.

'You won't confess?'

'No.'

'Very well! Good-bye—for ever!'

'Listen to me!'

Frederic turned on his heel.

'If you knew me better, you'd realize that my decision is final.'

'Oh, you'll come back to me.'

'Never, as long as I live.'

And he slammed the door violently.

Rosanette wrote to Deslauriers that she needed his presence urgently.

He arrived five days later in the evening; and she told him about the quarrel.

'Is that all? It's a blessing in disguise.'

At first she had hoped that he might be able to bring Frederic back to her, but now all was lost. The porter at his home had told her of his coming marriage with Mme Dambreuse.

Deslauriers lectured her, and showed himself strangely gay and whimsical; and, as it was very late, asked permission to spend the night in an arm-chair. The following morning he set out for Nogent once more; he told her that he did not know when they would meet again; there might be a great change in his life very shortly.

Two hours after his return Nogent was in a ferment. It was said that M. Frederic was going to marry Mme Dambreuse. At last, the three Auger girls could bear it no longer; and they went to see Mme Moreau, who proudly confirmed the news. It made old Roque ill. Louise shut herself in her room. A rumour went about that she had gone mad.

Yet Frederic could not hide his gloom. Mme Dambreuse was more assiduous than ever in order, as it seemed, to distract his mind. She took him out in her carriage every afternoon; and once as they were crossing the place de la Bourse, she thought it might be amusing to visit the public sale rooms.

It was the 1st of December—the very day when Mme Arnoux's sale was due to take place. He remembered the date, and showed his reluctance by declaring that the rooms were unbearable, because of the crowds and the noise. She only wanted to glance round. The brougham stopped. He had to follow her.

In the yard could be seen wash-stands without basins, bits of arm-chairs, fragments of china, empty bottles, and mattresses. there were villainous-looking men in blouses or dirty frock coats, grey with dust; some carried linen sacks on their shoulders; and they were either talking in separate groups or shouting noisily to each other.

Frederic pointed out the objections to going any further.

'Oh, nonsense!'

And they went up the stairs.

In the first room, on the right, some gentlemen, catalogue in hand, were inspecting pictures; in another, a collection of Chinese armour was being sold; Mme Dambreuse wanted to go down again. She looked at the numbers over the doors, and led him to the far end of the corridor, towards a room crammed with people.

He immediately recognized the two *étagères* that had been at the office of *Industrial Art*, her work table, and all her furniture. They were massed at the far end, with the tallest pieces at the back, and they formed a sort of sloping embankment stretching from the floor to the windows; while on the remaining three sides of the room carpets and curtains hung down the walls. Little old men, half asleep, filled rows of seats in the middle of the room. On the left stood a sort of counter, behind which the auctioneer, in a white neck-cloth, was nonchalantly waving a small hammer. Beside him sat a young man writing; and lower down stood a powerful fellow, looking like a cross between a commercial traveller and a ticket tout, who shouted out the descriptions of the pieces as they were sold. Three men placed the objects on a table, at which sat a line of brokers and dealers, both men and women. The crowd walked about behind them.

When Frederic came in, petticoats, scarves, handkerchiefs, and even chemises were being passed from hand to hand and turned over; sometimes they were thrown across the room and then a gleam of white would flash through the air. After that they sold her dresses, and one of her hats with a broken, drooping feather, then her furs, then three pairs of shoes; and the division of these relics, which still seemed vaguely to suggest the shape of her limbs, was to him an atrocity, as if he had seen crows tearing her corpse to pieces. The atmosphere of the hall, heavy with human breath, was stifling; Mme Dambreuse offered him her smelling salts. She said she was enjoying herself very much.

The bedroom furniture was exhibited.

Maître Berthelmot would announce a price. The assistant would repeat it at once, more loudly; and the three stewards would wait calmly for the hammer to fall, and then carry the article away into a neighbouring room.

In this way there vanished, one after another, the big blue carpet with its pattern of camellias, which her little feet used to skim as she came towards him; the little tapestry arm-chair, in which he always used to sit facing her, when they were alone; the two fire-screens, whose ivory frames seemed to have grown smoother from the touch of her hand; a velvet pincushion, still bristling with pins. As each thing disappeared he felt as if a part of his heart had been taken from him; and the monotony of listening to the same voices and watching the same gestures numbed him with fatigue, afflicting him with a deathly torpor, dissolving his very being.

He heard a rustling of silk at his ear; Rosanette was beside him. She had heard about the sale through Frederic himself. She had got over her grief and thought that she might pick up some bargains. She had come to watch, in a white satin jacket with pearl buttons, a flounced dress, tight gloves, and the look of a conqueror.

He turned pale with anger. She glanced at the woman at his side.

Mme Dambreuse had recognized her; and for a full minute they looked each other up and down, minutely, in order to discover the flaw, the blemish. One perhaps envied the youth of the other; while she, in her turn, was vexed by the extreme good style, the aristocratic simplicity of her rival.

At length, Mme Dambreuse turned her head away, with a smile of unspeakable insolence.

The assistant had opened a piano—her piano! Still standing up, he played a scale with his right hand and offered the instrument at twelve hundred francs; then he came down to a thousand, eight hundred, seven hundred.

Mme Dambreuse playfully described it as an old tin kettle.

They put before the dealers a little box with silver medallions, corners, and clasps. This was the very box he had seen at that first dinner party in the rue de Choiseul; it had passed to Rosanette, and then had returned to Mme Arnoux; his eyes had often rested on it during their conversations; it was bound up with his dearest memories, and his soul was melting with tender emotion, when suddenly Mme Dambreuse said:

'I say! I'm going to buy it.'

'But it's of no interest,' he said.

On the contrary, she thought it very pretty; and the assistant was extolling its workmanship.

'A jewel of the Renaissance! Eight hundred francs, gentlemen! Almost solid silver! Apply a little whiting and see it shine!'

She began to push her way through the crowd.

'What a peculiar idea!' said Frederic.

'Does it annoy you?'

'No. But what use can the thing be?'

'Who knows? Perhaps one could put love letters in it.'

She gave him a glance which made the allusion abundantly clear.

'That's another reason for not robbing the dead of their secrets.'

'I didn't think she was as dead as all that.' She added in a clear voice: 'Eight hundred and eighty francs.'

'You're behaving very badly.'

She laughed at him.

'My darling,' he said, 'this is the first favour I've ever asked you.'

'You won't make a very pleasant husband, do you know?'

Someone had just overbid her; she raised her hand.

'Nine hundred francs!'

'Nine hundred francs!' repeated Maître Berthelmot.

'Nine hundred and ten . . . fifteen . . . twenty . . . thirty!' yelled the assistant, scanning the crowd, and jerking his head back as he nodded.

'Prove to me that I'm marrying a sensible woman,' said Frederic.

He drew her gently towards the door.

Maître Berthelmot continued:

'Come on, gentlemen, nine hundred and thirty! Any advance on nine hundred and thirty?'

Mme Dambreuse had reached the doorway; she stopped and shouted: 'A thousand francs!'

A shiver went round the crowd—and there was silence.

'A thousand francs, gentlemen, a thousand francs! Any advance? No advance? A thousand francs! Going, going, gone!'

The ivory hammer fell.

She handed in her card, and the box was brought down to her. She thrust it into her muff.

385

Frederic felt his heart turn to ice.

Mme Dambreuse had not let go his arm; and she did not dare look him in the face until they were in the street, where her carriage was waiting.

She flung herself into it like a thief in flight, and when she had sat down she turned round towards Frederic. He had his hat in his hand.

'Aren't you coming?'

'No, madame.'

And, bowing to her coldly, he shut the door and motioned to the coachman to start.

His first feeling was one of joy at having regained his independence. He was proud of having avenged Mme Arnoux by sacrificing a fortune to her; then he was astonished at this action, and an overwhelming exhaustion swept over him.

Next morning, his servant told him the news. A state of siege had been decreed, the Assembly had been dissolved, and some of the people's representatives were in the Mazas prison.[1] Political events left him indifferent, so preoccupied was he with his own affairs.

He wrote some letters to tradesmen, cancelling several purchases connected with his marriage, which now struck him as a rather ignoble speculation; and he cursed Mme Dambreuse because, through her, he had nearly acted basely. He forgot Rosanette, and did not even worry about Mme Arnoux; he thought of no one but himself, just as he was—lost among the ruins of his hopes, sick and heavy with grief and despondency. In his hatred of the false world in which he had suffered so much, he longed for the freshness of the grass, the peace of the country, for a quiet, lazy, life, among simple-hearted people, in the shadow of the house where he was born. At length, on Wednesday evening, he went out.

Large groups of people were standing on the boulevard. From time to time a patrol would disperse them; they would join up again behind it. They talked freely, shouted jokes and insults at the soldiers, but did nothing more.

'What! Isn't there going to be any fighting?' said Frederic to a workman.

The man in the blouse answered:

'We 're not such fools as to get ourselves killed for the sake of the rich! Let *them* settle it!'

And a gentleman, with a sidelong glance at the workman, muttered

'Socialist scum! If only they could be stamped out for good this time!'

Frederic was baffled by so much hatred and stupidity. It increased his disgust with Paris; and two days later, he left for Nogent by the first train.

Soon the houses vanished and the country lay before him. Alone in his carriage, with his feet on the seat, he brooded over the events of the last few days, over his whole past. The memory of Louise came back to him.

'She really did love me. I was wrong not to take that chance of happiness. . . . Oh, well, let's forget it!'

Then, five minutes later:

'Yet, who knows? . . . Later on, why not?'

His thoughts, like his eyes, drifted far away into the distance.

'She was simple-minded, a peasant, almost a savage, but how kind-hearted!'

The nearer they got to Nogent, the closer he was to her. As they crossed the meadows of Sourdun, he seemed to see her under the poplars as in days gone by, cutting bulrushes beside the pools. The train arrived. He got out.

Then he leant on the bridge, and saw once more the island and the garden where they had walked one sunny day. Dazed by his journey and the fresh air, still weak from the emotions of the last few days, he felt a kind of ecstasy and said to himself:

'Perhaps she's out walking. Supposing I were to meet her?'

The bell of Saint-Laurent was tolling; in the square, in front of the church, stood a throng of poor people, and a barouche, the only one in the district, which was used for weddings. Suddenly, under the porch, amid a crowd of prosperous citizens in white neck-cloths, a newly married couple appeared.

He could not believe his eyes. But no! It was really she—Louise—draped in a white veil that fell from her red hair to her heels; and it was indeed he—Deslauriers—in a blue coat trimmed with silver, the uniform of a prefect. How could this be?

Frederic hid behind the corner of a house to let the procession pass.

Shamefaced, beaten, crushed, he went back to the station and returned to Paris.

His cabman told him that there were barricades up from the Château d'Eau to the Gymnase Theatre; so he went through the Faubourg Saint-Martin. At the corner of the rue de Provence, Frederic got out, intending to walk to the boulevards.

It was five o'clock; a fine rain was falling. The pavement

on the side of the Opéra was filled with well-dressed people. The houses opposite were shuttered. There was no one at the windows. Across the whole width of the road galloped a squadron of dragoons at full speed; they leaned forward on their horses, with their sabres drawn; and the plumes of their helmets and their great white cloaks, spreading out behind them, were silhouetted against the light from the gas jets, which flickered in the wind, through the mist. The crowd watched them in terrified silence.

Between the cavalry charges, squadrons of police came up to drive the crowd back into the streets.

Suddenly, on the steps of Tortoni's, appeared the figure of a man, conspicuous from afar by his tall stature. It was Dussardier. He stood there motionless as a figure of stone.

One of the policemen who was marching in front of his troop, with his three-cornered hat pulled over his eyes, threatened him with his sword.

Then Dussardier took a step forward and shouted:

'Long live the republic!'

He fell on his back with his arms folded. A scream of horror rose from the crowd. The policeman looked slowly round him, and Frederic, gaping, recognized Sénécal.

CHAPTER VI

HE travelled.

He knew the melancholy of the steamboat; the cold awakening in the tent; the tedium of scenery and ruins; the bitterness of interrupted friendship.

He came back.

He went into society. He had other loves still. But the ever-present memory of the first destroyed their savour; and, besides, the violence of desire, the flower of sensation itself, had withered. His intellectual ambitions had also dwindled. Years passed; and he endured the idleness of his mind and the stagnation of his heart.

Towards the end of March 1867, at nightfall, he was alone in his study when a woman entered.

'Madame Arnoux!'

'Frederic!'

She seized him by the hands and drew him gently to the window. She gazed at him, repeating again and again:

'It's he! Yes, it's he!'

In the half-light of dusk, he could see nothing but her eyes under the black lace veil that masked her face.

She laid a little red velvet pocket-book on the edge of the mantelpiece, and then took a seat. They sat there, unable to speak, smiling at each other.

Then he asked her many questions about herself and her husband.

They had settled in the depths of Brittany, where they could live cheaply and so pay off their debts. Arnoux was almost always ill and looked like an old man now. Her daughter was married and lived in Bordeaux; her son was on garrison duty at Mostaganem. Then she raised her head:

'But I've seen you again. I'm happy.'

He did not hesitate to tell her how, on hearing of the disaster, he had rushed to their house.

'I knew it.'

'How?'

She had seen him in the yard and had hidden.

'Why?'

Then, in a trembling voice, and with long pauses between her words, she said:

'I was afraid. Yes . . . afraid . . . of you . . . of myself.'

At this revelation he felt a kind of paroxysm of sensual delight. His heart beat wildly. She went on:

'Forgive me for not coming sooner.'

And pointing to the little red pocket-book, embroidered with gold palm leaves:

'I worked it specially for you. It contains the money for which the land at Belleville should have been the security.'

Frederic thanked her for her present, but reproached her for the trouble she had taken.

'No! That's not the reason why I came. I looked forward to this visit, and afterwards I shall go back . . . there.'

And she told him about the place she lived in.

It was a low-built, single-storied house. Huge box-trees filled the garden, and a double row of chestnuts stretched to the top of the hill from which there was a view of the sea.

'I go and sit there on a bench; I call it "Frederic's bench."'

Then, with greedy eyes, she began to examine the furniture, the ornaments, the pictures, in order to stamp them on her memory. Rosanette's portrait was half hidden by a curtain. But the whites and golds, standing out in the darkness, attracted her attention.

'I believe I know that woman.'

'No, no!' said Frederic. 'It's an old Italian painting.'

She confessed that she would like to take a walk in the street on his arm.

They went out.

The lights of the shops illuminated her pale profile, inter-mittently; then the shadows enveloped her again; and they passed among the traffic, the crowd, and the noise without hearing a sound, without thinking of any one but themselves, as if they had been walking together in the country, over a bed of dead leaves.

They talked about old times—the dinners, in the days of *Industrial Art*, the mannerisms of Arnoux, his way of tugging at the points of his collar and smearing his moustache with pomade, and they talked of other things, more personal and more pro-found. What rapture he had enjoyed, the first time he had heard her sing! How beautiful she was at Saint-Cloud, on her birthday! He reminded her of the little garden at Auteuil, of evenings at the theatre, a meeting on the boulevards, old servants, her negress.

She was astonished at his memory. Then she said:

'Sometimes your words come back to me like a distant echo, like the sound of a bell carried by the wind; and when I read about love in books, I feel that I am in your presence.'

'You have made me feel all the things that writers are supposed to exaggerate. I can understand Werther not disdaining the bread and butter offered him by Charlotte.'

'My poor friend!'

She sighed; and after a long silence:

'Never mind; we have loved each other truly.'

'But without fulfilling our love.'

'Perhaps it is better so,' she answered.

'No, no! How happy we should have been!'

'Yes, I believe it—with a love like yours!'

How strong it must have been to outlast so long a separation! Frederic asked her how she had found him out.

'It was one evening, when you kissed my wrist between my glove and my sleeve. I said to myself: "Why, he loves me . . . he loves me." But I did not dare make certain. Your reticence was so charming that I took pleasure in it as a spontaneous, unfailing compliment.'

He regretted nothing. His former sufferings were redeemed. When they returned, Mme Arnoux took off her hat. The lamp, standing on a console table, lit up her white hair. To him it was like a blow full in the chest.

To hide his disappointment from her, he sat down on the floor at her knees, took her hands, and began to talk tenderly to her.

'Your figure, your smallest movement seemed to me of more than human significance on earth. When you passed by, my heart lifted like dust after your footsteps. The effect you had on me was like a moonlit night in summer, when the world is all perfume, soft shadows, milky paleness, and dim horizons; when I repeated your name, I tried to kiss it with my lips; for me it contained all the joys of the flesh and the soul. I could imagine nothing beyond you. I loved you just as you were, with your two children—tender, serious, dazzlingly beautiful, and so kind! That picture blotted out all others. And I possessed more than my thoughts of you—for always, in the depths of my being, I kept the music of your voice and the splendour of your eyes.'

Rapturously she accepted this adoration of the woman she had ceased to be. Frederic, drunk with his own eloquence, came to believe what he was saying. Mme Arnoux, with her back to the light, leaned over him. He felt her breath caressing his forehead, and the vague contact of her whole body through their clothes. They clasped hands; the toe of her boot protruded a little from under her dress, and he said to her, almost fainting:

'The sight of your foot disturbs me.'

An impulse of modesty made her get up. She stood motionless, and then, with the strange intonation of a sleep-walker:

'At my age! He! Frederic! . . . No one has ever been loved as I have been loved. No, no! What's the use of being young? I care nothing for youth. And as for the women who come here, I despise them all.'

'Oh, they hardly ever come,' he said, to please her.

Her face beamed, and she wanted to know if he would ever marry.

He swore he never would.

'Really and truly? Why not?'

'Because of you,' said Frederic, taking her in his arms.

She stood still, leaning backwards, her mouth half-open, her eyes raised to his. Suddenly she pushed him away with a look of despair, and when he implored her to speak, she hung her head and said:

'I should have liked to make you happy.'

Frederic suspected that Mme Arnoux had come to offer herself to him; and once more he was seized with a stronger desire than ever—a frantic, ravening lust. Yet he also felt something he could not express—a repugnance, a sense of horror, as of an act of incest. Another fear restrained him—the fear of the disgust that might follow. Besides, what a nuisance it would be! And, partly from prudence, partly to avoid tainting his ideal, he turned on his heel and began to roll a cigarette.

She stared at him, marvelling.

'How chivalrous you are! There is only you! There is only you!'

Eleven o'clock struck.

'Already!' she said. 'At the quarter I shall go.'

She sat down again; but she watched the clock, while he went on walking up and down and smoking. They had nothing more to say to each other. At every parting there is always a moment when the beloved person is no longer with us.

At length, when the hand pointed to a little after twenty-five past, she picked up her bonnet by the ribbons, slowly.

'Good-bye, my friend, my dear friend! I shall never see

you again. This is my last act as a woman. My soul will never leave you. May all the blessings of heaven be upon you!'

And she kissed him on the forehead, like a mother. But she seemed to be looking for something, and she asked him for some scissors.

She took out her comb, and all her white hair fell about her. With a violent gesture she cut off a long lock, close to her head.

'Keep it. Good-bye!'

When she had gone out, Frederic opened his window. Mme Arnoux, on the pavement, beckoned to a passing cab. She got in. The carriage was lost to sight.

And that was all.

CHAPTER VII

ABOUT the beginning of that winter, Frederic and Deslauriers were talking by the fireside. They were reconciled once more, through that fatal element in their nature which always reunited them and made them friends.

Frederic briefly explained his quarrel with Mme Dambreuse, who had later married an Englishman.

Deslauriers, without mentioning how he had married Mlle Roque, described how, one fine day, his wife had run off with a singer. In an effort to free himself a little from ridicule, he had, as prefect, shown too much zeal for the Government and got into trouble. He was dismissed. After that, he had been, in succession, director of colonization in Algeria, secretary to a pasha, manager of a newspaper, and an advertising agent. He was at present employed as legal adviser to an industrial company.

Frederic, for his part, had consumed two-thirds of his fortune and now lived on a very modest scale.

Then they asked each other about their friends.

Martinon was now a senator.

Hussonnet had an important position, which gave him influence over all the theatres and the whole of the press.

Cisy, who had taken refuge in religion and was the father of eight children, lived in his ancestral mansion.

Pellerin, after experimenting with Syndicalism, homoeopathy, table-turning, Gothic art, and humanitarian painting, had become a photographer; and there were pictures of him on all the walls of Paris, with a tiny body and an enormous head.

'And your crony, Sénécal?'

'Vanished! That's all I know. And your great love, Madame Arnoux?'

'She must be in Rome with her son, who's a lieutenant in the Chasseurs.'

'And her husband?'

'Died last year.'

'Really?' said the lawyer.

Then, striking his forehead:

'Incidentally, I met our old friend Rosanette in a shop the

394

other day. She was holding by the hand a little boy she's adopted. She's the widow of a man called Oudry; she's become immensely stout. What a decline! And she used to have such a lovely figure.'

Deslauriers did not conceal the fact that he had taken advantage of her despair to find this out for himself.

'Besides, you did give me permission.'

This confession was to make up for his silence concerning his advances to Mme Arnoux. Frederic would have forgiven him, since he had not succeeded.

Although slightly put out by this discovery, he pretended to laugh; and the thought of Rosanette reminded him of Mlle Vatnaz.

Deslauriers had never seen her, nor many others who used to visit Arnoux; but he remembered Regimbart perfectly.

'Is he still alive?'

'Barely. Every evening, regularly, he drags himself from café to café, from the rue de Grammont to the rue Montmartre—feeble, bent double, a hollow shell, a ghost!'

'Well, and Compain?'

Frederic uttered a cry of joy, and begged Deslauriers to explain to him the mystery of the calf's head.

'It's imported from England. As a parody of the ceremony celebrated by the Jacobites on the 30th of January, the Whigs founded an annual banquet at which they ate calves' heads, drank claret out of the skulls of calves, and toasted the destruction of the Stuarts. After Thermidor, some Terrorists got up a similar society, which shows that stupidity repeats itself.'

'You seem much less violent about politics now.'

'The result of age,' said the lawyer.

And they went back over their lives.

They had both failed—one with his dreams of love, the other with his dreams of power. What was the reason?

'Perhaps we let ourselves drift from our course.'

'That may be true about you. But I went wrong because my mind was too rigid. I failed to take into account those innumerable subsidiary factors which are the most important of all. I suffered from excess of logic, you, of emotion.'

Then they blamed chance, circumstances, the period they were born in.

Frederic continued:

'We never expected to end up like this, in the old days at Sens, when you wanted to write a critical history of philosophy, and I a great medieval romance about Nogent. I'd found the subject in Froissart: How Master Brokars de Fénestranges and the Bishop of Troyes assailed Master Eustache d'Ambrecicourt. Do you remember?'

And, unburying their youth, at every sentence they said to each other:

'Do you remember?'

Once more they saw the school yard, the chapel, the parlour, the gymnasium at the foot of the staircase, the faces of masters and boys. There was one called Angelmarre, from Versailles, who used to make foot-straps out of old boots; there was M. Mirbal and his red whiskers; Varaud and Suriret, the professors of technical and artistic drawing, who were always quarrelling; and the Pole, the compatriot of Copernicus, with his planetary system in cardboard—an itinerant astronomer, whose lecture was rewarded by a free meal in the refectory; then there was a terrible drinking bout when they were out walking once; their first pipe, the prize-givings, the joy of the holidays.

It was during the holidays of 1837 that they visited the Turkish woman.

This name had been given to a lady who was really called Zoraïde Turc; and many people thought she actually was a Mohammedan from Turkey. This added to the romance of her establishment, which was situated on the river bank, behind the ramparts. Even in high summer there was shade round her house, which could be recognized by a bowl of goldfish and a pot of mignonette on the window ledge. Girls in white camisoles, with rouge on their cheeks and long ear-rings in their ears, used to tap on the windows as one passed, and in the evening they would stand on the doorstep singing softly in hoarse voices.

This haunt of perdition made a tremendous sensation in the whole district. It was described under euphemisms: 'You know the place I mean—a certain street—beyond the Bridges.' The farmers' wives in the neighbourhood trembled for their husbands; the richer women feared for their servants, since the sub-prefect's cook had been surprised there; and it was, of course, the secret obsession of every growing youth.

One Sunday, when every one was at vespers, Frederic and Deslauriers, having first had their hair waved, picked some flowers in Mme Moreau's garden, then went out by the gate leading into the fields. After a long round through the vineyards, they came back by the Pêcherie and slipped into the Turkish house, still holding their big nosegays.

Frederic offered his like a lover to his betrothed. But the heat, fear of the unknown, a sense of guilt, or possibly the very pleasure of seeing at a single glance so many women at his disposal, affected him so strongly that he turned very pale and stopped dead, without speaking. The girls all roared with laughter, enjoying his embarrassment; thinking they were making fun of him he fled, and as Frederic had the money, Deslauriers was naturally obliged to follow.

They were seen going out. Three years later the story was still remembered in the district.

They recounted it at length, each supplementing the other's reminiscences; and when they had finished:

'That was the best time we ever had!' said Frederic.

'Yes, perhaps you 're right. That was the best time we ever had!' said Deslauriers.

11. [1] Madame Lafarge was accused of poisoning her husband. She was found guilty, with extenuating circumstances, and condemned to life imprisonment.

    [2] Guizot (1787–1874), statesman and historian, was Louis-Philippe's most influential minister. His reactionary politics and his subservience to England made him unpopular with the Liberals and Nationalists.

27. [1] Electoral reform was one of the chief demands of the opposition to Louis-Philippe. At that period there were only 200,000 qualified electors out of a population of 30,000,000.

    [2] Humann was Guizot's Minister of Finance. The extralegal activities of his commissioners caused unrest and rioting in the provinces.

28. [1] Pritchard was an English missionary on Tahiti. When the French occupied the island, he roused the natives against them. He was arrested by the French admiral and some of his property was destroyed by the French forces. The British demanded an indemnity, which Guizot's Government eventually paid. The incident caused intense bitterness on both sides of the Channel, and Guizot's concession was deeply resented by French public opinion.

29. [1] Béranger, Laffitte, and Chateaubriand were associated with the Republican Opposition.

38. [1] An Opposition paper.

50. [1] The National Guard, recruited almost exclusively from the *bourgeoisie*, was for a long time one of the chief bulwarks of the July monarchy.

54. [1] In 1833 the Government had demanded a credit for the fortification of Paris. This was refused by the Chamber, on the ground that the forts would be directed not against foreign enemies, but against the population of the capital.

    [2] These laws, passed in 1835, imposed a severe censorship on the press.

    [3] So called from his Anglophile tendencies.

56. [1] Editor of the *National*.

113. [1] A fancy dress, based on the costume of the *débardeur* (longshoreman), was popular in the nineteenth century.

114. [1] Adam's opera of this name was first produced in 1836.

Page [2] Les Porcherons, a hamlet close to Paris, was the scene of a popular fair, which was frequented by society in the eighteenth century.

130 [1] The serious famine of 1846–7 resulted in the murder of two landowners at Buzançais by bands of starving people.

131. [1] In 1846 Louis-Philippe secured the marriage of two Spanish infantas to candidates favourable to France, thus incurring the displeasure of Palmerston.

132. [1] Barbès (1809–70) was an ardent and disinterested Republican. He was imprisoned in 1834, 1835, and 1839 —on the last occasion for life. He was released after the revolution of February 1848.

149. [1] M. de Genoude was editor of a pro-Bourbon paper. After the Orleanist triumph of 1830, he allied himself with the Republicans.

150. [1] On 12th May 1839 a Republican rising took place in Paris, organized by a secret revolutionary society called the Société des Saisons, and led by Barbès and Blanqui. The insurrection, which had little popular support, was easily put down.

161. [1] The melancholy hero of a play by Dumas *père*.

191. [1] Bou-Maza, defeated by the French in 1847, lived in honourable captivity in France.

197. [1] These two professors had been deprived of their chairs because they were associated with Radical ideas.

203. [1] Drouillard was a Parisian banker. Accused of having spent 150,000 francs in bribing the electors of his district, he was convicted in 1847.

[2] Bénier was accused of peculation in a Government department. The charge was quashed; but after his death (1845) a deficit of 300,000 francs was discovered in his accounts.

[3] Godefroy de Cavaignac was a lifelong Republican. After being prosecuted and acquitted several times, he was imprisoned in 1834; he escaped, lived abroad for some time, and died in 1845.

206. [1] Capercailzie.

217. [1] This was the original name of the Société des Saisons.
[2] Alibaud attempted to shoot Louis-Philippe in June 1836. He was tried and executed.

224. [1] The *carbonari* were a secret society of revolutionary Liberals. Originating in Italy, the movement gained ground in France under the Restoration. After the **fall**

Page of Charles X many former *carbonari* gave their adherence to Louis-Philippe.

244. [1] Banquets in favour of electoral reform were organized all over France in the latter part of 1847.

[2] The Kings of Piedmont and Naples and the Grand Duke of Tuscany had been compelled to make concessions to the Liberals early in 1848.

245. [1] Cousin's doctrines were taught in all the schools and universities of France. Although he was, as it were, the official philosopher of Louis-Philippe's régime, his pantheistic theories were not popular with the Clerical Party.

[2] Teste, Minister of Public Works in 1842, was accused of taking a bribe of 100,000 francs from General Cubières, in return for granting him a salt-mine concession. Both were convicted in 1847.

246. [1] The Duchesse de Praslin was found murdered in her bedroom in August 1847. The duke, charged with the crime, of which he was almost certainly guilty, committed suicide in prison before being brought to trial. The case provided much propaganda for the parties of the Left.

[2] The Liberal tendencies of Pius IX has made him popular with the French Opposition.

[3] *Rouget*=red mullet.

247. [1] A reference to a celebrated cartoon, showing Louis-Philippe performing a vanishing trick with three balls, marked 'Liberty,' 'Revolution,' and 'July.' The Radical Opposition considered that he had failed to fulfil the Liberal promises he had made when he achieved power, through the revolution of July 1830.

[2] Louis-Philippe, as Duc de Chartres, had fought under Dumouriez in 1792. After his victory at Valmy, Dumouriez had deserted to the Austrians.

[3] An allusion to the famous legend that Jeanne de Navarre, wife of Philip the Fair, used to lure handsome passers-by into the Tour de Nesle, in Paris, and, after a night's debauchery, throw them into the Seine.

254. [1] A *cause célèbre* of the period. Léotade was condemned to life imprisonment for the murder of a young girl. His guilt was doubtful, and the case aroused much controversy.

[2] In January 1848 the Sicilians defeated the King of Naples and re-established a Liberal constitution.

[3] A banquet in favour of electoral reform, which was forbidden by the police. This action was followed by a

Page stormy debate in the Chamber, in which the Government secured a majority of only forty-three votes.

258. [1] The promoter of the Reformist banquets.

[2] The attitude of the National Guard, in supporting the Republicans against Louis-Philippe, was a decisive factor in the revolution of 1848, of which this demonstration was the beginning.

263. [1] The Republican insurgents looted some houses that refused to supply them with arms.

264. [1] At six o'clock on the evening of 23rd February 1848 it was announced that the king had dismissed Guizot's Government.

268. [1] This was Marshal Gérard, reading the abdication of Louis-Philippe.

274. [1] Minister of the Interior in the provisional Government.

[2] A soldier who had distinguished himself in the Algerian wars.

[3] Representative of Liberal Catholicism.

275. [1] Lamartine, poet and politician, enjoyed immense, if transitory, prestige, as head of the provisional Government.

[2] Already the emblem of Socialism.

[3] Caussidière was appointed Prefect of Police after the February revolution. A Republican of the extreme Left, he created a police force consisting of men who had fought at the barricades.

276. [1] Dupont (de l'Eure) was a moderate Liberal; Albert, who was of working-class origin, represented the workers in the provisional Government; Louis Blanc and Blanqui were Socialists.

[2] Ledru-Rollin sent a circular letter to the Government Commissioners who were preparing the elections for the Constituent Assembly, in which he recommended them to support only those candidates who were trustworthy Republicans.

277. [1] Flocon was a member of the provisional Government. He was inseparable from his pipe, which made him an easy butt for caricature.

278. [1] The members of the Assembly were not to pass laws but to frame a Constitution, to replace the provisional Government.

283. [1] A demonstration of workmen had taken place against the provisional Government at the Hôtel de Ville, in which a minimum wage and the right to work were demanded.

[2] An Orleanist publication.

287. [1] Public prosecutor during the Terror of 1793.

293. [1] The editor of the *Presse* had asked what the provisional Government would do if the Constituent Assembly did not frame a Republican Constitution. This was resented by certain Republicans, who tried to wreck the offices of the newspaper.
[2] On 15th May demonstrators of the Left invaded the Chamber, demanding a new and more radical provisional Government.
[3] Conferences of workmen, presided over by Louis Blanc, to improve conditions of labour.
[4] A society of militant feminists.

294. [1] Public works instituted by the Government for the unemployed.

297. [1] Louis Napoleon had returned to France after the February Revolution.
[2] Marie had supported the Riot Act in the Assembly.
[3] De Falloux abolished the National Workshops.

301. [1] In his *Confessions*, Rousseau describes how his comic opera, *Le Devin du village*, was performed before the court at Fontainebleau in 1752. The ladies of the court were moved to tears, much to Rousseau's gratification.

306. [1] A suburb of Lyons.

322. [1] The two ministers responsible for crushing the June outbreak.

331. [1] Rateau had proposed the dissolution of the Constituent Assembly and the election of a Legislative Assembly.

335. [1] Probably Lachambeaudie, author of *Fables populaires* (see page 244), and a militant Republican

338. [1] Louis Napoleon had been elected President of the Republic in December, 1848.
[2] A popular outbreak, suppressed by Changarnier.
[3] A kind of topical revue, played at the Vaudeville Theatre, in which the Republicans were satirized.

355. [1] In February 1851 the Chamber had refused to vote an additional 1,800,000 francs to the president.

370. [1] The Liberal movements in all these countries had been crushed by the reactionaries.
[2] An allusion to the occupation of Paris by the Allied troops in 1815.

386. [1] This was Louis Napoleon's *coup d'état.*